CW00522377

The
TOMATO
RUNNER

Mark Smith

Independently published and available as paperback or e-book

Copyright © Mark Smith 2023

All rights reserved. No part of this publication may be reproduced in any form without the prior permission of the author.

This is a work of fiction. Names, characters, and places are the product of the author's imagination. Any resemblance to actual persons or places or events, living or dead, is entirely coincidental.

For my parents, without whom….

Other books by Mark Smith

Well actually, nothing at the moment. You see this is my first novel, but I am working on two more. So look out for them depending how soon after first publication you read this. They will probably be called *Messiah* and *Everytime I See That Bus*. Probably. Too soon to know for sure, but probably. Over use of *probably* and you've not even started to read the book yet.

See where the falling day
In silence steals away
Behind the western hills withdrawn:
Her fires are quenched, her beauty fled,
While blushes all her face o'erspread,
As conscious she had ill fulfilled
The promise of the dawn.

Another morning soon shall rise,
Another day salute our eyes,
As smiling and as fair as she,
And make as many promises:
But do not thou
The tale believe
They're sisters all,
And all deceive.

Tomorrow by Anna Laetitia Barbauld (1743-1825)

Chapter 1

Gavin drove the Hyundai coupe down the quiet lane and parked up behind what looked like a hedge verging on a sand dune. He did not know the place. He had driven about fifty miles to get here. It looked suitably pleasant and yet insignificant. A good place to die.

He went to the boot of the car and took out the flipchart tripod. It had paper already on it. He took it down onto the beach. It was an awkward thing to carry and banged against his legs on several occasions, but they were tomorrow's bruises so mattered little. It was early evening on a dull April day. Everything suggested he would not be disturbed. He set up the tripod and pushed its three legs into the sand. He had brought two pens. He placed them in the tray. He had brought a flask of tea. He poured himself a drink. The rest in the flask might be needed later. He sat with his tea and looked out across at the waves gently washing onto the mix of sand and pebble. There was something easy but evocative about drinking out of a plastic flask cup. Events in your life linked by taste and smell and touch of plastic on the lips as you sip the warm tea.

He stood up and took the red pen from the tray and at the top of the left side of the flipchart paper he wrote DIE. He preferred DIE to DEATH. DIE suggested action and that was what he had to consider. DEATH was final, all done, everything complete. DIE was an activity.

He took the blue pen and on the right side of the flipchart he wrote LIVE. Again, LIVE suggested the requirement to be active rather than LIFE which was a ubiquitous presence that just allowed itself to be taken for granted. Life is all around you but living comes down to the individual.

He stared at the two words. Did he need to focus on LIVE? Did he need to focus on DIE? He was not getting anything. He needed to think generally about everything and let that determine what to put where. He tried it. He flitted between trying not to think about anything and then overthinking with tort eyebrows. It produced nothing other than thoughts about how he must look. The words stared back at him. They taunted him. They challenged him. He found himself thinking about his choice of colour for each word. Red for Dying. Blue for living. Did that mean anything? What was he looking for? Then he saw the words again for what they were. They were verbs. They were about action. He had chosen action words. He had chosen activity and that would require him to live, to be alive. Perhaps he had never intended to die. Perhaps it was all a sham. Perhaps he was seeking attention. But from who? This was something that he was not going to share. But he realised then that he did not want to die. If his life lacked purpose, he would find purpose. If his life lacked meaning, he would find meaning. If his life lacked reasons to get up in the morning, he would change his alarm clock.

His commitment to living had to be based on action. He ripped down the first sheet along the perforated lines that never actually work. Well, they work but not neatly. He was left with two ripped pieces of flipchart paper. Then on the next sheet on the tripod he scribbled TOMORROW at the top. Starting tomorrow how would he live? Nothing grand. Nothing expecting too much. He sat down on what turned out to be a clump of grass protruding from the sand.

'What you doing mister?' The voice came from behind him.

He looked around at the boy. 'What does it matter to you?'

'Just asking.'

'How old are you?'

'Ten.'

'Come back and ask me when you're twenty.'

'Are you supposed to be here?'

'Are you?'

'I live over there.' The boy pointed in the direction where the tops of several houses could be seen.

'Why don't you go home?'

'Come to see what you doing.'

'Will you go if I pay you?'

'Of course not.'

'Why?'

'If you're prepared to pay me to go away it must be worth me staying.'

'Nothing to see.'

'I can wait.'

'You got nothing better to do?'

'Nope. Nothing to do round here. I reckon you the most exciting thing to happen round here since,' and he paused, 'since that fight between them two neighbours what been seeing each other.'

'Great.'

'Why you written tomato on that paper?'

'Tomato?'

'Yeh. On that paper.'

'It doesn't say tomato.'

'It does. At the top there.'

'That says tomorrow.'

'You a doctor?'

'No. I'm a famous murderer so be off.'

'Don't think so.'

'Why?'

'Murderer not be bothered with writing tomato on a piece of flipchart paper up there on that stand like you done.'

'It says tomorrow.'

'Still don't make you a murderer.'

'But can you be sure?'

'You a teacher or something?'

'Try something.'

'Why you got that flipchart?'

'Because it's my murder weapon.'

'Death by flipchart.' And the boy laughed. 'Reckon you must be a teacher. Flipchart paper. You look like one. And you don't know what you doing.'

'Sounds like you don't rate teachers that much.'

'Some of them are OK. Most of them. But a bit weird. Bit like you. That's why I reckon you're a teacher.'

'You like school?'

'It's okay.'

'Won't your parents be wondering where you are?'

'Probably. My dad knows where I am mostly. I always come up here.'

'Why's that?'

'Peace and quiet. Waiting for me tea. That's how I knew you were a stranger. Not seen you up here before. And don't know anyone in this place that'd bring that onto the beach.' He, of course, directed his look toward the tripod. 'Most people bring a bucket and spade.' There was a purposeful pause. 'Or drugs.'

'What do you know about drugs?'

'Nothing. But I've seen them over there.' He pointed to a spot amongst the trees on the edge of the beach. 'And they ain't building sandcastles. Anyway. What you doing with that?'

'Needed something to write tomato on,' said Gavin smiling.

'You like tomatoes then?'

'Yes.'

'They're okay. You having tomatoes tomorrow?'

'Not quite. Maybe. Maybe I will have tomatoes tomorrow.'

'Is that a shopping list then?'

'Does it look like a shopping list?'

'It would if you added bread.'

Gavin could see a figure in the distance. The boy caught his look and looked around.

'Shit. That's me dad.'

'You'd better be off then.'

'Thanks, mate. Good talking to you. Don't murder anyone. Not tonight anyways. Enjoy your tomatoes.' The boy laughed and then set off in the direction of the distantly approaching figure. He stopped, turned, and waved and then ran to his father.

At last, the boy had gone, and he checked to make sure that he really had gone, then Gavin looked again at the word TOMORROW. It does look a bit like tomato, he thought to himself. He also thought about how that boy of only ten years old seemed to be alive. Whatever his circumstance might be, and those houses over there did not look that inviting, the lad certainly had spirit and an interest in what was going on around him.

He took the red pen and crossed out TOMORROW and instead wrote TOMATO. He looked at TOMATO. Tomatoes were red, usually. He looked at TOMORROW crossed out. He didn't like tomorrow being crossed out. That wasn't a good omen. Had he written off tomorrow? Could tomorrow be replaced by tomatoes? He picked up the red pen again and wrote RUN below the battle that was taking place between TOMORROW and TOMATO. Why he had written it he did not know. But he did write it. It was a particularly active word. It was a word that denoted action. Tomorrow had become tomato had become run. Perplexed by the strangeness of his own mind, he packed everything up and returned to the car.

5

He still couldn't stop the flipchart tripod from banging against his legs. And this time it mattered, and it hurt.

He sat in the car. He poured the rest of his tea. It was tepid now. He thought about the boy. He thought about tomorrow. 'Bloody hell,' he said aloud. He remembered there would have to be a meeting tomorrow. Not a planned meeting, but the sort of meeting your manager wants when you've messed up big time and, apparently, he had messed up big time. That wasn't his opinion. In the minds of others, he was a big-time messer-upper. He had become the sort of person people have meetings about. This was a meeting he had not thought about. A meeting that there had been a chance he might be able to avoid by the convenience of being dead. Being dead can get you out of most things. It's amazing what a coroner's note can do for your need to attend work. Being alive changed all that in a damned inconvenient way. And it was going to be nothing other than a bloody awful meeting. That was something to write in the DIE column. Too late now. He finished his tea and put the plastic cup back on the flask.

He drove off and, as he did so, he reached into his jacket pocket and grabbed a handful of loose paracetamol and threw them out of the car window. Ten seconds later he was getting out of the car in search of all the paracetamol. It was an action that had no sooner happened than he had realised that the attempted suicide of half the local wildlife was not something he wanted to feel responsible for. In his pocket, he counted ten paracetamol. He collected twenty discarded tablets. He could not find the other two. He decided he could live with that. He got back in the car and drove off again.

For a turning point in his life, or indeed had it been so, a turning point in his death, he realised it had been a bit of a cock up.

Chapter 2

Several hours earlier.

Gavin headed down the stairs to reception where his foster carers were waiting for him. He liked Bob. He did not like Myriam. He got on well with Bob. They could talk openly about most things. Gavin thought he worked well with Bob. His relationship with Myriam was a car crash. On every visit, they always found something to fall out about. It could be a fostering matter. It could be childcare related. It could be politics. It could be the colour of the number forty-seven bus. They always fell out. It was as if she was waiting for him. Gavin could not dismiss the possibility that Myriam spent her days preparing and working toward her meetings with Gavin.

Bob and Myriam. Although it always seemed to be in the order of Myriam and Bob. Myriam and Bob were experienced foster carers. They were also experienced parents. The two did not always go together. The ability to parent your own child through to adulthood, University, or a job at B and Q was quite different to parenting a foster child. And it was Gavin's job to help bridge that gap. Gavin and Bob were on the bridge. Not the most exciting of constructions but a safe easy means of getting from one side of the river to the other. By comparison, Gavin and Myriam were to be found shouting at each other across the English Channel. And there was always a storm brewing.

'Hi, Bob, Myriam,' said Gavin, purposefully ordering them that way, on arriving in reception.

'Hi, Gavin,' replied Bob. Myriam just muttered something. It was probably not a mutter. It was probably a word or two. It was undoubtedly intentionally incoherent.

'This way.' Gavin led them through to the meeting room.

'Do we need to sit together?' enquired Bob.

'Sit anywhere. But yes, we could sit here,' said Gavin. They sat together. Bob sat between Gavin and Myriam. It required no preplanning. It just happened that way. It was always going to happen that way.

'You do know it's not my job to get you out of this mess,' said Myriam.

'Just tell it how it is. That's all you need to do,' replied Gavin.

'A mess, that's what it is. A mess. And you've done it.'

'That's it, Myriam. Tell it how it is.'

Bob tried to find a sitting position that didn't interfere with the dialogue that otherwise would be passing through him.

'I will,' said Myriam.

'I'm sure you will,' said Gavin.

Bob shuffled.

Sally Clark arrived. She was Gavin's manager. 'Hi, Myriam. Hi, Bob.' They returned the welcome. Then there was silence. Slightly awkward.

The silence was put out of its misery by the arrival of Sonya, the independent reviewing officer and the person who would be chairing the meeting. She was soon followed by Bernadette, who was the childcare social worker and remarkably not late. The child was Amy, or as named by her mother and long-absent father, Amy-Mae Atomic. She preferred to be called Amy. Amy was not invited to the meeting. She was in school… possibly.

'Thank you for coming,' said Sonya. 'I think we all know each other so let's get started.' They did all know each other. They did not necessarily like each other, but they did all know each other. It had the potential to be one of those meetings where personalities get in the way and past confrontations turn up with a cheery smile.

Sonya continued. 'My understanding is that the last time you visited Amy, Bernadette, she made a complaint. This was about the foster placement and about an incident when Gavin visited.'

'Yes,' replied Bernadette.

'Can you tell us first what the complaint was about the placement?'

'She said that Myriam was always telling her off and Bob overreacts to everything.'

'Can you give more detail, please? Be more specific. Any particular incidents?'

'Sorry, Myriam, but she says you tell her off for everything. She listed things but they were just everything. Not tidying up. Not washing up. Not cleaning her teeth. For swearing. For eating with her mouth open. For raiding the fridge. Just everything.'

'And Bob?'

'She said Bob just gets wound up for the slightest thing. Myriam will tell her off for not using her knife and fork properly and then Bob will storm off. That sort of thing.'

'Was there anything that concerned you? Anything that goes beyond what might be acceptable parenting?'

'I think she feels that it is constant. I don't think it's one thing. I think it's that Myriam constantly tells her off.'

'Is she happy there?'

'Hard to judge.'

'I'm struggling to find anything that we need to address other than Myriam perhaps needing to be aware of what Amy is saying to you, Bernadette.' Sonya paused to let that message sink in and then she continued. 'I can also appreciate that she is a black child in a white foster home.' This was the moment when everyone tried hard not to look at Bernadette. Bernadette was black and she knew that everyone was trying hard not to look at her. She was used to people trying hard not to look at her. It showed on their faces.

'Her African Caribbean heritage is really important and too easily overlooked,' said Bernadette. She looked at Myriam and Bob. Then she looked at Gavin.

'I'm sure Bob and Myriam are doing what they can,' said Gavin. He knew this wasn't true. He knew that Bob and Myriam didn't understand all that they needed to do. Their parenting knowledge and experience fell short of many things that Amy would need. He knew that for this reason and maybe other reasons this was the wrong placement. But he wasn't going to say that now. He'd said it when Amy was placed. He wasn't a strong voice on this because he let his nervous white perspective on the matter get in the way, but he'd said something. And he knew that Bob and Myriam were old school where you treat all children the same, except no one ever does.

'Bob, Myriam, do you have anything to add?' Sonya wanted to move things on rather than get caught in an issue about right or wrong placements.

Myriam spoke up. Bob knew better than to try. 'She's hard work. She needs telling. That room of hers is a real mess. Embarrassing. You wouldn't want anyone to see it the way she keeps it.'

'Okay,' said Sonya. 'Gavin, the reason for your visit?'

'Just a standard visit as Bob and Myriam's supervising social worker. Although I was aware that Amy has been saying things, but Amy is always saying things.'

'And do you take these things seriously?'

'Of course, but she is thirteen, she is in care, and she would probably rather be back with her mother.'

'Meaning?'

'Meaning I would not expect a thirteen-year-old in care who would rather be back at home to be a paragon of virtue.'

'Which I can appreciate but still requires us to take her seriously.'

'Of course.'

'Okay. Let's talk about the incident with the trainers. That seems to be the one that has caused the most problems. Bernadette, what did Amy say happened?'

'Amy said that first Bob threw her trainer out of her bedroom window. When she complained about this to Gavin, he threw the other trainer out of the window. And when she was not happy with that Gavin offered to buy the trainers from her.'

Myriam looked at Bob. Sally Clark looked at Gavin. They were similar looks.

'Okay. Thank you, Bernadette. Bob, can you tell us please what happened and why it led to you throwing the trainer out of the window.'

Bob smiled nervously which gave Myriam just enough opportunity to speak first. 'She is always in her room. We ask her to come down and join us for meals, but it's a real battle isn't it, Bob?'

'Yes.'

Myriam continued to take over. 'We keep asking her to tidy her room. It's a real mess. An embarrassment isn't it, Bob?'

'Yes.'

'I can accept so much but clothes are just thrown across the floor. Her bed is never made. I don't know what she has stuffed under the bed or in her wardrobe. It's a pigsty isn't it, Bob?'

'Yes.'

'Okay,' interrupted Sonya. 'Can we just hear from you please, Bob. What was the incident with the trainers?'

Two mouths opened. Sonya looked at Myriam. She closed her mouth. Bob was left to speak. 'We had called Gavin. To talk. Before he visited, I had gone up to talk to Amy about her room. It was a mess-'

'It was a real mess,' interrupted Myriam.

Sonya looked at her. 'Bob,' she said, inviting him to continue.

'We were just fed up. Everywhere clothes and I just picked up the nearest item. It was a trainer. The window was open. I threw it out. I told her that she needed to tidy the room and that was the only help I was going to give her. I left the room.'

'And how did she respond?'

'She slammed the door. I could hear it downstairs,' said Myriam.

'She slammed the door,' repeated Bob. 'Myriam could hear it downstairs.'

'And then Gavin arrived, didn't you Gavin?' said Myriam.

'Yes,' said Gavin, feeling like Bob.

'I think she heard him arrive because then she said she wanted to see him to tell him what she thought of us,' said Myriam.

'Gavin,' said Sonya, 'what happened when you went up to see Amy?'

'She told me that Bob had been winding her up and Myriam kept telling Bob to tell her off. I then mentioned that they had both spoken to me about the state of her room, so I asked her what she thought. She said she thought it was fine.'

'Did she mention what Bob had done?'

'She complained that he had thrown her trainer out of the window.'

'What did you do?'

'I threw the other trainer out of the window.'

Sonya and Sally Clark looked at each other. Sonya spoke. 'Why would you do that Gavin?'

'At the time it just seemed right.'

'Throwing a thirteen-year-old girl's trainer out of the window seemed right?' said Sonya, the disbelief sounding in her voice.

'At the time. Yes.'

'Really,' interrupted Sally Clark, unable to remain silent any longer.

'At the time I thought it would make the situation look farcical and we could all laugh about it.'

'I assume it didn't work,' said Sonya with a blatant measure of sarcasm in her voice this time.

'No. So then I tried a different tactic.'

'Which was?'

'I offered to buy the trainers from her.'

'So, after both trainers had been thrown out of the window, your response was to offer to buy them from her?'

'My response was to try and lighten the situation. I joked that I could do with a pair of trainers. I joked that I would buy them from her. I was trying to defuse the situation.'

'Except it didn't work.'

'But I didn't know that when I tried it.'

'But you made the situation worse.'

'No. I did not make the situation worse. I just did not improve it.'

'But she complained to her social worker that you were winding her up.'

'She's thirteen. She's in care. What else do you expect her to do but complain? It's like a hobby.'

'We have to listen to her, Gavin.'

'Of course, we do, but she's thirteen and there isn't much that isn't going to wind her up.'

'So, you're saying it's her fault?'

'Of course not. I repeat. She's thirteen. She's in care. Don't be surprised please when she says what she says. It's typical behaviour.'

'So, you think you behaved just fine?'

'I think I genuinely tried to do something about the situation. I don't think I made it worse. I think you are trying to make it sound like I made it worse. I think you are trying to blame me.'

'Seems to me you didn't exactly help.'

'Seems to me you think there was some easy solution that you are just so clever you would have known exactly what to do, but you think I am just not in your league.' The words just came out.

'I'm just trying to understand what happened.'

'It was a pair of trainers. They ended up in the back garden. No trainers were harmed in the making of this scene. She probably gained a great story to tell rather than being that upset. It was nothing like what she has experienced before. It was a trainer. I was trying to sort the situation by using humour. She probably can't wait for me to do it again. Give her something to tell at school. They'll all be waiting for her to tell them the next instalment. She'll probably complain now if I don't do it. I was just trying to be funny about it.'

'Didn't seem to work.'

'I know. I know that.'

'So?'

'So what! So what! At the time I thought humour would help. Try and lighten the situation.'

'Did you not think about trying to lighten the situation another way?'

'Of course, but I had to react. I couldn't exactly call a meeting and say I would get back to her. You can all sit here now and tell me what I should have done. But how do you know any of it would have worked? So bloody clever after the event. I tried humour. It didn't work.' Gavin looked at them all and then at Sonya. 'I was there. You were not.'

'Technically-'

'Shut up Myriam,' interjected Gavin.

There was silence. Gavin was still verbally high and was too agitated to outwait the silence. He continued digging his hole.

'Look at you all. So bloody clever now here in this meeting. Know it all when you have a meeting about it afterwards. What do you know about being there and dealing with it as and when it happens? You…' and he pointed at Sonya. 'You sit there in judgement without a bloody clue about real social work. Making decisions. Telling us all what to do. But you don't have to do any of it yourself. Too high and mighty for that.' He pointed at Sally Clark. 'You're just as bad. I reckon you became a manager just to get out of working with kids. Probably can't stand children.' He turned again. 'And you Myriam, the Spanish Inquisition have got nothing on you. Keep turning them thumb screws.' He finished off by saying, 'Sorry, Bob.' He stormed out of the room. He hurricaned through the building and tornadoed out through the doors into the street.

He walked. The sort of walk where you leave the building and make sure you do not bump into anyone. The sort of walk where you do not know where you are going, where you are, or where you've been. The sort of walk where you suddenly find yourself two miles away from where you should be, and you need to return for your bag.

Gavin crept back into the building. He said hello to someone who did not seem to be aware that he had just become pratt of the year. He went into the nearest unoccupied meeting room and took the flipchart paper, tripod, and pens. He was not sure why he'd done that, but the world had suddenly lost his confidence and the wad of paper was all he seemed to have any faith in. In desperation, he was turning to the power of flipchart paper. No one had questioned him leaving the building carrying his contraband. On reflection, it had probably not looked anywhere near as awkward as he had felt. He took the aforementioned items to his car and then had to return for his bag. This had possibly been a mistake but, whether he was going to need his work bag, he had never gone home without it, and so that had seemed the right thing to do. You leave the office; you take your bag with you.

'What the fuck have you done?' enquired Nichola sympathetically.

'Don't ask,' replied Gavin.

'She's steaming.'

Gavin grabbed his bag and left. So was he. And angry with the whole lot of them, the world, life, and every bloody thing.

He drove home, made a flask of tea, bought two packs of paracetamol from two separate shops, and headed in the general direction of the coast. Life was shite. With the e added for emphasis.

Chapter 3

It was four in the morning. Gavin was pacing around his house. It was a small, terraced house. Had it been a bigger house he might have restricted himself to pacing just upstairs or perhaps just in his bedroom. It was a small house. He paced everywhere. It did not take long. Front room, back room, galley kitchen, barely worth entering, he'd miss that out on the next circuit, bedroom one, bedroom two and bathroom. And again. He had chosen between life and death and now he had to choose between going into the office in the morning or staying at home. That it mattered was perhaps a positive thing. If you are going to live, then perhaps do not be a twat for the rest of your life. He had already given twatiness a fair share of his life so time to move on. A less twatlike approach to life seemed to be in order. But did the non-twat go to work in the morning or not?

Then he made a commitment to run. Give his life a pace. Give his life a purpose. Give him something to get up in the morning for, although preferably not this early in the morning. Did the person who was going to live go into the office in the morning? Would that be the right thing to do? The right thing to do. Now he was sounding like a politician. That was a completely different level of twatiness. Doing the right thing. The bath needed a good clean. That was the problem with pacing around the house. You noticed things. Clean the bath. That would be the right thing to do. Don't look at the ceiling in the small bedroom. Don't look at the ceiling in the small bedroom. What a mess it was. Damp and grey. He shouldn't have looked.

The problem with being awake in the night is nothing happens and time finds a winged chariot to hasten its passing. Before you know it, morning has arrived and you're knackered. Had the opportunity to go back to bed gone? Was it getting too late or rather should that now be too early? Still, if he was going to lose all this sleep, he needed to resolve the issue of work. Was he going back to work with his tail between his legs? Was he going to stay off work? He needed to think this through before his body took over. The first signs of that would be finding himself in the shower, technically the bath with a shower attachment that looked more like a garden hose, and then getting changed. If he was starting to make himself presentable then there would only be one reason for that. If you are going to take back control of your life you need to tell your body what to do and not have your body telling you what to do.

Finally, he reached a sufficient stage of night wakefulness to justify making a cup of tea and giving up on the next half an hour. He then settled himself on the settee and fell asleep. His tea went cold.

He awoke to sufficient worry about the time to know that he was planning to go to work and face whatever the music was. Worried he had overlaid, he rushed through to the kitchen clock and saw that it was only a quarter to six. He heated his tea in the microwave. He accepted that he was going to work and, in doing so, allowed himself the next hour to forget everything. Because after that, everything was going to hog the stage like the sparkling white teethed diva who thought this was the last night of everything and had a song to sing about it.

Gavin left the house twice. Once with the flipchart tripod and then again having returned the flipchart tripod. He had enough attention on him without walking through reception carrying a flipping tripod. He might as well go down the market and buy a great big hand with a pointing finger and sellotape it to his head.

Sally Clark was waiting for him. Maybe she had not been home overnight. Maybe she had been waiting for him all night. He was sure that this morning there was an unusually larger early arrival of other people, although he had made a habit of never getting in to work this early to know otherwise. No words were spoken. Her eyes sent for him. He followed her into her office. He closed the door behind him. The Four Horsemen of the Apocalypse were picnicking nearby.

Gavin's manager was a woman and the other five supervising social workers were women too. He wasn't sure if this mattered. There were no men to high-five or knuckle in the stomach. Had he been a man's man then at the end of every day he would have gone out into the world and evened it up with a beating of his chest and a war cry. Unfortunately, he was a wet blanket's wet blanket and therefore just more likely to drip everywhere and whimper.

'I wasn't sure we'd see you today or ever again,' said Sally Clark. She stayed standing. It showed the seriousness of the situation. Gavin sat down. He wasn't sure if he should have remained standing but had just sat down naturally. Now he could feel her looking down on him physically as well as disapprovingly.

'I'm here,' was the neutral response from Gavin. Under the circumstances, he had settled for safe and unprovocative. And as much as he might have felt ashamed for his performance yesterday, he was still hanging on to his belief that much of what he had said was true. Therefore, he was just guilty of saying it. He was also in two aftermaths. The trip to the beach had left its wake too. Better therefore this morning, after all he had been through, to be careful what he said. That meant saying as little as possible. Words got you into and out of trouble and right now there were too many of the wrong words bouncing around inside his head and asking to be spoken. Take what's coming and then find an empty field to swear in and a herd of cows to swear at.

'I've been wondering how to respond to your performance yesterday. What kind of disciplinary action I should take? What sort of expectations I should set out? How you should go about rectifying this? Do you understand?' During this speech, Sally Clark had wandered around her desk and sat down.

'Of course.' Safe and simple.

'Then I thought about why I was having to respond. Why I was spending my time trying to find the best action to take. This is your problem, Gavin. I'm not sure from what I saw yesterday why you have ever chosen to be a social worker. But that is your problem. So, as I understand it you are at work today and then off until Wednesday next week?'

'Yes.'

'In that case. I am sending you home today. And when you come in on Wednesday, I will be in my office at nine o'clock. What I do next will depend on what you do at nine o'clock on Wednesday morning. Is that clear?'

'Yes.' Gavin was not sure if it was clear. Had she an expectation of him? Was she expecting him to hand in his resignation? Was she expecting apologies or ready for action? Or was she just giving him time to think? But he had no wish right now to question anything. Therefore, the affirmative was what was needed. There was a herd of cows waiting to be shouted at.

'Go,' she said quickly, clearly, and loud enough to be final. He went.

Those in the office this morning, seemingly keen to make an early start, were not so busy that they could not look up, glance, or follow Gavin's movement. Remarkably no one was on the phone. They were all sat busy doing nothing on their computers and ready to look up once the office door was opened, quick enough not to miss anything, but slowly enough to make it look incidental. A raised voice had signalled this was about to happen. They all watched on. Gavin's next move involved bag collecting and leaving.

Once away from the office, he walked to his car and sat staring out of the windscreen at lots of other cars. Grey. Grey. Grey. Blue. Grey. Sort of green. Grey Grey. Those cars were telling him so much about life. He was now feeling numb. So much had happened. He had not slept well. He was feeling washed out. He decided to phone Sharyn.

Sharyn was a few years older than Gavin. She had two children, both girls. Anna was sixteen years old and Maria was fourteen years old. According to the content of an alcohol-induced discussion they had had one day, both girls were named after famous Unitarians and historic women of some influence. She'd told him the full names of these heroines, but he had never remembered them. Maybe Sharyn was hoping she was raising a couple of female protagonists so long as they would one day venture outside their bedrooms. Whilst they were too young to leave home, they had both reached that stage in their adolescent lives where they had left the lounge. They lived in their separate bedrooms and came out for special occasions, the chance to breathe fresh air and the obligatory Sunday lunch when Sharyn had insisted they all eat together. In truth, both girls, despite being independent and showing some rebellious behaviour, had a healthy respect for others and were maintaining and probably developing a good level of maturity. It was just a shame that Gavin rarely saw any of this. They made no secret of their feelings that he was an intruder. The lounge was still their territory not his, even if they had forgotten what colour the settee was.

Had he come into their lives with gusto, tales of great adventures, or even a hint of excitement they might have thought differently. Had he brought smiles, a cheerful hello, some gentle banter, or a bad joke or two, it would have been embarrassing but it would have at least given them something to respond to. Had he even brought them offerings from his own exciting life they might have had something to connect with. They did not expect gifts. They did not need platitudes. But he just seemed to be a spectre in the house, another body wandering around downstairs, or more likely a presence sitting in the same chair hanging around as if the world had taken the afternoon off. Anna and Maria had not taken to Gavin. They managed well in their task of avoiding him, much helped by Gavin's practice of not visiting too often.

'Are you free for coffee?' he asked. She was. As a vicar, Sharyn was particularly good at being free when people needed her. It came with the job. She was always free for coffee, tea, homemade biscuits, a walk around the garden, to see the new greenhouse, to meet visiting relatives who'd been asking about her, to confirm that the staining in the downstairs toilet really did look like an image of Jesus but that contacting the BBC was probably taking it a little too far. It was an unchallenged job requirement that she must be free at all times. She knew Gavin's needs were not religious, most people's never were, but he was a close friend and she was God's underpaid and overworked all faiths social worker. Besides this, Gavin didn't regularly contact her out of the blue.

Gavin arrived early and sat nursing his latte. He was early enough not to be expecting Sharyn's arrival. For the first time in the past twenty-four hours, his mind seemed free. Twenty-four hours of poorly executed confrontation, life-affirming and death considering calculations, agitated sleeplessness, and music facing. Now his mind was suddenly able to drift freely. It did not drift far. Had he really considered killing himself or was it just for effect? The sea would have been too cold for drowning. Thirty-two paracetamol washed down with Earl Grey tea was probably not enough. Most likely land him in hospital and puking up bergamot. Could he have swallowed that many tablets? And did any of it matter? He was where he was. Time out in his favourite coffee shop.

He had not rehearsed what he was going to say to Sharyn or how much he was going to tell her. At this moment in his life, it would be good to see her. He'd still got the flipchart upright in his lounge with TOMORROW crossed out and TOMATO and RUN written on it. He'd dumped it there when deciding not to return it this morning. It was a positive outcome. He had tomorrow now. He had some sort of commitment to run. Could he start physically running? Or would he just pick up the pace of his life? Maybe not the fast lane. But he could try running. He had never run before. He was not sure if he had the build for it. Did he have the legs?

'Hi, Gavin,' announced Sharyn, surprising him.

'Oh hi,' he replied.

'You looked lost in thought. What were you thinking about?'

'Oh. Just my legs. Both of them. Two legs.'

'Yes. I believe so. Helps us to walk or we would have to hop everywhere.'

'Or run.'

'Prefer walking. Not sure about hopping though.'

'Can I get you a coffee?'

'Let me get them. You look ready for another one and I'm still on my feet. Both of them. The usual, is it?'

He did not answer. They knew each other well enough to communicate that way.

Sharyn returned with a latte and a herbal tea.

'Can never really get into herbal tea,' said Gavin. examining the red content of Sharyn's cup. 'Never tastes as good as it smells.'

'We're all different.' That was almost a motto for Sharyn.

'I'm sorry if I've dragged you away from anything.'

'Just Mrs Parkinson. She invited me over to look at her hollyhocks but all she wanted to talk about was the Christmas nativity.'

'That was months ago.'

'Church politics. We ended up with two wise men, one shepherd and three Josephs. Technically two Josephs and a Josephina. She'd been holding back on wanting to say something about it. Anyway, I told her something had come up and I needed to leave early. Didn't even get to see her hollyhocks so she can use that one again.'

'Glad I can help.' Gavin smiled.

'You need to come round again. Seems a while since you visited us.'

'Never really sure that I'm visiting anyone other than you.'

'The girls will be there.'

'In their rooms. Staying out of the way.'

'Giving us space.'

'They certainly like giving me space. They just ignore me.'

'They ignore me too. They're at that age. We live in two different worlds. We live in the real world and they live in some sort of adolescent Alice through the looking-glass world where everything is the opposite of what we do.'

'Still think they ignore me at a higher level than you.'

'I didn't realise it was a competition.'

Gavin smiled and drank the remains of his first coffee and then lined up the one that Sharyn had bought him.

'Anyway. What's this all about? Why did you want to see me?' Sharyn asked.

Gavin told her everything about yesterday's meeting and the brief reunion with his manager earlier this morning. He told her nothing about the romantic evening spent on the beach with the flipchart paper and tripod.

'Sometimes you are a bloody fool,' Sharyn replied.

'Only sometimes?'

'Don't push me.'

'I can't say I didn't mean any of it. Myriam's a control freak. Sally and Sonya don't have to do the real work.'

'And why not tell them!'

'I know. I know.'

'So, what are you planning on doing?'

'Well. That's the problem, isn't it?'

'Is it?'

'Yes. Everyone will expect an apology with added remorse and double humility. Some would like me to fall on my sword or at least bake a cake.'

'Don't bake. The situation is bad enough already.'

'That's their answer to everything. Cakes. The first rule of social work. Learn how to bake. The welfare of the child is paramount but don't underestimate the power of cake.'

'I'm not going to argue against the power of cake.'

'But wouldn't that be hypocrisy if I meant what I'd said? And I can't apologise by saying I did mean it, but I'm just sorry for being honest enough to say it. Oh, and by the way, here's a cake. I've written sorry on it in blood-coloured icing.'

'That should work!'

'Cake and hypocrisy.'

'But that's life.'

'Yes. I know. No one says what they mean. You go out and visit friends and tell them what a wonderful evening you've had and then on the way home you discuss how much weight one of them has put on or how awful the lasagne was. I know that.'

'Exactly. You have to give people some respect.'

'And you see the best in everyone. That probably helps.'

'Certainly makes life easier. So, what are you going to do?'

'What do you think?'

'I think you have to apologise.'

'A dose of hypocrisy.'

'To all of them.'

'A triple dose of hypocrisy.'

Sharyn smiled at Gavin. 'I can't tell you what to do.'

'I know that. Against your religion isn't it: telling people what to do or what to believe. Ironic really when that is all religion has done.'

'That's why I prefer to consider myself a person of faith rather than some religious protagonist. Faith is about exploring what each of us believes. Religion, quite often, is about blocking that individual exploration. But of course, it's not that simple.'

'I wish I could have some faith to help me hold it all together.'

'It's not out of the question.'

'Not sure that I believe in God though.'

'That's up to you.'

'See. As reasonable as ever. Any other vicar would have just jumped on that opportunity. We've got a potential convert everybody!'

'I'm not sure it quite works like that now.'

'Anyway, I just needed someone to talk to. And have coffee with.'

'I had a fruit tea.'

They left the coffee house together but then parted with a hug and a kiss. Sharyn reminded Gavin that he was overdue a visit to them. Gavin promised to make that visit.

He then called in at a sports shop and kitted himself out. He was using the motivation of looking the part to give him the push to go for a run after he got home. He would run this afternoon. He had never run before, but he would have his first run this afternoon. His first run ever. He would also be wearing the gear. He was convinced that wearing the right gear would help him run faster or further. Or both. Writing RUN on the flipchart had not necessarily meant that he was going to go running. He had seen it as an active word that would make him think not about a steady slow walk through life but if he was going to live then he needed to set a pace. How he would run, in what way he would run, or how he would apply this philosophy, he had not been clear about. But he knew his life needed to be run and he would start this afternoon by going for an actual run.

Chapter 4

It hurt. It really hurt. He had been running for about fifteen minutes. And it really hurt. That was generous, possibly nearer to ten minutes. The first five minutes had gone fine. He had left the house looking like your regular jogger: leggings and some running top with strange fluorescent markings. He had wondered about a hair band next time or was he perhaps a few decades too late for that? But for five minutes he ran. And then, during the next five minutes, the pain started. He found himself breathing heavier. His chest felt tight. He kept going, briefly, and then, fearing he was about to have a heart attack, he stopped. Now he was sat, doubled over, so perhaps less sat, more foetal, and perhaps less foetal and more fatal, the way he was breathing. People made running look so easy. Slow or fast, they seemed to glide along the pavements and roads. You passed them in the car. They never looked like they were going to die.

He could take up walking instead. Or a class in yoga or Pilates, whatever that was. Surely it would not make him feel any worse than he did now. He was not fit, that much he knew, but he had not appreciated quite how unfit he was. And strangely, he also blamed his new gear. He'd expected his new leggings and his new top to have special powers. Now they just mocked rather than embellished his running credentials.

The pavement had got weeds in it. You only got to notice that if you were observant or your head was six inches off the ground. Gavin was not observant. He was still breathing heavily but had improved just enough to rule out a heart attack. Perhaps he had a health condition that he was not aware of. Perhaps he should not run for health reasons. There were ants on the pavement. They did not seem to be wheezing or doubled over in pain. The ants prompted him to move, so he sat up. Only now was he concerned enough to consider how he looked. What sort of sight was he? He had left the house trying to look like Mo Farah. Now he looked like the winner in a worst bedraggled scarecrow competition. Thankfully, those first ten minutes had got him as far as a quiet side street, so no one had had to walk around him, or ask him if he needed an ambulance.

He gathered himself further and got upright. He set off back home, walking this time. He now felt self-conscious, walking slowly, and looking like death briefly warmed up whilst, to any observer, he was wearing gear associated with running and looking vibrant. He needed to be home. That would be best for him and best for the reputation of the neighbourhood.

He arrived home and let himself back in the house, hoping to have done so unobserved. He slumped onto the settee. So that had gone well, he thought to himself. Running was supposed to make you feel good: physically and mentally. He'd busted that myth. He was glad to be home. It felt much safer here. He was now breathing properly too. The flipchart was still upright, dominant in the centre of the lounge. The word RUN was staring at him. He got up and grabbed at the tripod to steady himself, ripped at the flipchart paper, and then had to pull back against the tripod to further balance himself. He succeeded in ripping down the sheet of paper that was taunting him, but he only managed to tear across the bottom half, leaving TOMORROW crossed out and TOMATO intact and reducing RUN to a single R. TOMOTO and RUN were teaming up against him. Had they been animated they would have been laughing at him. He reminded himself they were only words. Annoying words, but just simple words all the same. He decided to give himself a few more minutes and then see if he could make it to the kitchen. He needed a mug of tea. And the problem with living on your own was that there was no one else to make it for you.

He returned to the comfortable anonymity of the settee with his tea and a packet of biscuits. Well, that was lunch sorted. The flipchart and tripod stood there. They were starting to look more settled than he was. The remote control could be reached with little further activity required and so he switched the television on and prepared for an abandoned afternoon full of quiz shows, other people's problems, third-rate soap operas, and over-repeated sitcoms. He could just about switch off from the flipchart which, whilst not in the line of sight of the television, did still hold a prominent position in the room.

He watched and considered if this was what life had brought him to. Watching and mocking the lives of others. He could settle for being an extra in a seventies sitcom or even the injured party in a mock court hearing. Before he drifted into ever-decreasing circles of self-pity and self-loathing, he decided he ought to phone Sharyn and thank her for meeting him this morning. He was not exactly doing anything right now. And it might stop him from finishing off the packet of biscuits. It would certainly drag him away from watching someone else looking to buy a holiday property that most of us could only dream of. And God knows where they got the money from. It also meant he needed to sit up properly. He dialled the number.

'Anna?'

'Sam?'

'No, Gavin. Who's Sam?'

'Shit. Sorry.'

'Who's Sam?'

'You won't tell Mum, will you?'

'Depends on who Sam is.'

'Someone.'

'Someone who?'

'You will tell Mum, won't you?'

'Maybe.'

'Shit. Sorry. Just that she'll kill me.'

'Sam's that bad, is he?'

'No. Just Mum doesn't know.'

'Not yet.'

'So, you are going to tell her.'

'I said maybe.'

'Which means yes.'

'Which means maybe.'

'Give me twenty-four hours and I'll either tell her or leave the country.'

'As long as you don't leave the country with Sam.'

'Funny.'

'Hope so. Anyway. How come you're talking to me?'

'I thought you were Sam.'

'I assume your mum is not in.'

'Correct.'

'How come you're not in school?' It had suddenly dawned on Gavin.

'Sorry. Back to not talking to you again.' Anna put the phone down.

'Anna!' The room heard the frustration in Gavin's voice. Anna did not hear it. Well, it was the longest conversation he had ever had with her. So that was a positive place to start.

Anna and Maria had different fathers. Gavin did not know much else about them. There had been no drunken revelations on this matter. Maria's father had stuck around for a while. But he was an atheist and more importantly, he was also, according to Sharyn, a complete bastard. Gavin had the feeling that Anna's father was a one-night fling or a short-term relationship. There were no clues as to whether he was a complete bastard. Sharyn was particularly private about all this. It did not match the Sharyn that Gavin had now known for the

31

past couple of years. However, Gavin recognised that he had no right to know, whatever the truth was, and he would not push Sharyn to tell him. To be honest, he did not have any great need or desire to know. Then again Gavin could not rule out that Sharyn had told him more about Anna and Maria's fathers. It was not beyond possibility that such conversations had taken place and that he had just not retained the information. He was not one for parking the unnecessary in his head. Now he was stuck in that place of not wanting to ask and hoping to rebuild what he should know through the sort of half conversations that bring back forgotten information. Other people's children and other people's children's fathers were a complete nightmare in the remembering game. He avoided it completely with his work colleagues. He had a vague idea who had children, much less idea as to how many, and no idea as to what their names were, although from the frequent conversations he overheard, rather than took part in, he was sure someone had an Arlo and someone had a Grace.

Perhaps this seeming lack of interest meant he was a complete bastard, thought Gavin. Or well-rehearsed and well on the way to being one. It was time to get up off the settee and out the door.

It was a fifteen-minute walk to Nap's house. He needed Nap. Nap lived on his own. He had been married once but that had not worked out and he was divorced now. There were no children. Gavin reckoned that if you were going to get divorced it was better if there were no children. Therefore at least Nap had got that bit right and kept it uncomplicated. Whether he was any happier was a different matter. The other thing about Nap was that he was always in. Gavin did not judge this as he found it useful.

They had met at University, but it had only been a passing friendship and more through association with others than by any direct connection. Then they had bumped into each other several years later in Tesco and realised that they were living close to each other and that they had both seemed pleased by the chance meeting. Nap was freshly divorced and, unbeknown to Gavin at the time, had started a spiral downward into some sort of agoraphobia. Soon occasional trips to Tesco were the only outings that Nap did. And then he discovered ordering online and that served any fear of open spaces or busy supermarkets well. It wasn't something that they talked about. Several years of social work training were not going to have Gavin going down that route. Nap did not go out. Nap was always at home. That suited Gavin when he needed to call round. And Nap always seemed upbeat and pleased to have him visit. They just left it that way. They got on well without any effort.

Gavin could easily trace back any problems that Nap had to his parents. Anyone who named their child Napoleon was already booking the therapy sessions. Gavin soon uncovered that Nap was the only person he knew who had worse parents than he had. It wasn't something they talked about, but they had shared enough in those incidental discussions and peripheral conversations to realise that they understood each other well enough not to worry about that bloody awful thing called life. And whilst they never really opened up to each other, Nap was the one person Gavin could fart in front of and that was worth more than a year's supply of therapy. There were times when aromatherapy might have helped though!

'Do you want a game?' asked Nap.

'Of course,' replied Gavin.

'I've got hold of the Derby County kit when Clough was in charge.'

'White shirts, black shorts.'

'That's the one.'

'You going to be County then?'

'Of course.'

'How about we have County versus Forest? You can have any player in your team that Clough managed.'

'What about anyone who played in both teams?'

'You mean like Archie Gemmill?'

'Yes.'

'I reckon he can play for both sides.'

'Okay.'

And so, Nap got out the Subbuteo pitch, goals and all the additional accessories that he had either bought or made over the years. Such was his enthusiasm that he had a special table for it all to go on. Derby County and Nottingham Forest were set up with the big white ball on the centre spot.

Derby County 2 Nottm Forest 1

By the time the final whistle had blown Derby County will have been wondering how they did not win this game by a larger margin. Part of the answer to that question will have been the quality of Des Walker in the Forest defence. He seemed to be everywhere and needed to be everywhere. Otherwise, it was an inability to find the target and too many shots going wide that let Derby down. Hector and Hinton scored a goal each, either side of halftime, to give Derby a two-goal lead, but both players were also guilty of missing good chances. With ten minutes to go a great cross from Robertson and an equally good finish from Francis made for a tense finish. But Derby County held on for a deserved victory. Play had to be stopped midway through the first half when the ball went shooting off the table and seemed to get lost behind the bookcase. The Forest manager might now be wishing that the ball had stayed there.

They had opened a bottle of red wine and a bottle of white wine during the game. However, the game was taken seriously enough by both for neither of them to have had much to drink until it was over. Now they could sit back in the lounge and put the world right. Nap was on the red wine. Gavin was on the white wine. For Nap, a whole bottle of wine was no challenge. Gavin was more of a lightweight, but he would give it a go.

'You were lucky,' said Gavin.

'No way,' replied Nap. 'You just couldn't handle Hector down that wing. Should have scored more.'

'But you didn't.'

'Do you know I've found a bloke on the Subbuteo forum who's got both Italy and Brazil from the 1970 World Cup final and reckons he's painted each player up to look like the real person. I'm trying to get him to sell.'

'Do you think he will?'

'I think he'll give in eventually.'

'How many you got altogether?'

'About seventy. Some can double up if you're not fussy. Others, like with Derby, I've added touches to give it a particular year.'

'You're too serious for me.'

'Can't believe we both used to play as kids.'

'Can't believe you still haven't grown out of it.'

'What about you?'

'Not as serious as you are.'

'Still like a game though.'

'True. But you're the collector.'

'Market out there for it. Still make them. A great game when we were kids.'

'The nearest you could get to the real thing.'

'Still a good game now.'

'But you've got all the computer games now.'

'On a screen yes. On a screen. But Subbuteo still gives you a physical connection with the game. Don't get that on the computer. Can't collect teams on the computer. Look at these accessories. You didn't tell me what you thought of the changes I had made to the scoreboard.'

'Impressive. Love the detail.' Gavin knew that Nap could talk all night about Subbuteo football. And with the wine beginning to flow that could be a long night. 'Did you ever hear back from your ex?' A change of subject was needed.

'Don't get me started.' But unfortunately, Gavin had got Nap started. 'I wrote about three months ago as you know and still heard nothing. Told her she's still got my collection of concert programmes. It wasn't me that walked away. It wasn't me that ran off with that dentist. The man with the white teeth living in that white house. All those fillings she was having. No one hangs out at the dentist.'

'You didn't suspect?'

'She comes home with a smile on her face, you think the dentist's done his job. I know what he was doing now. Should have been struck off. And now I bet she's sold my collection. I tell you, Gav, I've got no faith in dentists now.'

'How come she ended up with your collection? If she left you, aren't they here?'

'Ah, you'd think so, wouldn't you? You'd bloody think so. She came back and took them. Just for spite. She left me a note saying that as I hadn't been bothered to give her a child, she'd have custody of the programmes instead. And she took Stoke City.'

'Why?'

'God knows.'

'Stoke City!'

'I know. Always baffled me that one.'

'Perhaps the dentist was a Stoke fan?'

'We all know what he was stoking.' And they both laughed, but half-heartedly: Nap because it still hurt and Gavin because it didn't feel right to be laughing at Nap's misfortune.

'What concerts were they?'

'Loads. Slade. Duran Duran. Stones. Pet Shop Boys. Oasis. Beatles.'

'You never saw The Beatles. You're not old enough.'

'Didn't see any of them. Just bought the programmes.'

'Maybe that's why she left you.'

'Fuckin' hell Gav. You know how to cheer a bloke up. Can we talk about something else? What have you been up to?'

'That'll not help. Things are bloody awful at the moment.'

'Work?'

'Work and everything really.'

'We are a right pair.'

They were a right pair. There were many things they knew about each other and yet there were many important things that they had just never got round to discussing. But they were a right pair.

'How come we hit it off?' said Nap. 'You a left-wing communist socialist good guy if a bit wet and me a raging flog 'em all Tory.'

'Got most things covered there.'

'Perhaps sums up why we're both single.'

'Sort of.'

'Oh yes. I was forgetting about Sharyn. Can never work out what sort of relationship you have there.'

'Me neither.'

'You getting any?'

'I am assuming that you are talking about sex there.'

'That's the sensitive sort of guy I am.'

'More an emotional relationship.'

'So, the answer's no.' Nap laughed. 'Is it because she's a vicar?'

'Think it's just how we are.'

'Must admit the idea of sex with a vicar would put me off.'

'I'll let the Archbishop of Canterbury know the next time I see him.' They both laughed.

'Come on. We'll finish off the last of your wine and then I'll get us a whisky each.' Nap's bottle of red wine was empty. There was enough in Gavin's bottle of white for a small amount each which was soon gone. Nap returned from the dining area with a bottle of Jura whisky and poured them a glass each. 'Tell you what. Fancy a game of Subbuteo again and this time you can only have politicians in your team? Conservatives versus Labour.' The alcohol had taken them into the silly part of the evening.

They returned to the Subbuteo table. Nap offered Gavin a team in red and Nap took a team in blue. He then took a pen and paper. 'Who's in your team then?'

'Callaghan. Could play him up front with all his experience of strikers.'

'Winter of discontent?'

'You got it.'

'I'm going for Gove. You just never know where he's going to turn up.'

'Skinner and Prescott at the back. The Beast and The Enforcer.'

'Like it. Tebbit on the wing for me. With or without bicycle.'

'Corbyn on the left wing. Williams on the right wing.'

'Williams?'

'Shirley Williams.'

'Didn't she transfer to the Lib Dems?'

'Fair enough.'

'You having Wilson in goal?'

'Who's picking this team?'

'Just thinking of the image of the pipe-smoking goalkeeper.'

'Who's your keeper then?'

'Widdecombe.'

'Captains?'

'Thatcher.'

'Blair.'

'Interesting. They'll probably go for a drink after the game.'

Nap announced the teams in a mock stadium announcer voice and the match began.

Conservatives 4 Labour 1

Labour will be wondering why they started with both Milibands up front. They looked like they had never played together before. Several useful crosses into the box from both the right and left wings were easily dealt with by the Conservatives' defence. A breakaway from one of these soon had Tebbit on his bike and setting up Major for the opening goal. A brace followed by an energetic Hague. The second half started with Prescott bringing down Thatcher on the edge of the area. Heath scored straight from the free kick although Wilson complained to the referee that he had not been ready as he had been attending to his pipe. There was only enough time for a consolation goal from Castle when sadly after sixty-five minutes the match had to be stopped due to a giant glass of wine being overturned onto the pitch. Neither manager will have been pleased with their drunken behaviour. The game had to be abandoned due to a risk of serious injuries to both sides and a red wine-sodden centre circle.

'Don't worry. Do. Not. Wooooorry. I'll short it in the morning,' said Nap referring to the mess.

'I reckon, I reckon, I reckon I ought to go.'

'Yesh. Me tooooo. Been good to get 'gether. Musht do it more offen.'

'Agreed. Agreed. Thanksh Nap. I needed that.'

'You just make sure you gets home shafely.'

'And you jusht make sure you can. Make sure you can. Get up them shtairs safety.'

'Shafely.'

'That's it. Shafely shafely doesh it. Catch a monkey.'

'Will do.'

'Will do too.'

'Will do three.'

'Will do four.'

'What?'

'Dunno.'

Gavin set off home. It was an alcohol-induced walk. Not always in a straight line. Moments of self-induced hilarity sprang up from nowhere. At one point he broke out into a run but then ended up in a hedge. Come morning, life would take its revenge.

Chapter 5

The following morning life took its revenge. Gavin was reminded why he did not normally drink so much. The room was only just holding still, but his mouth was dry, his head hurt, his brain seemed to have reduced his IQ to that of a cornflake, and he was several hours short of a good night's sleep. His duvet felt like a straitjacket. His bed made him feel like he was sleeping upside down on the side of a mountain. And all of this was preferable to the thought of getting up.

So, he just lay there.

As good as the evening with Nap had been, it was always the morning after that made you wonder if it really had been worth it. Most of today would be lost in recovery. His body needed to regather from all the places it felt it had been scattered to. He would see it through this morning to such a time when he could arise and feasibly make it to a tap to quench his thirst. The first real stage of recovery. He waited and hated it. There was nothing he could do that didn't involve making him feel worse than he already did.

So, he just lay there.

Time passed by. Life passed by. His world for this morning was his bed. As good as he had felt last night, he was now back to feeling fed up with everything. He carried two Joker cards. They were Sharyn and Nap and he had already used them. As much as it hurt, as much as he did not feel like it, and accounting for the fact that he usually just preferred to lie there and let life get at him, this time he decided to fight back.

So, he got up. He sort of got up. He sort of moved. He sort of walked. It felt as if different parts of his body wanted to do different things and every limb was behaving as if they had been sewn on by a teddy bear manufacturer. His head had doubled in weight and abandoned all hope in trying to control any part of his body. And his stomach lurched and billowed with every movement. He felt as coordinated as a damp pop-up book.

He only made it as far as the settee and he was only half-dressed. But considering normally he would have not made the settee and would not be showing signs at all of getting dressed, then that counted for something. And being on the settee meant he had got up, and that counted for something more. He had dragged his shirt with him and a pair of socks. These he put on slowly and without trying to force any involuntary movement of his head. The idea was to avoid putting the shirt on his feet and the socks somewhere along his arms. He avoided that catastrophe. He was now fully dressed. He celebrated by crashing back on the settee. He still felt like yesterday's unwashed armpits. But that was progress.

Half an hour later and Gavin was making himself a mug of tea. Now he was beginning to pick up. The flipchart tripod was still in the lounge. He had hardly noticed it. It was becoming part of the scenery. It stood there like a great tower competing with him for ownership of the lounge. It was a bit like a lodger. It had the potential to become a friend. It had certainly seen him at his worst. He told it to fuck off.

And there was something in that moment of flipchart abuse that got him back onto a better level. Consequently, a second mug of tea and a bowl of cereal later, he set off on a walk.

It was a slow careful walk. It was an unusual walk. Gavin would have considered walking as something that got you from one place to another and at which point its purpose had been served. But this was just a walk. He did not know where he was going. He just walked. Having the complete lack of any destination in his mind did two things that were new to him. Firstly, there was no focus on getting somewhere, so he just walked. He just enjoyed the walking experience. This was a new experience. Secondly, he noticed things. Incidental though they were, he just liked that he could see things he had never thought about before. This too was a new experience. As bad as he had felt this morning. And he had felt bad. And even though he was not fully recovered, as he started this walk, he was already feeling the benefit. And then he realised he could stop and look around, or look above, or look below. And there were things to see. The colours of doors. Windows that had curtains. The shape of the clouds in the sky. He gave a good five minutes to watching two ladybirds mating on a leaf. He uncovered a world where you walked and stopped, walked and stopped. Walked when you felt like it. Stopped when you felt like it. And he was going nowhere, or he was going anywhere, so stopping was allowed. And he needed to stop. He needed to rest his legs, arms, and stomach. He needed to gather himself for the next bit of walking.

He knew where he was, but he did not care how he had got there. He passed shops and looked in the windows at things that he would never have any interest in buying. He assumed this was window shopping. There was a teddy bear he would not buy. There was a holdall he would not buy. There was a bust mannequin, that had seen better days, dressed in an orange blouse and a purple skirt, that did not go together. The other window had a brown jacket, a green shirt, and jeans. He would not have been seen dead in that combination, which was ironic considering what he was wearing. There was a book about Victorian dolls that he had no interest in at all. All this was in what turned out to be a charity shop. It did not tempt him to enter. The next shop offered him washing machines, tumble dryers and hoovers. The price of keeping things clean. There were deals to be had. Interest-free credit. He walked on.

He ended up at a café that he would never have known was there. He ordered coffee and cake. He marvelled at the ordinariness of both the coffee and the cake. The sort of coffee that involves a jar and a kettle. The sort of cake that needs coffee, any coffee, to help it leave his mouth internally rather than externally. The food and the experience revived him. The sugar rush helped too.

He got back into his stride and focused now on walking rather than stopping. He did not walk fast but he got a good rhythm going and, energised by processed sustenance, he was off. He took an unfamiliar direction and soon found himself walking across fields. Abandoned land soon turned into something slightly more attractive. Yellow was replaced by green. The discarded rubbish was replaced by, well, just less discarded rubbish. It was not exactly picnic territory, but it wasn't bad. He came round the back of a large modern building where there was a wide window that looked out onto the greenery. From inside, a woman, sat in a chair and looking out, smiled at him. He smiled back as if he had been caught out. She was an elderly woman. On closer inspection, he noted that she was not alone. He looked no closer and moved on before someone started regarding him with suspicion. He had done nothing wrong but the unusual way he had been behaving made him feel alien, and he was sure he stood out. He followed a well-trodden path out of a final field and found himself back on tarmac and then uneven pavement. He considered looking for ladybirds again, or maybe a beetle or two, but then decided that he had already had too much excitement for one day. He headed home.

He arrived back home and felt better. He was glad to be home. It was not a relief to be home. It was not home as a sanctuary from the world and its wild unremitting ways. It was home as a place to conclude and compliment his little escapade. He wasn't exactly Marco Polo or Sherpa Tenzing but this was his Base Camp and Gavin felt he had earnt his rest.

Over the next few days, Gavin kept himself to himself, and then it was the afternoon before he was due to go back to work and face some sort of music. He fancied The Flight of the Bumblebee, but it was going to be The Prodigy and Firestarter. Time for another walk.

This time he covered a bit of distance. Then he sat on a bench. A strange place for a bench, he thought. Then he thought, but I am sat on it so perhaps not the strangest spot. He looked around. Houses. A corner shop. Some garages. Yes, it was a strange spot for a bench and strange that he had chosen to sit here. But he was just starting to get to like strange. Strange was better than dull.

He set off walking again and turned as if to say goodbye to the bench. He said hello to the teddy bear in the charity shop. He avoided the café. He headed off across the fields where he thought it was a slightly more suitable place for a bench. But there was no bench. And then he walked past the great big window of the great big house which he had decided was a care home. And there she was again. She smiled at him. He smiled back. He took the initiative this time and offered a gentle wave. She waved back. He moved on. He walked home. She stayed where she was.

The following morning Gavin drove to work listening to The Smiths. As he had set off, he had realised, yet again, that he had not changed the CD. He could not be bothered to either stop and do this or to fiddle around with his left hand trying to get another CD out of the glove compartment and then all the hassle of switching discs and swapping sleeves and putting things away and then probably crashing the car. Consequently, he kept having to listen to The Smiths. He liked The Smiths. Originally, he had put the CD on because he wanted to listen to The Smiths. But that was several weeks ago, and he was tired of hearing Morrisey's take on the world. God knows, Gavin was already miserable now. He was driving to face a different sort of music.

Gavin supervised foster carers, which meant that he supposedly told foster carers what to do. The foster carers told the children what to do. The children told their social workers what to do. Their social workers told Gavin what to do. Sometimes though it went the other way round. The social workers told the children what to do. The children told their foster carers what to do. The foster carers told Gavin what to do. And Gavin just sat with his head in his hands. Whichever way it went round, Gavin was fed up with being the one that was always being told what to do. And then he had a manager telling him what to do. And sometimes other workers liked to tell him what to do. The only person that never told him what to do was Cora. She was the fostering team's business support worker. She used to be an admin worker and then someone decided to confuse everybody by changing the names of job titles. Now she was a business support worker. She still did administration-type things.

Everyone was in when Gavin arrived. His arrival in the office was greeted with 'mornings' all around. Then he had to find a desk. That was known as hot-desking. It was a bit like musical chairs but more dangerous and under consideration for Olympic Games status. Every year more desks were taken away and when the music stopped those finding a seat had to try to not look too smug when sympathising with those left standing. Wednesday morning. Team meetings across the service. Never a good day for musical desks.

And, of course, women had handbags. Not for carrying a whole plethora of what Gavin could not even think they might need. For him pockets were sufficient. Life had set him up to only need pockets. But handbags now seemed to have taken on a completely different purpose. They were territorial. You hung them on a chair and that claimed a desk for the rest of the day. The only thing better than a handbag was a cardigan.

The power of the cardigan was immense. With a cardigan draped on the back of a chair you could claim a desk for weeks. And shawls were the master stroke. They served two purposes. They announced sophistication. This was a real player in the game of hot desking. They could also easily fall off the back of any swivel chair and that put you in the territory of what to do next. Replacing a shawl on the back of a swivel chair is very much an underappreciated art form. Oh yes, shawls were the tool of choice in the game of hot desking. As Gavin owned neither a handbag nor a cardigan, or even a shawl, he often resigned himself to a dark corner somewhere else or returning home to work. And working at home. Don't even get him started on working at home. He had no desk. He had no swivel chair. He had no real identity with work. He did now have a flipchart tripod owning his lounge.

Already seated and holding their ground, with or without handbags and knitwear, were Nichola, Shirley, Kate, Naomi, and Rene. Gavin still did not know how to pronounce Rene properly. He tended to cough her name or, on a good day, either mumble it or lump it in with anyone else's name who was nearby.

Nichola was on the phone, and it sounded like she was trying to mollify foster carers who had had a bad night with the child from hell. The child from hell was on his mobile to his social worker complaining that he had had a bad night with the foster carers from hell. Soon Nichola would be getting a phone call from the child's social worker to argue over who the innocent party was and who it was that had been riding in from hell and trailing fire and all damnation.

Shirley and Kate sat at adjoining desks, around which there seemed to be some sort of forcefield that would always prevent anyone else from sitting there. Its special powers were derived from an array of unimportant personal items that had flaunted all hotdesking rules and established squatters' rights across this hallowed space. Shirley and Kate had been working together in foster care for so long that they talked a completely different language to everyone else.

Naomi was writing up an account of a visit she had made yesterday evening. She was the newest member of the team and the youngest. She had made a quick escape from front-line childcare into fostering and turned up suspiciously soon after Sally Clark had arrived as team manager.

Rene sat slightly apart from the others and seemed to be performing some task that involved her work mobile, the computer, and a stapler. She was the person Gavin knew the least well and yet he suspected that, if only he could get into some meaningful dialogue with her and get her name right, he would discover they had quite a lot in common.

They were all managed by Sally Clark. She was one of those people that when you are talking about them you always use their full name. No one talked about Sally. Everyone talked about Sally Clark.

His understanding of Sally Clark was that she had moved out of frontline social work and into fostering as she had got kids and thought this would give her more time. Something to do with the work-life balance. Gavin had never really understood what the work-life balance was. Work involved trying to appease a whole load of people he didn't like that much. Being at home involved no people. Life was just what passed you by. Maybe you needed to have kids to understand the work-life balance. He'd have to ask Sharyn the next time he saw her.

Sally Clark had her own office which was quite an achievement in these times. She operated a clear open-door closed-door policy on her availability. Her door was currently closed.

Gavin had arrived just before nine o'clock and, as such, following a cursory look around the office, he had given up any hope of finding a desk, even in the darker corners. He opted for lurking. This was the more awkward style of lurking that involved a lack of conversation with anyone. Much better to get into a conversation with someone and then give the appearance of belonging. However, everyone being busy and preoccupied had left him with the role of suspicious office lurker. He needed to calculate if he could make it to the kitchen or, did he have to wait it out until Sally Clark was ready. The kitchen was great. It always had a corner in which there were books that someone was trying to get you to put an order in for. Great for distracted reading but risky if you suddenly found yourself ordering something that under absolutely any other circumstance you would have shown no interest in at all. The sort of book that when it arrives you have forgotten what it was you ordered and the surprise is a disappointment. Something like '101 Recipes You Didn't Realise You Needed' or 'Yet Another Book of Sudokus'. Gavin stayed in the office and carried on lurking.

Sally Clark was on time. Her door opened. It was nine o'clock. This made a point. Gavin noted that in response to his misbehaviour she was presenting perfection. The sort of perfection that announces that we are the better people and you are just a bunch of wasted underachievers. The wasted underachiever entered the office and sat across from the perfection that was Gavin's team manager. He realised he was disliking her more than ever and this did not forbode well for the next half an hour. They had a team meeting in half an hour. She was unlikely to go beyond that time. She could not undermine her expectation of everyone else by being on time. Unless, of course, it was one of those occasions when she needed to use being late to underline her own importance. Gavin realised he needed to get out more.

'So, Gavin. Have you thought about what happened?'

'Yes.' Technically this was true. Gavin had thought about it, briefly. It was hard not to. But he knew he hadn't given it the sort of thought that Sally Clark was inferring.

'And?'

Gavin hated questions that consisted of just one word. And this was the King, or perhaps he should say, Queen of the one-word questions. It was like playing poker and asking the other player to show you their cards. He still thought that the whole situation was a mountain out of a molehill: less Everest and more Snowden, but a mountain all the same. But when you are seeing a mole and others are expecting Edmund Hillary and Tenzing Norgay with ropes, crampons, carabiners, and ice axes, and all you've got is a garden spade, then the route ahead is going to be a troubled one. Gavin was not sure that he cared any more. But there was still the consideration of making life easier or harder, both in the matter of ongoing relationships and for his conscience.

'I stand by the intention of what I did. I do not think I should be reprimanded for trying to be creative. I also think in the meeting I said no more than the truth.' He could sense Sally Clark tense up. 'But I have to accept that no one else seems to agree with me on either matter.'

Sally Clark gave a look that danced on the grave of anyone who could even think otherwise. This was followed by silence. The sort of silence that weighs heavier than a ten-tonne truck.

'So?' She was certainly looking to master the one-word questions this morning.

Gavin looked at his tormentor. Was she enjoying this? He couldn't tell. 'So.' He repeated the word back to her. 'You're expecting me to offer apologies.'

'It would help.'

'Apologise to a thirteen-year-old who's probably lapping all this up and playing us like some party game. Apologise to a foster carer with less warmth than an Arctic wind. Apologise to a social worker who has still probably got homework to hand in. Apologise to you.'

'I can cope without an apology. It's your cynicism that worries me. I can't force you to apologise. That is up to you.

But you do have working relationships to think about. Bridges to build.'

Myriam was not a place he had any desire to build a bridge to. Bernadette, he would just try and get along with. Amy, he would approach in his own way without throwing any more trainers out of the window. And Bob? Poor Bob.

Sally Clark cut to the chase. 'Do you think social work is right for you?'

'I'm not sure social work is exactly right for anyone.'

'I'm happy with it.'

Gavin was not too sure about this, but he knew better than to challenge. 'Well, it's certainly a complex profession,' he replied.

'It is but with some clear and expected standards.' She paused. 'Gavin, I'm not sure this is getting anywhere now. I have spoken to Carla and we have agreed that I should give you a verbal warning about your behaviour. It will go down on your file.' Carla was Sally Clark's manager.

Gavin nodded in acknowledgement of this. The sort of nodding that went on a little bit too long. The sort of nodding that was better suited to the parcel shelf of a car. The sort of nodding that was just simply avoiding having to say anything.

'I also think you should get counselling. I'm not sure what is going on, but I can't do nothing.' She handed him a card. 'This is our local authority counselling service. I think you should contact them. Even if just to see what they could do. Up to you. Again, it's up to you. Just do something, please.'

He looked at her and then looked away.

'The problem now Gavin is that people will be watching you.'

Gavin brooked any response that had reference to buying tickets or hoping to put on a good show. He was just keen to get out of the office.

Sally Clark sensed an ending to what little if anything had been achieved. 'Go,' she said, and Gavin did.

51

He walked out of Sally Clark's office, out of the larger office area, and out of the building. If Déjà Vu was running in the three thirty at Kempton, he would be putting money on it.

Chapter 6

Over the next week, Gavin did not attend any of his appointments with foster carers and missed a particularly unimportant meeting with some student social workers where he had agreed to bestow on them all his wonderous knowledge about the wonderful world of fostering. He did make a conciliatory visit to see Bob, Myriam and Amy. Myriam was not pleased to see him which was expected. Bob was indifferent. Amy was surprisingly pleased to see him and in good enough humour to ask if he was intending to throw any more trainers out of the window. The last pair Bob and Myriam had bought her were particularly awful and she wouldn't mind having them replaced. Did he have a good throw on him she asked, the sort of throw that could be far enough to make them hard to find.

Bob made him a cup of tea. Myriam gave him a piece of her mind. She didn't bake cake. Well, not for social workers. Amy went to her room and texted a couple of friends to let them know that the social worker who had thrown her trainer out of the window was visiting. It gave her a strange sort of status and she was going to milk that. She would update them if anything else went flying out of the window. And if it didn't, then she could make it up, or throw something herself.

It was a successful visit from Gavin's point of view because nothing had changed, and he walked away with no sense of needing to do anything. He liked visits that had you leaving with no further action needed.

Other than this visit, Gavin considered himself not so much absent from work as working very slowly. It was a job that brought you into the office regularly but often had you out and about or working at home. He was out and about and working at home. He had also made an appointment with the counsellor. Not willingly. Not with any sense of necessity. Not with any positive expectations. Just because it reduced the items on any list anyone had of the things he should be doing. He had expected a waiting list or that she would be busy. There was no waiting list. She was not busy. She was sufficiently not busy to be suitably available at any time. Gavin didn't like any time. It did not allow you to put it off. And so, he had agreed to an appointment five days hence. And that was six days ago.

'You going to be in trouble then?' asked Nap.

'Not exactly out of trouble,' replied Gavin.

'Will you get another appointment?'

'Not sure if I want another one.'

'Why d'you make this one?'

'Not sure. Perhaps I felt pressured.'

'Not like you.'

'Not sure what being like me is like anyway.'

'Join the club mate.'

'Is there a membership?'

'Just me. Chairperson, secretary, and treasurer. No wonder I don't know who I am.' They both laughed.

'Do I get a card? Any motto?'

'Loads of them. Eat Your Greens. Love Thy Neighbour.'

'Depends on who she is.'

'Depends on who she is.' They laughed.

'Life's a bitch and then you tie-dye.'

'Look Left. Look Right. Look Left Again. Fuck I never saw that coming!' The laughter continued.

'Don't look a gift horse in the mouth.'

'What?'

'Don't look a gift horse in the mouth. You've not heard that one? Surely you have.'

'What does it mean? What's a gift horse?'

'No idea.'

'Does it come wrapped?'

'You ever tried wrapping a horse?' And the laughter denied any chance of an answer to the question.

'Do you want to know what I've been doing?' offered Gavin. The laughter stopped.

'Is this getting personal? You know we don't do personal.'

'Don't worry. I'm not going to go beyond the boundaries of man talk.'

'That's good to hear. What have you been doing then?'

Gavin paused for effect, as if he was about to make some sort of announcement. 'Running.'

'Seriously? You've been running. You've upset someone have you?'

'No. I went for a jog.'

'How far?'

'Only about a mile, but I ran this time.'

'This time?'

'Tried it before and it finished me off. Had to walk home.'

'How come this time you didn't get finished off?'

'Done a couple of walks. Then ran this time. Probably slower than when I walked.'

'That seems a bit pointless.'

'Not really. Because I ran.'

'Bet that was exciting.'

'You know. It wasn't as bad as I thought.'

'Any chance of you doing it again?'

'That's the idea.'

'Can't you take something for it? See a specialist?' Nap laughed.

'You're my specialist. Napotherapy!'

It was a moment of humour that just sowed a few doubts. Nap tried to pull them back from going too far down the opening-up route. 'You know you can talk to me any time. Football. Politics. Cars. The weather. How to put up shelves. The best drill you can buy for under a hundred quid.'

'The best service station on the M5?'

'You got it. Captain Scarlett versus Thunderbirds.'

'Who was your favourite Bronte sister?'

'Careful now. Where's this going?'

'Sorry. Star Trek or Star Wars?'

'That's safer territory.'

'The best episode of The West Wing?'

'We're flying now!'

'Would you rather learn to fly a helicopter or a steam train?'

'Can you fly a steam train?'

'The Flying Scotsman.'

'Brilliant.'

'That's Napotherapy for you.' The laughter was freefalling again.

'Anyway. I never saw you as one of those joggers.'

'Me neither.'

'You got all the fancy gear then or are you one of those dressed-down joggers?'

'Bought the gear. Thought it might help me to run faster.'

'And did it?'

'Not sure. Certainly not the first time. Nearly killed me. Quite upsetting act-'

'Star Wars,' interrupted Nap before Gavin crossed that line that should never be crossed.

'What?'

'Star Wars. I preferred Star Wars.'

'Star Trek for me.'

'Star Wars. The effects. Big screen stuff. Princess Leia.'

'Star Trek. The characters. Spock. Data. Counsellor Troy.'

'Counsellor Troy. Good point. Counsellor Troy or Princess Leia.'

'The battle of the hairstyles.'

'Why don't we play a Star Wars versus Star Trek game?'

'Because we play real teams.'

'Not last time. Indulge me again.'

'Ok. I'll pick a Star Trek team and you pick a Star Wars team. You got enough players?'

'No problem if I put Jabba the Hutt in goal!'

And so, Jabba the Hutt ended up in goal, although he looked more like a plastic man in green and white stuck on the end of a long plastic stick.

Star Wars 2 Star Trek 2

This was a game of two halves. Star Wars took control of the first half and deserved the lead given to them by a brilliant solo goal with a forceful finish from Darth Vader. The second half looked like it was going to be more of the same when R2D2 scored an early second goal. However, a penalty confidently put away by Mr Spock brought Star Trek back into the game. From then on, they kept up the pressure and were rewarded when a great through ball from Captain Kirk left Seven of Nine with a simple tap-in to equalise. The pressure continued and it was only a couple of great saves from Jabba the Hutt that saw Star Trek fail to add any more. In the end, a draw was a fair result.

Chapter 7

The running continued. And the moments when he was enjoying it were getting longer. It was a great way to free think. Whatever came into your mind. And when he started to struggle, he allowed himself to walk. And those were the best walks. Although there were moments of guilt when he was being observed as underperforming for the gear he was wearing. He'd speed up if other runners were nearby. He'd note what they were wearing. It was fine when someone in tight leggings and a running vest went past him. It was a little annoying if they were wearing an old T-shirt and cheap supermarket shorts and especially if the shorts were pink and the T-shirt yellow or some other ghastly combination.

He regularly ran past the window of the care home. The next time he had stopped and made more of a point of waving from a standing position. It felt odd. But she waved back. And then she turned the wave into a beckoning. He stood there. He did not know what to do. He looked around which he knew was a pointless action. It just gave him time. He raised his arms and held his palms out as if he was calling on some omnipotent being to overwhelm him with the idiot's guide on what to do when an elderly woman you don't know is making contact. Then she had stopped waving and rested her arm back on her lap. He was close enough to the window to see. He moved back a step. He was too close to the window. He didn't want his actions to be misinterpreted. Then again, he didn't know how to interpret his actions anyway. He was still standing there.

Confused, he set off running again. He ran away from the situation, but he couldn't stop thinking about it.

Gavin stopped running. A young girl was sitting on the bench, the one he had sat on the other day. She was young enough to look like she should not be there on her own. Gavin stood next to her. 'Are you alright?'

The girl looked at him. She gave nothing away.

'Where's your mum? Or your dad? Your mum probably. Well, nowadays I suppose you could have a mum or a dad or a mum and dad or two mums or two dads. Hey, three dads! Why not?'

She smiled. It was better than the look she had been giving him.

'Any brothers or sisters? Are they younger, older, or the same age? Hey! I bet you're a triplet. No. A twin, or a quadruplet. I bet you're a quadruplet with three dads and a horrible aunty who lives somewhere in a forest where there are elves and unicorns and pixies.'

This time she laughed. Even better than a smile. 'You're funny,' she said, finally.

'Anyway. Who are you with?'

'Me mum. She's in that shop.' And she pointed at the bookmakers.

'She's left you here on your own?'

'She always leaves me here. She'll be out soon. She takes them money.'

'That's kind.'

'She always comes out in a bad mood. I just wait here.'

'How long do you have to wait for?'

'I don't know.'

'I was sat here the other day.' And Gavin realised what a ridiculous statement he had just made. It was the pressure of having to make conversation with the girl.

'Oh,' she replied, batting it back with all the disinterest it deserved.

Gavin managed to stop himself from referencing a personal history of all the benches he had ever sat on. Scarborough came to mind. And Plymouth, although that was too long to technically be called a bench. What was he doing? He tried to think of a funny story about a girl and a bench. Nothing was forthcoming.

'Do you want to sit down?' she asked him, moving along the bench.

This made Gavin nervous. And at which point he was shouted at from across the road.

'Oi. What do you think you're doing?'

'That's me mam.'

She didn't look like she was full of the joys of having taken the bookies to the cleaners.

'Time to go,' he said to the girl.

'See ya,' she replied.

The following day Gavin felt guilty about not visiting the old lady. He realised that he could walk away, or run away, but she could not. Well, she was there every time he went by, and he had not seen her out running! He made the decision this time to stop and take up any invitation to visit her. He dressed for the occasion. His running top matched his trainers. That was the best he could do. He would try not to sweat too much.

He set off again. He headed straight for the home. He felt daft. So far, he had just run without purpose and with no sense of destination. Out the front door and off you go. Now he had a destination and had set himself the requirement to look presentable. So far it had only taken five minutes into every run he had done before he no longer looked presentable. Turning up at the front door of the care home sweating, panting, doubled over, and asking to see a resident he'd never met before, that, he knew, would not look good. And up to now his relationship with her was through a large glass window. What would she think if he turned up sweating like a chocolate fountain? And then, if he turned up looking like he had made an effort, how would she interpret that? It all felt unnatural. Gavin was not one for giving too much thought to most social situations. And yet, here he was, outthinking Proust.

He was now not too far from the home. He took a diversion through a worn gap in a hedge and stopped. It was probably somebody's driveway. They had long driveways in this area. These were the sort of driveways that could easily be mistaken for roads. Big houses, big driveways, big gates, and no sense of humour. Gavin now found himself considering the mental state of the woman and making all sorts of judgements about her because she was in a care home. And more importantly to him, how she would respond to him turning up. Did she want him to visit? Did she remember him each time or was she just a friendly hand waver? And why was he thinking of visiting anyway? It was all getting a bit too much. He ran back through the gap in the hedge and took a different route, avoiding the home.

He was soon back outside his front door. He sat down. He was worn out from too much thinking. He went inside and got a glass of water and sat back outside again. He tried to stop thinking. He was now thinking about not thinking. He was not thinking about the old woman. He was not thinking about running past the window and waving again. He was not thinking about visiting her. He was not thinking about feeling guilty if he did not visit her. He was not thinking that he ought to visit her. He was not thinking about putting his glass of water down and running again. He put down his glass of water and set off running again.

He ran to the home and slowed down past the window. There she sat. She wasn't looking out of the window. She didn't know he was there. He stood and waited. She was looking at something else. Or she was asleep. Or she was just staring into space. Or that was where they had a television. But she wasn't looking out of the window. It was a big window. It wasn't a lot to ask that she might look out of the big window. She didn't.

Gavin paced. He was lurking. He was looking suspicious. He set off running again before his presence took on any semblance of stalking. He was disappointed. He ran and thought about his feelings of being let down. It distracted him from the effort of running. It helped him to run further. He ran back past the home and past the window on the assumption that she would be staring out of the window as was his expectation of her. This time she was not there at all. The chair had a different occupant. Gavin wondered how that worked. She couldn't have vacated the chair for long and now someone else was in it. She was always sitting in that chair. He assumed she had some sort of ownership. Would there be a fight? Could there be a fight? Would there be words? He was awoken from his surreal imaginings by an approaching woman.

'What do you think you're doing?' she demanded.

Gavin was not prepared sufficiently to answer and before he had the chance to gather any thoughts, she continued.

'You a pervert or something?'

'Just being friendly.' And, as the words left his mouth, he realised that, through his honesty, he was being set up like ten pins.

'Friendly,' she shouted and released her bowling ball, scattering all ten pins. 'Not around here you don't.'

Gavin set off running again to the fading accusation of perversion.

He ran home. He picked up the glass of water and poured whatever was left in it over his head. He needed cooling down. He needed a cold reality check. A few trickles of water taunted him. He went inside and filled the glass. He drank half and then poured the remaining half over himself. That drowned the taunting trickles and left him alert. He had run well. He had interacted badly. He had run away from both what he had intended to do and from his accuser. And now he felt bad on both accounts. He stayed home.

The next day Gavin had to work. It was a working day and he especially needed to counter the lack of effort of previous days with some sign of effort and commitment. He was only part-time. It suited him. He made two visits in between which he crept into the office, avoided Sally Clark, said hello to Cora and Shirley, had almost a meaningful discussion at the sinks in the toilet with someone he did not know and then left. He had sat in the car for ten minutes before his second visit. He had put the car heating on full blast to dry the splashes on his trousers resulting from not paying enough attention when he had been drying his hands. It looked like he had had an accident at the urinal. That was the problem with beige, it showed things up. Then he went home. He wrote up the details of his visits on his work laptop. He sent a few emails to make him look busy. Then he stopped work.

The events of the previous day had not wandered far from Gavin's mind and now they came back like toxic forgotten lovers at a wedding and as vivid as a disco ball at a nightclub. Just demanding to be entertained. He could not ignore them. He got changed into his running clothes: the combination of the slightly better top with the quarter-length jogging bottoms with socks rolled down and trainers that still looked new. He wanted to look like a runner. He wanted to look presentable. He didn't want to look like a pervert.

He set off running and headed straight to the care home. No window this time, just straight through the doors and ready to challenge the woman who thought he was a pervert. Of course, she was not there. There was no one in the foyer. He waited. There was a reception desk. Double doors were the way into the home, but they had a coded security lock. He would have to wait. It was right that he should wait. He was a visitor. This was a waiting room. Come to think of it, the whole place was a waiting room. It was a direction of thought that he abandoned.

Someone came through the doors. It was not the woman who thought he was a pervert. This woman was friendly. She had clearly not spoken with the woman who thought he was a pervert.

'Hello. Can I help you?' she said with a smile.

Gavin didn't know what to say. He was set up for a confrontation. It clearly would not be the right call to tell her he was not a pervert. He smiled back at her. She smiled again but with slightly less conviction. Gavin had to find the words before he messed up again. 'I was wondering if I could visit one of the ladies here?' And the words just all sounded wrong. He was heading toward pervert territory again.

'Do you know someone here?' asked the woman, hovering near the desk.

'Not exactly. I don't know what she's called.' Gavin paused to consider where he should go next other than back out the door. 'I go past the window and this woman in here often waves at me and I thought it would be nice to come in and say hello.' He wasn't sure where he had taken the conversation now.

'You mean Mrs Deakin?'

Gavin looked at her.

'You must be the man she has been waving to.'

Gavin responded with an uncertain smile.

'She has mentioned you. A nice young man in shorts. She often sits there. And you want to visit?'

'If that is okay. Just to say hello.'

'I will have to ask her. Might be helpful if I can give her a name.'

'Oh. Gavin.'

'Oh Gavin it is.'

'No. I meant just Gavin.'

'Just Gavin then.' Gavin was about to respond again but the woman smiled at him. 'I know,' she replied. 'It helps working here if you have a weird sense of humour.'

'I'm sure.'

'I'll ask her if she would like a visit from a young man called Gavin.' There was irony in the way she referred to him as a young man, as Gavin was clearly older than she was.

'That would be appreciated.' He was sounding more confident now.

'Just wait here.'

She disappeared into that world beyond the doors. He had never been in a care home before. He had all sorts of visions of what awaited him if he was allowed through. Chairs came to mind first. His first expectation of this place, of any such place, any care home, was chairs. The room they were in was secondary and a far far less important secondary to chairs. Chairs of dull colours. Chairs you wouldn't buy at home. Chairs that look like they are waiting to go to their final destination. He had a vision of a certain type of chair which, if you saw it in isolation, you would just know it belonged in a care home. He could see chairs.

She returned from Gavin's world of chairs. She held the door open. 'Follow me,' she announced. And he did. He entered that world and there were chairs. And in the lounge sat in one of those chairs and looking out through the large window was the woman that he now knew was called Mrs Deakin.

'You didn't wave,' she said before he had even arrived at her chair. He noted that her hearing couldn't be bad. Her eyesight too because she could see him wave, or not wave as the case might be. And her memory because she could remember that he had waved and that he hadn't waved. And then he stopped himself and realised that he was ticking off boxes based on all sorts of assumptions about her because of where she was.

'I could go out and wave if that will help,' he replied. Was he testing her sense of humour? Was he still ticking boxes?

'I'll leave you two to talk then,' interrupted the friendly woman. She smiled and walked off.

'No need,' said Mrs Deakin, continuing their conversation. 'You can run past and wave when you leave.'

'Seems fair enough to me,' replied Gavin.

'So, you're called Gavin then.'

'Correct. And you are Mrs Deakin.'

'I am, but that's just polite introductions. They like to give you a status here. They think it makes you seem more important. And then they knock you down again.'

'What do you mean?'

'Let's get you into bed, Mrs Deakin. Aren't you eating your peas today, Mrs Deakin? Never mind Mrs Deakin, we can clear it up for you. A title and then a stark reminder of where you are. Here, and in life.'

'I see.'

'I'm not mad you know.'

'Of course not.'

'Well, no more now than I've been before. There are many who would like to see me locked away. Spend half your life running away from madness. Never quite got me. Are you mad?'

'Not sure. Been close a few times.'

'Good to hear it. You're either mad and you know it or you're mad and you don't know it. I know which I would rather be.' She smiled at him. 'You not sitting down?'

He looked around. There was not a chair close enough. He pretended to sit on an invisible chair, balancing on his calves.

'What are you doing? I asked if you were mad. I didn't ask you to show me you're mad.'

He stood up again. She had disarmed him. Well, that and now he didn't know what to do with his legs.

'If you can move one of those chairs,' she pointed, 'then bring it over. Otherwise, you'll have to stand. But don't squat like you've been caught short on a country walk.'

Gavin managed to push a chair nearer and sat in it across from Mrs Deakin.

'Comfortable?' she asked.

'Yes,' he replied.

'Good. So, you're a runner, are you?'

'Sort of.'

'What does that mean? Sort of.'

'Just started running.'

'Did you get anywhere?'

'Not really.'

'Why do you wave?'

'You waved at me.'

'I'm stuck here with only this window. You'd wave if you were stuck here with only that window on the world. But you're not. You're free. You can go, and run, anywhere. So why did you wave?'

She had him with the question. Was it a simple question or was it a deep question? She seemed to have the capacity for simple and deep. Contrarily he was losing all capacity. And as if to prove the point he answered the question with little thought. 'I'm not a pervert.' Oh, how he wished he had given it more thought. Just enough thought to have not said he was not a pervert.

'That's a shame,' she replied.

'What?'

'A bit of perversion. Wouldn't do any harm around here. Remove some of that banality. They think we haven't done anything. They think we haven't lived. You get to eighty and someone removes your sense of humour. That's what they think. They replace it with incontinence. What I'd give for a pervert right now.'

67

Gavin was beginning to wonder what he had walked into. And now was not a good time to start being a pervert.

She could see his discomfort. But it was harmless discomfort, so she carried on. 'That's the problem today. When I was a girl, you had your dirty old men in raincoats. Girl at school got flashed at. Teachers told her to stop being hysterical. It started a competition amongst us all to see who could be next. For weeks after that, I walked home through the park. Nothing happened. Rita Fontwell claimed to have been bumped into by an old man, but we all told her that didn't count. She said he had a beard. Still didn't count. Finally gave up. But where are all the dirty old men in raincoats now?'

Gavin raised his hand, then put it down and added self-consciously, 'No idea.'

'I'll tell you where. Everywhere. Just stopped wearing raincoats. That's all. Most of them wearing suits now with silly ties. Probably married with wives who can't wait for them to leave the house and go to work and take their silly ties with them.'

Gavin found himself smiling rather than trying to find the right words to respond with.

'So. No suit. No tie,' she said. 'You can't be a pervert, can you?'

'I guess not,' he replied.

'Not sure if I'm pleased or disappointed. Bet you really do think I'm mad, don't you?'

'No,' he replied, not completely convincing in his tone.

'Well, you shouldn't have bloody well waved back. That's all I can say.'

Gavin was constantly lost for what to say. As soon as he had caught up with the conversation, she seemed to have moved along again. It was not the sedate polite chit-chat he had been expecting.

'So, you live here,' he said, trying to show some initiative but, instead, completely, and utterly revealing his lack of the gift of the gab that she had herself so ably demonstrated.

'Of course, I live here. You don't see Billy Butlins, do you? That's Reg over there in the red jacket but he's no entertainment. He just dribbles and complains that there is never enough sugar in his tea. Not exactly stand-up material. Can't even stand up.' She laughed at the joke. 'Can't even stand up myself. Mind you, I've still got my marbles. Unlike most of them in here. Not many people to talk to. And the staff are too busy to stop. To be honest we could have half a dozen perverts in grey mackintoshes wandering around the place and no one would notice.'

'Well, I suppose I ought to go now.'

'That's up to you. The day thou gavest Lord has ended.'

'What? I mean sorry. I mean…'

'A hymn. It's a hymn.'

'The Lord gives and the Lord takes away.'

She looked at him. It was a slow careful look, but it was the sort of moment that gave her time to wonder about him. And then she smiled. 'Your visit. The highlight of the day.'

And now he found himself torn about leaving. He had moved off the chair into a state of limbo. He was hovering above the edge of the chair.

'Come on. Sort yourself out,' she said.

He looked at her.

'Put the chair back. Then promise to visit again.' She smiled again. It was hard to tell if it was a smile of assurance or a smile of forbearance.

He put the chair back and promised to visit again. They were her words rather than his but he didn't rule out another visit. He gave a false wave.

'Ruth,' she said as he moved away. 'That's what my friends call me.'

'Gavin,' he said.

'I know,' she replied.

He was ready for leaving.

He set off running again once he had left the home. It was a gentle pace and the effort came easily. He had no real direction nor was he guiding himself home. The run was taken over by thoughts of the visit that had just taken place. Mrs Deakin. Ruth. Ruth Deakin. Not what he had expected. Had he had expectations? Whether he had or not, she had surprised him. She had challenged his unconscious bias. She was more than he had expected. She was greater than he had expected. She was more confident than he had expected. She was more lucid than he had expected. She was odd too. But odd in a nice way. Hopefully, in a nice way, he thought. He didn't know her yet. Yet? He considered that an interesting thought. Yet? It implied he would return. And she had asked him to come back which, to be fair, was a firmer invitation than a wave. So, probably, maybe, possibly, he would return.

Chapter 8

Sharyn had invited Gavin for a coffee at their favourite coffee shop. It wasn't the invitation that worried him. It was the tone of her voice. It was the way in which the invitation did not allow for him to turn it down. So, here he was, sat waiting. If he was in trouble, he had no idea what for, well other than the usual comments on his manner or his way with words. But those comments usually only appeared in general conversation and did not call for their own show. And they certainly had never resulted in him being summoned to their favourite coffee shop. Gavin was nursing his coffee anxiously. It was a cup rather than a cardboard beaker, otherwise he might have been squeezing it sufficiently tightly to have caused a serious overspill.

Sam ran the coffee shop. Sam owned the coffee shop. Sam loved the coffee shop. Sam loved coffee. She was a self-taught expert in coffee beans and coffee-producing countries. She offered lattes, americanos, cappuccinos, flat whites and her own special Samiano. A hint of ginger in the coffee and a smoothie cream-like topping with a hint of blueberries. Not one of her customers' favourites but she was working on it. She wanted to promote something different, something you couldn't get anywhere else. She offered various kinds of milk including soya, almond, oat and coconut. She was proud of the variety she offered. It was a good job, because she made little profit out of the place. She put a lot in and got a lot out. She had a pay-it-forward board. You could buy a coffee for a future customer and put a sticker on the board and Sam knew one or two local people who had become regular future customers. The coffee shop existed on a reputation of camaraderie. Everyone counted. Everyone was equal. Even Gavin. A place where everyone could find the right coffee and leave afterwards feeling warmer and alert.

Sharyn arrived, ordered her coffee, and started the conversation before she had even completed the process of sitting down and, more noticeably, without any welcome or introduction. She was normally good at welcomes and introductions. It came with the job.

'You knew about Sam?' said Sharyn.

'Only just,' replied Gavin.

'Only just? What does that mean?'

'She mistook me for Sam when I phoned the other day.'

'And you didn't tell me?'

'She said she would tell you.'

'She told me you were going to tell me.'

'I only said maybe.'

'What does maybe mean?'

'It means maybe. It means I don't know. It wasn't exactly the situation I was expecting when I phoned.'

'Well, you still should have told me.'

'Sorry. You know me. I mess up every time. Have you met him now?'

'What do you mean have I met him?'

'Well, this boyfriend. Sam. Have you met him?'

'He's not her boyfriend. He's her dad!'

'Oh!'

'Yes, Oh. And you can put double icing on that cake too.'

'Oh.'

'She seems to have traced him. Nothing from him for fifteen years. Now he's back.'

'You didn't keep in touch then?'

There was silence. The sort that shouts out loudly above all the noise. It drowned out the conversations at other tables. It hovered above counter activity, the clasping of portafilters onto groupheads, and the bubbling whoosh of the steam wand frothing the milk. It denied the noise of doors opening and chairs scraping across the floor. There was silence, awkward and full.

Sharyn broke the silence. 'You don't listen. I've told you about both their fathers.'

Gavin didn't know how to respond. He couldn't remember if he had been told or not. It wasn't worth pursuing even the slightest chance that she hadn't told him. 'Tell me again,' he said, hoping to rescue the situation.

'This is where most people would get up and walk out.' There was no denying the tone of frustration in the way Sharyn had spoken these words. She didn't get up. She sat opposite him across the table and, if the table was to be a battlefield, she had complete control of it.

Gavin nervously finished off his coffee just as Sharyn's latte arrived. They both smiled at Sam. She smiled back.

'Latte as usual,' said Gavin. He enjoyed a joke that no one else seemed to get.

And so probably not for the first time, Sharyn explained her encounters with love, trust, adoration, disappointment, sex, and sleepless nights for all the wrong reasons. And how all of this produced two daughters and consequently defined fatherhood and motherhood in her world. Through Anna's father, fatherhood could be described as providing some very friendly sperm and then making full use of a highly successful invisibility cape once it was apparent what those sperm had been up to. Through Maria's father, fatherhood could be described as initially helping out with one child who is not yours, then also helping out with your own child, claiming ownership and responsibility for two children until life becomes completely bogged down in wiping bottoms and

73

noses, pretending to be a whole host of imaginary characters again and again and again, and never going out without a thirty-minute stop-start process. Then he had enquired about the latest models in invisibility capes and bought the deluxe version. Sharyn had not heard from either father for many years. But now Sam was back on the scene. More than that, he was in communication with Anna. And Gavin was oblivious to any of it.

Sharyn decided to move on. 'And don't forget next Saturday the Walton's are coming for tea and you promised to come over the next time and this is the next time. Come to think of it, it is probably the next next time.'

'Oh. Yes.'

'You owe me, Gavin. Especially now.'

'I know.'

'And you will be nice to them.'

Gavin paused. 'I will.'

'Only, you remember what happened last time?'

'I thought we'd agreed to move on from that.'

'We did. We have. We always move on. Every time. But no repeat.'

'Anyway. You don't like them, do you? You only invite them because they're church people and you're their minister.'

'Part of the job.'

'I don't invite my foster carers for dinner.'

'Different job.'

'I'll be nice.'

'We could practise this evening,' suggested Sharyn, resuming the conversation.

'What?'

'Being nice.'

'I'm not practising.'

'Only over dinner.'

'I'm not practising being nice. It's bad enough that I have to be nice on Saturday. I'm not spoiling today too.'

'Just make sure.'

'I could go out and leave you to it. Tell them I've got something else on.'

Sharyn looked at Gavin.

'Tell them I've got someone coming to my house.' The reason for which Gavin did not need to conjure up, due to the continued look on Sharyn's face.

'No. We are meeting as two couples.'

'What about the children?'

'Mine or theirs?'

'They've got children?'

'Yes.'

'The Waltons have got children?'

'Yes.'

'I never knew that.'

'Well, it's not a secret.'

'Poor kids. Geez! They've got children.'

'Yes.'

'They've got children.'

'Yes. So be nice to them.'

'Because they've got kids?'

'No. Just be nice.'

'Are you sure you don't want me to go out, stay at home? I could visit my mother.' Gavin realised he was now pushing the alternatives too far. Sharyn looked at him. 'Maybe not,' Gavin added.

'Your mother!' Sharyn paused and looked at Gavin. 'No. I need you to be there. We are a couple.'

'But no kids.'

'They're coming for tea. The children can do what they like.'

'Yours or theirs?'

'Ours. Our children can do what they like.'

The subtle change of ownership of the children did not go unnoticed by Gavin. But even Gavin knew when to leave well alone.

'Will they be bringing their kids?' Gavin asked.

'No.'

'Who's looking after their kids?'

'Does it matter?'

'I suppose not.'

'Good.'

'They've got kids. The Waltons have got kids.'

'Yes. Yes. Yes.'

'How old are they?'

Sharyn had to pause. 'Ten and seven, I think.'

'Boys or girls?'

'One of each.'

'Names?'

'Why all these questions? Why are you interested?'

'Just…' Gavin paused. 'Just showing an interest.'

'Jack and Jill.'

'Jack and Jill? Who names their children Jack and Jill?'

'The Waltons do.' Gavin just thought he might have seen the slightest suggestion of an amused smile give itself away ever so briefly on Sharyn's face.

'They live near a hill?' asked Gavin.

Sharyn looked at Gavin, all hints of any sort of smile now completely vanished.

'Just kidding,' said Gavin hoping to break the look.

The look wasn't broken. 'Just be there,' she added.

Neither of them left the coffee shop feeling any warmer and they hadn't enjoyed their coffees.

Sharyn liked Gavin and she could see in him that there was a lot more than might initially be thought to be the case. However, there were times when he tested her commitment to their relationship and she knew it held her back, especially when her job could provide ample distractions. Gavin liked Sharyn. He just hadn't realised it yet.

Chapter 9

Despite some uncertainty about returning to the home again and some doubting thoughts on why he was visiting, Gavin quickly followed up the first visit with another. He ran past the window and waved. He slowed down which gave a slightly less absurd deportment. He wasn't sure what Mrs Deakin, Ruth, might have expected in terms of warning of his visiting, so this seemed to offer some sort of prior notice. He didn't want to assume that she had no preparation to undertake, although he was making this assumption. She waved back at him. That seemed to have covered all courtesies. His slow run became a walk. He went around to the reception side and, following a brief explanation of who he was, he was allowed through to visit again.

The same chair was vacant again. He moved it over and sat next to Mrs Deakin. He was thinking of her as Mrs Deakin with that air of respect that is offered to older people, but he recognised that she had introduced herself as Ruth and that familiarity seemed to have been agreed. Consequently, he sat down in the moved chair next to Ruth.

'You've come back,' she said.

'I have,' replied Gavin. Already he found the setting more familiar, without quite feeling at home, which he considered would have had all sorts of implications.

'I didn't frighten you off.' It was more a statement than a question.

'I'm here.' Gavin chose to answer. He looked around the room. The last time he visited he realised he had been so engrossed in the unfamiliarity of the visit that he had not taken in anything of the surroundings. Or indeed the other people in the room. He would not know if they were the same people or different, and he was aware that he was assuming not only the same people but sat in the same chairs, doing the same things. And it was an assumption that he could not easily dismiss. The walls were adorned with meaningless pictures. The wallpaper looked like it had been agreed by committee. It was a dull room.

'Welcome to my home,' said Ruth, in response to Gavin's scrutiny of where she lived. 'If you visit again, we could play a game of spotting anything that has changed.'

He understood what she was saying. That was the dullness. It was a room that no one lived in. It was a room in which nothing changed. It was decorated by a decorator. It was cleaned by a cleaner. It was overseen by a manager. And those people sat around, immobile and dependent, were residents. They were in the room but it was not their room. 'And would anything have changed?' asked Gavin, teasing out the obvious answer.

'Depends, if anyone dies before your next visit.' That had not been the expected answer. Gavin had expected some reference to flowers, vases, pictures, or tables and chairs all being the same: day in and day out. He had not considered those living there, other than someone sitting in a different chair. The idea that someone would never sit in the chair again was an unspoken possibility that Ruth had turned loose and spoken. The contents outliving the residents. She saw the vacillation in him. 'Come on Gavin. I know what the most certain thing about being in here is. There is only one way I am going to leave.'

'In a…' Gavin paused.

'If you are going to say coffin, I think that comes later.'

Gavin's mind was torn between the bravery of developing the conversation or the suitability of introducing a new topic. He chose silence and a lowering of the head to one side with lips clenched, as if he was torn between nodding in agreement or lowering his head in prayer.

'I can't work you out,' said Ruth. 'Or maybe I can,' she added.

'I'm not sure what you mean.'

'Well, what I know is you run but to be honest you don't look like you have been running for long. Life is so great that you want to visit someone who will be dying sooner rather than later. And yet there is a warmth. In your waving. In your smiling. And especially in your silence.' She looked at him with firmness. 'Am I getting anywhere?'

'With a mind like that. What are you doing here? I mean you're not exactly losing it are you?'

'I know people who would say I lost it years ago. And at least if you lose something you must have had something in the first place.' She allowed the silence to speak for both of them. Then to ease the situation she added, 'Unfortunately, my body is not in as good a condition as what is going on up here.' Her eyes opened a little wider to suggest that something was going on up there. 'My best friends in life now are a rotunda and a wheelchair. Perhaps I should give them names.' She looked at Gavin for a response.

He picked up the cue with a stifled cough and muttered back. 'Yes. Why not.'

'What would you suggest?'

'Well, they're your friends rather than mine.'

'One day. One day Gavin. You never know. Friends change. Not many people last a whole lifetime. I never thought I'd end up being best mates with two chunks of metal though.'

There was a brief interruption whilst one of the residents had a coughing fit and was attended to in an act of slow-motion kindness. The other residents carried on sitting.

'So, what's your story?' Ruth asked.

'My story?' Gavin replied.

'Yes. What's your story?' She laughed. 'Everyone has a story. I'm highly likely to be telling you my story if we keep on meeting like this. Especially as you never have much to say. So, before I tell you my story, I want to know what your story is.'

'I'm not sure I have a story.' Gavin paused. 'Maybe I haven't written it yet.'

'We all have a story. You can't grow up without having a story to tell.'

'That's it. I haven't grown up yet.'

'Perhaps some truth in that, but you are an adult. Past your best to be honest.' She laughed again. He could not deny her honesty. 'So there has to be a story.'

Gavin had nothing to say. Ruth could see the uncertainty in his mind. He had the look that showed a lack of words forming and an unlikeliness that anything of any value was about to be said. So, before he said something lacking any meaning, she continued.

'It might not be a complete story. Only in a place like this do you want a complete story. But you have a story. It isn't hidden. But you are not ready to tell it. To me, that is. Or to anyone. You have a story but no one to tell it to.' There was a friendly smile to accompany this observation. 'That is part of your story.' Ruth paused. 'Yes. I am certain of it. That is part of your story.'

'Maybe,' responded Gavin, having found the word of the day.

'Maybe,' further added Ruth. It was the word of the day. 'Okay. When you are ready and not stuck at maybe, then you can tell me your story. And after that, I will tell you my story. And I promise to try hard not to die in between.' She laughed.

'Okay,' replied Gavin.

'Are you normally this hard to engage?'

'I think I am just getting used to what to expect.'

'From me? Oh. Don't have any expectations from me. Any expectations you have are on yourself. Expect nothing and enjoy everything.' There was another smile. 'See. I have created a saying for us.'

'Expect nothing and enjoy everything,' Gavin repeated, as if he was her student.

'Exactly.'

For a few moments, silence settled between them. It was a comfortable interlude. Ruth gathered her thoughts. Gavin let his eyes examine the room as if he was in search of death's final secret. Four other people were sitting in chairs. He couldn't tell if they were preoccupied with thoughts, without thoughts, or just indifferent to his presence. He could have judged each one of them if he had taken the time to look properly. He would have been pre-judging though. He had no awareness of who they were or why they were there. Who had they been? What were their stories?

Ruth broke his musings. 'What's it like out there?'

'The sun keeps trying to break out,' he replied.

'No. I mean you live around here, don't you? What's it like?

'Oh. You don't know?'

'Yes. I get out most days.'

He sensed her sarcasm. 'You didn't live in the area?'

'No.' And she realised the misunderstanding. 'All I know is what I see through that window. And that view is regularly spoilt by some bloke running past and waving at me.' She laughed.

'It's probably the best view around here.'

'Not up to much then?'

'You could say that.'

'I mean, even those fields out there aren't the best-looking fields I've ever seen. They look abandoned. The sort of fields crying out to be built on.'

'I hope not.'

'I hope not too. Sounds like I've got the best view in this town. Until someone plonks some cheap housing there.'

'I'll have a word with the council.'

'Don't get me started on politicians.'

'Oh dear.'

'I've never trusted politicians. They are the sort of people who would persuade you to build a bridge when there isn't even a river. And they would just happen to know someone eager and willing to build the bridge for lots of money. Then they would persuade the people that they need to dig a river to go under the bridge but with minimal help and support. Finally, having divided the people to one side or the other of the river, they would charge everyone to use the bridge to cross the river.' Ruth presented a resting smile and then added. 'Do you know any politicians?'

'Not personally,' replied Gavin.

'I thought not. I've never met anyone who knew a politician. Politicians and people don't mix.'

Gavin decided it was the right time to leave, especially before Ruth had anything else to say about politics or before she moved on to her next bout of sagacity. He rose from the chair and managed a standing position straight away. 'I suppose I ought to make a move now,' he announced.

Ruth didn't challenge him. She was ready for a rest.

Gavin set off across the room and then turned around. 'Hansel and Gretel,' he said.

'What?' replied Ruth.

'Your wheelchair and rotunda. Call them Hansel and Gretel.'

Ruth smiled. It wasn't her story to be told yet, but Gavin had got a little nearer to it than he would have realised. She would call them Hansel and Gretel. It was a good link to her past. 'Thank you,' she said, but perhaps not loud enough for Gavin to have heard.

The run back afterwards was longer than usual. First, he was focused on the simplicity of expecting nothing and enjoying everything. He churned the words over and gave them a good examination. He wasn't sure what his expectations were. Like everyone he hoped for happiness and good health, but they weren't expectations. In terms of expectations, he had given up on them. His expectations were of other people rather than himself. And other people disappointed him. And as for enjoyment. He really couldn't say that he enjoyed life. He wasn't sure when he had last enjoyed life. He had never really pursued life as something to enjoy. There were moments of pleasure. There were moments, stretched to times, that had been good. But as for linking any of these moments together to form some sort of thread of enjoyment that ran through his life. That was not the case. He could easily admit that he did not get any enjoyment out of life.

By now Gavin had run far and intentionally taken himself on a course away from any familiar journey home. This meant there was still some distance to cover at whatever point he decided to head home. He now started to consider his second point which was what was his story. There seemed to be a natural link between not enjoying life and exploring what his story was. Ruth had provoked this. She had a story to tell. She had enticed him with her insightful wordery and then with her hint of having something to tell. But what was his story? This baffled him. He had nothing to tell. He lacked a story. She had said that everyone had a story to tell. But who was she to tell him that this was so? Why should she be right? Why couldn't she be wrong? He was determined to prove that she was wrong. He would think hard about what his story was. Then when he could not find one, it would prove she was wrong. The proof would be in the time it would take him. Time spent genuinely thinking hard about what his story was. Time that would finally run out and prove categorically that he had no story, and she was wrong. On that basis, Gavin set about trying to uncover his story.

Gavin slowed to walking. So much thinking already and so much distance covered, he was reduced to walking home. His body had endured enough running. His mind was still active. What kind of story was he looking for? A fairy tale? He was certainly no prince. A fantasy? Gavin in Wonderland did not stand up. There was no road to Damascus. There was no road to anywhere. There wasn't even a road. He was on a rain-sodden path to obscurity. He lived in the town of Nowtdoin. There was no Aladdin's cave. There were no lamps to rub. It took some time, but he was finally relieved to get home. And he still had no story.

That night he had a strange dream He was under fire, trapped somewhere. It was not clear who was attacking him. He was in hiding. There was a greyness to it all. He was hiding in a bunker. But, like the incongruity in many dreams, it was not a bunker. And he wasn't trapped, but he was hiding. He needed to escape whatever was out there. He could not stay in this bunker that wasn't a bunker, and a clear exit into a larger greyer world had now appeared, as if it had never not been there. He ran. He was on the back lanes of rows of houses. He avoided the fields: they were too open. He ran behind the houses. He used them as cover. He ran down an alleyway and then back behind more houses. They were terraced houses with no gardens. Or at least his dream did not let him see the gardens. He hid behind the houses. He hid in the gardens which now seemed to exist. He planned an escape. Then he ran again. And then he awoke. Still feeling melded into the drab insecurity of his dream he was cast into memories of childhood. He felt lost. And there and then he had his story. An absent father. A mother who wanted to save the world. And in the middle of all this was an only child who didn't belong to either of them. The story of the lost child.

Chapter 10

He went to work the next day. The lost child had become the invisible man. That evening, wishing for invisibility, he dined with the Waltons.

The evening with the Waltons was exactly as Gavin had expected. Sharyn had prepared a meal that, as a vicar, she knew had to balance humble simplicity with just enough effort to show how important you are. And two courses followed by coffee always seemed right. She had come up with lasagne. The dilemma with two courses was always starter or desert. Which to include? Which to omit? Inclusions and omissions, both being equally important in terms of people's expectations and preferences. However, by now, she had seen enough of most of her congregation at harvest festivals, pea and pie suppers, Christmas dinners, and attending meals with them or meals out, such that she knew where preferences lay. For the Waltons it was homemade Bakewell tart with the option of ice-cream. And at least with the Waltons there were no issues around gluten, dairy or nuts. Anna and Maria had eaten earlier and were safely ensconced in their respective bedrooms, thereby avoiding both the Waltons and Gavin for most of the evening.

Gavin turned up just before they arrived. He made it look like he had been there for a while so, when they arrived, he greeted them as if he was no less a host than Sharyn. He had been no help in the kitchen and a passenger in the setting of the table, but he was there and, for this, he hoped he was back in Sharyn's good books. He also knew how to open a bottle of wine and where to find the wine glasses.

The Waltons had been as boring and predictable as he had expected. They were not great conversationalists. They were the sort of people that answered questions rather than asked them. They were the sort of people who, when on leaving your company, you did not feel you knew any better than when they first arrived. Jack and Jill were fine. Gavin found that he had to ask about them separately as any thought of putting their names together just tempted an outbreak of the sort of guffawing that doesn't know when and how to end. As it was, he had had to leave the table twice. The first time, it was under the guise of a coughing fit on being told that Jack had been complaining of a headache all day. The second time, it was a protracted journey to the kitchen to bring an unnecessary extra spoon to the table whilst they were having their Bakewell tart. Apparently, Jill can be clumsy, according to the Waltons. Gavin had been full of admiration for Sharyn's straight face. The Waltons had seemed oblivious to any of it and much else that was happening in the world out there. Gavin admired their uncomplicatedness and found himself smiling when they left.

For the following day, Sharyn had granted him the sort of freedom that comes from not completely messing up the night before. He turned up that morning on Nap's front doorstep in need of something to counter the efforts of that night before.

'It went okay then?' enquired Nap.

'I guess so.'

'Did you like the Waltons?'

'Sort of people it's hard to like or dislike.'

'Mr and Mrs Neutral Personality.'

'Exactly.'

'So. If you named a salad after them it would be lettuce, tomato, and cucumber? A Walton Salad.'

Gavin laughed and nodded his head.

'Or a mild cheddar cheese.' Nap was on a roll.

'A slice of Walton please.'

'A straight Walton, no ice,' continued Nap.

'What?' replied Gavin.

'A straight Walton, no ice. A whisky!' repeated Nap.

'I don't get it,' replied Gavin.

'Hold the ice.' Nap started to laugh. He struggled to speak. 'I'll have it Walton style,' he finally managed to splutter.

'I still don't get it,' said Gavin.

'Oh,' said Nap. And this time they both started laughing. It was the merriment of friends. The reason, the source of the joke, had vanished. It was just two friends enjoying being blithe.

Gavin broke the laughter. 'Anna took me to one side last night and thanked me for not telling her mum about Sam. And then apologised that I got told off for it.'

'Is that good?'

'What do you think?'

'Good books with Anna.'

'Yes. But I can't have her doing that again though. I can't have her thinking I won't tell her mother anything she tells me. I mean, it could undermine my trust with Sharyn.'

'And you don't want to get caught in the middle.'

'Between mother and daughter. That I don't.'

'There's only one loser that way.'

'And that's me.'

'Afraid so. And believe me. They will both come out as winners. Mothers and daughters can fall out big time but only for as long as it takes for some poor fool to come along and then they can gang up like they've been together since the beginning of time.'

'And that's a long time.'

'Sure is.'

'Time makes fools of all of us.'

'Is that Shakespeare?'

'No Idea.'

'Do you think there are more sayings about time than anything else?'

'Well, that and sex.'

'Sex makes fools of all of us.'

'Now that's a good one.' Gavin picked his nose.

'I hope you're washing your hands before we play anything. We only flick Subbuteo players in this house.'

'Sorry. I'm sure you do.' Nap had a downstairs toilet and Gavin went and washed the offending fingers. 'Are you wanting a game then?' he shouted from the smallest room in the house.

'Unless you've got something else to tell me. Any big news? Nothing to shock me? Anything exciting?'

'What do you think?' replied Gavin, returning.

'I'll take that as a no then.'

'Fancy a game made up of teams of people you don't like?' Gavin asked.

'I thought we said next time we'd do a proper game?'

'Did we? Oh. I know, but I think I need a bit of therapy. You know. A bit like writing a list of people I hate and then throwing darts at it, or scrunching it up into a ball and kicking it around the room.'

Nap looked at him as if to ban both ideas.

'So, putting them on a football pitch and flicking them about sounds just as good too,' said Gavin.

'Can't beat a good idea.'

'Can't beat a game of Subbuteo.'

'Not sure I've got eleven people I don't like.'

'I can lend you a few.'

Nap's Enemies United 4 Gavin's
Detested Waste Of Timers 0

This was never going to be a friendly.
It was all over by half-time with a hat-

trick for Nap's Enemies United by his ex-wife. Gavin's Detested Waste Of Timers were then finished off by a late own goal from Gavin's mother. She went on a run down the left wing but ended up passing back from the half-way line where the goalkeeper was stood upside down. It was a moment of madness matched only by an unfortunate incident where two of Gavin's Detested Waste Of Timers were flicked across the room at full force and crashed against the wall. Sally Clark broke her arm and that annoying man at the desk at the far end of the office who might be called Pete became detached from his base. Both are now resting in their boxes but will be out for the rest of the season.

'Sorry,' said Gavin when they had finished. 'I think I owe you a team.'

'You feel better?'

'Not really.'

'I did wonder.'

'Did it show?'

'You tell me.'

Chapter 11

Work had been slipping. Even Gavin knew this. He was only part-time. He didn't have the sort of commitment some of his colleagues had. It wasn't that he had such an interesting and all-consuming home life either. He just regarded work as work. You went to work. You came home. Others went to work, stayed at work, socialised with work people, texted work people, put a few extra hours of work in, and competed to see who was the most over-worked. By his own admission, Gavin was underworked and not winning any prizes in the category of the most exhausted social worker.

He had a similar relationship with his foster carers. He preferred those who didn't want too many visits from him. This, when he thought about it, was most of them. It was some sort of unwritten agreement that if they didn't pester him then he wouldn't pester them. Most of the time it worked well, but when it went wrong and the fuse was lit, Gavin always seemed to be the one cradling the bomb.

There was the case of Mr and Mrs Downton. Leslie and Lesley. Les and Lesley as they were called. Great with babies. Not so good with nine-year-olds. And especially the sort of nine-year-olds that had seen more of life than Les and Lesley. No news should have been good news. But no news meant that things were building up quickly and patience was being tested, but they were coping. Until finally they weren't coping and Gavin got it full barrelled, torpedoed by a submarine. He got two things. He got all that had been happening. He got questions about where he had been when they needed him. They got that he was always available on the end of a phone and could come over any time. He got that he was never available on the end of a phone. They got questions about why they hadn't said anything the last time he visited. He got challenged about how long ago that last visit was. They still got challenged about not saying anything. He got challenged about the real reasons why they didn't feel they could talk to him. They got challenged that that didn't seem to be a problem now. He got challenged that it was different now because they were desperate for help. They got challenged that here he was. He got told to fuck off.

Michael and Dan were his favourite carers. Well, them and Maxine.

Michael and Dan were always pleased to see him. For a gay couple, Gavin had always considered them to be the least gay couple he knew. Then he had to admit that he didn't know many gay couples and therefore he was probably making this judgement based on the media, television, sitcoms, general gossip, specific gossip, and a whole load of who knows what coming from who knows where. They had taken younger children and moved at least two on to their new adoptive homes. It might have been more. He was the sort of social worker that easily lost count and confused children, especially if they were a similar height.

Maxine, he had inherited from a previous supervising social worker. She was an experienced long-standing foster carer who had seen and dealt with most things. She would have thrown the trainer out of the window, he thought to himself. Then again, Maxine would never let any situation develop that far. She always had the knack for knowing just how to communicate with any child placed with her. And she had certainly been presented with many challenges and risen to them all. Age was not a factor for her and she had taken a good share of older children and ones that it had always been harder to place. Whenever Gavin visited, she would not be shy of telling him all that had happened, but followed this with all she had done. He was superfluous. However, he sensed that, although she had a fantastic support network, he was the person with whom she could tell it as it was with no worry about sharing confidential information.

Gavin learnt from Maxine. So many times she had informed him of something that had happened and he had just sat back with his cup of tea and listened to her. It was like a training session for him. He had to admit that he would have had no idea how to deal with many of the scenarios she painted. Maxine was a star. And this was why she had been the person he had linked with Michael and Dan when they had first been approved as foster carers. It was a relationship that worked well. It worked so well that their problems were then often dealt with via well-informed and clear direction from Maxine and a whole load of energetic support. Maxine lived for fostering and that made Gavin's life so much easier because he didn't.

Gavin went to the office. The need to call in was not high on his agenda. Visits took him away. Writing up visits and events and reports he could do on the laptop from home. He would turn up for team meetings but otherwise found himself engaging less and less with his colleagues. This he considered to be part of the pressure they were all under to get work done, but he knew it was also because he had started to prefer it that way. The exception was Cora. She was business support or what used to be referred to as admin before they decided to issue everyone with new titles and confuse those that had been around for a while. Cora and Gavin passed moments together, but they were enjoyable brief conversations. And then they found themselves walking into town together. Initially, they were quiet as they tried to adjust from one-liners to real conversation.

'Are you out this afternoon?' asked Cora.

'Yes,' replied Gavin and then had to stop himself from asking her the same question. He knew she was office based. She wasn't going anywhere, unless she had a dental appointment, was due to see her doctor, or something more personal that would just be referenced as absent. He had to adjust what he was thinking of saying. 'Nice day,' he added and immediately chastised himself for such a mundane comment. Gavin found himself slowing to walk at Cora's pace.

'Unless it rains,' said Cora. It was the sort of meaningless response that Gavin's 'nice day' had deserved.

They walked on, briefly in silence. The shops would soon be there to end the uncomfortableness of the situation.

'Where are you going?' asked Gavin.

'The Co-op,' replied Cora. 'And you?'

Gavin had also been heading for the Co-op but now decided that he needed to have a different destination, or this could be dragged out along the aisles of the supermarket and way past any interest either of them seemed to have in developing the conversation. Observations on the cost of baked beans or how many custard creams you get in a packet were not going to save the situation. There had been moments when he thought Cora might be the one person at work he could talk to, and they could form some level of friendship. She was a little older than he was, but you reach a point in life when age starts to matter little. But he was going to have to shop somewhere else just long enough to hope he could go back to the Co-op as she was leaving. And he hadn't even answered her question. And he wasn't sure why he should avoid her. Although a lunchtime walk was a good opportunity to avoid people he knew. Just switch off and let the working brain unravel.

Then just as they arrived at the Co-op, Cora came to life. It was as if the pressure had been removed and they could part on something more whimsical. Except she made the sort of statement that held you. 'You've been quite the mystery character at work. Can't say people talk about you much, but when they do it's all about what you've been up to or how you are.'

Gavin looked at Cora. They had stopped now and were having a stationary conversation. Stationary conversations made it harder to leave.

And then she followed with a question that Gavin felt unable to duck. It hit him hard. It floored him. He felt compelled to give something back in the answer. She asked him, 'How are you?' And she pushed further and added, 'Really. How are you?'

Gavin didn't look at Cora this time. He turned his head slightly to the side and away from her. It was not a polite question. It was not a passing question. It was not setting itself up to be answered with one word or a mutter. Nor was it going to be deflected with the same question in return. Gavin felt the question and how Cora had asked it showed that she had meant it. That was unsettling: fixed to the spot outside the Co-op and being asked to explain how he was feeling.

'You know. Life could be better.' He was still looking away, but his eyes glanced at her just long enough to connect and then he looked away again. This was a genuine conversation now. He didn't do genuine conversation. He was stuck.

'If you ever want to talk,' she said.

He had never wanted to talk. He wasn't sure that he would ever want to talk. What was she doing even suggesting he might want to talk? What kind of thing to say was that? He didn't do talking. Not that kind of talking. He told himself to keep it together. It wasn't a trick question. It wasn't even a question. But it was loaded like a question. But it wasn't a question. He remained silent. It wasn't a question.

'It's just that I've got five girls. All grown up now. Just about. So, I've had so many conversations about so many things. Mother Hen, you see.'

And he didn't need a Mother Hen. He didn't need a mother of any animal variety. And he was a boy, not a girl. Didn't she realise that boys don't talk. It's all superficial and pointless with boys. That's why they invented football or rock music or cars. Something to talk about without actually saying anything. If he talked it was to discuss the diamond formation, the number of female backing singers some aged artist needs, or the merits of memory seats in your next car. If she'd had a boy, she'd have known that. He took the safest option. 'You've got five daughters?'

'Yep.'

'And no boys.'

'No boys.'

'Did you keep going thinking eventually you'd have a boy?' Gavin smiled to himself and then added. 'I bet the fifth daughter's got a boy's name with ella or etta at the end.'

'She's called Rose.'

'So much for that theory then. You could still call her Rosella or Rosetta.'

'Not really. Not when her father was Mr Stone.'

It took a while and then Gavin realised. 'Ah yes. Rosetta Stone. A bit like Henrietta Cake.' He stopped to think. 'Or.' But another example was not coming to him. 'But five girls.'

'I just love being a mum, so having five daughters was just great. It is just great.'

'Does your husband think the same?' Gavin knew that this was a loaded question, but the words just came out quite naturally. He wasn't fishing. He was being polite. He could do polite when he needed to.

'Unfortunately, he didn't stick around, so I guess he didn't.'

'Sorry.'

'Don't be. I've got five wonderful daughters. I couldn't ask for anything more.'

Gavin nodded his head. He was showing agreement but inside he was nodding to himself his approval of Cora's apparent happiness. He was not sure how he would have felt about five daughters. He had no children so he couldn't even consider what one child would be like. But he did know that five was a big number.

'You not got any children?' asked Cora.

'Never really found the right person to be a parent with.'

Cora smiled and Gavin had to decide if it was a smile of condolence or warmth. He settled for tepid sympathy, the smile of tepid sympathy. That probably summed up how the world thought about him. All the judges searching out the cards with lower numbers on them.

They were still standing outside the Co-op and Gavin seemed to have managed to avoid any proper conversation. Cora also seemed pleased to have made her offer should Gavin ever want to talk. It was an opportunity to part which they both took. Cora walked up to the entrance of the Co-op. Gavin went in search of a shop he didn't want to go to.

Following a brief return to the office with a newspaper he had not planned to buy, and nothing from the Co-op, the rest of the working day passed without anyone asking him how he was in any manner other than the usual cursory comment. He was fine. He didn't need a mother hen.

On his next visit to Ruth, Gavin had gone wondering whether she would be asking him about his story again which he recognised was a far more interesting way of asking him how he was. To everyone else he was fine, but Ruth had something about her that had made him want to continue to visit. If he stopped visiting, she couldn't come after him to ask why. She was not going to apprehend him in the middle of Asda, appearing from behind a stack of washing-up powder, to ask him how he's been.

When he got there this time, he was informed that Mrs Deakin was still in bed. He was asked to wait whilst someone checked that she was wanting to receive any visitors. On their return, he was informed that she wasn't receiving any visitors, but she would make an exception for him.

He arrived at room number eight which presented itself with all the appearance of a front door. He knocked on the door and Ruth shouted for him to come in. He opened the door and the small bedroom that greeted him seemed to make no effort to try and deny that there was not something more substantial hidden behind the convincing front door. It was a room with a bed in it, and there was a large, fitted wardrobe. To his immediate right, through a crack in another door, he could see that there was a toilet and some sort of shower arrangement.

'Have a look,' Ruth said.

Gavin did. It was a strange moment. It was a toilet. It was a walk-in shower or rather a wheel-in shower. It was clean. Not much else to say about it.

'What do you think?' Ruth asked.

'Yes,' replied Gavin, as if he was confirming that the toilet and shower were still there.

'Sit down.' There was a moment where Gavin thought she had been referring to the toilet. Her eyes indicated the chair. He made the brave decision to move the chair nearer to the bed so they could see each other. And then he sat in it without any fuss.

'Make yourself at home,' said Ruth. Gavin couldn't tell if she was being welcoming or sarcastic. He didn't dwell on it.

'Are you not so good today?' asked Gavin.

'It's hard work sitting in a chair all day. Sometimes I need a rest.'

Gavin smiled and nodded in response to her humour and then considered that she might be serious.

'This is my life now. A physical wreck. On a good day, it's a chair with a view. On a bad day, it's this.'

'Are you sure you're wanting me to stay?' enquired Gavin, appreciating that it was a bad day.

'I may not be as clever today and you might not get to stay long before I get too tired and, forgive my appearance, but I do appreciate the company.'

'Okay. Tell me when you've had enough.' He knew she would.

The new setting had thrown the conversation for Gavin. He did not know where to start. He also sensed that Ruth was less likely to initiate discussion. He had to admit that she did look tired. And here she was, in bed. He was talking to a woman he had only just met, and she was in her night clothes, and reclining in bed. It did confuse the situation. It didn't seem to bother her. Or maybe it did, he thought, but she was in no position to offer anything better. Gavin realised that he had not said anything. Ruth had remained silent too. He checked to make sure she wasn't asleep.

'What are you doing?' she asked in response to his eyes peering at her from her eye level. He was crouching and only half on the chair.

'Sorry,' he said. 'I was just making sure you hadn't fallen asleep.'

'Or died,' she added.

'What?'

'Oh. Lie still for too long in here and they're checking for sleep or death. It's interesting what becomes normal behaviour.'

'I didn't think you were dead.'

'That's because you don't work here.'

'I didn't think you were asleep either.'

'So, you are a pervert then.' This made them both laugh.

'Only in my spare time.'

'And is this your spare time?' She had him there.

Gavin looked around the room. This was supposed to be her personal space. This was not a place of chairs and bodies and insignificant fixtures and fittings. This was Ruth's world. Or at least some representation of it. But he noticed that there were no photographs. He decided that meant either the absence of important people or that they were regular visitors. He had a feeling that it was the former. There were two pictures on the walls. Had they always been there or were they of her choosing? One was standard issue. It looked like it had spent several months on the wall of a charity shop before being sold for either one pound fifty or ninety-nine pence. It was a cottage and a garden, all shining, due to the glass covering. The other was three distant people on a beach. Just vague figures. It looked like an original with paint rather than printed ink. There was the roughness of a palette knife. He asked her about both pictures.

'I'm not sure what they mean,' she replied. 'Someone put them there. Probably wanted to cheer me up. Maybe left by the last person.'

'Not yours then?'

'I like that. Someone else's choice. Makes you think about what they saw in them. Gives you a bit of a challenge. That one of the beach. I wonder who those three are? I reckon we could all put three people on a beach.'

Gavin wasn't sure who his three people would be. 'Who would your three people be?' he asked.

'Depends on when I'm looking at it. Tranquil though, isn't it? It feels safe.'

Gavin nodded and then realised she couldn't see him nod due to her supine position. 'Yes,' he muttered belatedly.

He didn't push her on the three people. She did not seem as engaged as she had been previously. He looked around the room once more. There was little to see. There was a chest of drawers but nothing on it. He noticed the absence of a television which could have been positioned on the chest.

'Don't you watch television?' he asked.

'Not really,' she said. 'I've got one at home. I'd have to bring that. They won't give you one.'

'I can get you one or fetch it if you want.'

'As I said. Not bothered about television. You can watch a programme about Africa, or you can go there. I'd rather go there than watch it on television.'

'Have you been there?'

'No.'

'What about a good Who Dunnit? Or a detective series? You can't exactly commit a murder yourself.'

'Who says I can't?'

Gavin wasn't sure how to respond to that. He looked around the room again, confirming how bare it was. Two pictures on the wall. Nothing else. A vase of flowers would have been nice on the chest of drawers. He made a note to bring flowers. He would need to bring a vase too. He picked up on something else she had said.

'You still got a house somewhere, have you?'

'Yes,' she replied.

'Nothing you want me to bring to put here?' he asked.

'No,' she replied.

'You don't want anything for your room?' he asked.

There was silence and then, 'No,' she replied.

Gavin was very aware that the room could have been anyone's. She did not seem to have claimed it. There was absolutely nothing to tell you anything about Ruth, other than what might be inferred from the lack of personal possessions. He wondered if she had any hope of returning to the home she had mentioned. If not, and she probably was realistic about that, then this room was a space that made Gavin feel sad. And Gavin was thinking of it as a space rather than a room or a home. So much for her own front door.

'I haven't forgotten,' said Ruth and then went silent. Gavin was about to ask her what she hadn't forgotten when he sensed that Ruth might have fallen asleep. He wouldn't blame

101

her. It had not been the most scintillating of conversation but at least he had avoided having to tell his story. He crouched down and tried to see her eyes. They were closed. She had fallen asleep. Or she was dead. He looked along the form of her body under the duvet and was sure he saw some semblance of regular movement. He felt he could safely assume she was asleep. Anything worse was someone else's problem. Anything else and he might never have to tell his story. That was what she hadn't forgotten.

Chapter 12

The next day Gavin found himself keen to visit Ruth again. First though, there was the matter of a visit to foster carers called Jane and Matt and an incident with Riley who was their foster child. Gavin was recognising that currently he was not a very good social worker. He had no pretensions that he had ever been up for social worker of the year, but he ought to do enough to keep his job. So far, he had upset most of the people he worked with, he had failed to turn up for his counselling session, he had a growing band of foster carers who didn't think much of him, he had a new manager who didn't think much of him, and he probably no longer met whatever the latest list of minimum standards for social workers was called. And all in all, he didn't care that much about any of it anyway. However, he was still trying to operate at a level that gave off some pretence of doing the job he was paid for. This meant keeping some of his appointments and trying not to upset absolutely everyone. He was going through the sort of motions that swim down sewerage pipes to the seaside. His life was full of it.

Riley had had four social workers so far during his time living with Jane and Matt.

The first one had seen him come into care, plonked him with these carers and buggered off around Europe for the following year.

The second social worker had been brilliant, both according to Gavin and in the eyes of Jane and Matt. Inevitably she got a better offer and rose to greater things with a private fostering agency somewhere nice.

The third social worker had been decent too, but soon went off sick due to stress and eventually left the profession altogether to pursue a much more rewarding career working on the cheese counter at Tesco.

And now Riley had his fourth social worker. She was vastly experienced, had stuck around in the same team for decades and carried the air of someone who was above all management machinations and corporate decision-making. Any new legislation, regulations, policies, or standards had assuredly been worded to work around her. She was armed with all the slings and arrows of traditional social work practice and she was not afraid to use them.

She had been pressing Gavin to do a joint visit. Gavin had been as awkward about this as he could be and presented her with a vast catalogue of excuses. In the end, she had conceded, under the restraint of time, that they do separate visits. Gavin hated joint visits. They usually occurred due to an impasse between the social worker and the foster carers. Both expected him to take their side and support their grievances. And there would always be plenty of grievances. He would end up pleasing neither and leave the house with an impossible list of things he had agreed to do, just to get through the front door and into his car in one piece. In Gavin's mind, you only did a joint visit if the earth was rupturing and the end of the world was threatening to happen, or the placement was on the verge of breaking down and the earth was rupturing and the end of the world was threatening to happen.

Jane and Matt were good foster carers. They got on and did the job. They had worked well with all the children placed with them and that had included some real challenges. They provided a safe and caring home. They did proper activities with the children. They integrated them into the wider family. They facilitated contact with birth family members. They took them on holiday. They never asked for respite care. Their only problem was that they didn't get social work theory. Whilst they were busy mopping up sick, repairing broken furniture or challenging unacceptable behaviour, social work theory flew thirty thousand feet over their heads. They were doers rather than thinkers. Ironically, this gave them much in common with many social workers. Unfortunately, Riley's current social worker assumed that if you had attended a one-day training course on dyadic developmental psychotherapy then you knew everything about therapeutic parenting. She never attended these training courses herself, for two reasons. Firstly, she had been doing social work way before any of this stuff had come along and she hadn't needed it then. Secondly, she was allergic to anything that involved group work. Her expectation was that foster carers should know all this, and that removed any responsibility from her. Anything, therefore, that the foster carers didn't know was Gavin's fault. And so was anything they did.

Riley had sworn at the neighbours and shown quite a selection of vocabulary when it came to his understanding of good old Anglo-Saxon jargon. Jane and Matt had told him off. Riley had told his social worker. His social worker had asked to be put on the phone with Jane and told her off for telling Riley off. Jane had told Gavin. Gavin had tried to ignore it. Riley's social worker had phoned Gavin and told him off. Gavin had tried to ignore it. Gavin's social worker had informed Sally Clark's boss as she liked to complain high. Sally Clark's boss had told Sally Clark. Sally Clark had told Gavin off and added that he had better sort it out. Gavin had carried on trying to ignore it. Riley's social worker had phoned Gavin to insist on a joint visit. Gavin had fended this off. Eventually, the forces were too great and under this mounting pressure, Gavin had finally decided not to ignore it and agreed to visit Jane and Matt on his own. Gavin's social worker had then wanted to know why Jane and Matt had not acted out the whole scenario with farmyard animals to find out what Riley had been thinking. What Riley had been thinking was that this nosey neighbour had better stop staring at him and asking him why he was in care. What Jane and Matt had been thinking was that Riley was having a bad day and no enactment with wooden cows or plastic sheep was going to help that. What Riley's social worker was thinking was that the dyadic developmental psychotherapy training course couldn't have been that good and she would need to be phoning someone high up about that. What Gavin was thinking was, get me out of here. As a compromise, he conceded the need to visit Jane and Matt. And this he did.

'It's just that, you know, people like that just don't listen,' said Jane.

'I know,' replied Gavin.

'And he needs to be told that. He can't grow up thinking it's alright to swear at people,' she added.

'We understand he's had a crap life,' added Matt. 'But he's been with us now for nearly two years and he can't keep using his past as an excuse. Out there as an adult they won't accept it.'

'He needs to start learning that now,' said Jane.

Gavin nodded his agreement to each statement. He was gathering his thoughts. He could hear Riley's social worker's voice in his head telling him to tell them that he is just twelve years old. 'Let's not forget he is still just twelve,' said Gavin, with limited conviction because he knew what would follow.

'Twelve going on twenty,' said Jane.

'Twelve going on twenty and on his way to prison if he doesn't learn otherwise,' said Matt. 'That's what happens to these kids and we don't want to see that happen to Riley.'

'We have a responsibility to learn him that,' said Jane.

Gavin tensed. It was a minor point. It was nothing to get annoyed about. But Gavin just hated it when people said learn rather than teach. It was also exactly how Riley's social worker would have said it too, so maybe there was more in common for them than they realised.

'I'm sure you're teaching him so many things,' said Gavin, hoping that Jane would pick up on his choice of verb, as much, if not more than the supportive statement.

'Exactly,' said Matt. 'So, what's the point telling us to learn him through bloody farmyard animals.'

Oh dear, thought Gavin. They were both at it now.

'I know,' said Gavin, trying hard to redact the word learn from his mental recording of the conversation.

'And he doesn't play with that stuff now anyway,' said Jane. 'He's moved on. Grown-up.'

'Can't stop him growing up,' added Matt.

'Which is why he needs learning what's right and wrong,' said Jane.

'And I'm sure you're doing that,' said Gavin.

'Of course we are,' said Jane. 'We've apologised to the neighbour too.'

'Not for the first time,' said Matt.

'Not be for the last time, but we will learn him,' said Jane.

'I'm sure you're teaching him well,' said Gavin. It was a battle of the verbs he ought to give up on, but Gavin was being driven by his inner pedant.

'So, can you get that bloody social worker off our back?' said Jane. 'She's the worst one he's had.'

'And that doesn't help. Him having different social workers,' said Matt. 'He doesn't like this one. I think he misses Rebecca. She was good.'

'She was,' agreed Gavin.

'Can't he have a different one?' asked Jane.

'That would be five then,' interjected Matt.

'Worth it if the next one was any good,' said Jane. 'She must be getting on a bit. Isn't she likely to retire?'

'She'll keep going forever,' said Matt.

'So, are you here to tell us off?' asked Jane. This had not been a planned visit. The foster carer's idiot's guide told you that if the supervising social worker was making an unexpected visit, then you were in trouble.

Gavin wasn't a telling-off social worker. He was barely a let's discuss it social worker. He preferred to be a let's skim the surface and leave it at that social worker. 'Do you need telling off?' returned Gavin.

'I bet that's what she wants,' said Jane.

'You're doing a good job,' said Gavin. 'And that's what matters.' He opted out of anything confrontational and, besides which, if he had to take a side, it would be with Jane and Matt.

'What was it last time?' asked Jane. 'Something to do with stopping him from seeing his mother.' She answered her own question.

'He didn't want to go,' said Matt. 'And she thought we'd persuaded him not to go because we wanted him to go out for the day with us.'

'We only took him out for the day because he was upset about his mother,' said Jane. 'He didn't want to see her. But she wasn't having that was she? She reckoned we'd stopped him going.'

'And when she asked him of course he said he wanted to go. He didn't want his mother to know he was angry with her and he didn't want to see her.' Matt kept the theme going. This was all too familiar to Gavin.

'And what does she say?' It was another question that Jane was going to answer herself. 'She reckons we need some training on WD40.'

'DDP,' corrected Gavin. 'Dyadic developmental psychotherapy.'

'Yes,' confirmed Jane.

'WD40's for old bangers,' said Matt. Gavin gave Matt a look to stop him from going any further. 'Don't worry. We know how to be politically correct.'

'At least with you we don't have to worry about that sort of thing,' said Jane. This was always where Gavin started to feel uncomfortable. Conversations with Jane and Matt always headed into dubious language territory and Gavin's challenge was to get out before they said the wrong thing. He would never report them. They were too good at the job. But he didn't want them to think that he was on their side, or others to think he was colluding with them, even if he was on their side and preferred collusion over confrontation. But Jane and Matt were the sort of couple who hadn't grasped the sensitivity of words and language. It happened at every visit. Gavin had to judge the moment when they were moving into unfiltered dialogue and get out, before it felt like he was being trapped in a dated sixties sitcom.

'Anyway,' said Gavin. 'I'd better go now.'

Pleasantries were exchanged and Gavin managed to get out through the door before his social work standards were compromised. He left wondering if the visit had served any purpose at all. He also knew that Riley's social worker would be after him to find out how it had gone and what kind of reprimand he had given them. He knew that she knew that he would not have challenged them. It was probably not serious enough for her to take it to the Director of Social Care.

After the visit, Gavin was ready for a run. It had been the sort of situation where previously he might have gone and visited Nap. But he knew the exercise would do him good. He was starting to feel like he was a genuine runner. He was also mindful of how Ruth had been on the last visit. He was not that familiar with old age. His appreciation of the differences between sleep and death was mere philosophical banter.

This time he ran past the window and was relieved to see that Ruth was back in her chair again. At least she wasn't dead, was a thought he managed to suppress quickly. They waved at each other. It was a gentle open palmed short movement from Gavin and a simple slightly raised open hand from Ruth. Yes. She was alive.

By now Gavin was getting to know some of the staff. The friendly woman from his first visit was called Linda and she let him through, acknowledging that Ruth was seeming to be a lot better today. He had not, since his first attempt to visit, seen the woman who thought he was a pervert. And no one else seemed to think he was a pervert. Well, if they did, they didn't say anything. He did wonder what they thought of his regular visits to the care home. He was not a typical visitor and his presentation might easily have prompted comment.

Ruth greeted him with a smile. 'Maybe those people were staying in the cottage,' she said.

Gavin had to think about this, and Ruth could see the uncertainty on his face.

'The two pictures in my room,' said Ruth. 'Staying in the cottage in one of the pictures and visiting the beach in the other picture.'

Gavin could see and hear for himself that she was much improved since the last visit. She had remembered their conversation better than he had. Mind you he did consider that he had more going on between visits than she did. Then again, Ruth did have the ability to surprise him. 'Maybe two of them are buying the cottage and the other one is the estate agent, and he is showing them the beach which is like their front garden,' said Gavin.

'Or they are drug smugglers using the cottage as a hideout and on the beach waiting for the boat to come that is bringing the gear.' Gavin was surprised by Ruth's choice of words. She knew some jargon. Films or real life, he wondered this time, and then remembered that she didn't watch much television. Although she did have a television at her house, then didn't everyone.

Admiring her creativity, Gavin responded in like. 'They're three sisters staying in the cottage but walking on the beach discussing how to kill off their respective husbands.'

'Maybe the husbands are in the cottage unaware of what their wives are plotting.'

'And the drugs that they are on the beach to collect from the boat are some sort of traceless poison.'

'But the husbands have known all along and they are the ones coming in the boat to seek their revenge.'

'Or it is mum, dad and little Ellie who are staying in the cottage on holiday and just gone for a nice family walk.'

'I hope not,' said Ruth. 'That would be too boring.'

'But more likely,' suggested Gavin.

'Not in paintings,' offered Ruth. 'Paintings are a chance to create a story.'

'And we certainly did,' said Gavin, not spotting the trap.

'So then,' said Ruth. 'What's your story?' The trap was sprung. Gavin was caught, tied up and dangling from the tree. Or he was enveloped in gorse and shrubbery and had landed in the pit. Or he was on the end of the line about to be dropped into the fishing net.

Gavin paused, but he had been too chatty up to this point, so suddenly going quiet was not an option. His usual escape route had been blocked.

'Tell me about your parents. That's where the story usually starts.'

Gavin made a noise that was part cough and part grunt. It was that tell-tale sign of someone trying to dissipate the brain-fog and search out a safe but honest answer.

'All my mother seemed to want to do was save the world.'

'And did she?'

Gavin smiled. 'She's still trying.'

'Do you see much of her?'

'Not if I can help it.'

'She's your mother.'

'Just about.'

'And your mother wanted to save the world' repeated Ruth, now less as a question and more as a statement.

'Yes.' Gavin felt the safest thing to do was to answer the statement.

'And were you in this world she wanted to save?'

He froze. Something so obvious. Something he already knew. But to hear those words spoken aloud to him, so easily found, and as a simple question. He couldn't move. For a moment he was less mobile than she was. She could see his discomfort. There was the sort of silence that shouts and screams and demands attention. She was not going to take it away from him. He could hold it for a while. Let it simmer. Then let it settle.

'And what about your dad?' asked Ruth. The simmering and settling were washed away. There was a tide, a riptide, and a possible drowning. Gavin remained helpless.

'And what about your dad?' repeated Ruth.

Gavin had heard the question but did not care about it. He was still drenched by Ruth's earlier dive into his childhood.

'My dad left home when I was about eight,' he answered, trying to find a way out. 'Probably to save himself,' he added.

Ruth could not tell if Gavin was being serious or amusing. A bit of both, she conceded.

Gavin found himself wondering about his father. This was a man he had never really known. This was a man he had dismissed. This was a man he had tried not to think about. And he had failed miserably. Of course he thought about him.

'Do you still see him?' asked Ruth.

'He left when I was eight. I think he came back two or three times after that, but that was it.'

'So, you've not seen him since then?'

Gavin had seen him in his dreams. He had fantasised stories. He had wondered where he was and what he was doing. But he had let all those meanderings drift away. They

112

were a tide, ebbing and flowing, but he had never set sail to explore anything further. Gavin could feel himself welling up. This, he knew, was why he never let any of this wondering develop. It would only result in tears, not answers. And he had no idea what answers he was after. He had no idea what the questions were. There were questions, not always clearly defined, but he knew them to be angry ones. So, he left them alone.

'You keep asking questions,' he commented, attempting to pull himself together and trying to dull the conversation. He could just walk away. Out the door and off was always an option. She had no right to be doing this to him. He did not need this. But he stayed. And that was the biggest confliction of all. He didn't want to walk away. What was it about Ruth that could hold him here? His feet were stuck. They stood their ground. They were not moving. He was letting her quiz him.

'Seems to be the best way with you,' she answered.

Gavin just muttered. He had lost the thread of the questions. His head was full of thoughts. These were notions well short of being anything clear or focused. They were messages thundering around his head. His mind was like a caged animal, prowling and waiting to be set free. He clawed at whatever space was left for any thought and sought a way to escape. 'Must be getting near for your turn to talk,' he said, trying not to give away the discomfort in his voice.

'Patience,' she said. 'You will get to hear it.' Ruth could see that she had provoked Gavin. His face said it before his voice added verification. She considered if she had gone too far. She had suspected that Gavin had demons. Most people did. And most people hid them away and pretended that they were not there. However, Ruth knew she would soon be dead. And she had never lived life lightly. There was never time to pussyfoot around. That was one of life's teachings and she had always had it up there in her ten commandments, alongside thou shalt not tell me what to do and thou shalt not eat with thy mouth open.

Gavin was silent. He considered that Ruth was no threat. She was no threat at all. Was it because she was in a care home and had nowhere to take his story? Was it because she would die soon and take his story with her? Or was it her? She fascinated him. And it was enough to keep him there. He was vulnerable. She had made him vulnerable, but he was choosing to stay vulnerable. But then, he considered, this exposure should be shared and consequently had earnt him the right to hear her story. That had been the deal.

She broke his thoughts. 'You're expecting my story now, aren't you?'

'Well, yes,' he replied. She had read his thoughts. That was how exposed he was. 'I've told you mine.'

'Not much though.'

'Enough for now.'

'I can see that. And you're expecting me to talk.'

'Wasn't that the deal?' It had all got a bit serious, so he smiled.

'And what did we discuss last time about expectations?'

She had him. It was like a game of chess, he thought to himself. He didn't like to swear, even within the confines of his own head, but there were times, and this was nearly one of those times. But there would be so much anger to follow through, so he needed to plug that hole. She was playing him as if he was one of the pieces. He might hope to be a bishop or a knight, but he was a pawn stuck on the same square waiting for a great big hand to come down and move him forward. 'I give up,' he announced.

'Great,' she replied. 'You give up. You have no expectation.'

'Not now.'

'All expectations are gone?'

'Yes. All gone. Out the window, out the door, and up the chimney.'

'In that case, next time you come we will start.'

He wasn't sure if this was genuine or if she was delaying. Then again, she did not seem to be the sort of person to trick him. Well, not like that at any rate. And he had to concede that they had talked for a while and she was entitled to a break. And he needed a break. But this was not a sulking and walking off the stage break. This was a well-earnt break. She had battered him into near submission, but he had not thrown in the towel. He needed the towel to clean up all the mess.

'Oh,' then said Ruth. 'I've never asked you what you do for a job. That should have been at the top of my list.'

'Social worker,' replied Gavin.

'So now you're trying to save the world.'

And Gavin had to leave.

Chapter 13

Gavin booked into a hotel. He had made two decisions. The first was to drive somewhere that he did not know. The second was to stay overnight in the best hotel he could find. Although this decision did have a price limit.

He wanted to have nothing familiar around him. He wanted to see no one he knew. He wanted no conversations other than the practical politeness of hotel staff. He didn't want to be at home. He had been home to get changed and to pack the smallest of bags. He didn't want to be distracted by anything recognisable. He did not want to cook. He did not want to make that effort, and he did not want to fall back on the usual easy meals. And he was in a hotel which had more than one menu. He wasn't used to places that had more than one menu. He was in his room. The bag was at the bottom of the wardrobe, with its few contents inside. There were no toiletries. He would rely solely on what the hotel provided. This was a decent hotel, so they provided shampoo, conditioner, soap, and a hairnet. He liked that they were different to his own shampoo and conditioner. He kept taking the tops off the little bottles and smelling the contents. He didn't get high, but he did get a little overwhelmed with citrus. The hairnet he left alone.

He stood in the middle of the room, looking at himself in the mirror. Everything he wore he had bought a couple of hours earlier. New jeans. New shirt. New socks. New shoes. New underwear. He had managed to get a haircut. Nothing drastic. There wasn't much to cut anyway, but just that sense of having a fresh head was sufficient. His old clothes were in the bag in the wardrobe. He looked at himself in the mirror and offered his mirror image an embarrassed half-smile. He did the daft thing of smiling back. This made him look away and then walk away.

This was not a new start. He was not abandoning anything. He needed to remove everything that connected him with himself. Gavin wanted to neutralise his life just for tonight and maybe for some time tomorrow. He wanted to be free of himself.

The hotel was good enough to have its own restaurant and an all-day bar menu amongst others. He had not booked into the restaurant when asked on arrival. He preferred the informality of the bar and the unpretentiousness that came with a bar menu, rather than choosing different courses or expensive meal deals off the a la carte menu. If the worst came to the worst, he would take the microwave over the chef. The seating was more comfortable in the bar. He found his place on a sofa with views of the street in front of the hotel. He ordered a local beer and chose the ubiquitous beer-battered fish and triple-cooked chips. What difference it made to cook them three times rather than two he did not know. Nor did he expect to taste the difference. It just sounded like they cared more. They cared enough to cook your chips three times for you, and they wanted you to know it. If you asked them kindly, they would probably boil the soup three times for you or wash your lettuce three times in spa water. It seemed to matter in this modern world. Gavin wondered if there was a hotel somewhere offering quadruple-cooked chips or gin-battered fish.

The bar attendant brought him a knife and fork, serviette, and a smile. This was followed by his beer and another smile. She was half his age and felt sorry for him. He did not look like he was staying overnight on business which accounted for most single residents. He'd spotted one in the restaurant and another sat on the other side of the bar. He had made a mental note not to catch the eye of either of them in case they were the type of businesspeople who might seek out conversation with a fellow lone traveller. He had no wish to know what they were selling, where they lived, which celebrity they had met in a bar in Llandudno, how long they had once spent stuck on the M25, or what had befallen them on that fateful Spring morning in Milton Keynes and how they had wriggled out of the whole fiasco. He was not looking for company. He wanted to be left alone.

He stretched out on the sofa. This was the great advantage of not sitting in the restaurant. There he would have been sat upright at a table and visible to everyone. His verticality would have led to him having nothing better to do than make observations around the room and would have given him a feeling of being watched, consequent to which he would have been required to take the time between courses to look occupied and composed. He would have stood out. On the sofa, there were no between courses. There was no structure to his meal. He could be timeless, shapeless, and slouched on the sofa. He could blend into the room. He was just part of the scenery. No one would notice him. Restaurants announced your presence. Bars gave you inconspicuousness.

He sipped his beer. Ruth had got to him. He had needed to escape to free himself to think and to do whatever seemed pertinent in the circumstance. If he was going to have to think about past baggage, he wanted no present-day baggage.

He remembered his father leaving home. And that already was a strange phrase. His father didn't leave home. His father took home with him and left Gavin and his mother in the house, homeless. He would think about his father. He was prepared to give some consideration to his father and who he was or who Gavin thought he was. However, that was for later. What he could remember of those first eight years as a family was limited. He knew from his job that you didn't remember things. You remembered remembering things. The original memory often became a montage of following reminiscences. His scrapbook of earliest memories seemed pleasant and uneventful. He could remember walking down streets. There were images of school. There were the names of some of his first school friends: Danny, Adam and Parky (whose real name he had now forgotten). There was his first girlfriend, Anna. Well, not really a girlfriend, but just someone who, when you are seven years old, you are going to marry and go and live with in Australia where you will raise kangaroos. There was a memory of running up and down a hill somewhere. His mother liked playing patience with a pack of cards. That seemed to fall into those first eight years. His father teaching him to ride his first bike and it did seem a real memory that his father did that usual thing of letting go of the bike without letting you know. Then again, was that just a group memory that we all have. And there was a holiday with a beach and a cottage that had a strange blue window. The clearest recollection being the strange blue window. He had decided that it had strange magic powers and so, both loved it and feared it with equal measure. But all of this was incidental. How important it all might have been only became apparent by comparison with what happened when his father ran away with their home. Thereafter his mother's influence became clearer and less incidental. His father was left to compete with a blue window. In the film of his life, Gavin considered that Bettie Davis would play his mother and someone on the verge of becoming a minor character in a soap opera would get ten minutes at the beginning as his dad.

The beer-battered fish and thrice-cooked chips arrived, accompanied by a small pot of peas that had had something done to them that Gavin could not figure out, but was further evidence that they cared. Perhaps they were double-mushed peas or crushed with some mint concoction. He soon discovered that they tasted like peas. He tucked in, which was the simplest approach to what was in the end simply fish and chips.

He was left being raised by a mother who Gavin now recalled was full of what she could do to make the world a better place. She started by wearing a long kaftan dress. And when this didn't change anything, she started writing letters. These were letters to anyone who had a letterbox and covered as many of the world's problems as she could find the time to think about. She went on marches. She saved cardboard to write slogans on. She formed passing friendships. He was never introduced to people. They just seemed to be around more often. They sometimes spoke to him and then they were gone. The only person he got to know was Sheila. She stuck around for longer than anyone else and she tried to engage with him. Gavin considered that there was about a year in his life when Sheila parented him more than his mother. This did not reflect any significant willingness or passion for the task but stood out against his mother's lack of enthusiasm for painting, playing games, reading bedtime stories, and getting covered in the sort of sticky gooey mess that seems to seep out of most children.

His mother did things. She made posters. The house was full of posters. Many of them displayed on windows and walls. She phoned people up. She argued with people. She shouted at the television. Sometimes she put the television on just to shout at it. And then Sheila would explain to Gavin what this was all about. He didn't understand, but he welcomed the conversation. He escaped to school during the week and at the weekend he would go for walks and no one would notice he was missing.

His mother was emotional about everything. She hated men. She hated politicians. She hated the couple next door. She hated the police. She hated breakfast television. She hated The Rolling Stones. Then she loved The Rolling Stones. Then she hated them again. She hated the Americans. She hated whoever supplied the gas. She hated bankers. Then one day she hated Sheila and Sheila was gone.

He got another smile as the bar attendant cleared away his plate and they both agreed that he would welcome another beer.

His mother finally had a breakdown. She didn't go anywhere. She shut herself away. Gavin was seventeen and studying for his A levels. He had chosen three and was struggling in two of them. He excelled at English. At this point in his life, literature gave him places to escape to. He read books and he enjoyed the debates they had in school about them. It was an interest that did not last. But for this time in his life, fictitious worlds seemed more appealing.

Gavin sipped his beer, which he suddenly realised was there, having not noticed it arrive. The bar had also got busier. There were groups of people gathered and talking and the noise level had risen. He remained undisturbed and master of his sofa and table. The sofa on the other side of the table was not inviting anyone unless they were fellow slouchers.

Gavin could not recall being upset by his mother's illness. There was insufficient attachment between them for it to matter. Besides which she was around him more and he was now the one to ignore her. He had well and truly established his independence. A year later he took this independence a step further and left the house. He had not felt guilt at leaving his mother. He felt that she had left him many years ago. Nor had any guilt arisen in the following years. He visited her about once a year and this, every time, was a chore. They sent each other Christmas cards. Gavin sent a card from a standard selection box of twenty. His mother sent something similar. They exchanged robins and reindeer and little else.

Gavin's mother had moved house. There had been a significant relationship with someone called Martin. Martin had died and left the house to Gavin's mother. Gavin had only met Martin on three occasions. They had been together for three years before he died. Martin had always been ill. Gavin assumed that his mother had tried to save him but failed. Now, she lived alone in the same house. She had once sent him a letter. She needed him to know that, although she had lost the only three men in the world that she cared about, she was fine. She had not named the three men, but Gavin had assumed them to be his father, Martin and possibly himself. If not himself, he was not sure what the letter was about. Gavin had replied with a postcard of some Van Gogh flowers but no condolences.

Gavin did think about his father. There had always been three questions. Why did he leave? Who was he? Where is he now? The discourse around these questions had changed over time and in line with Gavin's own experiences of life as an adult.

Why did he leave? Over time Gavin had learnt to consider this question in terms of both leaving and arriving somewhere else. Had the grass somewhere else been greener or had he been fed up with the foliage at home? Having endured his mother as a necessary part of his childhood, Gavin could sympathise with a desire to leave. He got out as soon as he could. But his father had also left Gavin and this he could not understand and did not want to think about too much. And he had not only left, but he never maintained contact and this, more than anything else, was what hurt Gavin. Or it would have hurt him if he had allowed himself to dwell on it. Most of the time he succeeded, but he couldn't always ignore the feeling that never went away which was that, when it came down to basics, his father had abandoned him.

Who was he? He had no idea who his father was, other than the paternal title and some vague memories. His mother had told him nothing. He had not bothered to ask. As a child, he had been resigned to not knowing about his father. As an adult, he did not wish to have that level of dialogue with his mother. Face to face evocative chatter across the table was not on the cards. Before any discussion of who his father was could take on any meaningful level, there would need to have been some discussion about why his mother had been so ineffectual in his life. Gavin's mother lived in the here and now with little regard for the past. Consequently, working out who his father was gave Gavin a blank page. His father could be anyone or anything he wanted him to be. But such thoughts never ended well. They were unsubstantiated. They were pointless. They were fantasies best left alone.

Where is he now? This was not just a question about geography or locations that might be near or far. He found himself considering the places and people that might be around his father. Who were they? What were they? These thoughts had changed as time went by. People changed. People moved. And then the possible answers to this question had to consider whether he was even alive. Was he buried somewhere? Had he been cremated? Like every subject related to his father, it was best left alone.

He'd supped his beer. He had spent the time without interruption. Slouching worked. Gavin went back upstairs and returned to his room. He stood in front of the mirror. This time it was a leary smile. The person in the reflection was both real and distant. He wondered how much he might look like his father, and especially now that he was not much older than when his father had left him. Part of the way he had been parented meant that there were no photographs. His mother painted, printed, and scrawled logos onto cardboard and cloth, but she did not take photos. Consequently, the only photos Gavin had from childhood were two school photos: a school year photo on which he appeared second from the left on the back row and something taken by a friend's mother which she had insisted he had a copy of. From his childhood all he had were images in his memory of his mother, posed photos of himself, and nothing of his father.

In bed, he admitted to himself that most of what he had been remembering was now a reconfiguration of what had happened. It was like putting together a jigsaw puzzle and each time you do it a piece is taken away. Had someone offered him the box with the picture on it he would have turned them down. He assured himself that he was better off in the dark. He switched the light off and went to sleep.

The following morning Gavin awoke to realise what a good night's sleep he had had. He ordered breakfast in bed. He did this because he had never done it before. He sat upright against the pillows, waiting for the knock on the door. He didn't put the television on. He didn't read anything. He just waited. He did nothing and found that he enjoyed letting time go by. He wasn't impatient or expectant. He just was. What he was didn't matter. He was alive and breathing and now was all that mattered. He was enjoying the present. The past had happened. The future would happen. This was all about being in the here and now. I am. Not I was or I will be, but I am. He was without connection. Gavin breathed. Gavin breathed. Gavin breathed. Gavin breathed. Gavin breathed. Gavin breathed. Gavin breathed.

There was a knock on the door. Breakfast had arrived.

Chapter 14

Gavin returned home. He had enjoyed his night away. As if to prove the point, he went to work the following morning. He skipped into the office. He even made them all tea. Some of them had wanted coffee. Some of them would have preferred their own mugs. He couldn't even remember if he had a mug, and if he did, where it was or what it looked like. He borrowed one. He went for the most plain-looking mug he could find and when he found a group of them huddled together on the same shelf, he felt he was in safe territory. He decided that some mugs were like sheep, off-white and they liked to stick together.

Having put in a full day's work, Gavin spent the evening watching rubbish on the television with an Indian takeaway on a tray on his lap. It was the sort of pointless evening in that feels good because you have done something worthwhile in the other part of the day. He didn't move the flipchart and tripod. Its presence made him smile.

The following day he made sure all his case notes were up to date. He undertook an unannounced visit to one of his foster carers. He was required to do this once a year. Normally he'd think about when the safest time would be to call. He didn't want to uncover anything untoward. If they were secretly worshipping Satan, then best for him not to know. And Satan wasn't as bad as people had made him out to be. Anyway, this unannounced visit he did without any thought or planning. It went well.

Gavin was just starting to wonder if life might be worth living when life decided to give him the sort of kick up the arse that really hurts and reverberates up through your body telling your brain it should start connecting way over the usual number of synapses to remember to do all it can to make sure that doesn't ever happen again.

Gavin went to visit Ruth. He didn't run there. He dressed himself up a bit. He had been a bit tentative about this visit. The last visit had had an impact on him. Yes, it was her turn to tell her story, but he knew she had a devious side. He wanted her story. He didn't want the devious side. He was keen to learn more about her. Who was she beyond the walls of the home? He decided he needed to take charge. He arrived at the home looking smart. Something halfway between a chat show host and a pimp.

He was greeted in the reception by a familiar face. It was the woman who had called him a pervert. And she hadn't forgotten. This became clear when she repeated the accusation and told him there was no way he was coming in. The last thing these old folk needed was a pervert. He tried to point out that he wasn't a pervert. It just made him sound more like a pervert. Through a combination of words and a top-to-bottom perusal of what he was wearing, she made it clear that he needed to remove himself. He said that he was there to see Mrs Deakin. She said that she didn't doubt it and that the poor woman had suffered enough without having visits from perverted folk like him. He further protested his innocence. He was getting nowhere. Eventually, defeated, he left.

He paced up and down in the car park. His pacing took him around the side, onto a side street, and eventually into the field where the large window looked out and where he usually ran past or waved. Ruth was sat in her chair. She waved. He waved back. And then his rage took hold. He raised his arm and pointed over her to the back. Then he straightened his arm in the air, bent it back and straightened it again, then bent it back and straightened it again. He did this several times. He broke into the demonstration to wave at Ruth again. She needed to know from him that the love child of Adolf Hitler would not let him in. She didn't wave back. She didn't seem to be getting in. Then he started goose-stepping in front of the window. He stopped and once again pointed over her to the back. He forced a smile. He waved. Then he left.

Only as he walked away did he start to wonder if he had gone too far. He was angry that he had not been allowed in. He wanted Ruth to know that he wanted to visit. He wanted Ruth to know that the woman in reception wouldn't let him in. He wanted Ruth to know that the woman was a Fascist. He knew she wasn't a Fascist. But he was angry. The woman in the reception had completely spoilt everything. He assumed Ruth would understand. Ruth knew he wasn't a pervert. Gavin considered that the whole situation was ridiculous. He went back to the window. Ruth was there. So was the woman who wasn't a Fascist. She spotted Gavin. He waved. She didn't wave back. She gesticulated in such a way that Gavin was clear that he needed to go. He shuck his head in disbelief. As he walked away at quite a pace, in case she was on her way out to confront him again, he realised that the disbelief included his own behaviour. With a time-lapse that could be measured in nanoseconds, he faced the stark realisation that it had not been his finest hour.

He didn't go home. He just walked with a head full of contrition. He had overreacted. There were better ways of miming to someone that the person in reception won't let you in to visit because they are the devil's child and born to spew evil all over the world. He had gone too far. However culpable he was feeling, he was not going to let the woman in reception off the hook. He could conjure up all sorts of arguments in support of her being the real evil monger. That satisfied him just enough to ease him on his way. He could walk proudly in the knowledge that he was the lesser of the two demons. If

Beelzebub was interviewing for an assistant, then she would get the job before him. These were the thoughts that finally brought him to Nap's door.

'Is there ever a good time to give a Nazi salute?' asked Gavin, when Nap opened the door.

Nap let him in. 'Something happen?'

'You could say that,' replied Gavin. He was here at Nap's house. He had come to Nap's house. He wanted some assurance that he hadn't gone over the top. He wanted to take what had happened and what was going around in his head out of his head. But he didn't want to tell Nap that he was visiting Ruth. He wasn't ready to share that. Something about forming a friendship with an old lady in a care home felt too unusual to be told, even to Nap. It would have felt like he was confessing.

'You joined the Nazi party then?' joked Nap. 'Because I don't want you goose-stepping around here. Got to think of the neighbours.' He laughed. 'Mind you that bloke down the road that's always twitching at his curtains. He'd probably join you.'

'Thanks,' replied Gavin, with mock sarcasm.

'Thought you'd be more of a communist,' continued Nap.

'Just keeping my options open.'

'I hear there are vacancies at the Women's Institute.'

'Don't think they'd have me.'

'Why ever not?'

'Don't know how to make jam and my pans aren't big enough.'

'Think they've probably moved on from that sort of thing now.'

'Guess so.'

'Are you going to tell me what's happened?' This was as close as Nap could get to inviting any sort of meaningful dialogue between them.

'Don't think so,' replied Gavin, likeminded in his determination to avoid the unintended meaningful dialogue.

The conversation moved on, with both feeling that they had offered the level of support that their friendship expected, but without them having to go through the emotions of talking about it. It suited both parties.

'Apparently, The Beatles are going to reform,' said Nap confirming a completely new subject and moving back into the more comfortable arena of comic wistfulness.

'They got a resident spiritualist at The Cavern, have they?' replied Gavin. The effort of trying to be funny was just enough to stop the brain from dwelling on past misdemeanours, however recent they were.

'And she sings vocals and plays lead guitar.' Nap played air guitar to demonstrate the point.

'You got an itch down there?' said Gavin.

'Very funny. That was my best guitar riff.'

'Looked more like crabs to me.'

'Lennon or McCartney?'

'I didn't know we were naming them?'

'Naming what?'

'The crabs.'

'I mean. Who was the best?'

'What at?'

'What at! What at! Swimming the channel. What do you think?' Nap looked at Gavin and raised his eyebrows.

'Musician? Singer? Songwriter? Let's face it Ringo would have been best at swimming the channel.'

'How come?'

'All those drums to keep him afloat.'

'Who was the best songwriter?'

'But they wrote songs together.'

'Imagine or Mull of Kintyre? Give Peace a Chance or Frogs Chorus?'

When you put it that way,' answered Gavin. 'Lennon.'

'Lennon.'

'But then when you consider the stuff McCartney did with Wings. I'd have to say McCartney.'

'Yoko Ono or Linda?'

'Don't even go there.' Gavin retorted. 'Harrison,' he added.

'Harrison, Yoko Ono or Linda McCartney?'

'No. The best songwriter. Harrison. While My Guitar Gently Weeps. My Sweet Lord.'

'Something.'

'Anything.'

'No. Something.'

'Yoko or Linda?'

'George.'

'Well, he was the best-looking Beatle.'

'And he mortgaged his house for those Monty Python films.'

'So. Harrison wins everything.'

'I bet he was crap at Subbuteo though!'

'Are we going to then?'

'Will it make you feel better?' asked Nap.

'Already feeling better.'

'Why don't we play this one?' Nap produced a programme from a game played in January 1967. It was Mansfield Town versus Scunthorpe United. 'Ray Clemence in goal for Scunthorpe before he went to Liverpool. FA Cup second round. Do you want to play the two teams?'

'Do you know the score from the real game?'

'The real game? This will be the real game.'

'You know what I mean.'

'No idea. Would sort of spoil it to know the real score.'

'But afterwards, let's look it up and see what it was.'

'If we must.'

'We must.'

Mansfield Town 4 Scunthorpe 1

The joy of the FA Cup came alight this afternoon at Field Mill. Two teams fighting for a place in the third round and an opportunity to face one of the big guns. Mansfield started well. The Stags piled on the pressure and in the fifteenth minute got their reward when Curry scored from twenty yards. Clemence got a hand to it but it was not enough to prevent Mansfield from taking the lead. More pressure continued but it was Scunthorpe who got back on level terms against the run of play. Some great play down the left by Colqhoun and what might well have been a shot was deflected and fell to the feet of Burrows who did not miss from five yards out. The rest of the half saw a resurgent Scunthorpe take charge but without further reward. The second half belonged to Mansfield. Their lead was resumed when Curry got his second although it was a shot that took a wicked deflection off Birkinshaw and completely deceived Clemence in goal. Hall scored the Stags' third goal after sixty-three minutes. Thereafter Scunthorpe were forced to take risks and finally made to pay in the eighty-second minute when Morris scored from a corner. The ball had fallen to him in the area and he tucked it away with ease. The game then slowed down, the outcome

clear to both sides. Scunthorpe had
nothing to offer. So, it will be
Mansfield who will be keen to see
who they can get in the third round.

'So, what was the score when they played it on grass and
not on your table?' asked Gavin.

'Give me a chance,' replied Nap. 'I'll have to look it up.'

By now, Nap had poured them both a glass of brandy.
Gavin sipped his and waited for Nap to report back on his
findings.

'Game postponed due to snow. They never played it.' Nap
looked at Gavin.

'What?' replied Gavin unsatisfied with the information.

'Only joking,' replied Nap. 'Of course they played it.'

'And?'

'And Mansfield won two one. Scorers for Mansfield were
Brace and Mitchinson. Doesn't say who scored for
Scunthorpe.'

'And in the third round?'

'You don't want much do you.'

'No. Just who they got in the third round.'

More brandy was supped.

'Middlesborough,' Nap announced. 'Which Mansfield
won two nil.'

'That must have been a cup upset.'

'You'd have thought so.'

Nap looked at Gavin's empty glass. 'Don't want to be
chucking you out and I know it's still early, but I've got a box
set of *Game of Thrones* calling me.'

'I can take a hint.' Gavin tried to take a sip of brandy from
his glass and only when it reached his lips did he realise that
the glass was empty. He followed through and pretended to
drink what wasn't there.

'Thanks,' said Gavin on leaving.

'No problem,' replied Nap, and closed the door between them before either of them could say anything too emotional. It was a relationship that worked better that way. Doors had always been a most underrated component in keeping relationships going.

Chapter 15

Gavin kept his head down over the next few days. Whilst this was not unusual, he was trying to keep his head that little bit lower than it might normally have been. Somewhere near his ankles. He busied himself with work and got more done than had been the case for quite some time. He got all his records up to date. He surprised people with visits. He was seen in the office on consecutive days. He even bought a mug and tea bags. If there was a tea fund, he owed big time.

Gavin always made a point of not visiting Nap too often. Their friendship rested on regular contact with sufficient time in between to suggest they both still had better things to do. Even if quite often neither of them did have anything better to do. He had never asked, but it was always a matter of some concern to him that Nap might not do anything between visits. He was probably on eBay searching out concert programmes or rare Subbuteo teams that hadn't been hand painted, or if they had been hand-painted, that they were then a work of art. So often these self-painted figures looked worse than the box they came in, the paint peeling off their shirts, with badly daubed shorts that have extended past their knees, nearly meeting stucco socks coming the other way. Most lads had at some time or another had a go at painting a favourite strip and quickly learnt that it was better to save up your pocket money, or wait until birthday or Christmas lists were being requested.

Gavin and Nap had developed a good understanding of what a relationship between two men as friends should be like.

Yes, there were times for a bit of off-loading and a touch of soul searching, but never anything likely to risk hugs or a pat on the shoulder. And God forbid that there should ever be tears. The nearer they ever got to anything emotional the more determined they were in following visits to keep it mundane, routine, and inconsequential. Friendships like that between Gavin and Nap didn't do consequences. When you parted there should be no more in your head than a new statistic or a cheery anecdote. Gavin and Nap had their relationship sussed.

Gavin made no contact with Sharyn. His relationship with Sharyn served him well in terms of giving him some link with the fairer sex. That took away all the pressures and expectations from others around dating, or not dating, or having someone trying to fix you up with someone else equally committed to avoiding anything too messy. She was also his ballast. If he went one way, she had the habit of pulling him the other way. She calmed rocky waters. She brought wind to the doldrums. She set the sails and then when it got too windy, she hauled down the mainsail. And currently, she was making him feel seasick. But, then again, that was Gavin and relationships. Sharyn was the one person that gave him expectations. Never anything too difficult, but a connection that kept him in check. And he was allowed to fall short of those expectations. In many ways, it seemed like the best of both worlds. He had a relationship, and he didn't have a relationship. Commitment without commitment. When he thought about it, he didn't have any idea what his relationship with Sharyn was.

There wasn't anyone else. Cora had started talking to him recently, but that wasn't a friendship outside work, although he suspected it had potential. Other than that, the only other person he had any conversation with was the postwoman. She initiated this and usually it was related to him taking a parcel for a neighbour. The neighbour seemed to be out more than they were in, which Gavin regarded as impertinent when they

135

received such a regular supply of packages. He guessed that talking to your postwoman did not count as a real friendship.

He realised that without Nap and Sharyn he had no one to talk to. He wasn't thinking about companionship, although that was important, but actual conversation. Without Nap and Sharyn, the only place where he needed to speak, the only people who needed to hear his voice, were at work. And they didn't count. Without Nap and Sharyn, he might as well be mute. They were the people that gave him the reason for speech. Otherwise, he might as well live inside his own head.

During these last days, he did not visit Ruth. He wasn't sure whether this was due to fear of any consequences following on from his goose-stepping around the grounds outside the window like some demented out-of-practice fascist, or that he needed a break. If he was going to be honest with himself, he was sure, and it was both.

He did think about where Ruth fitted into his limited social circle. His charitable visits, his kind volunteering to see her, his thoughtful giving of time to her, his generosity in regularly turning up, the way he put himself out for her benefit, the saint that he was for all this doing of good deeds. It was complete nonsense. Could it be that he needed her more than she needed him? Indeed, she didn't seem to need anyone. He had never met someone so content. Stuck in that home, in that chair and in that bed, she had more life about her than he had ever had, and he was running free. She was the tortoise and he was the hare. He wasn't sure if that fitted the bill, but he liked the analogy. Or rather, on consideration, he didn't like the analogy. He was running in circles.

Ruth was already fascinating to him. She sat there in her chair unable to get up. Physically she had no power over him, but she pulled him in. There was something about her that called him back. He wanted to know her story. He was ready to hear her story. But he would wait.

So, for a few days, Gavin kept, with much success, a low profile.

And then his cover was blown.

Chapter 16

They stood outside the heavy wooden chapel doors on which, in bright red paint, was sprayed the word 'Nazis' in great big capitals, except for the last letter which was smaller and trailed off. The word was clear and could be seen from a hundred metres away. They were about five metres away. There was no need to examine the situation from any other vantage point.

'And someone's put a swastika on the hall room front door,' said Sharyn.

The hall room door was around the corner from the main entrance to the chapel, but the evidence of one piece of offensive graffiti did not warrant any doubt about another example somewhere else. 'Seriously?' responded Gavin. He was shocked. But he had just the slightest, tiniest, teeniest, weeniest little worry scratching away there, and this accounted for his natural shock pitch rising by a mere semi-tone.

Sharyn looked at Gavin. Gavin withered.

'We need to talk,' announced Sharyn.

Not again thought Gavin. 'We do?' he replied.

'We do,' re-affirmed Sharyn.

Gavin was caught in a place where he could not stem the flow of guilt washing over him, even though he was not sure quite what he had done. There was a link, but it was tentative. He was not a racist. He knew enough about it to appreciate that there were many perspectives on what constituted racism and what that meant for white people. He knew that by only

138

the most extreme of these views could he be considered a racist and then it was along with the whole white community. Otherwise, he was a pretty understanding and unprejudiced sort of guy. When it came down to it, he had nothing to say and nothing to hide.

'Someone at the church says you are to blame,' said Sharyn, getting straight to the point.

'What?'

'Yes. My reaction too when they said it. So. Answer me this.'

Gavin looked at Sharyn wondering what was coming.

'Did you go down to that care home and do a Nazi salute to the old people?'

'Shit.'

'Gavin!'

'How…' and his voice trailed off in search of somewhere he could hide for the rest of his life.

'I'm a vicar, Gavin. You'd be amazed at who I know and what people tell me.'

Not any more, he thought to himself, and then considered that she ought to have some sort of responsibility not to share information given in confidence or confession or was that a different church? Why couldn't Sharyn be a Catholic priest or whatever they call themselves and keep it to herself? Gavin was stuck. She had connected him to what was right in front of them and condemned him for it. Part of him was feeling the rising anger of being a victim. Whatever he had done several days ago. However he had behaved in a mad moment, he had not intended to be part of anything like this. He was as harmless as John Cleese doing Basil Fawlty to laughing millions. He was not in any way whatsoever, a Nazi. It had been a message to one person that had now, if not gone viral, was certainly feeling more than a sneeze from a bad cold let loose. 'Can't we go for a coffee and talk this over?' was the best he could muster, trying to buy time to digest what was happening.

'No. No. No. No. No.' replied Sharyn. 'We talk right here right now.'

'You're sounding like Fat Boy Slim.' And as soon as he had said it, he knew it was one of those moments where his sense of humour was hanging him.

Sharyn walked off. He called after her. He knew this needed to be dealt with. He knew they needed to talk. He needed to explain. He needed to get into a conversation and try and understand it himself. He didn't want any delay. He called again. She turned and slowly came back to him.

'Sorry,' he said.

'And what are you apologising for?' she said.

'For the joke. For the bad inappropriate joke.'

Gavin could see that she was looking for more.

'I can't apologise for this,' and he pointed at the doors. 'I didn't do this. Do you really really think I would do anything like this? Do you really think that expresses my views? You know me. You know that is the opposite of how I feel about these things.' Gavin needed to say this. He needed to make a statement that re-asserted his dislike of intolerance.

'I do know you. I know how stupid you can be sometimes.'

He could not disagree with that.

'Someone said you had upset the old people at a care home somewhere and that you had now been banned. Now I'm full of questions, starting with, why are you visiting a care home and ending with why are you impersonating Hitler and scaring the residents?'

'How can that be connected to the church? How do you make that connection?'

'Someone at the church had heard about the home and they put two and two together and made a pretty convincing four.'

Gavin did not know what to say.

And then a figure came around the corner and called out to Sharyn. It was George Rampling, the chapel treasurer. 'Ah, Sharyn,' he said.

'Yes, George,' replied Sharyn. The thing about church people is that whilst they might use first names when in conversation with each other, once you start referencing them to someone else there is a strange requirement to use full names or titles. George, therefore, was always George Rampling. If Sharyn spoke to Gavin about the chapel treasurer, he was always George Rampling. If she spoke about the chapel secretary, she was always Miss Wakeling. If she spoke about the chapel chair, he was always Gilbert Peterson. The organist was Mr Russell. The caretaker and keyholder was always Rebecca Simpson. Had Sting or Shaggy attended the church they would have been Mr Sting and Mr Shaggy.

'And, Gavin,' George Rampling said, turning to an initially relieved man, about to enjoy a brief period of respite. 'Nice to see you,' he added. Gavin would not have recognised George Rampling as they had only met a couple of times, but as the *friend* of the vicar he suspected he was more easily recognised and remembered by most of the congregation. And it was nice to see him. Very timely. It was a pity Miss Wakeling, Gilbert Peterson, Mr Russell, Rebecca Simpson, Mr Sting and Mr Shaggy hadn't turned up too.

'We're here for the same reason,' said George Rampling, directing his gaze at the monstrosity that stood before them. He then looked away as it felt uncomfortable to see the word written there across the doors of the chapel he had been attending for over twenty years.

'And around the corner,' added Sharyn.

'So I've heard,' replied George Rampling. 'What an awful thing to do.' George Rampling addressed this to Gavin.

'Absolutely,' replied Gavin. He meant it. It was awful in so many ways.

'Why does someone do something like that?' George Rampling said. 'I mean what have we ever done?'

'All sorts of people out there,' said Sharyn.

'We need to get it off as soon as we can,' said George Rampling.

'We're here to help,' said Sharyn, looking at Gavin.

Gavin's look was not that committal, but he knew where his feet would be taking him. He was telling himself that he had nothing to feel guilty about. He had not done it. It signified absolutely nothing that he agreed with. But, of course, he would help. Partly because he was there, on the spot. And partly because he had to be clearly on the right side of this issue. And wholly because he wanted the matter finished as quickly as possible.

The swastika on the hall room door was seen by Gavin when they went through that way to get buckets and hard brushes. George Rampling positioned himself at the hall room door with brush and water. Sharyn and Gavin returned to the chapel doors, fully armed.

'So,' resumed Sharyn. 'Firstly. Why are you hanging around this home? Do you know someone there?'

Gavin explained how his jogging had turned into visiting.

'You've been visiting this elderly lady in a home for the past two months, but you don't even go and visit your own mother.'

'But you know what she's like.'

'I know, but she's your mother. Who's this other woman?'

'She's not the other woman. That makes it sound, you know.'

'I know. How do you want it to sound? You're not married so you can't be cheating on your wife.'

'So now you're saying I'm cheating on my mother.'

'That could be one way of looking at it.'

'I prefer visiting this elderly interesting lady in a care home rather than getting a load of abuse from visiting my mother.'

'I'm just pointing it out.'

'I'll go and visit my mother if that helps.'

'That's up to you. I'm not telling you to visit your mother. I'm just making the comparison.'

'It takes a day to visit her. Half an hour of suffering and then the rest of the day in rehab.'

'She's still your mother.'

They were an unhappy couple and it showed in the effort they were both putting into cleaning the doors. Sharyn had worked away most of the N. Gavin was heading toward her from the other side and having cleared the s he was now starting on the I.

'And second,' continued Sharyn. 'Why the ridiculous behaviour? Why?'

Gavin explained about the woman working there who seemed to have taken a dislike to him and that he had only intended to demonstrate to Ruth that she was not letting him in. He decided that Sharyn didn't need to know that she also thought he was a pervert.

'And you thought you'd help the situation by saluting and goose-stepping in front of all the residents.'

'I was only trying to get over to her that I thought the woman not letting me in was behaving like a Nazi. Well, not a Nazi but, you know, like she was some sort of unreasonable crazed authority figure. And it wasn't all the residents. Only those in the lounge. And only those that could see, that could see me.' It was a correction that Gavin knew made no difference to the accusation.

'And-' started Sharyn, but she was interrupted by George Rampling.

'Done the hall door.' George Rampling stopped and looked. 'I can see that you too are nearly done here too. Much appreciated, Gavin. Hard work, isn't it?'

'Glad to help,' Gavin replied. He could feel the words being shredded by Sharyn and falling to the floor in rags.

'I would offer you both a drink but I'm keen to get off. You have a key with you?' George Rampling looked at Sharyn.

'Yes,' she replied.

'Thanks again,' said George Rampling and then left.

'At least I'm in someone's good books,' said Gavin.

The look Sharyn gave him was more than enough to replace any words. Gavin returned to the last of the paint on the door and resumed his exertions. She left him to it and paced around the grounds. It was an old chapel and had a small amount of land on which were occasional tomb stones, some upright and visible, others hidden amongst years of growth. No one maintained the grounds and it was down to occasional efforts on the part of certain chapel members. It was tidy but lacked any planning or aforethought. They were a church not a garden centre, but Sharyn felt that they could do more for what people saw outside, as well as stimulating their thoughts inside the chapel. The inside of the building was well maintained but there were always battles with damp and peeling paint, often ignored if they were in the darker corners and crevices. It was a second home to Sharyn, but her work and demands were with people. And that very much included Gavin.

'Finished,' he shouted. Gavin picked up the two buckets and brushes and balancing everything awkwardly, he returned them to the kitchen area in the hall. She followed him in and they put everything away. They came back out and Sharyn locked the door. They walked off together into the town centre. They had both parked in the usual car park. They came to Sharyn's car first.

'This isn't over,' she said to him, as she unlocked the car and climbed into the driver's seat.

Gavin smiled, and how he said good-bye to her confirmed that he knew he was on the bottom rung of any ladder to salvation. It was a long ladder too. He found his car and drove off.

He returned home to a note on the door and the apparent nailer of the note sitting on the doorstep below it. There was initially silence between them. It took the seated figure a couple of seconds to twig that the house's owner had returned. It took Gavin a couple of seconds to take in the scene before him. It took him more seconds to weigh up his options and to wonder what to do. Consequently, the nailer's review of the situation concluded first.

'You live here?' enquired the man who was barring Gavin's way into his own house. That was something else that Gavin had not had time to weigh up.

Gavin stalled for just too long to avoid any get-out clause. He offered his best mutter.

'Big Ron's looking for you,' threatened the nailer. He stood up. He was small in stature. He was big in girth. He had moved off the step which only served to confirm his compactness. He stood his ground. There was no way past him.

Gavin looked at this character who seemed to have entered his life when everything else was taking a strange direction. He did not know what to say.

'He's got big hands. He got the sort of hands that could strangle two men at the same time.' The nailer waited, expecting a response. 'Even if they were in different rooms.'

Gavin looked him up and down, which didn't take long.

'He wants to see you.' The nailer looked at Gavin.

Gavin looked at the nailer. Briefly, their eyes met.

'You don't want to mess with Big Ron.'

Gavin still had nothing to say. He was still staring at the man.

The nailer was finding the lack of response a bit discomforting. He was running out of threats. The situation was losing its shadiness. 'Big Ron is, I mean, he's big. And nasty.'

Gavin looked again at the nailer. It took a few more seconds and then it came to him. 'Satnav.' It was released with a feeling of sanctuary and peppered with genuine delight. 'Satnav,' he repeated.

And Satnav realised that he knew Gavin. 'No one calls me that now. They call me by my proper name.'

Gavin had to think, but it did come to him. 'Jacob,' he announced proudly. In his job you came across many children and remembering them, never mind their names, was an impossible task. But he had always remembered Jacob. His foster carers had nicknamed him Satnav because he always got lost. It had been a warm and friendly joke and Jacob had revelled in it as it had given him an identity which in turn had meant he was important. But that must have been ten years ago. Gavin had been his social worker for several months. He considered how old Jacob must be now and what had happened to him. 'Do you want to come in and tell me what this is all about?'

Jacob was reluctant. He had always liked Gavin. Gavin was never a social worker. He had just been an older person looking out for him. But this situation was different, and he knew what Big Ron expected. He had also heard what Big Ron did if you let him down. Jacob liked having four fingers and a thumb on each hand, all four limbs, and a reasonably formed face.

Gavin read the hesitancy. 'Tell you what. Shall I bring us a couple of beers out here?'

Jacob assented. It felt strange and yet powerful sharing a beer with his former social worker.

'Big Ron really is a bastard,' said Jacob. He paused after swearing to see if Gavin might admonish him, although Gavin, the social worker, had never really told anyone off for anything.

'So, why are you working for him?'

'It's not work. He don't pay me. He just slips me things every now and then and I do a few jobs for him.'

Gavin showed some alarm.

'No, not anything illegal. Not those sorts of jobs. Just errands.'

'Like this.'

Jacob did now look a little bit embarrassed. He wasn't going to tell Gavin anything though. That was his own business. 'He said to put it on the door somewhere and wait and let him know that you'd got the message. I didn't know it would be someone I knew.'

'Don't worry,' assured Gavin.

'You need to worry though. Big Ron is seriously not good. If he asks you to do something, you do it.'

'Sometimes you have to stand up to people, Satnav, Jacob.'

'Not Big Ron. You don't want to mess with Big Ron.'

'Do you know why he wants to see me?'

'Not really. But he is really upset. I don't think he wants to see you. He wants to beat you up. Done it before. Or he'll get someone else to do it.'

Up to this point, the conversation had been an interesting connection for Gavin with his past work. You rarely got to see what had happened to any of the children or young people you had worked with. But now it turned back to the reason for them coming together in the first place. Jacob also sensed the change and was concerned not to do anything that would get back to Big Ron, and he was keen not to disclose to Gavin what a mess his life was. The message had been delivered and that was what he had been expected to do. Better to get away before it all got too nice.

'Anyway, I'd better go,' said Jacob.

'Take it with you,' replied Gavin, seeing that Jacob was about to put his can down on the doorstep.

'Thanks,' said Jacob, and he set off. He turned around, 'Big Ron is not good news. Be careful.' And he walked off.

Gavin watched him walk up the street. Then he took down the note and read it.

'No one upset my mother and get away with it you are dead mate'.

The last word looked like mate but could have been meat, such was the style of the scribbled writing. Mate sounded friendlier. Either way, it sounded terminal. And whose mother would be giving out instructions that Gavin needed a good beating? He might have upset a few people recently but surely not to that extent. He would sleep on it.

The following morning there was a knock on the door. It was the sort of knock that doors were not made to withstand, and it was accompanied by the sort of aggressive bellowing that could break down a door all on its own, without any assistance from hands, fists, or knuckles.

'You in there? I know you in there,' was what Gavin could decipher, along with other reverberations as voice and door competed to be heard.

Gavin decided to do whatever one should do when somebody needs convincing that you are not in. He made a concerted effort to do nothing. He put a lot of effort into doing nothing and into not being there. He quickly got himself to a place where he could not be seen and then he stayed still, kept quiet, and waited. He was playing the part of person not at home.

'I know you there,' repeated the caller. 'You dead mate.'

Gavin could not tell if he was saying he was dead meat or dead mate. His oral communication was as bad as his writing, considered Gavin, before acknowledging that he was focusing on the wrong thing. Gavin's mind was racing. His heart was beating fast. He was undertaking a lot of internal activity for someone trying ridiculously hard not to be there.

'I know you there. I can smell you shitting yourself.'

Gavin had to think. Did he know he was there? How would he know he was there? Was it a bluff or had he been seen? He preferred chess to poker. There was more certainty

148

with chess. There was more to go on. Poker taunted you and teased you. It thrived on doubt. Could he sit it out? Should he sit it out? He still didn't move. He could feel his heart beating faster and faster.

There was another bang on the door. It made him jump. He was considering how strong the door was. This person who he knew must be Big Ron, with big fists, big arms, big muscles, and big intentions. How far was he prepared to go?

'I know you in there. I'm coming back.' There was a further thud of something hitting the front door. The house reverberated. It could have been a fist. It could have been Big Ron's head. It could have been the body of someone who had just been passing by.

Gavin had no reason to doubt it. Would he even go away? Was he waiting outside? Gavin dared not go and look. He was still focused on pretending he was not at home and if you are not at home you don't go looking through windows or twitching at curtains.

He had told Jacob he needed to stand up to people. He considered that to be a load of old nonsense. If Plan A was standing up to Big Ron, then he was already onto Plan B. And Plan B was looking like sitting still and pretending you are not there. Gavin knew that Plan B had a limited amount of time before he would have to give it up for Plan C. Sooner or later, he would need to respond to a physical need. The way he was feeling, it was the toilet that would give him away before the kitchen. He couldn't spend the rest of his life hiding away. Well, it had never worked before. His thoughts continued to race. He was keeping still. But that could only be a prequel to doing something. And if Big Ron could show any potential to live up to the reputation that Jacob had given him then he would break into the house sooner rather than later. He could only pretend not to be at home for a brief time. Eventually, he would be found to be in. And what would happen then? He'd be dead meat, mate. They'd find him on a hook on the wall.

The television would be on high to drown any last sounds. He'd probably utter his final breath in front of an average episode of The Chase. Or even worse, Pointless. His mind was racing. Who needs drugs when you've got Big Ron. Plan B had no future. Plan B had no future. It was racing through his head. Plan B had no future.

He abandoned Plan B. According to a rough version of Plan C, Gavin left via the back door and over the fence into an adjoining garden. He scratched his arse and left leg on a rose bush and scarpered.

Chapter 17

There were four of them.

None of them came on horseback. There were no winged messengers. They hadn't come far. They didn't bring gifts. Unless you counted a packet of custard creams. And it seemed that none of them had ever met before.

The police officer wasn't too clear what this was all about. It was another of those unimportant points of contact with the public that they were always sending him out to. It wasn't that he didn't like the public, although he wasn't much for interacting with anyone, the public or his police colleagues, but it was more the lack of excitement. Again, he had been in the force long enough to have learnt that you were better off avoiding trouble rather than going out looking for it, but, just occasionally, a stake out or being part of the team surrounding the building would have been nice. He knew he wasn't very good at the job. And he knew that was why he always got sent to schools, community centres, and the sort of situations that would otherwise have sorted themselves out eventually or been bettered served with a life-size cardboard cut-out of a police officer. It wasn't as if he liked the job. He didn't. He had started hating the job after two days of doing it. And here he was, several years on, sitting in the lounge of someone's house, having been let in by someone else who did not live in the house, but had a key, And the only excitement was his usual doubt about whether or not that gave him the right to enter the house. He was a crap police officer. He had no time for the public and he had never got his head round all those laws and protocols and what would be the right thing to do. Any remaining excitement in what he did had bolted over a decade ago. Now he offered little more than the aforementioned cardboard cut-out. He just cost more and was less likely to get soggy.

Jake lived next door but one. He didn't work. Because of something to do with his heart. He lived with Sam. Sam had three different jobs and worked a shift pattern, the algorithm of which would have had Pythagoras reaching out for a handful of paracetamol. If he wasn't working at the newsagents he was working at the council tip, and if he wasn't working at the council tip he was working at the fish and chip shop, and if he wasn't working at the fish and chip shop he was probably at home falling asleep, in the arms of Jake, in front of Coronation Street. Jake had the time that Sam didn't, and Jake liked to know what was going on. And this unexpected meeting and invitation was an opportunity not to be missed.

Cora worked in what was now called business support. It used to be called admin. There would be a future change of name on its way, possibly to something like technical interference or general dog's body. Whatever it might be called, Cora typed and sent emails and did minutes and made phone calls and answered phone calls and booked meetings and cancelled meetings and apologised for people not attending meetings and apologised to people who had attended meetings that had been cancelled and had brief moments of respite before the next demand was made. It was on her way home. They were concerned enough to send someone, and she was that someone. She had to admit that she too was a little concerned. She hardly knew him. They had had a couple of brief conversations, but that was two more than anyone else had had recently.

Sharyn had let everyone into the house. Enough time had gone by for her to have started to become worried. She hadn't seen or heard from Gavin for eight days. She'd been to the house. It had looked abandoned. His car was where he usually parked it. She'd tried his phone and then that had rung back at her from down the back of his settee. She'd spoken to his work. They had to agree that, whilst he was an odd sort of character, this was a different level of oddness, and he was off without having booked any leave. Everything had given Sharyn a sense that something wasn't quite right. And then there was his front door. There was recent damage and it was not inconsequential. Her job gave her both contacts and a level of respectability and so this meeting had been agreed following discussion with someone she knew in the police force. They weren't guaranteeing they would be able to send one of their best officers, but they would see what they could do.

They were sat in the lounge, equipped with tea and an offering of biscuits. The flipchart and tripod stood in their midst. Whilst Sharyn had sorted out refreshments, they had tried to make small talk around it. Someone was always having to crane a neck, or stretch to the left, or move a buttock, so that they could see someone else properly. This was not their home and so it had seemed impolite to suggest that the tripod was moved.

As Sharyn had settled into her chair it was at once clear that the flipchart was going to have to be moved. She got up and moved it in front of the fireplace. The police officer had half got up to help her and then found himself caught in the dilemma of whether that was appropriate as he was a man and she was a woman, but then again he was a police officer so that meant he had a potential responsibility to help which was professional rather than personal, but then would she see it that way and would everyone else see it that way and after all no one else had moved, and by which time the tripod and flipchart had been moved and Sharyn had already sat back down.

It was clear to Sharyn that the police officer was showing no signs of taking charge. This had been clear from the way he had sloped from outside the house to inside the house and marked the juncture with a nervous cough. He wore his uniform as if he was hiding inside it and hoping no one would come too near to check. She recognised the need to take the initiative.

'Hi everyone. I'm Sharyn. A friend of Gavin's and a vicar. But here as Gavin's friend.' She looked across at the police officer and opened out her hand and arm as if to invite his introduction.

There was a cough. 'PC Mike. Call me Mike. Mike. A police officer, of course,' although he had never been that sure about it. There was no point in adding his number. 'Just call me PC Mike. Call me Mike.'

'Cora. I work with Gavin. Although I don't know him that well. He's very quiet at work. When he's there. But I've spoken with him a couple of times. Been in a lot recently and then not for a while.' Cora stopped abruptly, wondering if she was speaking too soon.

'Jake. I live next door but one. We don't see much of him. Keeps himself to himself. Sam and I have never really spoken to him.'

Cora was black. Jake seemed to be gay. He'd have to listen and observe a bit more to be sure. He lived with Sam and Sam was one of those names that God had created just to confuse people. And Sharyn was a woman priest. PC Mike Call Me Mike found himself considering all the possible pitfalls that he thought this combination could set. He had never been able to fathom what was the right or wrong thing to say. To him, people were people and it was just that some people were more like him and other people were less like him and you couldn't beat the people that were more like him that he met every so often at a **Dr** Who convention or a gathering of the diminishing number of Trekies. And they really were an odd assortment. All ears, badges, and sonic screwdrivers. That was your real diversity.

'Thank you,' started Sharyn. In the game of who's in charge, the vicar had sunk the police officer without a trace. That said, PC Mike Call Me Mike had always considered that being in charge wasn't about speaking but more about letting other people speak and he was very good at letting other people speak. Once he got back to the station, he could tell them that he'd been at a meeting where there had been an equal number of women as men, one gay man, and one black woman, and that he'd let the woman take charge. How respectful of diversity had he been! But then again, that sort of comment had previously been more likely to get him into trouble rather than out of trouble. Political correctness baffled him however you looked at it, and he'd found that over the last few years how you looked at it had changed. He'd readily accepted that he was never going to be Earth's greatest ambassador. Although, he had seen every episode of *Star Trek: The Next Generation*, and that had to count for something.

'It feels odd sitting here,' said Sharyn. 'Not only in Gavin's house, and I really do hope he turns up whilst we're here, but also because I'm not sure what the situation is. I'm not sure if he's missing, if he's lost, if something has happened, or if he is just being more obtuse than normal.' The word, obtuse, rang around the room with no one daring to ask what it meant. 'I asked PC...' she looked at him and stalled, 'Mike, to come in case we do need to do anything. I don't get the impression that either of you know him well.' She looked at Cora and Jake. 'But you cover work and home. He has a friend Nap who I don't know. And I don't know where he lives. And that is all as far as I am aware.' She looked at each of them in turn. 'Does anyone have anything else to add? Is there anyone else?'

Three heads shook from side to side. PC Mike Call Me Mike added a cough.

'I know he had visited some old lady in a care home recently,' added Sharyn. 'I don't know who she was or if it related to work in any way, but I'm not sure it can be that significant.' Sharyn hadn't wanted to add anything else. She wanted to share information to see if they could unravel what had happened to Gavin, but she also wanted to leave him with most of his privacy intact. 'When was he last at work?'

'I'm business support. I'm in every day. It was strange because for a few days he was in a lot. Not a lot, but a lot for Gavin He also made tea. He's always looked a bit…' and she hunted for the word, across fields and over hedges, and finally settled for, '…sad. Not really sad, not unhappy, but not happy either. A bit lost. But in the last few days, he was more upbeat. He'd had a bit of life about him. And that was about a week ago. And not seeing Gavin for a week is not unusual. But Sally Clark says to tell you, that's his boss, she says to tell you that he has missed appointments. He's not answering his work phone.'

'Probably down the back of the settee,' said Sharyn.

'Maybe,' replied Cora.

PC Mike Call Me Mike shuffled as if he had just found it.

'And here?' asked Sharyn, addressing Jake. 'When did you last see him?'

'It's got to be over a week ago. He usually sits on the doorstep to put his trainers on. Sometimes, anyway. Can't think that we've seen him for at least a week.

PC Mike Call Me Mike wasn't sure if he should be writing any of this down, or if he ought, at least, to be seen to be writing some of it down. He could remember it so far, if they asked him. Missing a week. That about summed it up. 'What about the door?' he offered. 'Do we know when that happened?'

'Did you hear anything?' added Sharyn. She looked at Jake.

As much as Jake liked to know what was happening on the street, he had to confess to himself that he had missed this one. He must have been out. That could be the only explanation. But as to when it was, he had noted it. 'Well. I didn't see or hear anything. And why would I? I'm not a nosey neighbour. But, and this is going to be interesting, I reckon it must be about a week ago. It's recent damage. Was not like that before. About a week ago I noticed it.'

'And have you seen him since you noticed it? asked Cora.

'No,' replied Jake. 'Now that's funny, isn't it?' He seemed pleased with the observation.

'Do you think it's on purpose?' asked Cora. 'The door?' she added and turned to PC Mike Call Me Mike.

How did he know? He didn't do scenes of crime or any of that science stuff. It was just a damaged door. Splinters and paint missing. Granted, you were unlikely to damage your own door, but he had attended enough of those Star Trek events to know that there was often more happening out there than people realised, and people from across the universe could do very strange things, including damaging their own door. 'Could be,' PC Mike Call Me Mike replied.

'By Gavin or by someone else?' added Jake, rising to the intrigue. Something now to tell Sam when he got home from work.

'Not sure why Gavin would do it,' said Cora.

'No,' replied Sharyn. 'But then this is Gavin.'

'And what do you think that means?' said Jake, pointing at the flipchart. He was starting to see himself as some sort of sleuth now. Deerstalker, pipe, mac, monocle, trilby. He'd have to think about the accessories later. 'Got to be a clue there.'

They all looked at the flipchart leaning up against the fireplace. It stood out. And so did the words written on the paper.

'What does that mean? Tomato?' said Cora.

'I think it says tomorrow,' said Sharyn.

'Tomato,' repeated Cora. 'I think it says tomorrow above it crossed out.'

'Why would it say tomato?' said Jake. Definitely a trilby, he thought.

'Why would it say tomorrow?' said Cora.

'Maybe he was planning something tomorrow,' said Jake. 'Which has now happened and as a result of which he has disappeared.'

'Or he was going to plant some tomatoes,' suggested Cora.

'In which case why write about it?' added Jake. 'And what about the R where the rest of the word has been torn off?'

'R for red,' offered Cora. 'Red tomatoes.'

'Could just as well be Robot or Robin,' said Jake.

'Why?' replied Cora.

'I mean it could be R for anything,' said Jake.

'Okay,' interjected Sharyn. 'I'm not sure what it says or why and I don't think it is helping.'

PC Mike Call Me Mike found the very existence of the flipchart in the man's lounge to be odd. He also felt that Sharyn had justified his silence. He had often found that the best way was to say nothing. You could avoid most things that way. The quiet approach. He was in the wrong job. He wasn't sure what the right job would be. Libraries were quiet places, but then they had all those books to manage and all that knowledge to keep an eye on. Anyway, tomato or tomorrow. R for Rudolph. What did it matter? He wasn't sure why he was here at all. This Gavin was an odd chap. He would turn up. He'd probably walked past him at an event somewhere. A chap with a flipchart tripod in his lounge needed to attend a few more Dalek conventions.

'If he was brainstorming ideas he didn't get very far, did he?' said Cora.

'Unless he was preparing a presentation,' said PC Mike Call Me Mike and then wondered if he had said too much.

They all went silent. Jake was running out of ideas. His private detective ambitions were faltering. Cora couldn't get the association with tomatoes out of her head. PC Mike Call Me Mike was thinking he might have tomatoes on toast for tea. Sharyn wasn't sure if any of this had been worth it. Was Gavin in trouble, or had he just gone on some jolly jaunt and given everyone else his usual lack of consideration? Although she then considered that that was unfair. Gavin was considerate. It just came out the wrong way.

'We need a plan,' Sharyn said and broke their thoughts. She looked at PC Mike Call Me Mike and then addressed him first. 'Would the police do anything in this sort of situation?'

This put PC Mike Call Me Mike on the spot. There had always been the possibility that this might happen. This was the problem with being a police officer. People expected you to know what to do. It was the thing that spoilt the job more than anything else. Often, he didn't know what to do. And that was when he started to feel like a police uniform with a body rattling around inside it. He did what he usually did in these situations. He coughed. It sounded like he was clearing his throat and thus suggested he might have something to say. This made him scratch his knee. Another cough. And then he spoke. 'Depends.'

They had been looking at him. They were looking at him. And he was overwhelmed by the likelihood that they would continue looking at him until he came up with something better than 'Depends'. 'If he was reported as missing it would be a low priority.' He scratched both knees at the same time. 'Is he missing?' The smugness about the way he had put this question back amongst them and removed himself from such machinations had him sitting upright in his chair. It was as if he was saluting himself.

Jake didn't know Gavin. Just observing one or two departures or arrivals at the house gave him nothing. He'd given up on the trilby now. Cora had felt that something was not right, but she could not claim to have enough knowledge of Gavin to allow that to lead her to any interpretation.

The question landed firmly in Sharyn's lap. It arrived there with the sort of inevitability that could be matched only by the complete lack of any certainty regarding the answer. Was Gavin missing? The very question implied not being where you should be. It was hard to come up with where Gavin should be. He had seemed stressed recently. And there had been some bad decisions which brought back the image of the writing on the chapel doors. But he was a regular when it came to making bad, or perhaps to be a bit fairer, strange decisions. He kept a lot to himself, so he was not an easy person to understand. And when he did explain himself, it all seemed to come out at once and probably in the wrong way. And when she thought about it, she had to admit that he often seemed lost. But had he now got so lost that he was missing?

'Perhaps it's too soon to say he's missing,' said Sharyn. She wasn't that satisfied with the answer but felt it was the best response for now. 'However, I would like to see what enquiries we can make. And if there are any clues as to where he could be.'

Jake had moved on completely now from the detective ambitions. He might have some interest in being a freelance journalist if the story could be developed.

'What about his car?' asked Cora.

'It's still here,' said Sharyn. 'I checked.'

'Isn't that a bit strange?' questioned Jake.

'Is he using it?' said Cora.

Sharyn wasn't sure but she had the feeling that it had not been moved. She'd spotted it twice now. In the same place. A four-seater Hyundai coupe with a sloping back that meant that the back seats were designed to take only small people, or someone prepared to arch their back or lie down for the length of the journey. Those sorts of people weren't that common. In Gavin's world, there weren't any of them. The front passenger seat looked like it was just an additional space for rubbish. It was a sporty car that did not match the mediocrity that Gavin otherwise struggled to achieve.

'I don't think he's used it,' said Sharyn.

'We don't seem to have anything clear either way,' said PC Mike Call Me Mike.

'I agree,' replied Sharyn. No one else said otherwise. 'Should we perhaps meet in two or three days and see what we can come up with?'

Jake nodded, although he wasn't sure that there was anything he could offer to do other than twitch at the curtain occasionally. Cora nodded, although she could only report if there was any contact with work.

'Back here in three days. Same time?' suggested Sharyn.

PC Mike Call Me Mike nearly offered a room at the police station and then thought about the added paperwork or computer work. He decided he didn't want to find out. He kept quiet and nodded his agreement. He assumed he would be given the time to attend. They seemed to let him make that kind of decision, occasionally.

'If I can,' replied Cora. For someone in business support, it was like being a social worker. She should think about it. Then again, she had five daughters keeping her busy enough.

'Should be okay for me,' said Jake, unable to think of much to prevent him, and by then it might just have got a little more interesting. It made him wonder what some of his other neighbours might have been up to and whether he had missed some other fascinating stories to be told.

PC Mike Call Me Mike scratched a knee, coughed, and then nodded sufficiently to assume that his response had been noted. Then just in case it hadn't he said, 'Yes,' and coughed again.

Sharyn let them all out of the house and then closed the door behind her, as she walked up the street to her car. Where are you, Gavin? she asked herself. And what are you up to? She wasn't one for swearing. So, she didn't. But she could have. So easily she could have. Gavin! she screamed inside her head.

Next stop, eighty-seven-year-old Frank Dodger and a friendly visit that will need a moment when she asks him to explain to her why it isn't appropriate to say to Mrs Jenkins some of the things he has been saying to Mrs Jenkins. And then a visit to Mrs Jenkins to say that she has spoken with Frank Dodger. Bloody hell, Gavin!

Chapter 18

Three days later they were assembled in the living room again. The gang were back together. They'd all made it. It must have been the custard creams. Sharyn had brought Bourbons this time.

PC Mike Call Me Mike hadn't been sure if they would have let him come for a second meeting, but they had said they could spare him for a couple of hours. He was out of uniform and brought no new information with him. There had been no Gavin at the Dr Who gathering he had attended. Several contenders. There would always be contenders, but no actual Gavin. They had met someone who had played a Dalek when Colin Baker had been The Doctor. He would hold on sharing that information in case they weren't as keen as he was. But no Gavin.

Cora could only confirm that they continued to have no contact with him at work. He had not communicated in person, by email, or by phone. They were none the wiser.

Jake had been on the lookout and taken several walks to what he understood to be Gavin's car. No sign of him. The car hadn't moved. He'd been there enough to be sure of it.

Sharyn had managed to find Nap. That was the wonderful thing about being a vicar. You could go to the strangest places and make the weirdest enquiries, but if they knew you were a vicar it sort of made sense to them somehow. And everyone wanted to help. Even though most people had nothing to offer they wanted to, at least, give a thoughtful look or some

163

reference to once seeing or hearing something about something that might be something but then wasn't anything. In the end someone knew someone who had an idea who Nap might be and where he lived. None of them believed in God, but this was a vicar, and she was wearing that compelling scent that these religious people must wear to make you talk. And she was a woman priest. That made it even more compelling. Nap knew about the chapel door and the incident at the care home. He didn't know much else. He had also lent his car to Gavin and had seen neither the car nor Gavin since. The only information she felt worth sharing was concerning the car.

'Why would he borrow a car when he has his own?' asked Jake, on behalf of them all.

What followed was a conversation that explored all sorts of possibilities, weird and wonderful and where everyone had a different knowledge about cars, their colours, and their specifications. None of it left them any wiser.

Sharyn had managed to find the care home, but the woman she had to deal with there was having none of her aura of divine priestess or whatever god incarnate she was trying to exude the beatification of. She had identified who Sharyn was referring to and recommended that she leave him well alone. He might have visited someone here, but that racist pervert was never going to get past her. Sharyn had no reason to doubt this proclamation. However, had she known to come back a couple of hours later she would have discovered that the fire-snorting winged gatekeeper was off duty and off home to her lair, and her chances of getting in, or getting the right information, would have increased dramatically. Sharyn decided that she would keep this to herself. No one needed to know that Gavin was viewed as a racist pervert and, even though he could be quite the annoying maverick, she knew he was caring and loving. Yes, there were times when a good throttling wouldn't have gone amiss, but she could forgive him. Of course, she did. Although right now, this was being tested.

'We don't seem to have much,' said Sharyn.

'So, what do we do?' asked Cora, which once again prompted the question of whether he was missing to raise its head.

PC Mike Call Me Mike only just heard the question. He hadn't come back down to earth since meeting the Dalek actor. He coughed his way back into their presence and finished a last splutter with, 'I'm still not sure if he's missing. A car you say. Borrowed a car. Now if he'd stolen it.' And he paused for effect. There was none.

'Can you put the number plate number out for people to look for?' asked Jake.

'It's not stolen though, is it?' returned PC Mike Call Me Mike. He scratched his left knee.

'Technically though, if he's not returned it?' offered Jake.

'Like a hire car,' suggested Cora.

PC Mike Call Me Mike scratched his nose which made his nose itch, so he scratched it again. 'But they're friends and he borrowed a friend's car.'

'I suppose so,' conceded Jake.

'I just feel helpless,' said Cora. She realised that she quite liked Gavin.

'I know,' said Sharyn. 'I am starting to worry now. If someone disappears for a week that feels like, I don't know,' And she didn't know. She thought about it.

'A holiday,' suggested Jake.

'Exactly. People disappear for a week on holiday. Yes, they usually tell you they're off somewhere, but this is Gavin.' Sharyn could feel herself getting upset.

'And he hasn't booked any leave,' said Cora.

'And his front door doesn't look like he's just gone on leave,' said Jake.

'I am beginning to worry now,' said Sharyn. She looked at PC Mike Call Me Mike.

PC Mike Call Me Mike could feel a shift in the mood of the room. Time to forget about Daleks. He still didn't think there was a lot he could do but he probably needed to offer something. And after all, he was part of the when-everything-else-fails service. They had come to a dead end and there was no borrowed car parked there. 'I really can't promise anything,' was how he carefully opened. 'But I will talk with my sergeant and see if any action is warranted.' He liked that. A good old police word was *warranted*.

'Thank you,' responded Sharyn.

Cora smiled.

'Hopefully…' said Jake, offering the best unfinished sentence he could think of.

PC Mike Call Me Mike sat for a while without scratching anything and just wondered about the powers of the word *warranted*.

Sharyn got up. She wasn't sure that they had achieved anything. She was worried about Gavin. Nothing was happening to resolve the situation. She would pray tonight. She wasn't one usually prone to praying in such a situation. Most things were about life and allowing life to play itself out. But unusually she felt helpless. She wasn't sure where this was going. A little bit of Almighty guidance would not be amiss. And was she being selfish? That wasn't for her to dwell on or decide.

Everyone else got up. They all left the house and gathered outside.

Chapter 19

Eleven days previously, Gavin had scarpered.

He sat up against a tree trunk in a small field. It was the sort of place you could drop without drawing too much attention to yourself. The field barely justified such naming as it was awash with discarded cardboard, paper, glass, and life's single-use detritus. But it offered a location for contemplation and time out. And it was time that was hanging over Gavin and he did not know what to do with it. The scratches that he had incurred during his escape were now starting to hurt. The pain had initially combined with the adrenalin of escape and given him concentration and focus to jump fences, cross gardens, and finally get out onto the road where he could move quicker. But he felt more conspicuous. Now, under the protection of a rogue tree, the pain added to the misery of the situation he was in.

He had left through the backdoor. He had locked the backdoor. His only possession was the backdoor key. That wasn't going to get him far. He didn't fully understand from what he was running. But the threat was clear. The threat was real. He did not feel safe.

He knew he would have to go back. He needed to pack some things. He wanted to check the state of the house. He feared what the state of the house might be if they had got in. What he would do if the house no longer had a front door, he did not know. There were potentials here that he did not want to contemplate. He wanted some assurance that the house was alright. He did not want to stay in the house. He wanted to gather some things and then... well that was another problem. He did not know what he was going to do. He could not live under a tree.

An order of events formed. Go back and check the house. Pack some things. Go somewhere else. Disappear. Never be seen again. It wasn't a great order of events. And it involved going back through those gardens which, now he was planning it, made him feel like a trespasser. Leaving that way was just an uncomplicated action with no time to consider the right or wrong of it. Going back that way, intruding on people's private property, now seemed awkward. But he dared not go down the street and through the front door. Come to think of it, he did not have the front door key. Unless there was no front door. But he could not take that risk in case Big Ron would be waiting for him. It had to be the back door and the gardens route that led there. He did reconsider if the return home was needed at all. Could he find another way of getting a report on the state of the house? Could he live in the clothes he was wearing? Could he borrow money? The answers to these questions were not positive. He would have to go back and reacquaint himself with the rose bushes. He did think about the way back in, but he had left by the quickest and safest route, and so he would need to return that way too. He was dreading the next few hours.

He took a circuitous route back to the house where his earlier escape had eventually reached the pavement. He looked down the side of the house and past the garage. He was lingering, so he moved on. He did not want to attract suspicion. He could not believe how hard it felt contemplating a route back home through the neighbours' lands. He stood out. He might as well have been wearing a fluorescent red cape and a hat with a whacking great arrow pointing down on it. He was not a natural intruder. He paced up and down a side street.

168

He was looking guilty now. He walked on to gather his thoughts, but these were the very same thoughts that were making him think too much about what he was wanting to do. He revisited the extent to which he needed to get back to the house and matched it against six months for trespassing, burglary or whatever the charge might be. He was certainly failing any audition to join the criminal fraternity. He stopped right next to a post box. He was tempted to pretend to post a letter. He needed to look like he was meant to be where he was. He wasn't sure that posting imaginary letters would help. He decided that he needed to get on with it. When it came down to it, the choice was between Big Ron or the Neighbourhood Watch. He chose the Neighbourhood Watch. They twitched behind curtains. They wrote letters. They had secret meetings. They liked to know other people's business. But they didn't break down doors and put you in hospital. Not in his neighbourhood anyway.

He walked back to the house with the garage at the side. It was the obvious way in. He walked past. He cursed himself. He got to the corner of the street and went round it, out of view. There he stopped again. There he chastised himself for being such a spineless fool. 'Neighbourhood Watch,' he said out loud. 'Here I come.' And he charged.

Over a wall, around the back of the garage, sideways over another wall, and then facing him was the big fence and the last hurdle before he was back in his garden. He looked at the fence and wondered how he ever got over it. He wondered how he was going to get over it this time. He noted the rose bushes. He ducked down to hide and surveyed the garden. Near enough was a garden table and two chairs, looking worn but stylish with blue and white tiles: a hopeful touch of Greek culture in a colder climate. There was no sign of activity around the house. He moved the table against the fence. It would do. He climbed onto the table, avoiding the roses, and he pushed himself up and over the fence, abseiling down and falling into a heap on the other side, next to an overturned garden chair.

He was relieved to have arrived back in his garden, at the back of the house. Then he remembered why he would not be staying. He reached into the back pocket of his jeans. The key was not there. That's where he had put it. He checked his other pockets but without conviction because he knew the key would not be found there. It was missing. The realisation was that it must have fallen out. He had had it on the street because he had kept checking it as part of his nervous preparation. Gavin could see no answer to its whereabouts other than it had fallen out during the flit across the gardens. He looked where he had landed and around his garden, in the hope that he might uncover it nearby and without any need to revisit the sights of his just accomplished and harrowing trek. He did not find it. He moved the overturned chair into position against the fence and peered over but could not see it.

'Can I help you?' came a voice from the opposite direction to that which he had just been surveying. It startled Gavin. It was the neighbour whose garden table he had moved. She did not seem to have realised what he had been up to.

'Looking for a key,' replied Gavin, too quickly and not sure how he would explain its loss.

The neighbour looked at the table. Gavin looked at her looking at the table. She then looked at him. She shuck her head. 'I can't believe how many times George has moved this table. And why he'd put it here is beyond belief. He's not even moved the chairs.'

Gavin made strange noises with his mouth as if to sympathise with her.

'He's never satisfied,' she carried on, feeling empowered by Gavin's muttering. 'I always preferred it over there,' and she pointed. 'What key?'

'Ah, yes,' replied Gavin. He was about to resort to more sound effects and competing with George for fool of the year in this neighbour's eyes when words took over. 'I threw it in the air. Don't ask me why. Caught it a few times. Just passing time. Then I went for a high throw and it's gone over there somewhere.' He pointed to the two gardens he had just come tumbling through, which included hers. 'I feel such a fool.' And he did.

'Let me have a look,' replied the neighbour.

'Shall I-' but she stopped him mid-sentence.

'You stay where you are,' she replied.

Much to Gavin's relief the key was found. 'Here you are,' she said, passing it over. 'Make sure you don't go throwing it in the air again.' She smiled at him.

'Thank you,' he said, as she turned to go back to the house.

Gavin unlocked the backdoor. He did so quietly although the conversations with the neighbour would have been the sort of alert he had wanted to avoid. He assumed that Big Ron was not around. Then he considered that he could be inside the house rather than outside it. The front door would clarify that. Carefully he entered his home and soon felt the relief of seeing a front door still in its rightful place. The rest of the house showed no sign of unwelcome guests. Memories came back of only a short while ago when he had fled. The reality of that experience spurred him to be organised. A visit to the toilet came first. That had been long overdue. Then he found his rucksack. It was the one he had never used. He'd bought it with all sorts of ideas about travelling the world and it had ended up in a cupboard under the stairs. It wasn't a particularly large rucksack, so he had probably not intended to go far.

He did not know what to pack. What should you pack when going on the run from some maniac who was out to do you some serious harm? And should you be seasonal? He had to be practical. This was not the occasion for his Rolling Stones sweatshirt. It needed to be jeans, shirts, one ordinary sweatshirt, pants and socks and something for running. From amongst these items, he picked fresh clothes to change into. The rest went into the rucksack.

He picked up his wallet. He took the car keys. He did not intend risking trying to make it to the car. The keys though had the front door key and work keys, and they carried the sort of responsibility that required him to keep them safe. The keys also gave him options. Although those options did rule out sleeping at work, well for now anyway. He grabbed a handful of dry roasted peanuts and went out the back, locking the door behind him, and stopping to put the key onto his keyring and into his bag.

And then, before he had had the chance to plan his exit across the gardens, he heard footsteps coming down the passageway and getting louder as they got nearer. He panicked. He threw his bag behind the dilapidated wooden building that was far from obviously a garden shed. He followed the bag and squeezed into the furthest point. There were voices.

'You sure he's not in?'

'I've heard nothing.'

'I told you to wait. Not to come and get me.'

'You said to let you know.'

'I said to wait. You need to listen.'

'Sorry Ron.'

'You will be.'

The voices filled the back garden. Someone tried the backdoor. The upright chair against the fence was spotted.

'He's gone,' said the grating voice that Gavin now recognised as Big Ron. It was not as threatening or loud as the last time he had heard it, but it was etched into his brain. He kept still. He could feel his heart beating. 'He won't get far. He'll be back.' Gavin cursed an imagination that was sending his brain all sorts of images of body parts swapping places and limbs being used as baseball bats. 'He's gonna pay for upsetting my mother like that.'

The other man coughed.

'Check behind that shed and make sure he ain't still here.'

Gavin could feel his whole life slipping away as he tried to do his best impression of some strange bush that you just might find growing around the back of an abandoned shed. He didn't move. He tried to look shrublike. He hoped and prayed that he looked as green as he was feeling.

His eyes met the eyes of Jacob. Jacob smiled at him. There was not enough light in the narrow space for Gavin to tell what kind of smile it was. Jacob turned away.

'Nothing,' said Jacob. Gavin made a note to thank Jacob at whatever point in the future he would have a chance to do so and whatever that future might be. He held back his relief and remained quiet and motionless.

'He's dead. She ain't well and he upset her. No one does that.' The proclamation was followed by footsteps that faded back down the passageway.

Gavin was too fearful to make a move. He was considering how long would be safe for him to wait. Would Big Ron hang about? This seemed unlikely if he thought Gavin had gone. Would Jacob hang about? Did that matter? He listened out. There was no noise. He pictured the two of them talking on the street, waiting, and then walking off. He tried to figure out if that was what would be happening. He tried to calculate a length of time that seemed sensible for him to wait. This dead time had him wondering if it would be safer to move back into the house. They had not tried to break in. He could live at home like a quiet hermit. He would not answer the door to anyone. He would ration what food he had. He could read books. Books didn't make any noise. He would turn the pages quietly. He would need natural light though. He would have to live upstairs where no one could look in on him through the windows. He wouldn't put on any lights. He was going mad. This was pointless. He needed to move.

He gathered the rucksack. He climbed over the fence, with the help of the chair on one side and the table on the other side. He threw the rucksack to the ground and jumped down. She caught him jumping off the table. She came over. She seemed to have appeared from nowhere.

'Sorry,' said Gavin and thinking quickly added: 'Thought you'd like me to move the table back to the chairs for you.' He smiled at her. 'Save George having to do it.'

She looked at him. She was puzzled but also appreciative. 'That's very kind of you,' she said. 'You could have come round the front.' She noted his rucksack. 'Especially with that to carry.'

'No problem,' said Gavin. He was about to move off and then realised he needed to act on his story. He put down the rucksack and took the table back to where the two chairs were. He put it down.

'Actually, I would prefer it over there if you don't mind.'

How could he mind?

Back on the street, Gavin headed for Nap's house. He abandoned any desire to further use people's gardens, but he did feel the need to avoid the main routes and stick to pathways where possible. He wasn't sure if Big Ron would recognise him but that was something he was not prepared to put to the test. He was sure he would recognise Big Ron and then Big Ron would be able to assume that this quivering wreck was his prey, and it would be ambulance time.

'You look bad,' said Nap on opening the door to Gavin. 'Never seen you look so edgy.'

'So would you, if the local mafia were after you,' replied Gavin.

'The local mafia? What are you on about?'

'Come on. Let me in and I'll tell you.' Gavin was quick to get indoors and to make sure that Nap did not delay in closing the door properly.

Gavin gave Nap a vivid explanation of what had happened. If in doubt, he left it in.

'You're in a mess then,' was Nap's response.

'Thanks,' replied Gavin.

'My pleasure.'

'You'd have a funeral to go to.'

'Nah. I'd watch it on YouTube or something.'

'Probably be on the news.'

'There you are then.'

'What should I do then?'

'Are you wanting to stay here?' Nap had noted the rucksack.

'Not sure that works. I think I need to be a bit further away.'

'Phew!' Nap laughed. 'I thought we might be about to become a couple.'

'Careful now.'

'And you did say he could strangle two men in two rooms at the same time.' Nap spread his arms out. 'And I've got two rooms!'

'Too risky then.'

'Too risky.'

They were sat down by now, but Gavin was trying to manage an overactive right leg.

'Can I get you anything for that?' asked Nap, directing a look at the offending leg as it tapped away at about two hundred beats to the minute. 'A whisky?'

'Better not. Not sure what I'm going to do yet.'

'You've not got the car?'

'Correct. Daren't risk the front of the house.'

'Thought you parked down the street a bit?'

'I do, but that's too near.'

'Borrow mine if it helps.'

'Does it work?'

'Of course it does.'

'But you don't use it do you?'

'You never know. Rev it up twice a week. Never failed yet. Sit in it and listen to The Smiths.'

'I bet the neighbours think you're gassing yourself.'

'One of them did once knock on the window. I smiled back at them. They've not done it again.'

'Is it insured?'

'Of course. MOT about six months ago. Should be fine.'

'You driven it lately?' It was a reluctant question. Gavin thought it unlikely that Nap had driven it anywhere. Nap had become such a hermit that it was hard to understand why he had a car at all.

'Would do me a favour taking it out. Not been anywhere since Mick took it for its MOT.'

'You sure?'

'Of course.' Nap smiled at Gavin and added, 'Are you sure you're not taking this threat too seriously?'

'Can't take it too seriously. I don't want to end up looking like my front door. You might have to identify the corpse.'

'And the front door!'

'Funny.'

'Well, it would probably do it good to have a proper run around.'

'I'll put some petrol in.'

'Probably needs it.'

Keys were handed over. They nearly hugged, but Gavin escaped before either of them showed the sort of emotions that they would have regretted for the next hour, and which would have needed some back tracking the next time they met up. Gavin sat in the car and wondered. He also felt some warmth for Nap which was fine because he was contained within the car and Nap was contained within his house. There were at least two doors between them. It made Gavin smile. Then he wondered what to do.

Chapter 20

Gavin drove Nap's car down the quiet lane and parked up next to a space where a hedge and a sand dune were competing for the same piece of land: a battle repeated across the area. Fifty miles to get here again. A nice feeling this time of familiarity. He knew what was waiting for him. Sea, sand, and a fair number of pebbles too. A good place to think. Different thoughts this time. But a good place.

This time he did not have the flipchart with him. That was still in his living room. Perhaps Big Ron could beat ten shades of whatever out of the flipchart and its accomplice the tripod. Do them both a favour. He'd have no sympathy for a well-beaten tripod and shredded flipchart paper. And if it made Big Ron feel better then so be it. Gavin was almost regretting not having left a message on the flipchart paper inviting Big Ron to do this. He could even have drawn a picture of himself or pasted a large photo if that had helped. The mangled frame and littered paper could lay testimony to whatever childhood trauma or catastrophe had made Big Ron the mild-mannered citizen he now was.

Gavin sat on the beach and realised that he was missing the flipchart and feeling guilty for his destructive thoughts. This brought home to him the state of things and the realisation that life was certainly having fun at his expense. This was where he had written the word RUN. Instead of running, he was now on the run. The irony of this was unwelcome. That he had chosen to return to this place was not something he felt sure about. The journey had given him something to do and the destination a focus, but now that he had arrived, he was not sure what was supposed to happen next. It felt safe, but he could hardly make this beach and the nearby tree his home, with a shifting sand dune for his pillow. He reflected on what had happened since his first visit. He had just started to mull over what Ruth would say or tell him to do when he was interrupted by a familiar voice.

'You back then, are you?'

Gavin looked up. 'I guess so,' he replied. He couldn't help considering if the lad lived on the beach. He certainly seemed to have developed an interest in lurking and waiting to pounce on unsuspecting visitors. Gavin had to wonder if other sad figures like himself made it all worth the lad's while. Was this the place of lost souls?

'My dad told me off for talking to you last time. Said you could have been a paedophile.'

'Not again,' replied Gavin.

'You mean you are?' The lad sounded intrigued rather than concerned.

'Of course not. I told you last time, I'm a famous murderer.'

'Better than being a doctor.'

'A paedophile or a murderer?'

'Both.'

'A murdering pervert.'

'You don't look like any of them.'

'That's good.'

'You just look weird.'

'Safer that way.'

'Better not let me dad see us though. Looks suspicious a second time.'

Gavin contemplated what sort of father a lad like this would have. Knowing his luck, it would turn out to be some relation of Big Ron. Seaside Sam with hands like mallets. 'I guess your father would not approve of you talking to a famous murderer.'

'It's not so much that. He just don't like me talking to anyone he don't know.'

'Sensible.'

'He don't like me talking to people he knows either.'

'Oh.'

'He don't like a lot of the people he knows.'

'Sounds like he doesn't like you talking to anyone.'

'He don't.' The lad looked thoughtful. 'He don't like anyone.'

They both became preoccupied. The conversation had taken them to places of introspection. The lad did not want to stay there long. 'Why you here then?' he asked. 'Where's your paper with tomato on it?'

Gavin decided it was not the time to debate the quality of his flipchart writing. 'God knows,' was his dismissive reply.

'Not sure I believe in God,' said the lad.

'Not sure I do either,' said Gavin.

'Yes, but you're an adult.'

'What difference does that make?'

'My dad reckons you shouldn't be allowed to decide if you believe in God until you are an adult.'

'Makes some sense.'

'He says, if you can't drive until you are seventeen, can't drink until you are eighteen, can't have sex until you are sixteen, and can't vote until you are eighteen, then you shouldn't be allowed to go to church until you are one of them ages. He reckons sixteen because you can marry then and would have to go to church to get married.'

'Your dad sounds as if he's clever.'

'Not really. Last week he got a rope burn hanging out the washing.'

'How'd he do that?'

'Don't know, but he was swearing a lot. He's not been the same since me mother left.'

'Sorry to hear that.'

'Yes.' There was a sad look on the lad's face. 'They call me Tank Top. Only you didn't ask last time.'

'Sorry. You're not wearing one though.'

'Not got one.'

'So how come they call you Tank Top?'

'Don't know.'

'Oh.'

'Wait here.' Tank Top got up and wandered off.

Gavin had nothing else to do so he waited. He didn't have to wait. He owed the lad nothing. He had made no promises or commitments. He just had nothing better to do. He stared out across the sea. The horizon was hazy. It was a dull day. He could not make anything out. The horizon leant itself to the imagination. What was out there was at the behest of the inspiration of the onlooker. Consequently, Gavin saw vague shapes and different hues of grey. He could make nothing of them. There was not about to be a great disembarking or monster invasion. There were no Vikings or ancient seafarers. Pirates weren't ahoy. Brigands were not smuggling. There was no tsunami about to wash them all away. It was just a bland greyness that he could see. The lack of clarity was fitting.

'This is Twiggy,' were the words that interrupted his imaginings. Gavin looked up to see that Tank Top had returned with two other children, both younger. 'And this is Taylor,' he added, turning to the girl, which confirmed that it was the boy who was called Twiggy.

Gavin found this confusing but resigned himself to modern names in modern times. That's what happens when you get older, he considered. Names no longer match the same faces.

'My dad calls him The Twigster, but we all call him Twiggy.'

180

This time Gavin acknowledged Twiggy with a careful smile.

'And my dad calls her Stitch,' said the lad, and then stopped as if he might be expecting a question about this.

Gavin didn't ask. He got the connection.

'So, everyone calls her Stitch. She says she's nine, but we all know she's only seven.'

'Twiggy and Stitch.' Gavin finally said. They sort of smiled back. 'You sound like a children's television programme.' It went over their heads. They were still quite small.

'I told them about you, but they didn't believe me.'

'Where's the flipchart?' asked Twiggy.

'He's not brought it this time,' said Tank Top.

'Is it true that you brought a flipchart to the beach?' asked Twiggy.

Gavin was unsure how to respond. They had arrived over thirty years too late for him to befriend them. 'Shouldn't you be in school?' he asked.

'It's a training day,' said Tank Top.

'I thought it was an insect day,' said Stitch.

'Don't you mean inset day?' corrected Twiggy.

'No,' replied Stitch tersely. 'We got an insect day.'

'We're at the same school,' said Tank Top.

'Well, I was told it was an insect day.' Stitch turned away.

'What you doing here?' asked Twiggy.

'He says he's a famous murderer,' said Tank Top.

'Who you killed?' asked Twiggy, more excited than frightened.

Gavin thought he ought to avoid the conversation going in the wrong direction. 'I haven't killed anyone.'

They seemed disappointed.

'Why you bring a flipchart?' asked Twiggy.

'As you can see, I haven't.'

'But he said you did.' And Twiggy turned to Tank Top.

'Last time,' Tank Top said.

'What you write on it?'

'I told you,' interrupted Tank Top. 'He wrote tomato on it in big red letters.'

'A bit like tomatoes,' said Twiggy.

'What?' replied Tank Top.

'Big and red. Like tomatoes.' Twiggy gave Tank Top a look and then added. 'Why d'you write tomato?'

'It was an insect day,' said Stitch, turning around to add emphasis to her certainty.

Gavin decided it was time to show some adult sense of taking charge. 'Won't your parents be wondering where you are?'

'That's what adults say when they've had enough of you. Did you know that?' said Tank Top.

Gavin knew. Tank Top knew. Twiggy and Stitch now knew. 'Do you all go to the same school?' asked Gavin, attempting to halt any sense that he was trying to send them on their way.

'Yes, but we're in different classes,' said Tank Top. 'We live on the same street.'

'His dad lets us come round,' said Twiggy. 'My parents never know where I am anyway.'

'What about you?' Gavin asked Stitch.

Stitch looked at him. She gave a half-smile. Gavin wasn't sure if it was a lack of confidence or a lack of trust, or probably just good common sense since he was a confessed famous murderer.

'I don't like tomatoes,' said Stitch.

'He's not got any tomatoes,' said Twiggy. 'You've not brought any tomatoes, have you?' Twiggy briefly looked at Gavin, but before there was any need to reply he continued. 'He just likes writing tomato on paper.'

'Anyway, even if he had brought some tomatoes, he's not going to force feed them to you, is he?' said Tank Top.

'I want to go home,' said Stitch.

'That's how he murders people. Death by tomato.' Twiggy laughed at his own joke. Tank Top joined in.

'It's not funny,' said Stitch. 'I don't like tomatoes.'

'We know,' said Twiggy, showing the first signs of impatience.

'So, what do your parents do?' asked Gavin trying to distract them.

'What you mean?' replied Twiggy.

'What do they do?'

'They don't do anything.'

'He means jobs. Work. What work do they do?' said Tank Top.

'Oh,' responded Twiggy, confused by the matter.

'No one works round here,' explained Tank Top. 'Our parents don't do anything. The only people who work round here are teachers.'

'And they get loads of days off,' added Twiggy.

'And they finish early,' said Tank Top.

'Reckon I could be a teacher,' said Twiggy.

Gavin wasn't sure about Twiggy's motivation, but then he was at the age where most children were only considering a handful of ways of earning a living and that list included footballer, astronaut and train driver. It was something, if his parents weren't working, that at least he had not completely given up himself.

'Stitch's mum used to work but then she got the sack,' said Tank Top.

'Oh dear,' replied Gavin. He didn't feel he needed to know any more.

'She got caught taking stuff,' continued Tank Top.

Gavin faked a slight look of interest.

'Her boss caught her,' continued Tank Top.

'We used to get free chocolate,' added Stitch.

'Of course you did,' said Tank Top.

'We don't now.' Stitch turned away.

'That's because your mum can't nick it anymore,' said Twiggy.

'She never nicked nothin',' said Stitch.

'She was always nicking stuff,' said Twiggy. 'She probably nicked what you wearing now.'

'No, she never.'

Gavin was mindful of how it looked with him engaging on the beach with these young children. Recent events gave him caution too. He was aware that Tank Top's dad could come along at any time, and he'd already had more than his fair share of people jumping to wrong conclusions. The situation could only get worse if there was a fall out that he might have to referee. Taking charge of other people's children was never a good thing. And succeeding in the audition for the roll of interfering suspicious male was the last thing he needed right now. There was no Oscar to be won for that part. Gavin decided that it was time for him to leave.

'Thanks, kids,' was the best farewell he could conjure up.

'She knows what she's like,' said Tank Top.

Gavin looked puzzled.

'She knows what her mother's like,' Tank Top added.

'Oh,' replied Gavin. He moved away from them at a slow sympathetic pace.

Their entertainment over, Tank Top, Twiggy and Stitch set off back along the beach.

'Let us know if you come back with your flipchart,' shouted Twiggy.

Gavin returned to the car. It was a reminder that he had borrowed Nap's car. Seeing it there, parked up against the hedge, made him feel disconsolate. It was a scene that might begin a low-budget film about some lone figure driving between towns trying to find somewhere to belong and some way of connecting with life, but for whom it never quite works out. Except this wasn't a movie, it was the very state of Gavin's life. No Oscars for this role, just Twat of the Year for the fifth year running.

The Twat of the Year realised that all the day now left for him was one last possibility. It was not what he wanted. It was all that was left to him. He had no wish to seek out Sharyn. She was mad at him. She had no room for him. She had two daughters that would just see his turning up as confirming whatever opinion they had already reached about him. He couldn't match their expectations. He didn't know what they might anticipate, but he was sure he would fall short. And if Big Ron found him there, it didn't bare thinking about. A piece of Sharyn's mind versus Big Ron's bunches of fives was not something Gavin wanted to witness. The only choice loomed before him like death's pageant. He anticipated what was to come with all the joy of seeing a herd of elephants stampeding toward you and someone's tied your shoelaces together.

Chapter 21

This was the final resort. He hadn't seen her for several months. He'd probably missed her birthday. It wasn't too far to drive. It had never been too far to drive, not in miles anyway. It was a little further from where he was now. He didn't mind that. The longer it took, the better. Or would it be better to get there and just get it over with? Or should he just not go? Or should he book a hotel nearby just in case? There was no just in case. He couldn't afford a hotel, not for the rest of his life. Not even for a few days, which might be all he had left if Big Ron was to catch up with him.

It was a slow tortuous journey. He made it slow. He was taking as much time as he could. She made it tortuous. Just the thought of arriving was playing havoc with his digestive system. By the time he got there, he would have nothing left of his stomach. He didn't put any music on. He hadn't even checked to see if Nap had left any CDs in the car. There was nothing he could listen to that would not either worsen the mood or make him feel like he was being mocked. Sad music to finish him off. Happy music to laugh at him. They both liked The Smiths so there was one of their CDs somewhere. He might as well have played the funeral march and be done with it. He tried the radio. Through the crackling, he could make out that something by Earth Wind and Fire was playing. Even with some of the elements on his side, he was still four horsemen of the Apocalypse and the entire cast of Braveheart short of entering his mother's house with sufficient support. He switched the radio off.

He had driven part of the way back along the route he had taken to the beach. Then he had cut across unfamiliar lanes. Now he had joined the usual roads to the land of God knows what he was doing. It was one of those journeys that supplied an ever-growing list of familiar landmarks, each one a reminder that, although he was getting closer, he could still turn around and go back. The Overlit Chinese Restaurant of Foreboding. The Are You Sure Traffic Lights that always take ages to change. The Hillside and Quaint Cottage of Doom. The Last Chance Farm with Broken Gate. The You Can Still Turn Around Now Roadside Parking with Mobile Burger Van. The hidden Left Turn Down the Road to Wanton Self-Destruction, that he didn't have to take. And finally, The Now You've Done It Pick Your Own Strawberries Field. By this time, he always felt like the bastard son of Dame Misery and Lord Mockery.

The house was set alone. And if that didn't tell you something.

It was a farmhouse, or once was a farmhouse. A three-bedroom property on two levels and in much need of renovation or repair. It had outbuildings, although Gavin did not know what was in them, or what purpose they served. He could not be sure if his mother even owned them or had access to them. The house was surrounded by fields, though Gavin had never worked out who owned what. Nor had he stayed around long enough to meet any wandering neighbours to find out, except for the occasional stray animal. He suspected that his mother did not own any of the land, otherwise there would have been placards set up asking you to save some aspect of the world that you had never come across before: bees in Rwanda or a coffee plantation in Peru.

He knew she would be in. For someone who wanted to save the world, she spent a lot of time at home. He knocked on the door. He looked around at the untended yard and a garden area that showed promise. Some grass was recently cut. Flowers fighting weeds. He did this at every visit. It helped him to be prepared. The door opened.

'Oh,' she said.

'It's me,' said Gavin.

'Yes. I can see that.' They stood there for a few seconds. 'Do you want to come in?'

Gavin replied with a look of misgiving.

'Of course. Yes. Come in.'

For a woman in her sixties, there remained a healthy spriteliness about her. Gavin had a habit of noting this every time he saw her. Whilst he had seen his mother age, she did not change in figure or the clothes she was wearing. They went through to a room that Gavin always considered to be the lounge. It was hard to tell the rooms apart as they all served similar purposes. There were three rooms downstairs. One was a kitchen. The other two rooms both had settees, a separate armchair and in one, a bookcase, and in the other, a small table with a computer on it. They were in the room with the bookcase. The kitchen also had two easy chairs and a large tea chest full of wood. It was therefore only distinguishable from the other two rooms due to the additional kitchen paraphernalia, although some of that did seem to seep into those rooms.

Gavin's mother had disappeared to make them a cup of tea. Gavin hadn't been asked what he wanted. This was done out of habit. Time for them both to adjust to the situation. Fortunately, Gavin was ready for a drink. He was thirsty and in need of a prop. He could easily pace the room. Instead, he would have a cup to pass from hand to hand and to grasp and hold. Every moment of bringing the drink to his mouth would be a response to his uneasiness.

'Here you are,' she said, passing him a mug. 'Sorry. I'm out of tea. I forgot. Will coffee do?'

'Yes. That's fine,' he replied.

For a while, they both supped their coffees. Gavin glanced at the room. His mother was comfortable in the art of doing nothing. The bookcase was overflowing. Gavin was sitting in the armchair. His mother sat at the far end of the settee.

'So, what's brought you here?' she asked.

It was a question that Gavin could have answered in a hundred and one different ways. It was a question that had more layers than a skip full of super onions.

'Come to see you.' Given skirted across the surface.

'That's good.' A statement that neither of them thought had any truth in it. Gavin had felt let down by his mother since childhood, and she had felt let down by Gavin since he had been an adult. Gavin had sensed a shift in the blame as his mother had got older. That she could put any of the faults for their poor and intermittent relationship on to him had just fuelled those already wind-caught flames.

'How are you?' asked Gavin.

'You know. Fine.'

'Good.' There was a pause. 'Good,' repeated Gavin.

'You been doing anything?' asked his mother.

Of course he had. People were always doing something. Gavin had things that he was doing. But what were the things he was doing that he was going to share with his mother, and what were the things that he was going to keep to himself? And did it matter anyway? It wasn't a question that cared about the answer. 'Work. Keeps me busy.'

'That's good to hear.'

It was slow and tortuous, but then it always was.

'And what have you been doing?' Gavin knew the answer to this question was that his mother seemed to do less and less. As a child, he remembered a house full of people and activities, the purpose and results of which he had never understood. But he had not appreciated what was happening. He had been a child and excluded from any explanation. Over the years he had seen a lessening of people attending around his mother and in any fighting for causes. There had been the time Sheila was around. He might ask her about that. He was more aware of her relationship with Martin as he had seen that through adult eyes, albeit from some distance.

'Not as much as I'd like to be.'

'I guess not.'

The questions and answers were mundane. Each word was carefully crafted and positioned to block the wrong leitmotif escaping. But they both knew that there was no banality to be found in the thoughts in their heads. Behind each other's eyes, they could see the danger. The setting, the presence of his mother, and recent events, it was all treading the boards that formed the stage in Gavin's head. And this play was no comedy. Serious actors only. Although the potential for it to all end up in a heap on the floor was never going to be far away.

And so it was that Gavin felt the need to settle in. 'Haven't you got anything stronger?' he asked, gesticulating with his empty mug. It was a request for alcohol. It was also a statement of intent. It was his way of notifying his mother that he intended to stay over, without actually having to ask the question which came with all its historic awkwardness, and without the need to await whatever form the answer might have taken.

'You're not driving?' It was the devil's own response, teasing him and wrapping him up like blindman's-buff. Then setting him off in a direction that reorganised his senses.

Gavin looked at her. 'Yes, but I thought I might stay over.' The words were out. Let her do with them what she willed. If he had stayed over before then it must have been a long time ago and wiped from his memory.

They looked at each other. It was brief and was followed by a looking down and a looking away that hid nothing. There had been enough for both to see in each other the fear and wonder at what the forthcoming hours were likely to bring.

190

'Over there,' and she pointed to a box near the bookcase. She held back on comment and put up no fight over his staying the night. Nor did she smother him with indifference. He felt the sense of occasion rising around them like a mist from the floor. It was both exhilarating and intimidating. This was a new world opening up before them. Gavin found a bottle of brandy. He directed it at her. She nodded. He filled both their mugs and emptied the bottle. If they were going to get through the rest of the evening, they would need it. He'd noted a bottle of something else just in case, but that might put them on the wrong side of a precipice and they were already into uncharted territory. A desert lay before them that neither of them was prepared for, and they were drinking cheap brandy.

Now the silences were replaced with elongated moments of sipping between easy questions and generic answers. References to the weather were followed by some vague nod to the wallpaper. The benefits of eating all your vegetables got a look in. The size of elephants' ears popped up. There was a reference to politics and the lack of charismatic leadership, the content of which suggested similarities between them and which itself then became slightly unsettling. Any discomposure was abated by a discussion on the unsightliness of wellingtons, followed by a hundred and one uses for cardboard. And then the brandy took hold and tongues were loosened.

'Why did you and my father split up?' Gavin had wanted to call him dad but that implied a level of intimacy he could not concede.

'That's none of your business.'

'Of course it's my business.'

'That's between me and your dad. That's about our relationship. It's not about you.'

'Of course it's about me. I'm your son.'

'You were a child. We were adults.'

'I was your child.'

'Leave it, Gavin.'

'No!' But the conversation came to a halt. Gavin dwelt on his mother referring to his father as his *dad*. He preferred the more formal title of *father*. This reflected the distance between them as two people who had not seen each other for decades. He didn't have a *dad*, but somewhere out there was someone he could refer to as his *father*. They had a biological relationship and nothing more. 'You were an adult. You experienced it. I was a child. I only know through snippets. What I remember is meaningless. What I need to know isn't.'

'What you need to know is that your dad and I were together and then we weren't. End of.'

'No. It's not the end of. It's the beginning of.' Which Gavin knew didn't quite work but it kept the ball in the air. And this ball was all about his father.

'Look.' She drew breath. 'We were young. We had you. It didn't work out. Us that is. Not you.'

Gavin wanted to challenge his mother's comments that implied that he didn't qualify for the didn't-work-out support group, but he could see that she had more to say.

'You're a social worker, Gavin. Don't even pretend that you don't understand the complexities of relationships. Your dad and I were different. We were different people. We were always different people. We were just too young to realise it. And when we did realise it, we separated. Not straight away, of course. You don't separate when you should. You keep going for too long. Far too long. It isn't hope. It isn't any belief you can get it back together. You just put off that day when one of you finally calls time. And then, through all the misery, you look back and wonder how it took so long to end it all. Then you think about all the time you wasted. And yes, you were in the middle of all that.' She stopped and looked at Gavin.

Gavin was unsure what to say or what to do. It wasn't the content that halted him. It was that he had never heard his mother talk like this.

She could see Gavin's perplexity. She was his mother. In many ways it didn't feel that way, but she was. She was his mother. She had given birth to him. Whatever he thought, she had suffered for him. And that gave her the standing to carry on. 'I'm not sure how your father and I came to be together. I don't mean the events that led up to it. I mean as a choice. I can't remember when we chose to be together. It just seemed to happen. And that's not a good sign. That's not how a relationship should start. But what did we know? Suddenly…' She stopped and thought about it. 'No, it wasn't sudden. Just, there came a time when we were together. And was it great? Was it a wonderful thing? No. It was never any great deal. Did I love him? You want to know. Did he love me?' She looked at Gavin. He remained the lost soul that thought he had sat down at the theatre to see a light comedy and had been hit by some tragic drama unfolding before him. He was clutching his mug as his only source of reassurance.

'I don't think we did,' she continued. 'I'm not sure we even liked each other. We just came together and there was nothing else in our lives to make us do anything about it. It lasted. There were some good times. I suppose we kept going. There was nothing else. We got used to it. It became every day for us. And for a time, we were a family.'

Gavin doubted this. 'But I can only remember it being busy. The house was a busy place. Not a family place.'

'We were a family. But you're right. Other things took over. Your dad and I didn't have enough with each other. We found other things. That was what made it all seem busy. There was probably a lot happening around you.'

'And I lost out.' It was a statement with only a hint of a hidden question.

'You're probably right. To be fair your father did spend time with you.' She stopped. There were memories. There were feelings. These she was not going to share. She was a mother, but an adult too, and entitled to the same right to some privacy as anyone else. 'We were a family, a bit different to most others. And yes, your dad left. Then we were a single-parent family. And different to most single-parent families. Probably nothing different today though.'

Gavin's mug was empty. He went over to explore the other bottle. He needed to move. His body needed to shake the rigidity that had become his defence against the unexpectedness of what was happening. And he couldn't walk properly. It wasn't the alcohol, not in the main. The immensity of the situation made him feel as clumsy as a giant striding across worried farmland and overcautious about every step he took. He got so far.

'Here. Have mine.' She offered to pour her brandy into Gavin's mug. He let her. So, it hadn't been the alcohol talking. His mother was either reacting to Gavin or just choosing to speak in a way he had never heard before. It was unsettling. It might have made him cautious. It might have made him considerate of where this might be heading. But then he had been drinking what was more than his share of the brandy.

'I need to know who my father is,' he said, when he sat back down again.

'You know who he is.'

'I mean, know him. As a person.'

'No, you don't.'

'Yes, I do. Who was he? What was he like? I only have vague memories.'

'He was fine.'

'Great.'

'We were all fine. We were all just normal parents. Nothing exceptional. Nothing inappropriate. Just fine, fine, fine, fine, fine.'

'Not a great advert for parenting though, is it?

'It could be a lot worse. You should know that.'

'And you still haven't told me anything about my father.'

'No.'

'I don't even know who you are.'

She took a deep breath. 'I'm your sixty-six-year-old mother and I live here all alone. Surrounded by people I don't know. And the people I do know don't come any more. Including you.' It was as if she had risen from the settee with an accompanying tempest, overcome him like some winged beast, devoured him, spat him out, and returned to her cave for a satisfactory breather.

There was silence. Loads of it. The sort of dinging silence that attacks all your senses at once. The sort of silence that wants to dance on your grave but for now will make do with your living body. A silence you can feel. A silence you can smell. A silence you can taste. A silence that has you screaming out into a void. A silence you can hear. A silence that overshadows the room. The conductor stands with baton frozen in the air and the orchestra is held captive, awaiting intervention that feels like it is never going to happen.

Gavin's head was having a battle between staring his mother out for all she had done to let him down and lowering his head in the shame that she was sending his way in bucketloads. He was also inebriated to the point of feeling that his head was about to depart his shoulders and resolve the whole embarrassing situation by blowing up. His hands rose to cover his face. It was conformation that he was still whole as well as a non-committal avoidance tactic. It could be a pose of despair or guilt. The alcohol made his mind up for him. All filters suddenly rushed off, as if they had somewhere better to be, and abandoned him to his rage.

'What do you expect!' he shouted. He stared at her. A whole load of expletives were ready to erupt but a renegade filter had remained and held him back. His body contorted with the effusiveness of what he wasn't saying.

And the silence was once again deafening. They both sat there, held by what they had said, and trapped by what they had heard, but even more, they were captive to what they had not said.

Gavin stared into his mug at the remains of what brandy was left. He finished it off. 'I remember Sheila.'

'Forget Sheila.'

'But she was the only person who I can ever remember explaining anything to me. She talked to me when the rest of you were too busy making placards or painting ripped sheets with slogans. She took the time to engage with me.'

'That was a mistake.'

Gavin shook his head. It didn't make him feel any better. And it did make the room go out of focus. He needed to steady himself.

'You don't need to know. She was not what she seemed.'

'Well, she seemed nice to me.'

'Fine. Keep it that way. Have good memories, if it helps.'

He wanted to say that they were some of his best memories but decided to restrain himself. Sheila was the person that took him to places. Sheila played games. She took him to the cinema and bought ice-cream. And that was more than once. Meanwhile, his mother was still saving the world and had never noticed whether he was in or out. Had he been a baby at the time, he suspected that Sheila would have been the chief nappy changer. She would have fed him too. Assuming he wasn't breast fed. This he didn't know. This he felt to be something that was superseded by other more important things he wanted to know about.

'I miss Martin,' said his mother, breaking Gavin's reverie. He suspected that she had known where his mind was.

'Martin?' was the best and simplest response that Gavin could give to this unexpected statement.

'Yes. Martin. This used to be his house.'

'I know who Martin is, or was, or...' Shut up, he told himself.

'I wish you had got to know Martin.'

'I would like to have got to know my father first,' said Gavin quietly, but sufficiently to have been heard.

'I'm sure. And I would like you to have got to know Martin. I think you could have got on.'

'Maybe I could have got on with my father too.'

'Maybe.'

'Maybe.'

'Martin made me happy.'

And that was a loaded statement. Too many options to form a response in Gavin's head. He remained silent. It had been a long evening and the effect of the brandy was on the turn, switching him from animated and empowered to tired and slow.

'Anyway,' he paused. 'I'm off to bed.' And Gavin got up, although he was not too sure where his bed might be. He did not know the house that well and he was certainly not up to date with how the rooms were currently used or set up. He assumed that the second bedroom still had a bed in it, and that it would be accessible.

'Up the stairs. Take the middle room. Bathroom at the end. Not sure what the room will be like, but it will do.'

It will do ought to be the family motto, thought Gavin. He would make do with whatever the room offered. And he did.

Chapter 22

Gavin had slept in most of the clothes he had been wearing when he first arrived. Too much brandy had made bedtime an occasion for no change of wear other than basics and that which could be discarded quickly in the slow drop from upright alcoholic to supine snorer.

It had been a fitful sleep. A promising start deceived him and was the precursor to several hours of tossing, turning, and imagining, before finally falling asleep again, and then being woken prematurely by unfamiliar noises.

His imaginings were those nocturnal meanderings that came as journeymen, travelling between the lowlands of light sleep and the highlands of hazy restlessness. They brought tales of abandoned children, crying fathers fighting vague mythical beasts, and mothers marching in circles, going round and round. One tale had a baby in the middle of the circle of marchers. Another tale had babies marching around a poor desolate mother figure. And then there was a great meeting of figures through a mist, a calling of the clan. And for a while, there were brothers and sisters. It wasn't clear if they were kin or brethren. It was hard to let go. It suggested paracetamol for breakfast.

The morning noises were internal and they were coming from Gavin's mother knocking about somewhere and making more din than she needed to. Dull thudding sounds reverberated around the room and echoed in his head.

Imposters, space invaders, and a drum corps that he needed to release.

Gavin got up and wandered down to the car and took his rucksack up to the room. He changed into his running clothes and bumped into his mother in the kitchen where he had been taking a drink of water and she had walked in. Of the two of them, Gavin decidedly looked the worse for the wear of the night before. Then he remembered that his mother had not had that much to drink. He had decided that he did not want to hang around, but he knew he was still probably over the legal limit for driving and, therefore, a run would help get him to a state that felt safe enough to take control of Nap's car as well as using a bit of adrenalin to perk him up.

'Just going for a run,' he said to his mother.

'Good for you,' she replied.

They both avoided eye contact. Gavin got through the front door and as he was about to set off, he did a half turn around which served no purpose at all. He was then on his way.

He took the lane that had led him up to the house and then he made a turn down a different road. He was soon into unfamiliar territory. He was amidst what had previously only been the scenery when driving to or from his mother's house. It was a lane with the extent of greenery growing down the middle that suggested some, but little, vehicular activity. It was peaceful and scenic. It made running simple. Gavin's mind wandered between easy thoughts, taking in the surrounding countryside, and the occasional reminder that it was still requiring an effort to maintain any pace. There were thoughts about last night. There were thoughts about how his mother had seemed. There was a field and a gate and another field beyond that. There was the trudge trudge trudge of his trainers on the unkempt tarmac. There were thoughts about last night again. More trudging. Another field. There was a wooden sign. He had come to a turn-off. He had been running for a while.

He needed to consider how to return to the farmhouse. Back the way he had come. Or this public footpath that seemed to go in the right direction. He risked the footpath. Thoughts of brandy. A decided effort not to think about the brandy. The different shades of green and brown across the vista. Trudge trudge trudge. There had been something different about his mother. A cow. Trudge trudge trudge. His mother's situation. Two cows. His mother's… A herd of cows. They were ahead of him. They didn't seem to be too bothered about him. But they were cows, and he didn't know cows. He stopped running. He needed to think. He was thinking and walking backwards. It made sense to return the way he had come. He knew the way. If he continued, he couldn't be sure where he would end up. Better safe than sorry. He didn't know cows.

He returned the way he had come. He got back to the house, got a shower, and came downstairs with his rucksack. His mother was in the kitchen. There were two bowls on the table.

'Porridge?' she asked.

'Oh,' Gavin replied.

'You must eat before you go. It looks like you're leaving.'

'Yes,' he confirmed.

'Well, sit down and I'll finish off warming this porridge.'

He sat down. There was no conversation. The last time his mother would have made him breakfast he would have been a child. He waited. Silence and time did not keep good company. He kept wondering about how the porridge was progressing. It was taking a long time. Hidden behind his mother he could imagine a large spoon turning the milk and oats around the pan. Surely it was thick enough and hot enough now. The bowls were waiting. He was waiting. He should have left when he could and got breakfast on the way. He looked at his rucksack. He couldn't go. The porridge had got him. She had played the porridge card. And now it was ready, poured and brought to the table in silence.

They were sat at the table together. Each with a bowl of porridge. Each with something to distract them away from any suggestion that any topic from last night could be resurrected. Maybe the size of elephants' ears was as good as it could get, but then that could end up putting all last night's subject matter back on the table. There was only room for porridge on this table. It's hard to hold a conversation when your mouth is full of porridge. And that made the silence seem more acceptable. Gavin was committed to full porridge concentration. His mother, whilst seeming more at ease than he was, did not seem to be opposed to the silence. It struck Gavin how comfortable she seemed to have been with everything. He dared not wonder too much about how she was feeling, for fear it would have him looking across at her, trying to see into her thoughts. He kept his head down. He filled his mouth with porridge. She seemed relaxed enough to have moments where she wasn't needing to eat porridge. He still mustn't look at her, he reminded himself.

'You don't have to go,' she said.

His mouth was full of porridge. It gave him time to think. It meant a sensible answer would be expected and he just wanted to give a muttered rebuff of the offer. But you can't mutter when you have had time to think. Time means words. And what was she doing inviting him to stay longer, inviting conversation, inviting discussion about so many things that he just was not ready to talk about? And now the porridge was gone from his mouth.

'I do,' was the sum of all his time and thoughts. He needed to go. He looked down at the remaining porridge in his bowl. There was just one greedy mouthful. He shovelled it all in. He felt like a boy again, furtively misbehaving at the breakfast table, under the disapproving glare of his mother. Except she wasn't glaring, and she didn't disapprove. She stayed still.

'Okay,' she said. But it wasn't okay. None of it was okay. The whole damn situation was completely lacking in okayness.

Despite her ease. Despite her lightness. Despite her offering nothing he could object about. She was the mother who had let him down. And if there was an elephant in the room, that was it. He suspected she saw no elephant. Meanwhile, he could see its trunk and the size of its flapping ears. And it wasn't going anywhere.

He got up from the table. He moved toward his rucksack. She cut him off at the pass and hugged him. This was out of the blue, completely. This was out of character, completely. This was not what they did. It had not been close or lingering, but she had put her arms around him. He had responded by resting his hands on her shoulders. It hit the whole okay problem for six, out of the ground and into unchartered space. He needed his rucksack. He carried it in one arm. It was a shield against any further onslaught. The car keys were his spear. They led the way. He went through the door toward his car, well Nap's car.

'You look like him,' she said. He was her quarry. She had gone in for the kill. He did not turn around. He did not respond. He could pretend he had heard nothing. He walked up to the car. They both knew what she had said. They both knew he had heard her. All he could do was get in the car and go.

With his head full of too many thoughts, he crunched the gears and was off away from the farmhouse and on to the free open road. And the thoughts he took with him were many. The hug, his father, the father he looked like, his mother and how she seemed to have calmed down, and the whole bloody question of why, oh why, he had come here in the first place. Frying pan and fire came to mind. The roads were clear, but he was not free. His head was a traffic jam. Cars, lorries, buses, double-decker buses, trucks, rickshaws, and tuk-tuks. He had the lot in there, converging on his hippocampus. He kept driving, just to get further away. He knew he would have to stop, but he needed to make some distance. Not just distance between them, but a different place. Somewhere else. Somewhere unconnected to it all, like the couch of a good therapist.

Finally, he pulled over in a lay-by, the sort that is hidden behind a small green island of trees and bushes. He got out of the car. He climbed a fence and sat against the fence from the other side. This was his place of therapy. It was everything he could do not to cry.

He sat. He stared across a field but saw nothing of what he was looking at. His head dropped down. He breathed heavily, in and out, in and out. His head dropped on the out breaths and rose on the in breaths. Finally, following an in breath he let his head stay raised and he looked across the field and beyond. Hedges and trees. Hedges and trees. Such wonderful hedges and trees. Wonderful, because that was all they were. Hedges and trees. The hedges had always been there and they had always been hedges. Just good old reliable hedges. And trees. Trees just stand there, unmovable, unflappable (give or take a few thousand leaves that is), but strong and firm and just trees. Trees are trees. Hedges and trees. They were his relief.

Why had she hugged him? It came back to him. Why had she done that? Was it for her? Was it for him? Was it a positive thing? She'd never hugged him before. Certainly not adult to adult. And not that he could remember as a child either. It was not like her. It was not what she did. But she did. It wasn't false. It wasn't warm and comfortable. But it wasn't false. It was a real hug. And he was not ready for a real hug. He'd had over twenty years to prepare himself and that was nowhere near enough time. She must have known that. But she'd hugged him. Arms around him. She'd held him. She had made time stand still. The hug lasted forever. The letting go lasted forever.

Of course, he looked like his father. That should be no surprise. Father and son win lookalike competition is hardly frontpage material. Even local papers don't have to stretch that far. But there was the age factor. That did it. That was what it was all about. He was leaving this morning similar in age to when his father had left. He looked now like his father looked then. Was that what she was telling him? Was it a plea? Had she wanted him to stay? Had it been a trigger for her? And why was he now feeling all the guilt? Was she shifting the blame? Or was that just complicating things? Was that unfair? Was that unfair to both of them? It was like time travel. He had left just like his father did. Mind you, he'd only stayed one night. His father had been there... And there was a problem. He had memories of his father but nothing to tell him how his mother and father had lived together. Were they always together? Were they apart a lot? His mother seemed to have suggested that it was not a close relationship. Did he leave often? Was there just that one final leaving? Did she know it was final? Did he? Too many questions. Too few answers. But, of course, he looked like his father.

And then his thoughts returned to his mother. Just the two of them for that time. It was always going to be risky. She had seemed sad. It wasn't that he had ever remembered her as happy. She was more... busy, preoccupied, and distracted, but not exactly happy. But now there was an ordinariness about her, and she looked lost. It was true that in recent years her house had become less busy, but now she was a small figure in a large space. Gavin was not prepared to feel sad for her. There was still way too much to be angry about. But he had spent the last twenty-four hours with someone it just seemed that little bit harder to be angry about. But he was angry, and he felt he had the right to be angry, and there was a whole history of things to be angry about. But it was an anger that did not rest as easily as it might have done before.

And then, finally, he reminded himself why he had gone there in the first place and what he was now going back to. Life had lit a cigarette, taken a deep drag, and smirked at him. No.

Life had lit a whacking great Cuban cigar and was belly laughing in his face. He was on the run from everyone and everything. That was his life.

Dejected, fed up, weary, and wondering what it was all about and whether any of it was worth it, he got back into the car and headed wherever the turns seemed to want to take him. Not so much autopilot as subconscious pilot.

Chapter 23

His subconscious pilot took many turns which finally returned him to a familiar road, albeit it one he knew better from running rather than driving. He got out of the car and walked to the care home. It was risky, following on from what had happened last time. He had little to lose though. He tried hard not to be seen and tried equally hard not to walk as if he didn't want to be seen. He wasn't sure why he was visiting Ruth during this time of flight, but he felt the need to be the recipient of her very particular weird view on life. Especially when it was his life and someone had turned up the absurdity dial way past ten. He also assumed he would be safe, as long as he could avoid anyone who thought he was a pervert or a fascist.

Carefully he walked into reception. Linda was on duty. The world owed him something and Linda was on duty. She asked him how he was and let him in. Gavin found Ruth in the lounge. His arrival upset her. He was doubting already his decision to return to the scene of his crime.

'You need to go.' The words were matched with some urgency. 'Come back in fifteen minutes and I will be in my room.'

Gavin left. He smiled at Linda on his way out. He said he would be back in fifteen minutes and then wondered if he should have imparted that information. What was happening? Was he being set up for a lynching by the old folk? Would the carers look on whilst he was wheelchair rammed and stick poked from every direction?

'Okay,' replied Linda. There was no suggestion of her knowing something that he didn't.

Outside was not a safe place to be wandering about for fifteen minutes, so he went back to the car and kept his head low.

Twenty minutes later, he returned. He managed to get through to Ruth's room without any assault or abuse taking place. There were no errant wheelchairs or smiting sticks. There she was, waiting for him. Someone had put her in the easy chair.

'What was that about?' Gavin asked.

'What do you think?'

'I seem to have gained something of a bad reputation.'

'Well, you don't help yourself do you.'

'What are they saying?'

'All about your performance the last time you were here.'

'News travels fast,' said Gavin.

'News travels slow round here, but it gets there in the end. You should see us play Chinese whispers.' This made them both laugh. This came as some relief to Gavin. She was still on his side. Gavin could not help wondering about the incongruity of her intellect and the setting she was in. He had not expected her, or indeed anyone in such an environment, to be so clever. This was many standards above the levels of coherency that he had associated with those in care homes. Again, it had come down to expectation. She was in the home because of her body. Mentally she was a queen and he was a pawn with no prospects. She had the con as they would have said in Star Trek. Well, in the later series anyway. To boldly go, he thought.

'Just so I know what to expect. What have you been hearing?' Gavin asked.

Ruth told Gavin about one resident, in particular, who had been upset by his behaviour. She had needed a lot of consoling. Gavin told Ruth about Big Ron. Two and two made an uncomfortable four. Even more so when Ruth informed

Gavin that this Big Ron he was referring to had been known to visit his mother here.

There was a question that Gavin couldn't resist asking. 'And is he?'

'Is he what?'

'Big?'

Ruth gave him a concerned look. There might have been humour in it, but the smile barely hid a teasing warning. 'I'd say so. Then again, most people coming here look big at the sides of us. We've all shrunk with old age. And we're usually sat down or bent over. You look big to us. But I'd have to call you Little Gavin next to him.'

Gavin couldn't help feeling she was taunting him. It was all right for her. She hadn't upset anyone and, even if she had, she was unlikely to be strangled whilst sitting with a plate of over-cooked state-sponsored cottage pie. He'd seen it. It was the sort of cottage pie that would have you thinking you were regularly chewing on a piece of rotted garden fence.

Ruth could see that Gavin was uncomfortable. 'Look. I'm sure he was very upset, but these things usually calm down. And he's not going to do anything to you in here is he?' There was no reply from Gavin. 'You can always hide in the wardrobe. No one ever looks in the wardrobe. No one ever uses the wardrobe. I think they only put it there to make the room look better. There's probably a spare duvet and pillow in there. Move in if you like. I won't charge rent.' Gavin smiled. He realised it was an offer he might need to take her up on.

'My turn,' she said.

'What?'

'My turn to tell you my story.'

'I guess I'd better listen.'

'Exactly.' Ruth smiled. 'I'm two people. I have two stories-'

'She hugged me,' interrupted Gavin.

'Sorry?'

208

'She hugged me.'

'Who hugged you?'

'My mother.'

'I thought it was my turn to tell my story. Do you want to hear it?'

'Sorry. Yes. Of course.'

'I was two people. There is me now and there is-'

'She said I looked like my father.'

Ruth stopped. She stared at Gavin. It was a friendly stare. 'Your mother, I assume.'

'Yes. She said I looked like my father.'

'And do you?'

'I don't know. That's the point.'

'Well, I'm sure you do. We inherit looks and personality whether we know who our parents are or not.'

'I guess so.'

'So, where was I?'

'I can't remember.'

'No. That doesn't surprise me.'

'Sorry.'

'Today's word, I think.'

'Sorry?'

'Exactly.'

'Exactly?'

'Sorry. Today's word.'

He looked at her.

'Forget it. Never mind. Where was I?'

'She's changed.'

'Who's changed? I haven't mentioned anyone yet. I've not had the chance to tell you about anyone.'

'My mother. She's changed.'

'Okay. Okay. Your story again it is.'

'Sorry?'

'Exactly!' She smiled at him. He smiled back but he wasn't sure why. 'How has she changed?' she asked.

'Calmer. More relaxed. Less distracted. On her own.' He thought about the last observation. Ruth picked up on it.

'On her own? I think we all spend time on our own. That's not unusual.'

'No, not that,' he replied. 'I'm not saying she's lonely, but I'm used to seeing people around her, or people coming and going. Some sort of activity. It wasn't there. It wasn't happening.'

'Lonely?'

'Maybe. Alone. She was alone.'

'And you've never seen her alone like that?'

'No. I've seen her on her own, but there has always been that feeling that she was between things happening. This time I didn't get the feeling that anything much had happened before I visited. And I don't think anything was going to happen when I left. She was alone. I've not seen that before.'

As the words came out, Gavin found himself contemplating what it all meant. What it meant for his mother. What it meant for him. He had a mother who was alone. No. More than that. He had a mother he didn't like, and she was alone. Then again. No. It wasn't that he didn't like her. Yes. He felt let down by her. Over forty years of being let down. But that didn't lead to not liking her. That just kept you aloof. That just made you hold off. It neutralised your feelings. And now he'd seen her in such a way that those neutral feelings might feel tempted to awaken something within him. And that was a whole can of worms. That was a factory full of canned worms. That was some factory. The sort of plant you would see taking up more than its fair share of land on the outskirts of some industrial city.

'Do you think she was lonely?'

Gavin was reluctant to reply. This was awakening the wrong senses in the wrong way. This he was not ready for. This he had not expected. Suddenly being beaten half to death by Big Ron seemed to carry the threat of less pain than opening up about anything relating to his relationship with his mother. This was something that he was not ready to embrace. But she had hugged him. His mother had taken hold of a great big can opener and was waving it around in the general direction of the canned worms factory.

Ruth was leaving Gavin to his thoughts. She waited for him to come through the other end of wherever he was.

Where Gavin was, was a place of anguish, turmoil, torture, and downright fearsome uncertainty. And it was a damned nuisance. This was not a good place. This was the sort of place that welcomes you in and then hangs you from the ceiling by your testicles. He was hanging there, swinging.

'Tea?' the voice outside the door was followed by a woman stepping ahead of a tea trolley. She had the sort of carefree smile that Gavin just wanted to punch. But she was offering tea.

'Yes please,' said Gavin returning from the devil's own territory.

'No thank you,' said Ruth, knowing that the tea usually tasted like it had been brewed somewhere near the devil's own territory.

Gavin took a cup of dark brown liquid and realised that he was still making bad decisions. Out of intrigue, he took a sip. This he soon regretted. He waited for the nice welcoming woman with the happy smile to leave and then he put the mug onto the chest of drawers. He apologised to his mouth and internal organs. He didn't apologise to the chest of drawers. It was in a place where it ought to be used to having just about anything put on it.

Ruth smiled at Gavin. It told him everything he should have known about institutional beverages. The days of the great big silver tea pot, stained dark brown inside and several sizes too big for anyone to handle safely, were not yet over.

'Sorry,' said Gavin. 'I've come here and just put a downer on things, haven't I?'

'Well, you can take the tea as your punishment,' replied Ruth.

'Come on. I haven't been that bad.' There wasn't laughter, but they looked at each other as if to acknowledge life's tragedies and that it was time for a bit of light entertainment.

'Where's Bruce when you need him,' said Ruth.

'Bruce who?'

'Bruce Forsyth. You know Bruce Forsyth?'

'What? The old man who sits in the yellow chair in the lounge and looks like he's never moved.'

'Of course not. You don't know who Bruce Forsyth is?'

'Of course, I do. Anyway, he's dead now.'

'True.'

'And I prefer Ricky Gervais.'

'Can be a bit crude.'

'But clever. Very clever.'

'Do you know how old I was when Hitler came to power?' Ruth decided that she needed to play different cards to the two people hand she had declared earlier. Reference to Hitler could usually do it. Gavin needed knocking out of the melancholic world he was trying to find rented accommodation in.

Gavin was knocked out of the melancholic world where he thought he had put down a deposit on a nice two-up and two-down with a rusted swing in the garden and dilapidated fencing. This was a question that he had not expected, and this was information that he did not have. He had no idea how old Ruth was. He might have known when Hitler had come to power but, like most people, he supposed he did not. Would a guess be impertinent? Did age matter at whatever age Ruth was? He shook his head.

'You could speak rather than shake your head.'

'Sorry.'

'Three,' she said. 'I was three. He came to power on the thirtieth of January 1933. It was my third birthday.'

Just as most people would, Gavin did a quick mathematical calculation to work out how old that made Ruth now. He said, 'I don't suppose he knew it was your birthday.'

'I don't suppose he did. Might have made a difference if he had waited a few years and I had been five or six and it had been my birthday. Then we might have clashed.'

'I think if he had waited a few years, a lot of things might have been different.'

'Men like that can never wait.'

'So, are you telling me you are German?'

'Do I look German?'

Gavin had to consider if this was a trick question. Or if it was Ruth's way of having a bit of fun with him. He looked at her.'

'Have a good look,' she said.

He had a good look. 'I wouldn't have noticed but now that the question has been asked, I would say I can see something. Although to be honest, I'm not sure how I would differentiate between different countries like Germany or Austria or Switzerland, you know. And our noses and mouths and faces are now such a mixture. Skin colour and all that. So hard to tell now. Maybe some countries are a bit paler or darker and-'

'I was called Ruta,' she interrupted, to put an end to his going on a bit too much. 'Everyone called me Ruth. A lot of things changed. Ruta spoke German. Ruth could only speak English.'

'So those are the two people.'

'You were listening then.'

'Just about.'

'Yes. I was Ruta in Germany. I was Ruth in England.'

'What happened then?'

'What happened is my story.' She looked at him. It was a special moment. She would share her story with him. She could see that he was ready to listen. And she was ready to tell. But

213

not now. Not today. She was tired. The story could begin the next time they met.

Several years of social work had been sufficient for Gavin to be able to read body language and poignant moments of silence. 'But another day?'

'Another day. Later today. Another day. Whatever.'

'I look forward to it.' And he did.

'Will you be sneaking out?'

He didn't know if she was joking or not, but the real world came tumbling back into focus. 'I'm going to have to be careful.'

'What will you do?'

'I don't know.'

'You seriously aren't going home then?'

'No.'

'And your mother's house?'

'No. No. I'm not ready for that again.'

Ruth could sense that she had darkened the mood. Quickly she tried to bring back some lightness. 'Well don't forget the wardrobe is still available.' They both laughed.

Gavin left. He moved slowly and carefully across the threshold of Ruth's room and then cautiously and watchfully, but with more haste, through the rest of the home, before finding himself outdoors and still feeling vulnerable. It was as if he was someone's prey and they were waiting to pounce, two great hands destined for his throat.

Sometime later, having wandered here, there, everywhere, done nothing, been nowhere, seen nothing, been seen by no one, and completely having wasted the rest of the day, he was back at the care home.

'Is the offer of the wardrobe still on?'

Chapter 24

It took him a few seconds to realise where he was when he awoke. It had been a terrible night's sleep. Fitful for several hours before complete exhaustion sent him on his way for the last few hours. There had been a duvet and a pillow. He had laid down in such a way that both were more protection against the frame of the wardrobe rather than being there to cover him. The room, as always, had been warm throughout the night. It was a battle for comfort rather than warmth. He could not tell what time it was. It just seemed far enough into the morning to accept that, despite how tired and weary he felt, he was not going to get any more sleep.

He popped his head out through the gap between the wardrobe doors.

There was a knock on the door. 'Can I come in Ruth? Are you awake?'

He quickly popped his head back inside the wardrobe and carefully pulled the doors together.

There had been a slight delay before Ruth had answered. 'Yes. Come in.'

'How are you this morning?'

'Fine, thank you,' Ruth replied from her bed.

'Are you ready to get up?'

'Yes please.'

'What would you like to wear?'

He could hear them moving Ruth out of bed and into a chair and changing her from nightwear into daytime clothes.

215

The voice of the carer did not sound like the woman who had thought him to be a pervert. But now felt like the right time to pray to any God that would still accept him. He didn't care what the terms were. He would stand, sit, kneel, recite liturgies, or whatever you called them. Give him the costume. Give him a bell to ring. Anoint him with a thousand and one oils. Just please don't let it be the woman who thinks he's a pervert and please please don't let her find him in the wardrobe. It was like being in the house with Big Ron banging on the door. But worse. Everything depended on his ability to act out again the whole charade of not being there. This time the stakes were different. This time it wasn't a beating he was trying to avoid. This time it was the sex offender's register. What would they call him in prison? He dared not think. What would they do to him? He should never have returned to sleep in the wardrobe. He tried hard not to do anything. He tried hard not to listen, but the more he tried not to listen the more he listened. And he needed to listen. He needed to know what was happening. There were clothes in the wardrobe. Surely, they would need to come to the wardrobe to get fresh clothes. Had that moment not arrived? Could he curl up into a tiny ball? He knew the answer. The answer was he could not move or do anything. If they opened the wardrobe, he would be well and truly caught and prison bait. He had gone from prey to bait overnight. This was now his life. One moment he was a shrew running across a field trying not to be caught by a watchful owl, the next he was on a fishing line, waiting to be netted.

'You can come out now.'

Oh my God, thought Gavin. They know he's there. Of course they knew. You can't hide in a wardrobe all night and not get caught. What had he been thinking? He was a fool.

'Out you come.'

He crept out with his hands raised. He felt completely guilty and devoid of any mitigating argument or explanation for his presence. He was a man appearing out of an old lady's wardrobe. What could he say to explain himself?

Ruth had to try hard not to laugh. She stifled the sound as best she could and sufficiently to avoid drawing any attention back to the room. She sat in her wheelchair and watched as Gavin appeared, arms raised as if he had just been caught by some enemy.

Gavin looked up and around. The door was closed. There was only Ruth. She was trying hard not to laugh and he could see it. There was no one else. They had left. He felt relieved, shameful, and angry. He wanted to tell her off. He wanted to leave. But it wasn't Ruth's fault. And he couldn't leave without knowing what was happening.

'She's gone,' said Ruth. 'She won't be back for a while. I told her I needed a bit of time before I left the room.' Ruth wasn't sure what Gavin would have heard from the comfort of his wardrobe. 'And they're too busy around here for her to rush back. It will be a late breakfast. If we play it right, you can look like an early visitor. You might even be offered breakfast.'

Gavin could still taste the stewed tea from yesterday. Or was that the stale feeling of the inside of the wardrobe? 'I'm not sure about that.'

'I can charge you for bed and breakfast then.' Ruth laughed. Gavin didn't. 'You look like you could do with a couple more hours in the wardrobe.'

'I'm still coming round.'

Ruth was back in her wheelchair and Gavin was in the spare chair. Neither of them had much to do. Well, Gavin ought to have had lots to do. There was so much he should have been doing but he wasn't. They had both decided that it was too soon for him to leave, and that he might as well wait and see if he could get any breakfast.

'So,' started Gavin. They had time to kill. 'Tell me about Ruta.'

217

'Ruta was born in Germany. I have memories of my parents but there is nothing clear. I cannot recall their faces. I seem to have lost any images I might have had. My father I remember little about. Distant recollections that I am not even sure about now. In all senses, sadly I have nothing to remember him by. I must have been closer to my mother. I remember being with her. In a house. Walking somewhere. But again, nothing distinct.'

'So, what happened?'

'The war,' she answered and looked at him like a contestant getting the easiest question on a quiz show. 'Have you heard of the Kindertransport?'

Gavin shook his head.

'I was one of them. Children from across Germany and other countries, but mainly Germany. Just before the war started, we were moved to England. Probably Wales and Scotland too. Most of the children were Jewish. We had to leave our parents behind.' She stopped at this point. It called for time out.

'It must have been really difficult.' It was a statement that sounded like a question. It was a combination of words that acknowledged what Ruth was telling him, but which Gavin knew could never match what she had to say. 'Do you remember coming over here?' Gavin added carefully, whilst trying to invite further information.

'Of course. I would have been eight.'

They were interrupted by a voice at the door. 'Breakfast Ruth?'

'Yes please,' replied Ruth.

The voice entered the room. 'Oh. You have a guest.' She looked at Gavin. 'You're an early arrival.' She was still looking at him. 'I didn't see you come in.'

'No,' he replied.

'Would there be any spare breakfast?' asked Ruth.

'I should think so,' replied the carer. 'What would you like?' The question was directed at both of them.

'Cornflakes, toast and orange juice please,' replied Ruth.

'That would be great,' added Gavin.

'I'll see what we can do. Here or at the table?'

Ruth could read Gavin's mind. 'Here please.'

A short while later, breakfast was served. And a little later after that, breakfast had been consumed.

Recognising that it would have been rude to leave straight after sharing breakfast, Gavin resumed their earlier conversation.

'Do you remember the journey to get here?' Gavin asked again.

'I was an eight-year-old girl. I said goodbye to my parents. We were all children saying goodbye. In most cases it was forever, I think. I think that fear was there too. When will I see you again? Will I see you again? Parents can't hide that sort of leaving. I remember my mother crying. She held me and then she let me go. I see the meaning in both actions now. She held me because I was hers. She held me so that one way or another we would be together always. It is my most vivid memory from childhood. It defined my mother for me. She gave me that forever. And then she let me go. She gave me my freedom to live. And strangely, I think, she gave her own freedom to me as well. I took it with me. My father wasn't there at the station. I never knew why. I can only guess now. But I'm not going to guess.'

Gavin just listened.

'But at the time I think we all thought we would come back. We were only children. We didn't understand what was happening. Kristallnacht happened. I'm not sure our parents knew what it meant. Not fully. Not what was happening. But things were changing. Things were bad and things were going to get worse. As children you notice change, you notice difference. And you see it in your parents, in those nearest to you. I do have a distinct memory of hiding in the attic with my mother whilst outside there was noise and activity. My mother wanted us to keep quiet, which we did. I can't remember how long we were in the attic, but it was a long time. No one came to find us. I think I was protected from the worst of what was happening. I am sure most children were. And even adults must have been trying to work out exactly what was happening, and why. So initially we thought we were going away but going to come back. I'm not sure if our parents were so confident. We weren't confident, we just had no reason to think otherwise. But as I said, there was something in the way my mother held me and there was something in the way she let me go.

'My mother called me Ruta when I was born. When I became Ruth, in England, that was the name her freedom gave me. I am both people. One does not replace the other. They both exist. I am both Ruta and Ruth. Ruta is the eight-year-old child who hugged her mother forever. Ruta never lost or left her mother. Ruth was my future. The girl she let go. And if you like, the journey to England was my second birth. Although the journey was not straightforward.'

'How long did it take?'

'About nine months.'

'To get to England?'

'No. To be somewhere in England. To be Ruth.'

Gavin shut up again and returned to listening mode.

'The actual physical journey was train and ferry as I remember. I can remember getting on the train and being on the train. I can remember the excitement of being on a ferry. I don't remember seeing the sea. I think I can remember the feeling of the sea but I'm not sure now. Time does that to you. It makes you forget. Which is good and bad. Then we were taken to a camp. It was cold and damp. I kept my clothes on at night. I had a case which I kept with me. That was it. I was only in the camp for a few days. I can't remember much, but just a sense of being on my own. There were other children. We must have talked but I don't remember anyone else. I just wonder now about the futures all those children had before them. What we didn't know and what we know now. Who were they? What happened to them?'

'Then where did you go?'

'To a horrible place. Let's just say they didn't seem to want me right from the start. I just remember this horrible couple. I'm not sure why they offered to have me. Or I wasn't what they expected. I was quiet. I'm sure I must have been in shock. I bet they thought I should have been grateful. It was all about me fitting in with them. No thought about an eight-year-old girl and the world she brings with her. That was all gone. And I had to let it go. I was German. I spoke German. They were English. They didn't speak German. I didn't know what they were saying. I didn't know what they were doing. I didn't know what I was supposed to do. But it was down to me to fit in with them. They lived on a farm. I can't remember any animals. I don't know what kind of farm it was. And one of them had a big nose. But I can't even remember who. I told you it took me months to arrive because this was a place where I didn't belong. I suppose they might have expected me to speak English. It was a horrible place, and they were a horrible couple. And it is a place I have no desire to remember, so I've let it go. I think he had the big nose.'

'So, did you leave?'

'Yes. Eventually. I'm not exactly sure what happened but I think they probably gave up. Well, they never got started, did they? They must have not liked me. I know I didn't like them, so the feeling was mutual. But I moved and then my new life began. I was nine years old and I was called Ruth.'

She paused at this point. Gavin wasn't sure if she was being drawn back to thoughts and feelings of the time or if she was tired from the exertion of storytelling. There was energy in her accounting of what had happened. He could appreciate that one way or another it was an undertaking for her. But her memory was good and she seemed to be enjoying having the opportunity to share her story.

'Do you want me to leave?' said Gavin, trying to be considerate and then, in case she might think he was being unappreciative of what she was sharing with him, he added, 'I'm really really fascinated by what you're telling me. Your story certainly puts my story to shame. You are tiring though and I can come back later.'

'Don't compare stories. That's like comparing lives. Everyone's story is important and most important to them.'

He was told off.

'I just want to tell you about the person I moved to, and why that was much better. The place where Ruth was given birth to. Then I will have said enough for now.'

Gavin nodded and waited. Ruth took some time, to revive a little and to find the words to continue the narrative.

'She was older. That was my impression of her. But then when you get old yourself, age becomes relative. But she was older. She was single. She was old enough to be noted as being single. And it didn't seem to bother her. I never got the feeling she was looking for someone. I called her Aunty Aggie. Everyone called her Aggie although her real name was Agatha. She never expected me to regard her as my mother. I think she realised the dilemma that would have caused.' Ruth stopped and checked the look on Gavin's face to make sure he was showing the sort of response that would substantiate that he understood the dilemma too. Gavin being Gavin, she wasn't sure, but she moved on.

'She was small. I bet she didn't quite get to five feet. She was friendly. She got on with everyone. I think she did what she could for me. I felt I belonged. I accepted being Ruth. But I never felt that I was allowed to get too close. I'm not sure now if that was just her. She was single, so did she not want anyone to get that close? Or was she just over-concerned with never trying to replace my mother? She was too sensitive. And I don't know if she was right or wrong. There wasn't an example to follow. I arrived. I felt welcomed. I felt accepted. In a strange way, I did feel loved. But I had a mother and father in Germany.'

'What happened to them?' This question had been ricocheting around Gavin's head. He had been cautious about asking, but he felt it was a necessary part of the picture that Ruth was presenting him with. He could have waited to see if she told him. He sensed though that it was one of those pieces of information that was waiting to be asked about. And they had come to a moment where the question seemed less intrusive.

'In truth, I don't know. Realistically, it seems inevitable that they were got rid of. I'm not sure how I want to word it.'

Gavin was about to interject with apologies and give her permission to stop. Why she needed his permission was a thought that did not have time to develop as she showed that she wished to continue.

'I had a letter from my mother. It was given to me when I was on the farm. It was in German, of course. So, I could read it then. It was carefully written. There was no mention of my father. That stood out. My mother asked me to make sure that I was polite and kind to the people looking after me, and that I should be thankful that they were keeping me safe. I always remember the reference to not being afraid to make new friends. There was something about the way my mother had used the word "new" which even at the time stood out and has stayed with me. The letter was important to me, but it did not replace the hug. Its significance also became clear when I did not get any more letters or cards. And the hug then established itself as being for Ruta. Then with Aunty Aggie, I found Ruth. Was it a new beginning? Was she a new friend? You'll have to wait for another time to find out.' Ruth laughed at her cliffhanger.

'I can wait,' replied Gavin.

'Good. I need to rest now. On your way out can you ask someone to come and move me?'

'Of course.' And Gavin left the room, passed on Ruth's instruction, and carefully removed himself from the building.

Whilst Ruth rested, slept, or just switched off from the world for a while, Gavin returned to Nap's car. He drove off, found an unassuming spot, and went to sleep. He didn't sleep well. You don't in the back seat of a car. He was mindful of traffic, noise, and being disturbed. But he did rest. The remainder of the day was spent achieving nothing. It was a combination of wanting to hear more and having created a world in which he couldn't do anything or go anywhere that returned him to Ruth's room. She wasn't surprised to see him. She was already in bed, such was the time and such was her expectation that he might return.

'Well, this isn't a surprise,' she said.

'I thought it wouldn't be,' replied Gavin, in like manner. 'Not too late, is it?'

'Of course not. Bedtime for me is decided either by how tired I am or when someone is free to sort me out. Have you done anything exciting?'

'No. Why d'you think I'm here.'

'Not sure how to take that.'

'With a pinch of salt. Anyway, I've come back to hear more about Aunty Aggie.'

'Aunty Aggie,' responded Ruth, whilst she gathered her thoughts and memories.

'She had a friend called Daisy. She was really called Emmeline, but everyone called her Daisy. She was so full of life and energy, so they said she was as fresh as a daisy. And that's how the name came. Good job she wasn't daft, or they might have called her Brush. That's an old joke, by the way. I thought of that years ago. I didn't know her real name was Emmeline for quite a while. No one ever called her that. She was just Daisy. It suited her. They were a partnership. Aunty Aggie was the responsible parent. She made sure that things happened. She made sure I was safe. She fed me. She watered me. Made sure that I was in on time. Made sure I went to school. All those things. Then Daisy oversaw the entertainment. She made me laugh. She made me cry. She showed me how to live. I think they were just friends. Aggie was older and never married. Daisy did get married eventually. But she was a free spirit, so it never lasted.'

'Did you keep in touch with them when you left home? As an adult?'

'Aunty Aggie died. I would have been about thirty. I don't think that gave me the real chance to get to know her: adult to adult. She was only ever Aunty Aggie. When I think about her now, it is strange to be considering someone in my life who now I am older than she was then. It changes your perspective. It gives you a different understanding. I can think about her as another person: woman to woman. I didn't go to her funeral.'

'Why?'

They were interrupted by a conversation taking place outside the room but too close for comfort.

'How is she?'
'She's fine Mr Wicker.'
'Well, I hope I don't ever see that Nazi around 'ere.'
'I'm sure he didn't mean what he did.'

Gavin could feel his whole body tense up.

'Well, if I ever find him… He's dead meat. No one upsets my mother like that and gets away with it. You shouldn't have people like that coming 'ere.'

Gavin reflected that it wasn't a good time to have resolved that bit of handwriting. He was dead meat if Big Ron came in.

Not that Big Ron would come into Ruth's room. He was just dead meat if he left the room any time soon. And in the room, he could feel himself getting increasingly anxious. He looked at the door as if it was about to burst open. He tried to reassure himself that Big Ron was not going to enter Ruth's room.

'No one upsets my mother like that and gets away with it. You shouldn't have people like that coming in here. I wouldn't let them in.'

'Tea, Mr Wicker?'

'Two sugars.'

Gavin kept looking at the door. He could only imagine the scene on the other side. And he could imagine the scene on the other side were he to be on the other side. In that case, Big Ron would be attacking more than a sweet cup of tea. He needed to be on this side of the door. And not for the first time he was overcome with the need to be silent, that special skilled effort in actively doing nothing and actively saying nothing. He was becoming quite practised at it. He was sure they must have moved on by now. They could only have been passing Ruth's room. However, being sure and being alive, or being in a state of not having yourself receive a sizeable pounding, were not guaranteed to go hand in hand. At which point, Gavin thought about the enormity of Big Ron's hands. He had no wish to make any effort to move anywhere else right now.

'Well, looks like I'm stuck here another night then.' This Gavin said quietly.

'The wardrobe do you?'

'Will have to.'

'I don't think they've changed the bedding.'

'You just can't get the staff!' If Gavin laughed, it was quietly done.

'If you're going to stay another night you might as well set out my clothes for tomorrow and then you're less likely to risk being disturbed and, besides which, I will need a change of clothes. We stink enough at this age without having to wear the same clothes every day.'

Having set out Ruth's clothes in the chair he had been seated in, Gavin settled into the wardrobe for a second night. 'I hope I won't be joined by a lion and a witch,' he said.

'Goodnight, Gavin,' replied a tired Ruth.

'Goodnight,' replied Gavin. All bets were off for who would get to sleep first.

Chapter 25

For the second time, Gavin was awoken by a combination of lack of sleep and discomfort. He couldn't believe he'd been daft enough to do it again. He had to assume that Big Ron hadn't stayed overnight. There wouldn't be a wardrobe big enough.

The night had been spent more awake than asleep. Although it was the sort of awake that finds you drifting through time, creating imaginings and notions in a pea souper of mind waves, with a brain that feels like all the wrong connections are being made. Ruth had to escape the Nazis and come over here. It was clear what had happened to her parents. More than one person thought that Gavin was a Nazi. He was a bloody fool for behaving in such a stupid way. He had meant nothing by it. He hadn't thought about what he had done. And now he was in fear of his persecutor. Well, Big Ron wasn't a Nazi. That wouldn't make sense. But he was after Gavin. And now he found himself hiding in a wardrobe. Oh for that bloody lion and witch to turn up and make a mockery of it all, and then he could just go home. But, despite several strange hours wondering about it, including his unlikely access to Narnia, he was once again greeting the morning from a situation that could not last. He had thought he'd heard a voice, but that might just have been a hangover from the hallucinatory night-time experience. He only seemed to be just about hanging on in there in the real world.

'You can come out now.' The words confirmed that he was back in the real world.

He came out. And he was greeted by Linda. 'Oh,' he managed to offer.

'Oh,' she replied.

'I wasn't expecting you.'

'And you think you should be more surprised than me?'

He couldn't argue with that. Gavin couldn't work out if she was being serious, or just slightly funny. He knew a lot depended on which it was.

'I'm not sure I even want to ask what this is all about,' continued Linda.

'It's because he's an idiot on the run from another idiot,' offered Ruth from her bed.

'This is all to do with Mrs Wicker, isn't it?'

'Big Ron. Mr Wicker. Mrs Wicker.' He worked it out. 'Yes.'

'He is rather big,' confirmed Linda.

'I knew it,' spurted out Gavin.

'But you can't stay here. There are so many reasons why we can't have you moving into one of our wardrobes.'

Gavin was still trying to gauge from Linda's words what her response was going to be. He decided he needed to avoid humour and focus on serious and careful dialogue.

'I'm going to have to think what I should do about this,' said Linda. 'I suspect we don't have a policy on who can sleep in wardrobes.'

'Guests can visit anytime,' said Ruth.

'They can,' said Linda.

'And stay as long as they like,' said Ruth.

'Yes,' said Linda.

'And Gavin just prefers wardrobes to chairs.'

'It would appear so.'

They fell to silence. Each of them was wondering about the situation, who they were, and what they ought to do. Linda felt she had some professional responsibility. Ruth didn't care. Gavin wanted to walk away with at least a smidgen of his self-respect intact. It was looking unlikely.

'I have it,' declared Ruth. 'My house. I don't want to prolong your being on the run any longer than you need and, in my opinion, it has already gone on too long. But you can stay in my house, if,' and the last word was given special emphasis and then repeated, 'if, you have to maintain this farce.' And then she smiled. 'Although to be honest, I am finding it rather entertaining. Better than anything on the television.'

For the first time, Linda smiled, which gave Gavin some hope that there was not to be any punishment other than the diminished regard that people would have for him. And that said, Ruth was enjoying the whole farce, as she called it. He wondered if Linda was grateful for something to break up the usual routine and monotony of most days in a place like this.

Ruth addressed Linda: 'I can give you permission to give him the key, can't I?'

'I suppose so. Yes,' replied Linda.

'And if he promises to sleep inside no more wardrobes?'

Linda remained in thought about the whole situation. There were rules and there were people. The rules always seemed to win. She wasn't a job's worth. It wasn't clear that any rule had been broken. It was clear that that was only the case because no one had ever thought that they ought to write up a prohibited list of places where you are not allowed to sleep: under beds, under tables, in bathrooms, and especially in wardrobes. And they were allowed visitors at any time.

'I do promise,' added Gavin. 'I have no wish to repeat that experience.' He didn't look at Ruth.

'There's so much here that I don't need to know,' said Linda, although she was human and intrigued by the mess that Gavin seemed to have got himself into, and a bit more information would have helped compensate for any soap opera she had missed on the last shift.

'Please,' said Gavin. Ruth had no intention of pleading. They had both had quite different life experiences and hers did not allow for pleading.

Linda looked at them both in turn. 'I'll fetch the key.'

'Thank you,' responded Gavin.

Once Linda had gone, Gavin turned to Ruth. 'Are you sure about this?'

'Well,' she started. 'You're getting to know more and more about me. I'm not sure my house will hold any secrets. I do trust you to be respectful. Although it won't be tidy. It will smell. It will need a good clean. And it might make you want to get back to your house and sort yourself out. You can stay there, but it is a short-term answer. See it as an alternative to the wardrobe rather than an alternative to your own home.'

Linda returned with the key. Gavin left, making a special promise to visit later and report on the house, as well as wanting to hear more about Ruth's story.

It took an hour to drive to the house and, much to Gavin's relief, it was away from anywhere he knew.

Chapter 26

The house turned out to be a bungalow, which indeed is a house and was once a home. It now looked like an abandoned derelict hideout that was beginning to give up hope of ever being saved. It was one of four properties set apart in a small cul-de-sac, pleasantly positioned just off the main road. This implied privacy, except amongst the occupiers of the four houses. The other three houses were another bungalow but of different shape and design, a dormer bungalow, and a detached house. Ruth's home was the smallest. The other properties looked well cared for. They were waiting for Ruth to die so that someone would then clean, renovate, or knock the whole thing down and start again, and make sure they were back to the best-looking cul-de-sac in the town.

Gavin had parked on the main road, preferring to arrive at the property on foot, for reasons he was not too sure about, other than wanting to make less of an entrance. He had anticipated being seen but wanted to give the appearance of a reluctant visitor rather than an eager tenant. He hadn't yet worked out what he was doing and therefore didn't want to give the neighbours too much to ask about.

He opened the gate, that is to say, he pushed it against months of growth, and set off along the short path through wild unchartered territories in search of a door.

'Hi there!' were the words that came from a head that peered over the fence. There was assumedly the rest of a body below, but out of view.

'Hi,' replied Gavin.

'Can I help you?' asked the head.

Now Gavin considered this to be an awkward question. He didn't need help. But that wasn't really the question. The question was 'What the fuck do you think you are doing?' or more mildly put, 'I say, do you think you might be in the wrong place old chap?' The answer to which question simply required the use of Ruth's name. However, he needed to form a polite sentence. He wasn't sure how long he would be staying, and these were, for that duration, his neighbours.

'I'm Gavin. A friend of Ruth's.'

To which the head disappeared and then reappeared, at the gate and attached to the whole body. 'Mick. But my friends call me Mick.' Mick laughed. Gavin feigned a laugh. 'A bit of a mess.' He pointed to the overgrowth.

Mick was immediately joined from the dormer bungalow by someone who announced herself as Daphne. She apologised on behalf of her husband for not asking how Ruth was. Gavin gave them an update which served to set up his true credentials. They were soon joined by Bert who lived in the detached house and by Doreen and her friendly dog who lived in the other bungalow. Both were given repeat updates on Ruth.

'How do you know Ruth?' asked Doreen. The dog was called Puddles and Doreen sought Gavin's reassurance that he didn't mind friendly dogs. He didn't have much choice. Puddles was set on checking out the new person.

'Leave the poor lad alone,' said Bert. 'He's just got here.'

'I'm only asking,' responded Doreen.

'If you're going in there, you'll get a shock,' said Daphne.

'Got to find the door first,' joked Gavin.

The four neighbours backed off. It was a step or two but symbolic of letting him know he could go. He found the door. The key worked, which was a relief, especially with an audience only a few metres away.

'Good luck,' shouted one of them, most likely Mick, he thought.

The door opened and introduced him to a pile of post and a stale damp smell that was unpleasant and strong. He stepped over the letters and leaflets. He was in a hallway. There was a shallow bureau and a photo of Ruth when she was younger. 'Well, the neighbours seem friendly,' he said to the photo. He wondered what they knew of Ruth and what she knew of them. On closer examination, he decided that it wasn't a photo of Ruth. It was a woman, in middle age and taken several decades ago. Other than that, it was hard to date either the person or the photo. He assumed it was likely to be either Aunty Aggie or Daisy. Unless there was someone else that Ruth was yet to tell him about.

The front rooms on either side of the hallway seemed to be bedrooms. It at once struck Gavin that Ruth had two bedrooms. The hall led to an archway and a door. The door took him into the lounge which overlooked the back garden. The archway took him into a dining kitchen area. Unusually the bathroom was set off from this area. It all seemed quite dated. The smell was everywhere. The state of the whole house gave away the need for a thorough and deep clean. Gavin wondered about her leaving the place for the last time and how that must have felt. She knew she wasn't coming back. It made him feel grateful for what he had, not least his health.

Having examined everywhere with the interest of a visitor's eye, he now contemplated what staying there would involve. On closer examination, it was clear that one bedroom had been used and the other must have been set up for visitors. The latter was where he would sleep. He also decided to not go back into Ruth's bedroom unless he had to. He wanted to offer privacy. He had not brought any food with him and the kitchen did not invite preparation anyway. Every surface had marks and stains. There were cupboards which had tins and packages. There was a bread bin which was incubating new life forms. There was a bin, half full, and exceeding even the success the bread bin was having. It struck Gavin that, on leaving, Ruth had had no one to come back to the house and attend to its upkeep. This must have been how she'd left it. It stood for some sort of legacy. It was a museum of her life. It was a piece of art. This was Ruth. This was not a place tided up for visitors. This was Ruth in life. Or rather, this was Ruth toward the end of her life. He wondered how the house might have been presented when she could get about freely and easily.

He went back to his car to get his rucksack. Mick caught him on the way out and on the way back with questions about what he had found and how long he would be staying. Gavin was vague on both accounts. He decided to leave the car where it was. There was a driveway hidden under various plants and some debris. He wasn't sure what else there might be there. It struck Gavin that no one had made any attempt to break into what was an empty property. Then again, they'd have to get past Mick.

Back in the house, he turned on all the taps, remembering something he had heard about people returning from long holidays to water that was infected with legionella, salmonella, or rubella. No, that was an illness children got and not from taps. Something bad anyway. He also realised that the water was on, and the electricity was on. Ruth must still be paying bills.

There was a knock on the door, which he had left partially open to release some of the foul air. 'Hello,' shouted a voice. Gavin went to the door. Doreen was there holding a mug. 'Tea?' she said. 'I wasn't sure, so I've put milk in, but no sugar. That's how most people take it now, I think. Hardly anyone has sugar nowadays.'

'That's really kind,' replied Gavin.

'I thought the state of the place, you'd not want to use anything in there, and I didn't see you come with any shopping either.'

'Thanks,' repeated Gavin.

'It must be over five months since they took her in. They came and then we never saw her again. I'm glad she's safe and well. Can't be the same though, in that sort of place. I hope I die at home.'

'In my sleep,' replied Gavin.

'What? Oh yes. Me too.'

'This is kind of you,' repeated Gavin.

'Tell me if you need sugar next time.'

'Hopefully, I can get it a bit sorted in there and make you a cuppa next time.'

Doreen looked past Gavin into the house and was doubtful about drinking or eating anything coming from there for quite some time yet. 'Have you run the taps?'

And Gavin realised they were still running. 'Thanks for reminding me.' He disappeared inside to switch them off. He returned outside where Doreen had been joined by Mick. Gavin picked up his tea.

'Where's mine?' joked Mick.

'Daphne's always got the kettle on, making you drinks,' said Doreen.

'She does spoil me,' replied Mick.

'And what do you do?'

'I reward her by staying out of the way.' Mick turned to Gavin. 'Are you married, or do you have to make your own tea?'

'What sort of question is that?' said Daphne, appearing very quickly from nowhere. 'I have to keep my eye on him,' she said to Gavin.

'What's this? A party? And I didn't get an invite.' Bert completed the gathering. 'What did you find in there? No dead bodies I hope.'

'Bert!' was the admonishment he got from Doreen. 'You've been single too long. You need a good wife to keep you in check.'

'What do you think Mick?' said Bert.

'I couldn't possibly comment. I'll tell you when she's gone.' Mick and Daphne gave each other a look that confirmed that most of what they said between them shouldn't be taken too seriously.

'And I'm not going anywhere,' replied Daphne.

'Where d'you keep his lead?' asked Bert.

'Next to my bed in the hallway,' joked Mick. There was laughter from all of them. Gavin half joined in, trying to be friendly, but not too intimate on account of not knowing them. There were echoes of a couple he'd once met on holiday. Laughter, jollity, drinks for everyone on the first day, and then on the second day he'd discovered how obnoxious and racist they were. He'd spent the rest of the holiday trying to avoid them. And holidays are not the best place to be avoiding people.

'Anyway. Come on. Let's leave him to it,' said Doreen, trying to gather the clan. 'There'll be plenty to do in there without us holding you up.'

'Thanks,' said Gavin, returning the mug. He returned himself to the house and decided, on entering again, that the next thing to do was to open all the windows and doors. This sortie through the bungalow done, he confirmed to himself that the spare bedroom and the lounge seemed to be the least affected by human absence and that these would be the places he would use. That said, he found utensils and a range of cleaning products and set to work on improving the kitchen. He dared not aim so high as to expect to clean the kitchen, but he could see where sufficient restoration could be undertaken as was needed for his temporary residence. That Ruth had only been absent from the property for about five months had meant that time's relationship with grime, dust, cobwebs, and such like had not been allowed to develop too much. But the place still needed a good clean and Gavin would give it a clean, but only reserving extra hard work for special places such as in the kitchen, the bathroom, and the toilet.

A few hours later, having achieved his goal, Gavin put the kettle on, found a clean mug and one of several abandoned tea bags and set up to make himself a simple cup of milkless tea. Instead of completing this task, he fell asleep on the settee. Finding the settee significantly more comfortable than any wardrobe, he slept well and for quite a while.

When he finally awoke, he realised that he had slept through to the late evening and had now left it too late to go back and visit Ruth. He felt guilty at not keeping his promise but made a severe mental note that he would return in the morning and reassure her about the house. He was hungry though. He decided to set off in the car in search of fish and chips. He then decided to eat them in the car. The smell in the house was still too strong for him to want to eat there. And he dared not eat them outside for fear of having to share with the constantly appearing neighbours.

Never had fish and chips tasted so good. He had also found a late shop and returned to the house with provisions for the next couple of days. He couldn't get the television to work. He found a CD player and introduced himself to George, Frank, Tony and Petula. And then, not for the first time that day, he fell asleep, but in bed this time, albeit one that had been waiting months, if not years, for someone to pull back the sheets and hop in.

Chapter 27

Gavin awoke the following morning feeling like a corpse. The room was dull, dank, and depressing. He was wrapped in white linen that had, throughout the night, felt just a little on the fusty side. And for a moment he didn't know where he was. He had quickly ruled out heaven and hell. He had ruled out heaven first which told him something. Then he remembered where he was. Consequently, he knew that he was not dead, he just felt that way. There had been no need to get up in the night. There had been no disorientation. And had there been, he would have been sure that Mick would have appeared from a room somewhere and pointed him in the right direction with a quirky comment or two.

He got up. Switched on the immersion heater, which seemed to work, and made himself a mug of tea and a bowl of cereal. He didn't want to return to the mausoleum spare bedroom and so he sat in the lounge, staring out of the window. It was a large window across most of the far wall. There was a decent garden with the remnants of a fountain in the middle. It all backed on to the gardens of other people. A bit like life, he philosophised. Big gardens, small gardens, long gardens, short gardens, gardens hidden behind hedges, behind walls, behind fences. Gardens touching other gardens. Gardens hidden away. Public gardens. Gardens surrounded by other gardens. Gardens in isolation. The water must be hot by now, he thought.

He ran a bath. It wasn't as hot as he would have liked but, like most things in Gavin's life, it would do. He chanced a bottle of strawberry bubble bath. He lay in the tepid water wondering what bills Ruth was still paying: all of them most likely on direct debits. Was this what it came to? Whatever happened to you in life, the utility companies still got their share. He would visit Ruth this morning. He wouldn't take her any post. It would fill a bag and most of it was probably rubbish.

It was a strange journey back to the care home. He was returning equipped with a new perspective on Ruth. The house, the décor, the furniture, the garden, the neighbours, the area. It all brought her more to life. It also gave him a sense of her as a person who was not too dependent on others. There were three people now: Ruta in Germany, Ruth at home and Mrs Deakin in the care home.

She was in the lounge when he arrived. He couldn't help comparing lounges. The one this morning where he had sat staring into the garden and this one where Ruth sat staring out of the window and where he had first seen her. Did she miss her home window? Did she miss the garden? He didn't ask her.

'How's the house?' she asked.

'Could be better, could be worse,' he replied, which was the sort of observation that was both true and pointless.

'Still there then?'

'I didn't count all the bricks but it looked complete to me.'

'Good.'

'Do you think I'm safe in here?'

'Well that's Bill over there and he used to be a security guard, but he's got dementia and can't remember anything now. I don't think he carries a gun. That's Judith and she's still got her own teeth so I suppose she could-'

'I mean with Big Ron being around,' interrupted Gavin.

'I know what you meant,' responded Ruth. 'Of course you're safe. I don't reckon he visits that often and, even if he did, he wouldn't dare do anything in here.' She paused. 'So. In a bit more detail, please. How's the house? And the garden?'

'The house smells a bit. Damp. Lots of post. But I would say in good order really and considering no one's been there for several months.'

'About five months since they took me away. And the garden?'

'A bit overgrown at the front. The back garden looks nice. Great view from that window.'

Ruth smiled.

'Grass needs cutting. Beds need weeding. Fountain needs some repair.'

'That's always needed repairing. I got used to it that way. Less a fountain, more a piece of art: a garden sculpture.'

'I'll get it sorted for you.'

'Yes, because I'm bound to be going back.'

Gavin looked at her, wondering if he'd made the wrong offer.

'Sorry,' she replied. 'I was being sarcastic. It would be good to know it's not been too neglected.'

'I didn't bring any of the post.'

'Probably bills and leaflets.'

'I didn't like to open anything.'

'Wise decision. Who knows what you might have discovered about me.' They smiled at each other.

'I slept in the spare room.'

'I should think so. I can't have strange men sleeping in my bed. Chance would be a fine thing anyway. Can't remember the last time anyone slept in there.'

'Your bed or the spare bed?'

'Getting a bit personal, aren't we? I'll leave that one unanswered. Hope the bedding was okay.'

'It was.'

'Have you met the neighbours?'

Gavin nodded.

'Of course, you have. Mick doesn't miss a thing. Mick and Daphne. They met at the Blackpool ballroom. He swept her off her feet. She's been sweeping up after him ever since. Never had children. Too late now. Bert divorced his second wife about five years ago. Can't believe he's still got the house. He must be worth a lot. You know he's an actor. Well, he used to be. Thinks he's important because he's been on television. He appeared in a bad film. He doesn't like to talk about it, but he did. Then he got offered second dead body in Casualty and he never looked back. Became an expert in playing dead bodies. Even got a run on the West End playing the corpse in some play where the dead body has to be on the stage all the way through. He always said the best bit was when he got up at the end and got a round of applause. Poor him a brandy and you'll not stop him telling you about all the famous people he's met. Not sure he met them as such, but he's been a dead body in the scenes they were in. Doreen's lovely. She's into animal welfare, animal rights, that sort of thing. Has she made you a cup of tea yet?'

'Yes.'

'How did it taste?'

'A bit different.'

'Soya milk. Or sometimes oat milk. You get used to it.'

'I wouldn't have known.'

'Sometimes it's down to the water or the kettle. In Doreen's case, it's the milk.'

'She seemed very kind and thoughtful.'

'Probably thought you were a bit of a stray.'

It was the kind of statement that needed no response. It broke the conversation and gave them a brief time-out. And it was the sort of statement that lay so close to the truth that it could not be knocked by humour, distraction, or any well-intended sensitive afterthought.

'I saw the photo in the hallway,' said Gavin, after a while and restarting their conversation.

'That's Daisy.'

'I did wonder.'

'Let me tell you about her.'

Gavin had the picture in his head which set him up well to hear about her.

'That photo was when she was about thirty years old and I was twenty or so. We went to the seaside by train. She always did things with me. She gave me experiences. Both when I was a child and as an adult. You don't become an adult at eighteen or twenty-one do you.'

'Not at all.'

'Interesting that we have two ages for becoming an adult. I think you could add twenty-five, thirty, and forty to the list.'

'That lets me off the hook a bit.'

'Lets us all off the hook.'

'But it doesn't.'

'No. It doesn't. Which is why we should all be a little kinder to each other.'

'And Daisy was that kindness?'

'That and so much more.'

'And what happened?'

'She got married.'

'Oh dear.'

'No. marriage suited her. It's just that single life suited her even more.'

'Did things change?'

'Naturally. Naturally, they did. As much as I loved her and appreciated her companionship, I am sure she felt the same. I know she did. To start with she played a part in looking after me and bringing me up. Then as I got older and became an adult we became friends on more of an equal footing. The way I guess a lot of parents and grown-up children do. She was my equivalent of that. She knew both my pasts. In exchange for that she shared things with me. We were close friends. But naturally, that changed when she met John. He pruned her a bit.'

'Can you prune daisies?'

'Not easy.'

'But they were a happy couple. I still saw her, but not as often. Sometimes with John. Sometimes on her own. It was best when she was on her own. But even then, she was this married person. She retained a lot of the Daisy I knew but she also became Mrs, whatever it was she was called. I forget. She died about twenty years ago and I went to the funeral. That was the first funeral I had ever been to.'

'The first?'

'I'd said goodbye to a whole country and a family in that country. There'd been no funeral for that. Why would I go to any other funeral? But for Daisy I did.'

'Not even Aunty Aggie?'

'How could I go to her funeral when I couldn't go to my own parents' funerals?'

'You could have said goodbye to everyone. Your country of birth and your family there.'

'No. You see. Like I told you. There are two of me. Only Ruta could have said goodbye to Germany or her parents. Ruth had to move on. And yes, I've never fully moved on. I haven't dealt with everything. But does anybody? Eventually, we all have to move on. What happens is that you live your life a little faster. People find you harder to live with because their lives are not at the same pace. But I'm not going to slow down and they're not going to speed up.'

'Does that mean you never met anyone? Did you never get married?'

'I did.'

'You did!'

'Trevor.'

'And was he as fast as you?'

'No. He was a lumbering idiot.'

244

'I'm assuming it didn't last.'

'Longer than it should have.' She looked at him. 'You remind me of him.'

Gavin couldn't hide a sense of disappointment.

'Only joking,' she said. 'Well, you have your moments, don't you?'

He had to suppose he did.

'So, what happened?' asked Gavin.

'Life. The realisation that one and one didn't make two. It just made a mess. Not the worst sort of mess. I think, despite everything I've said, I think there are times when your past does catch up with you. He was a bit older than me. I don't know if that was part of the attraction for me. I don't know if I was seeking in him something I had never had or something I had lost as a child. Or it was just that we were not a great match. We weren't terrible together. We just weren't sufficiently right for it to work. Or I was not ready. I'm better on my own. So many reasons when I think about it.'

'And he was a lumbering idiot,' repeated Gavin.

'That was unfair of me. But he did have a train set and insisted on having a room to put it in.'

'Say no more.'

'When we divorced, I got the house, and he got the train set.'

'Really?'

'Maybe.'

'Maybe?'

'Does it matter?'

'I suppose not. Did you keep in touch?'

'No. It was an amicable marriage which is not what a marriage should be and it was an amicable divorce which is not what a divorce should be either. And we went our ways. There was nothing to keep us together, nothing to keep in touch for. Not sure I have had anyone to keep in touch with.'

'Daisy?'

'Old Daisy, but not new Daisy.' There was a thoughtful pause. 'What are your ties?' she asked him.

'What do you mean?' Gavin replied.

'Well. What is it that holds you back? Your parents are usually ties, one way or the other. They hold you back. They stop you from doing things.'

'I'm not sure that my parents stopped me or helped me like that.'

She looked at him. 'We all have ties. But the extent and power of these ties varies enormously from person to person. If you had a good upbringing, then you had strong ties. This means your parents stopped you from going off and doing things that would not be good for you. But.' And it was a poignant break. 'But. It can also stop you from going off and doing things that might challenge you or make openings for you.' 'So many famous people make it because they had difficult childhoods. They didn't have strong ties holding them back.'

'But that isn't necessarily a good thing. I mean drugs as well.'

'Yes. Weak ties lead to doing things that most people wouldn't do. In the worst scenario that would be drugs and crime. In the best scenario, it could be a stage, films, or music. And how often do we see both drugs and fame? Parents keep us safe, but they also hold us back. Without ties, we are set free. But that freedom can lead in good and bad directions. The most interesting lives usually come from difficult childhoods. I have always been half a free spirit.'

It was a lot for Gavin to think about. As usual, Ruth's sermon showed how much more she was than he had first expected. It challenged his preconceptions about where she was and who she was. They both went quiet.

'I suppose you had better go and tidy that house,' said Ruth after a while.

'I suppose I had,' replied Gavin.

246

'And garden. I used to love sitting in that garden. I was a decent gardener you know. The only roots I felt comfortable enough to put down.'

'House and garden,' confirmed Gavin.

'See. Big Ron didn't turn up.'

'Thanks for reminding me.' Gavin got up to leave.

'Say hello to Daisy for me.'

'I will.'

And he did.

Chapter 28

Gavin spent a further seven days in the house. Or to be exact, in the house and in the garden. He was rarely alone. All the places he might try to hide were covered. But briefly, he became part of that small community. The whims and ways of its residents he soon accepted in contrast to his own mundanity. He developed a liking for quirkiness, albeit with a fair sprinkling of damp ordinariness.

On that second day. Following his return from visiting Ruth, Gavin was met by Mick, appearing from behind a rhododendron bush. For Gavin's return from the shop, Mick jumped out from the side of the garage. For Gavin's return from a short run, Mick appeared from the other side of a pagoda offering him a wheelbarrow. With the offer of the wheelbarrow came Mick who was volunteering to help Gavin make some improvements in the front garden. They set to work. Mick offered direction and some work. Gavin took direction and did most of the work, possibly all of it. It seemed that every time Gavin looked up, Mick was examining a flower or some weeds and muttering vague possibilities about what could be done. They took a rest and were soon joined by Daphne, Bert, Doreen (who was arriving with a tray of drinks) and Puddles. They all seemed to have a second instinct for knowing when to come together.

They were sat, either on the ground or in travel chairs, kindly provided by Mick and Daphne. From various positions of discomfort, they were surveying what had been achieved in the past hour or so. The discomfort, it might be added, was due to a combination of their means of sitting, age, and the limited places that the improved but still somewhat unkempt garden was offering.

'This is very kind of you all,' repeated Gavin, not for the first time.

'Kind of you too,' responded Doreen. 'Ruth did like her garden. Especially at the back.'

They all muttered confirmation of this. Gavin couldn't tell if it was polite acknowledgement or part of a plan to have them all next in the back garden repeating the same performance.

'I understand you two met on the ballroom floor at Blackpool,' said Gavin.

Daphne and Mick looked at each other and then Daphne said, 'Who told you that?'

'Ruth,' replied Gavin.

Mick laughed. 'We met in Blackpool. Well on a trip to Blackpool. We were on the same coach and kept bumping into each other when we were in Blackpool. I wouldn't exactly call it dancing.'

'Have you seen him dance?' said Daphne.

'You wouldn't get me anywhere near a dance floor like that. I'm not exactly flashy suits and light on my feet,' replied Mick. 'Ruth tell you anything else?'

Gavin looked at Bert. 'She said you're an actor. Played a dead body in casualty.'

Mick roared with laughter. Daphne, Doreen, and Bert smiled.

'I've never been near the stage or a camera,' replied Bert.

'Seen a few dead bodies though, eh?' added Mick lightening his hilarity.

Gavin now looked confused.

'I used to work for a funeral company,' added Bert.

'Looks like Ruth's been having a bit of fun with you,' said Mick.

'That's Ruth,' said Bert. 'Good to see she's not changed.'

'What did she say about Doreen?' asked Mick.

'She said you were into animal rights and used soya milk.'

'Oh,' replied Doreen.

'She is and she does,' said Mick.

'Into animals and uses soya,' added Daphne.

'Can you tell?' asked Doreen, referencing the tea.

'I can tell,' said Gavin. 'It's creamier, but I like it.'

'Got us all on it,' said Bert.

'Still working on animal rights though,' added Doreen lightly, but not lacking some meaning.

'You're going to have to watch her,' said Mick. 'Ruth,' he added, seeing that Gavin had looked confused.

'Did you know she was German?' asked Mick.

'So that's true then?' replied Gavin.

'Oh, I don't think she'd make anything like that up.'

'Knowing Ruth,' started Daphne, 'she just elaborated a bit about us to see what would happen. Nice really. She can't be here, but she can still have fun with us.'

There was general agreement and approval of this.

'So back to work is it?' announced Bert.

'Nearly done here and then you can get round to the back garden,' added Mick. Gavin did sense that Mick was also thinking about the neighbourhood.

Gavin and Mick got back to work in the garden. Bert disappeared. Daphne busied herself back at her own house. Doreen returned home with cups to wash. Puddles followed.

'She liked her garden,' said Mick. 'She would have been upset to have seen it like this. She'd be pleased to know you were tidying it up.'

'With help,' acknowledged Gavin.

'She'll not be coming back?' Mick asked this question in a way that predicted the answer.

'No. She knows that. She would like to hear that it's all in a decent condition though.'

'I'm sure she would.'

'I could elaborate a little bit for her, but I'm not good at lying.'

'No need to. We'll get it done.' Mick had the look of meaning that, whatever part he might or might not intend playing in it. 'Bet she's not had many visitors.'

'Just me, I think. Not seen anyone else. She's not mentioned anyone else.'

Gavin had picked up that Mick was the cul-de-sac's local reporter. He was gathering information for them all. It seemed fair enough. He could sense only warmth toward Ruth and genuine interest in how she was. And that Ruth had teased him with those false tales suggested she was aware that they would be talking to him, and therefore reminding them that she was still capable of mischief.

'That'll have to come up,' said Mick pointing at something that Gavin had no idea about. Gavin had always approached gardening like tidying, rather than having to know much about what was in the garden. As Mick moved toward the shrub, plant, or whatever it was, Gavin noted that they did seem to be moving around the side of the house to the back garden, and that Mick seemed to be in charge. He didn't mind this and it did seem to be the best for the garden. Mick was the sort of person that knew about most things. He had that practical awareness of what needed doing. Gavin didn't.

Another hour was spent weeding, removing, digging up and trowelling and then Doreen appeared with tea, cakes, and biscuits. Daphne and Bert soon followed bringing empty stomachs. And such was the rest of the day, with Mick telling Gavin what to do and others interrupting at useful intervals. Six o'clock was the magic hour when they all disappeared indoors to do whatever their lives expected of them that did not require the very local residents' committee approval. Although Gavin sensed that Mick could still reappear at any moment. He was probably hiding in a cupboard somewhere.

On the third day. Gavin decided to do more indoors, not least to avoid too much company. He knew that as soon as he stepped outside, he would not be on his own. And, although indoors, he was regularly waiting for a knock on the door. He considered that Daphne must be very well practised at telling Mick to give people a break. Then again, it took him away from her and gave her a break.

Gavin found a hoover and put it to use in the lounge, spare bedroom, and hallway. If anyone came to the door now, he wouldn't hear them. He wondered about keeping the hoover on even after he had finished using it. A daft idea, he decided and, besides which, he had enjoyed the company of Ruth's neighbours.

He played a bit of George whilst he cleaned the kitchen. It was a reminder that he might want to return with something different. He couldn't go home, so he would have to think about buying a couple of CDs. That said, there was something about the easy humour of Mr Formby that he found preferable to The Smiths.

Halfway through the morning, Gavin sat with a mug of tea and a couple of biscuits and stared out of the lounge window onto the garden. It was improved but nowhere near what Ruth would want her back garden to look like. The more he looked at the garden the more he knew that that was where he should be. Such were the workings of Gavin's mind, and especially when stimulated by tea and ginger biscuits, that he could accept two reasons for abandoning the inside of the house and resuming yesterday's work on the outside. One related to doing his best for Ruth. The other related to his newfound, even if temporary, neighbours. Both related to Gavin. Much of the knotting, chiselling, scratching, and general banging around in his head related to Gavin.

Gavin could see now that the house represented Ruth's head. Inside it was a show of who she was. This was personal and private and not for general viewing. It contained the dirt and grime of her life as much as the colour and charm. It was the best and worst of her. It was all of her, there to be found, and therefore to be respected. It should remain, if not untouched, at least unaffected by his presence here. He could see that. This was not his house. This home did not represent him. Whether she returned or not, it did not matter. This was Ruth. It was not for him to change anything. The garden, on the other hand, was what she wanted others to see. For Ruth and for Gavin, he needed to be in the garden.

And why did he shut himself away? That was the focus of his second reason. He had met the neighbours. Ruth had, by her cheeky deception, given him permission to engage with them. They were decent people. They undoubtedly had thoughts and opinions that would cause disagreement, but who didn't? And Gavin could disagree with the best of them. These were people who just liked to get together. It was as simple as that. But, also, it was as important as that. They were friends. They were being friendly. They asked for nothing and got something every time. Right now, and maybe for only a few days, but right now, they were offering to be his friend and for him to be their friend. For Mick and Daphne, Bert, and Doreen and for Gavin, he needed to be in the garden.

The hoover was returned. A glance into the kitchen confirmed it would do. Gavin opened the backdoor and walked up the garden to the abandoned fountain. He looked at water that offered no reflection. It was a thick, brown and green soup that no bird would risk getting too near to unless it never wanted to fly again.

'I'll get the hose,' said Mick.

Gavin smiled. 'Thanks.'

On the fourth day. Gavin visited Ruth again. The house still holding on to the personality of its owner, the garden having received supervised renovation, the neighbours happier and updated on Ruth's health and continuing sense of humour, Gavin headed off on his visit. Mick popped up from behind a tree and wished him a good morning. Gavin slowed down to return the compliment.

'Give Ruth our best wishes,' said Mick.

'Will do,' replied Gavin.

It was a light-hearted visit, welcomed by them both. Nothing too serious and a chance not to hide behind their respective stories. It brought them a little bit closer in a different way. Gavin updated Ruth on the garden. And this time Ruth told Gavin that Doreen had buried three husbands, Mick and Daphne were spies, and Bert used to play soccer for some American team. Gavin didn't believe a word of it, but later that day it was further amusement for them all, sipping tea and eating homemade cake provided by the serial husband burier.

The suggestion was that the next time he visited Ruth Gavin should go with tales of what had befallen them all. Bert was dating an American porn actress half his age: most porn actresses were probably half Bert's age. Mick and Daphne had won the Irish lottery and out of some weird sense of obligation were planning to move to Ireland. Doreen had run away with a Portuguese fisherman. That was Doreen's suggestion. She liked the idea of running away with a Portuguese fisherman. She had to confess that a seed had been planted. She had to admit that it wasn't going to happen. She couldn't abandon Puddles.

On the fifth day. Gavin, on his way to his car to go into the town centre, was ambushed by Daphne, appearing from behind a previously referenced rhododendron bush. It served the purpose well and got frequent use. Gavin did wonder if there was a pair of binoculars stashed away or some secret passageway. A few seconds later, but belatedly, Mick appeared from another part of the garden. He had the look of someone who hadn't been doing his job properly He might easily have apologised to Gavin for not having fulfilled his responsibility for popping up here there and everywhere. He could have thanked his assistant for standing in for him. He could have promised to do better next time. Should he resign there and then on the spot and hand the responsibility on to someone else? He did none of these, but he did have that look of realising that his reputation could so easily have been on the line.

Gavin returned from town with a few new items of clothing bought from several charity shops, except for underwear and socks which he wasn't going to risk buying second-hand, or second foot, or second bottom, depending on how you looked at it. Mick appeared out of thin air to ask how the shopping had gone. There was a sense that world order had been restored.

Later, Gavin visited Ruth. He was always anxious about getting caught by Big Ron, but once again it didn't happen. Visiting Ruth was one of those risks that he was prepared to take. He was living in her house. His obligation to visit was the rent. He would have visited anyway. It was safe territory until they were outside, and then he should be able to run faster, especially now. He was tempted to call at home but decided that that risk was still too great. He updated Ruth on the neighbours which made her laugh. She told him that Bert was gay, so the porn actress gag was not going to stand up anyway. Gavin didn't know what to believe anymore. He didn't care. It didn't matter.

'I did miss him you know,' said Ruth.

'Who?' replied Gavin.

'Father Christmas! Who do you think?'

'Trevor?' Gavin wasn't sure.

'Yes. Trevor.'

'I didn't think you were that close.'

'That's not quite what I said, I don't think.' She thought about it. Gavin let her think about it. 'He wasn't a soul mate. He wasn't much of a lover. He didn't know one end of a hoover from the other. He couldn't cook. He could be a bit of a pratt. He could be a lot of a pratt. And he had that bloody awful train set. But he was there. For a significant part of my life, he was there. And then he wasn't. You miss that. Despite all his faults, he was genuine and kind. Like I said, you remind me of him.'

Gavin reflected on the list she had just read out and wondered where the likeness did and didn't exist. Ruth looked at him. She knew she was teasing him. She had soon come to realise that Gavin was very much can-be-teased material. She saw it as a strength in him.

'He wasn't just someone to have a meal with or watch a film with. We went to places. It feels much better looking at the Leaning Tower of Pisa when you are standing next to someone you know. The Taj Mahal on my own or Battersea Power Station with someone you care about? I'd take the power station every time.'

'Really?' said Gavin, although he hadn't seen either the Taj Mahal or Battersea Power Station. He was beginning to wonder if he had missed out. He noted that Ruth cared about Trevor but did not mention that she had loved him. 'Was Trevor the person you were closest to?' was his way of approaching that thought.

'Not been that close to anyone. I think that's a shadow from my past cast over my life. Different relationships but none of them lasting. Ruta's parents. Yes, I know, my mum and dad. Aunty Aggie. Daisy. Trevor. And some blithering idiot called Gavin.'

The last name shook him. Ruth didn't interrupt the shaking. She let Gavin take that in. He was surprised. They hadn't known each other long. Then he considered that they had, though, got to know each other well. Maybe not a surprise. Gavin thought about the people he was closest to. Ruth would be on that list. This came to him as quite a revelation. He was on her list. And. She was on his list. It made him feel slightly uncomfortable. Up until now, they had just talked. Yes, it had been about themselves and each other, but it had been talk. But it had never been just talk. It had never been just a conversation between two people. They had formed a friendship. There was trust between them. Gavin looked at Ruth and saw a friend.

'What are you staring at?' she said, finally breaking his thoughts.

'You,' he replied. And then he stopped looking because enough was enough.

'You see. I'm right,' she said. 'We have a relationship. And you're a blithering idiot.'

'Never known what blithering means, but I'm not going to argue with you.' He rose. 'Time for me to go.'

'Thought it might be,' she said.

He looked at her.

'You need to walk away like you're coming back. I hope I haven't scared you too much.'

Gavin smiled at her.

'You see at my age, and in this place, you stop caring too much about what you say or who you might upset. You start to enjoy upsetting people. Well, I do. Sort of a hobby. Too late to worry otherwise. Way past being a sport. Never was that good at it anyway. But now you discover how good it is to speak your mind. It's like there are new rules when you pass eighty. It's a great age for discriminating and upsetting people. I'll give you that to look forward to. Mind you, you seem to have started early!' This made Ruth laugh.

Gavin grinned, took his cue, and walked away, trying to walk like he would be coming back, which he decided meant going slower and stretching out his steps. He looked like a blithering idiot. It probably sustained Ruth's laughter.

Gavin drove home. He realised he would rather be stood looking at Battersea Power Station with Ruth than looking at the Taj Mahal on his own.

On the sixth day. Gavin did nothing. He rested. He might have got his days in the wrong order, but he rested. This meant he got up late and took ages over breakfast which morphed into brunch. He didn't shave. He washed at noon, cleaned his teeth at one and got changed at two.

The afternoon was spent sauntering between places to repose. He decided that he had a particular liking for the view from the lounge window. It allowed him to stare out onto the world without making any commitment to anything out there. Then he could relapse into meandering thoughts, weaving different threads in his head. He wondered why none of the neighbours had visited Ruth or even approached him about the possibility of a joint visit. Mick and Daphne were young for a retired couple. They were probably in their fifties so visiting death's waiting room ought not to have had them fretting. Bert had worked with dead bodies, so he ought to have found it refreshing to see them still breathing. And Doreen seemed to have enough about her, mentally and physically, to be assured that she was many more life experiences yet away from ending up in such a place and, when she did, she could hope that there would have been a significant improvement in the presentation of institutional tea and biscuits.

He couldn't work out why Ruth had not had the fountain repaired. The garden looked nice, probably not as good as when Ruth was living there, but in a few days, they had given it an acceptable appearance. He thought about their friendship. He recognised some slight discomfort when this had been brought up but now, away from her, although in her home, it made him feel good. It also made him think about the people that would be on his list. Sharyn and Nap. Was that it? What kind of list was this? Did Cora count? Did the postwoman count? Should he add his mother? Just the thought made him go in search of the rulebook. Thinking of Nap made him wonder if he could get a list of eleven people to play Nap at Subbuteo. They would both struggle to put together teams for a five aside game. He and Nap had a lot in common, Nap just approached it from the same old sofa. This got him thinking about home, his real home, and his real life. And what did he think he was doing? And what was he going to do? Eventually, he had to face the music. And it was sounding more like a death metal band rather than soothing lullabies or something written for gentle flute and ethereal keyboards. And then he thought about Big Ron and that created a whole new picture. It was the fullness of his real life with everything in it, and that included the good and the bad. How good was the good and how bad was the bad? This current situation was a fantasy. At best, it was a vacation from reality or time out from facing reality. He knew he would have to go back. Relationships, work, his home, they had all been abandoned. But sooner or later this had to end.

He went to bed that night granting himself one more day, or maybe two at most, or he could re-evaluate after two days. But no more than three.

On the seventh day. Gavin took Bert to the hospital. He dropped him off at two o'clock. The agreement was that Gavin would be at the Costa Coffee, that every hospital seems to have, at four o'clock. This seemed sensible, as they had worked out that as Bert's appointment was for two, he probably wouldn't get seen until three and would then not be finished until four. If early, Bert could wait with a coffee. If late, Gavin could wait with a coffee. At five o'clock, Gavin was wondering if they shouldn't have made a better plan. It was also a reminder that there were better places for mobile phones other than in the glove compartment of your car (the one you actually own which is parked miles away), down the side of the settee, or in a drawer somewhere. Bert didn't have one. He thought those tall red boxes still contained telephones. He was a man who still valued his Polaroid camera and thought coffee came in bottles. Gavin had a mobile phone but used it once a week and never knew where he had put it last.

Gavin was considering the possibility that Bert had been so efficiently dealt with that he must have finished by three and got a taxi. He would have been home just in time to have stopped Gavin setting out. But Gavin hadn't returned to the bungalow. Gavin had parked up amid some trees in what had seemed to be a forest or woods or conservation area, somewhere green. He had spent the time walking and considering life, death, the price of biscuits, and why, as every year went by, Friends, the television programme, had seemed less and less funny and more and more annoying.

At ten past five Gavin decided to head home to cover the possibility that Bert had invented Plan B and got a taxi and was now either at home watching television or knocking on Gavin's door, sorry, Ruth's door, wondering where he was. At fifteen minutes past five Bert walked along the hospital corridors to find Costa Coffee, grateful that it was all over and eager for his lift home. Consequently, whilst Gavin was checking out Plan B, Bert instigated Plan B. After a reasonably short wait, Bert picked up a taxi and arrived home at six o'clock, which, coincidentally, was the same time that Gavin then arrived back at the hospital. Gavin returned to Costa Coffee full of doubt that Bert would be there. His doubt was justified. Bert was not there. Bert was at home putting the kettle on and making a nice cup of tea. To be fair, Bert had called at Ruth's bungalow to see if Gavin was there and Bert had been concerned that something had gone wrong when no one answered the door. But with no way of contacting Gavin, he did not know what to do. The idea of getting a taxi back to the hospital did cross his mind but he assumed that Gavin would finally give up. By quarter to seven, and feeling restless and jittery from too much coffee and two slices of chocolate cake that was one slice of chocolate cake too many, Gavin did give up. By twenty minutes past seven Gavin was knocking on Bert's door.

By twenty-one minutes past seven Gavin and Bert were having hysterics. There was so much laughter that all the neighbours were soon calling round, and this was past the magic hour of six o'clock when they should all have been truly settled in for the evening doing whatever they all did after the magic hour had come upon them. They didn't stay long but each wanted a share in the story.

Later that evening, finally settled in on his own and with a can of beer in his hand, Gavin was stunned by his reaction to the whole escapade. Old Gavin would have been apoplectic. Bert would have had several pieces of his mind. But this was new Gavin, laughing about it, making light of what ought to have been considered a wasted afternoon, but instead, it was funny. The whole event was funny. He found any consideration of the difference between the two Gavin's bewildering. Bert was a friend, not an antagonist. And this was becoming a most odd and funny old world.

On the eighth day. Gavin offered to take them all out for a meal. This didn't go down well. It was appreciated. It was a kind and generous offer. It was very thoughtful of him. But it would have meant them all leaving the cul-de-sac at the same time and they had never done that before. They had no recollection of ever leaving the place unattended. It didn't seem right. It wasn't what they did. It would also have meant them all sitting around a table together and having to make conversation. This, Gavin learnt, was completely different to gossiping in the garden with tea and cake. They compromised and agreed that Gavin could bake them all a cake. Doreen brought him a recipe book with the correct page turned over at the corner. Daphne brought him all the ingredients and a few extra just in case. In case of what, Gavin was not sure. Bert said that if it wasn't ready by five o'clock, he would be getting a taxi and fetching his own cake. This made Bert laugh. It eventually made Gavin laugh when he finally got it. He needed to laugh. He'd never baked before.

The agreement was that Gavin could not come out of the house until he had baked the cake. The fear was that they would never see him again. Very quickly he was drawn into the world of recipe chaos. Were words such as whisk, beat, and fold, strict terms? Or could they be interpreted loosely? Why a specific order of adding ingredients? How exact did measurements need to be and did anyone really have that amount of patience? What length of time constituted pre-heat? Did forty minutes mean exactly that, or could you give and take a few minutes either side, especially if you needed to visit the bathroom exactly on the fortieth minute? And would this thick mess that he was pouring into the tin look anything like a cake? Were ovens places of magic? Did he need to invoke some incantation? Was there a God of Cake that he needed to pray to?

By the time he had put the mixture into the oven, Gavin had to concede that the kitchen looked to be in a far worse state than it had ever been and he despaired of what cleaning was needed. The only difference was that the various ingredients that had landed across many surfaces and places had just arrived and had not had several months to congeal. Gavin had always thought that once the cake entered the oven the baker could sit back and relax. He calculated that the baking time was probably equal to the cleaning time he would need. They didn't tell you that in the cookery book. Forty minutes of preparation. Forty minutes in the oven. Forty minutes to clean up.

Thankfully, on cooling, the cake did generally loosen from the tin and left behind only mere fragments of itself. It survived the transition from tin to plate, keeping its circular shape reasonably well. A couple of cracks appeared. Gavin assumed that the special powers of icing would sort that out. If not, he was sure Ruth would have some polyfilla somewhere. And what about the icing? This he made. It took about ten minutes trying first a spoon, then a spatula, and finally a knife, before he could get it spread reasonably evenly over the top of the cake. Then he saw the state of the kitchen once again. There was a thin layer of white dust everywhere. He would be cleaning up icing sugar for the rest of his life. Gavin was stunned by how something so minor could have such a major impact on its surroundings. It was like it had been snowing. All he was missing was Father Christmas and a snowman.

But finally, he had a cake. It looked like a cake. It smelt like a cake. So…

The testing was put to his neighbours. Gavin walked out of the house carrying the evidence across the front garden as if he was Salome presenting the head of John the Baptist.

'Do we need to dig a grave?' asked Mick sarcastically and appearing once again from behind the rhododendron bush.

They were soon joined by Daphne and Bert who wasn't going to miss out. Doreen turned up with a pot of loose-leaf tea as if she was giving the occasion special status. Gavin had to believe that they had all been in a state of high alert, ready for his grand entrance.

'Chocolate cake à la Gavin,' he announced. He was proud of his creation. The true test would be in the tasting, but for now, he could be pleased with what, on the plate, was claiming to be a chocolate cake. It looked the part. He had achieved that much.

'A knife?' asked Daphne.

'So he can commit suicide when we've all died of cake poisoning?' questioned Mick. It got a look from Daphne and a laugh from Bert.

'Ah yes,' replied Gavin and returned to the house, coming back out with what was probably a bread knife but better than some of the other implements in, what could loosely be called, the knife drawer. It could have been called the large spoon drawer or the there's nowhere else to put it drawer.

'Plates?' asked Doreen.

'Oh' responded Gavin and repeated the same journey, returning with five plates this time.

'Serviettes?' asked Bert.

Were they taking the proverbial, wondered Gavin. He looked at them. They laughed. They were taking the proverbial.

'Are you cutting or shall I?' asked Doreen.

'I'll let you,' replied Gavin.

The cake was cut and shared out. No one was sufficiently concerned to ask for only a small piece. No one died. No one started rolling around clutching their stomach and beseeching some lesser god to release them from excruciating pain. Everyone agreed it wasn't a bad first effort. Mick and Gavin had seconds.

Gavin went to bed that night with a real feeling of satisfaction and a potential case of indigestion. Once back in the house, he'd had a self-congratulatory third slice.

On the ninth day. Everything changed.

Chapter 29

On the ninth day. Gavin hadn't slept so well. He'd had a chocolate cake induced nightmare about being chased down streets, which he knew in the dream, but that he didn't know outside the dream. He didn't know who was chasing him, but he ended up hiding in a barn with a woman who was and wasn't his mother. And then the dream ended and Mick popped out of the bedroom wardrobe. This turned out to still be the dream. When he did awaken, it was with such regard for the bedroom wardrobe that he had to get up at once and check for any hidden Micks. He opened it and looked inside. There were none.

That morning he had felt the need to visit Ruth. Maybe his time was up. There were no crossroads. Realistically there was no choice. Eventually, he had to get back into the real world: his real world. He couldn't keep putting it off. He had to go back. There were people that mattered, perhaps even more now. His job mattered, if he still had one. They always needed social workers, especially in child protection. On second thoughts he would have to get down on his hands and knees and beg. He wanted his old job. And possibly he needed to reconnect with his mother. Not something he was comfortable with. And could Big Ron strangle two people in separate rooms at the same time? Were his hands really that big? Surely not. Then again, Gavin was only one person and more a stick than a trunk. He would snap. But somehow, he had to say hello to who he really was and where in the world that put him. Some questions needed addressing. Ruth would have the answers. He needed to visit her. He had walked out last time as if he was coming back. He needed to go back.

He drove to the care home more aware than ever that he was still driving Nap's car. Nap, whom he hadn't seen for quite a while and whose car he had just about stolen. He saw Nap often enough for quite a while to be too long. It just added to how he was now looking at things.

On arrival, the best wishes of Mick, Daphne, Bert, and Doreen were passed on. Ruth smiled. Gavin smiled.

'What have they been up to now?' asked Ruth.

'Well. Bert and Doreen have run off together. It turns out that Doreen was a porn actress in a previous life. He recognised her from a film he had just watched. Mick and Daphne have bought their houses off them and set up a home for Yemeni asylum seekers And Puddles has opened her own parlour.'

'Ah yes, Puddles. Nothing would surprise me.'

'Oh,' replied Gavin, in a manner that did not match the humour in their conversation. His face could no longer hide the thoughts he had been having.

'You look troubled,' said Ruth. 'More so than usual.'

'I just don't know what to do,' said Gavin. 'I've run away and found a life that I quite like.'

'Quite like?' questioned Ruth.

'Okay. Like a lot. But I have to go back, don't I?'

Ruth allowed the silence to make further enquiries for her.

'I miss Sharyn. The only real friend I've got is Nap. I miss him. I think I might miss my job. But I've messed up there. God knows what they now think of me. Everyone. Probably be best if Big Ron did make a balloon animal out of me.'

Ruth kept the silence going, although she had been tempted to ask which balloon animal he would prefer.

'I probably ought to go back and see my mother.' He held the thought too long. 'Probably.'

The silence had a smoky tinge. Ruth broke it. 'Have both worlds. Add them together. You can still borrow the bungalow. My niece will get it when I die. But until then you can live there or use it as a holiday home or in whatever way you want. I can put something in writing if that helps. My niece will get it so don't worry about keeping it perfect.'

'Your niece?'

'Trevor's brother's daughter. She lives somewhere in Sidmouth. Don't see her. Never really liked her. Trevor didn't leave much, and I'd agreed when he let me have the house that it would go to his family when I died. She'll get it. She'll sell it. Then she'll forget all about me. Would much rather it went to some charity, but I promised Trevor.' There was a sour look on Ruth's face. 'Della.' It was spoken with a loathing that Gavin had not previously associated with Ruth.

Gavin looked confused.

'Her name. My niece is called Della.' Ruth returned to her previous suggestion. 'Have both worlds.'

'So. Bring both worlds together. The opposite of what you did?'

'I didn't say I was right. That was my way of coping. I had to move on. You don't. Your past is still there. Not the past and not another country. You can combine both worlds. I had no choice.'

There was now a distinct smell of burning. It interrupted the conversation.

'That doesn't seem right,' said Gavin.

'Nothing coming out of the kitchen normally smells that bad,' added Ruth.

The alarms rang out.

Gavin carefully but purposefully opened the door. The smell was stronger. Staff were running around. No one seemed to know what to do. 'In the kitchen!' someone shouted.

'What?' shouted Gavin quickly.

'Fire in the kitchen.'

'What do we need to do?' asked Gavin, looking for something precise.

'Get everyone out.'

Gavin could see that the staff didn't seem to know what to do. They were either not well-rehearsed or were panicking about a real situation. This wasn't the occasional Wednesday two o'clock alarm practice.

'We're moving the walkers.'

'What about those that can't walk?' asked Gavin. He was not the only one coughing.

The same woman looked at him.

'Get them into wheelchairs,' shouted Gavin. 'I don't know how to do that. Get them into wheelchairs and then I'll wheel them out.'

'In here then,' said the woman.

Gavin followed her into the room. The resident was sat in her riser chair. There was a rotunda. The carer transferred the woman from the chair to the rotunda and then into the wheelchair. Gavin swiftly took the wheelchair and wheeled the woman out through the corridor, through the main doors, and out into a far part of the car park where others were gathered. He went back into the building.

Another woman shouted to him. 'Down here.' He ran and wheeled another resident out, taking the same route. He was back again, and wheeling someone else to safety. He was coughing through the smoke which now was everywhere. He came back in for a fourth person. On wheeling this person out, he was met by a firefighter coming into the home. An ambulance had now arrived and was taking someone on board. A second ambulance could be heard.

Gavin turned to go back in but was stopped by a member of staff. 'No,' she shouted at him. 'Two left. Firefighters are getting them.'

'You sure?' Gavin replied. He wanted to go back in to be certain. He couldn't stop.

'No,' she repeated. She meant it.

Gavin stopped. 'Ruth!' he said aloud.

Gavin couldn't see Ruth anywhere in the car park. 'Anyone know where Ruth is?' He was asking them all. Residents and carers looked stunned. They were all coughing. Gavin was coughing. They all smelt of burning smoke. 'Ruth?' he asked again.

'In the ambulance,' said a woman. She was one of the carers. There were now three ambulances, one leaving, one operating stationary and one just arriving. It soon became clear to Gavin that Ruth must have been in the ambulance that had gone. He felt sick. It was the smoke he had inhaled, and it was the worry about what might have happened to Ruth. It was a situation where no one looked good. Just some were worse than others. He would have to find out what had happened to Ruth. But he was coughing and exhausted and not feeling good. Gavin sat down. He needed air. He could not tell any more what was happening. Another ambulance probably arrived. Someone took him by the arm. He just gave way.

Gavin wasn't sure if he had passed out or switched off, but he had a sense of coming round. He was still struggling to breathe, but the air around him seemed to be better. The emergency services had taken charge. Everyone seemed to be getting some form of attention. Gavin was reassured to see that some sort of order had been resumed. He switched off. He didn't pass out. He sat there. He cried. Tears rolled down his cheeks. This was the moment when it had all become too much. He cried for Ruth. He cried for Sharyn. He cried because his life had been a mess. He cried because there had been good times. He cried because Nap never went out. He cried for the broken fountain. He cried because he'd never seen the Taj Mahal or Battersea Power Station. He cried because the world was shit. He cried because the world was good. He cried for all the children in foster care. He cried for world peace. He cried for the state of the world. He cried for the state he was in. And he cried for his mother.

'You okay?' a friendly voice asked. She was a paramedic.

'I will be,' he answered. 'I will be.'

'You okay?' another friendly voice asked. It was Linda. 'They called me in. What a mess.' She smiled at Gavin. 'Do you want to come with me?' she asked.

He looked at her.

'I'm going to the hospital. I can drive you there. They've taken several residents. I need to find out what's happening. Including Ruth.'

'Yes please,' replied Gavin.

Linda helped Gavin up. He could walk. He was still coughing but he felt better. It was a slow careful walk to Linda's car.

'I felt like this the first time I went running,' he said, as they got in the car.

'Surprised you carried on,' she replied. 'I thought exercise was supposed to be good for you.'

There was silence for most of the journey. Gavin had worn himself out and Linda was astute enough to see this and to know that he needed to switch off. She switched on the stereo. It was Earth Wind and Fire. 'Sorry,' she said.

'No problem,' he replied. 'Rather appropriate.'

Gavin drifted. It was the car passenger's repose, neither asleep nor awake. He felt peaceful. He found himself revisiting his dream and back in the barn with his mother. He wondered what they would talk about. He wondered why it was a barn. He found he didn't care. He listened to the music. His thoughts were wandering. He was back in the smoke, reliving his bravery, but this time from the safety of a car seat. He felt proud. He had done something. What should he be afraid of? This brought back thoughts of Big Ron. Where had Big Ron been when he was needed? Little Ron, more like. Big Gavin. But he was too fatigued to be big anything. And Big Ron had big hands. Big enough to push two wheelchairs. He was back in the smoke. He didn't even know if he had wheeled Ruth out. The whole thing was one big, blurred image of pushing elderly people about and being praised for it. He drifted off…

'We're here,' a voice said. Time had performed its hypnotic trance on the weary traveller.

Gavin came round. He apologised for his lack of conversation and was forgiven. Of course he was. Linda made him feel easy. Even when he was sleeping in wardrobes, she had a smile on her face.

Once in the hospital, Linda left him in Costa Coffee. Gavin made a note not to overdo it on the chocolate cake this time. Although it was a different hospital and a different time, and irrelevant in so many other ways, Gavin still found himself looking out for Bert.

Bert wasn't two elderly ladies that came by. He wasn't a man in a wheelchair. He wasn't the person that looked like she was probably a doctor or some consultant. He wasn't the young man pushing the wheelchair whose occupant seemed to be well covered up. Maybe there was no person. Perhaps it was a bomb. Was there going to be another fire? There was one chap that reminded Gavin of Bert, and then the chap turned around and he looked nothing like him and probably several decades younger. There seemed to be different coloured uniforms for different jobs. It was hard to tell the hospital staff from the patients. Sometimes it wasn't. Sometimes an authoritative gait beat a slow lost walk. Other times it was a sense of purpose against enquiring looks. Those that worked here and those that were just visiting, or maybe staying a while. He decided it didn't matter. And none of them was Bert. It was life passing by and he was enjoying watching it.

'They're keeping her in.' It was Linda. She hadn't been that long. Although time had become negated over these past minutes or hours or however long it had been. 'She's asleep. I'm not sure how concerned they are. I think you'd be better off coming back tomorrow. Probably better for both of you. Don't like to say it but you need a bath and a good tidy up.'

Gavin had been getting one or two strange looks and it wasn't because of how he was drinking his coffee.

'I'm staying, but I've enough time to give you a lift back.'

'No. I can get a taxi. I appreciate what you've done already.'

'What I've done. I appreciate what you've done. A real hero. I'm giving you a lift.'

She was too forthright for him to disagree. The best he could offer was, 'Are you sure?'

'Have you seen the state you're in? No taxi's going to take you.' She was right. Gavin looked like he needed to arrive at a hospital, not leave one.

Linda dropped Gavin off back at the care home. He decided that he would go back to his house. The journey to the bungalow was too far and he no longer cared about any risk to his life. He'd just done that and got the T-shirt. He left Nap's car where it was and walked home. He knew it well from all that running. It was just some time since he had done it.

Gavin trudged. If he'd had a tail it would have been between his legs. He felt like he looked. He looked terrible. His hair gave the impression that it was trying to escape from his head, different clumps trying to depart in different directions. His face must have lost a fight against a rabid gang of chimney sweeps. His clothes would have shamed any skip. He didn't care. It didn't matter. Not much, anyway. He was heading home.

Chapter 30

Gavin stood at the top of his street. It might have been the bottom of the street, but he was looking down so that gave him the feeling that he was at the top of the street. House numbers one and two on either side also confirmed the status of his position. He was on the road. It wasn't a busy street. On the road he stopped, slightly nearer to number one than number two. Number one was called 'Apple Blossom'. Number two didn't have a name. The things you noticed when life was presenting you with a different perspective. He'd never noticed any apple blossom on the street or approaching the street. Might as well have called it the Taj Mahal, he thought. Then he remembered the conversation with Ruth. He realised that it didn't matter.

He looked down to where his house was. He didn't move. Once he reached the house he would be returning to that world. For now, he just wanted to stand apart from it. He wanted to see his world before he stepped back into it. This was a safe distance. No one knew him at this end of the street. Here he was a stranger. Then again, he realised, he was a stranger all the way down the street. Was that due to him? Were they having secret parties without him? Was he the subject of drunken conversations? Or were all the people on the street strangers to each other? Was that how people lived now? Modern life: house to car, to work, to car, to house. Where did walking, talking, and socialising come into it? And when he did leave the house without his car, he was running. Running past houses. Running past people. Avoiding getting to know anyone. He thought about Mick and Daphne, Bert, and Doreen. How different that had been. How much he had enjoyed their company. They were different to him. He might not have sought any of them out in a group. He probably had the potential to fall out with each of them. But he didn't. He had only known them for a week. But give him a year and he knew that he would not fall out with them. It was sad to be standing here and not on the cul-de-sac, but here was his home. This was the world he needed to return to.

He could smell the smoke on his clothes and in his hair. He liked it. That wasn't how people should smell. Cologne, perfume, a splash of something, but not smoke. And he had the appearance to match. He felt different. And he liked the difference. It gave him status. It was the look and smell of a man who had done something. He had never been a man who had done something. And he hadn't done much to get this current manifestation, but here he was, the result of being a different Gavin for just a few minutes. And then in the aftermath, in the time after the fire and the rescue, he had carried on feeling different. And yes, he would be getting a shower and a change of clothes and possibly clearing away new Gavin and going back to being old Gavin. But for these moments he wanted to stay here in the guise of new Gavin. He liked the smell of burnt residential home aftershave.

Eventually, he would have to face Big Ron. Let those hands do their worst. Perhaps he'd end up in the same hospital as Ruth. Could he ask for adjoining beds? Did they do mixed wards? Hopefully, she'd be out soon anyway. But he had to stop running away. He would have to face Sharyn. The longer it took the worse that reunion would be. And, as understanding as she could be, she also had the knack of finding him out eventually. She had an overwhelming ability to reference disappointment in such a way that that one word had the power of a string of expletives. Not even the raised voices of

Satan's choral ensemble or a belter of a sermon could match that one-word killer. And she was no mean sermon teller. It was the complete character assassination that comes with how she tells you that you have disappointed her. He would need to return Nap's car. Whatever problems that might have the potential to cause, he reckoned that could be put right with a game of Subbuteo. Their disagreements didn't go any deeper than what could be sorted out by twenty-two buoyant plastic figures kicking an oversized football around on a green velvet cloth. If he still had a job, then he would have to face up to work. Sally Clark would be beyond any hope for him. As for the others, he had spotted the extraordinary powers of cake when it comes to overcoming professional conflict amongst work peers. Cream cakes in extreme circumstances. Or a good moist over-iced chocolate cake. He would return with both.

But, above all this, he had to face himself. It was like going to university and pretending to be someone else and then having to go home in the breaks to family and friends who had no idea what it had been like to have been God's gift to the social scene and the person most likely to go to lectures in a purple onesie. It was like going on holiday, eating, drinking and damning the real world and then you have to come home and the real world is waiting for you: dead-end job, a freezer that keeps switching itself off, and the return to the neighbours from hell with the washing that never comes off the line. And he was going back to face his real world. There was nothing he was looking forward to. It wasn't that it was negative. He hadn't missed his home or anything in it, but that wasn't the house's fault. He couldn't blame the television or the fridge. He hadn't missed work. But he couldn't blame his foster carers or his work colleagues for that. He hadn't missed his friends but that wasn't down to them. Nor was it about the relationship he had with them: all two of them, when he thought about it. Nap was Nap and Sharyn was Sharyn, but unfortunately, Gavin was Gavin, and that was what he was going to have to face. He couldn't ask for anything different from Nap. He couldn't ask for anything more from Sharyn. He would have to ask it of himself. He had put his life on hold and found it to be a better place. But that was a holding bay. You can't live in a holding bay.

The top of the street was the edge of that bay and he needed to move. He could do it, house by house, brick by brick if needs be, nearer and nearer. Each movement forward would be the coming together of two lives: the one he had been enjoying for these past days and the one that just went round and round and round.

He moved. It was one step. It lacked conviction. And then his attention was drawn to figures who had come out onto the street. They were leaving a house and it was suspiciously near to his. He could make out four of them. He needed to get nearer to see if he could identify anyone. And he could. And he felt like running. He felt like running away and he felt like running to her. He didn't need to recognise her face or her shape. He could tell Sharyn straight away by her body movement and her stance. What was she doing there? Which then seemed like a daft question considering the questions people must have been asking about him. He assumed they had been. He found himself hoping they had been. It was Sharyn and now another figure who looked like Cora from work which really did unsettle him. The other two he couldn't recognise. He was close enough for it to be too late to turn back.

The four figures had been talking on leaving the house. The only person facing up the street was PC Mike Call Me Mike, so he had no idea about the significance of the person coming toward them, although he had been alerted by the way he was walking diagonally across the pavement and how his pace seemed to constantly alter. He was probably drunk. And if not, then maybe he had mental health problems and once more PC Mike Call Me Mike was thrust into that world of prejudgements and the things that he could never work out what you were allowed to think or say. Or could you think one thing and say another. He hoped the man was drunk. It would be easier.

Gavin came near enough to be noticed by them all. They could smell him too.

'What?' started Sharyn.

Gavin gave Sharyn a big hug.

She hugged him back. She meant it. 'I might be hugging you,' she whispered in his ear, 'but you are in so much trouble, and we need to talk.'

'I know,' he whispered back.

'You smell,' she said.

'I know,' he replied.

'Am I to assume…' started PC Mike Call Me Mike.

'Yes,' replied Sharyn, as she let go of Gavin and gasped for fresh air.

'And the smell?' enquired PC Mike Call Me Mike.

'It's a long story,' replied Gavin.

'It certainly is,' said Sharyn.

Cora smiled at him.

'What are you doing here?' Gavin asked Cora, although it could equally be addressed to all of them.

Sharyn stepped in to answer the question. 'We're all here because we've been concerned about you.' She turned to each of them as she introduced them. 'This is Jake: your neighbour.'

'Oh yes,' replied Gavin. He tried hard to recognise Jake. He couldn't match him with any house on the street.

'This is…' and she paused. 'This is Mike: a police officer.'

'Really,' replied Gavin.

'Oh yes,' said Sharyn. 'Really. You've been missing.'

'Yes, I suppose I have.'

'And Cora you know.'

'Unexpected though,' said Gavin, in response to each of them and all of them.

'Not as unexpected as you going missing,' replied Sharyn. 'Where have you…' and she paused. 'No. You can answer that later.'

Gavin had probably hoped that he could have returned to his real world slowly. Get home. Say hello to the furniture. Clean himself up. Then decide over the rest of the day and night and even the next morning, if he needed it, how to make contact with people again. He had not expected a waiting committee.

It was PC Mike Call Me Mike who then spotted two more characters coming down the street. Little and Large, he thought to himself. He didn't fancy tackling either of them. But they seemed to be heading for this gathering that they had now created.

And then Gavin spotted them. One small but wide and one tall and decidedly big. The small man he soon recognised as Satnav or should he now call him Jacob. The tall man he assumed must be Big Ron. He had still hoped that Big Ron would turn out to be one of those names applied in humour to someone who was small. This was clearly not the case. Then again, whether he was big or small, it was probably only down to a choice of having either your nose or your ankles reassembled. Up until now he had heard about Big Ron, he had experienced Big Ron pounding his front door, and he had overheard him talking. None of it had prepared him for the size of the man as he came upon them all.

'That's him,' announced Jacob, reluctantly. The hold Big Ron had over him was clear. He had pointed at Gavin. Gavin wondered what the point of the last eleven days had been, only to be got now. He just assumed that present company might prevent anything too horrific happening. There was a policeman. And surely Sharyn could call on divine intervention. There were too many witnesses for a beating.

Big Ron came up to Gavin and enveloped him in his huge arms. Gavin found himself waiting for the big hands to strangle him or a dagger to be thrust into his back. What did Big Ron care about an audience. He could feel the man's chest pressing against his own feeble effort. It was like a takeover. He was like a slice of thin cheese in a Big Ron sandwich. Maybe Big Ron was going to squeeze the life out of him. There seemed to be so many ways for this to end unfavourably. And then Big Ron kissed him on the top of his head. It was unexpected and bizarrely frightening.

'I 'erd what you done. She'd a been dead meat.' This Big Ron said as he let Gavin go. He felt like a stress ball trying to reform. And he had a wet head.

Gavin wasn't sure if he'd said meat or mate. And he'd been kissed on the top of his head. 'Done what?' Gavin asked carefully. He sensed that everything with Big Ron needed to be careful. And his body was still trying to find its original shape.

'Big Ron,' said Jacob. His eyes signalled to the left.

'So I gather,' replied Gavin. He wouldn't forget the voice and he had the build to match. And he'd nearly been crushed.

'He's forgiven you,' said Jacob.

'Oh good,' replied Gavin.

'I 'erd what you done,' reasserted Big Ron. 'As probable saved 'er life.'

'As probable,' repeated Jacob.

Gavin was still not sure and he didn't think that Jacob was going to enlighten him further.

'You smell of smoke you do,' said Big Ron. He nodded his head as if to confirm that he was right. Then he grabbed Gavin and kissed him on the top of his head again. Big Ron let go and breathed in as he did so, taking in the fumes as if this was some sort of ceremonial connection with Gavin.

'Smoke,' repeated Jacob.

By now the others had just about come to terms with the realisation that the Earth was spinning slightly differently and they had found a way to stop falling off. PC Mike Call Me Mike was relieved that nothing had kicked off and was readying himself for leaving. Cora recognised that she had been witness to enough already. Jake was happy to hang around and, if he had to go, then he was near enough to keep an eye on proceedings from his front room window. Sharyn felt the need to seek some clarification. The last eleven days could wait a little while. The last few seconds she wanted to understand better.

'Can someone explain to me what you are talking about?' she asked, and switched eye contact between Gavin and Big Ron.

Despite having their reasons, the question meant that no one left.

Gavin looked at Big Ron. Only Big Ron knew what he was talking about. Jacob seemed to be no more than an attachment. Gavin could speak up, but Big Ron had the story. It wasn't clear how well he could tell it though.

Big Ron wasn't one to stand on ceremony. 'You saved my mother. They told me. You got her outta that fire.' And Big Ron gave Gavin another bone crunching hug. Gavin felt himself implode. It was the sort of squeeze that only a cartoon character would normally survive. Big Ron didn't kiss him on the top of his head this time.

'He likes you,' said Jacob.

'You went in that fire and got her out,' said Big Ron, as he allowed Gavin to breathe again. 'Big time mate, big time. What you done.'

'Big time,' repeated Jacob, with all the understanding of an echo.

Sharyn looked at Gavin for an explanation. So did everyone else, but with less exigency. Although they were still hanging around, which gave its own sense of expectation.

'It was nothing,' started Gavin. 'I was at the home. There was a fire.'

They all nodded at this point due to the connection between how Gavin looked and smelt and what he was saying. He'd brought the evidence with him.

Gavin continued: 'I helped get some of the people out. Pushed them outside. Several people, but I don't know who they were. One was your mother, I guess.' Gavin addressed Big Ron.

Big Ron replied with a heavy nod. It provoked a less weighty nod from Jacob. Indeed, everyone else seemed to follow suit with diminishing nods.

'I'll 'ave that fixed for ya.' Big Ron pointed at the front door.

'It's fine,' replied Gavin.

'I'll 'ave it fixed,' repeated Big Ron.

Jacob smiled.

'You can 'ave a different colour if you want it.'

'Any colour,' added Jacob.

Big Ron looked at Jacob. It was a reminder that Jacob was safer repeating what Big Ron had to say rather than suddenly going off with words of his own choosing.

'The colour it is now is fine,' said Gavin. In truth he had returned to a front door that did not mean a great deal to him.

'I'll sort it,' said Big Ron. The statement was not to be challenged.

'He'll...' started Jacob, and then decided the safer option was to curtail adding anything.

Big Ron left, but not without giving Gavin his final bear hug. Jacob followed with a big smile on his face. This was a good day. Not every day was a good day. Most days weren't. But for Jacob, this was a good day.

'I think I'm going to go now,' said Cora.

'Me too,' said PC Mike Call Me Mike.

Cora and PC Mike Call Me Mike left.

It left Jake realising that his own little street soap opera was over for now. Well, this episode at least. There was no point waiting for the music or credits to start rolling. 'Yes. I guess I should go now,' he said with some reluctance. And so he did, slowly. It was as if he was waiting for something else to happen or an invitation to take place.

Gavin watched to see which house Jake disappeared into and made a note that that was Jake and that was where he lived. He'd try and remember.

They were still at the front door. Sharyn unlocked the door and invited Gavin into his own home.

Gavin was pleased to go inside. It didn't feel like home. It did feel safe, or safer than it had done. It was the destination at the end of a drifting and sprawling journey. But it no longer felt quite like a home. It was a house he knew well. He could tell you where everything was and how everything worked. But none of it had he missed, other than it was the place he owned, the place he lived. It was somewhere to come back to. He was pleased to be here. He was ready to be here. But as he looked around, there was nothing he wanted to reconnect with or nothing that he couldn't do without. He was in the lounge, but he had no desire to rush into the kitchen or check on his bedroom. If he went to the bathroom, it would be because he needed to go to the bathroom. The sink was just a sink. The toilet was just a toilet. The bed was just a bed. They could all wait to offer him any welcome home.

'So where have you been?' Sharyn asked. It was put to him like the main question in a seated exam.

In less than an hour, Gavin told her everything. By the end, Sharyn knew Gavin better than she ever had. And by virtue of how he told the story and how she had listened, Gavin too felt that he knew Sharyn better than he ever had. But the greatest revelation was that Gavin found that he knew himself better than he ever had.

It didn't help him get to sleep. Sharyn had left with him promising that it wouldn't be another eleven days before she saw him again. And he had gone to bed with a head full of the lives of two people. When he had finally found sleep, he awoke in the night, only to be disorientated by the unfamiliarity of his own bedroom. Then he found a deeper sleep and let the world go by without him.

Chapter 31

Gavin awoke to a new day. He had not had a bath or shower before going to bed. He had just given in to the way it had all eventually caught up with him, which needed little effort and no consideration of anyone else. But this was a new day.

He showered, which he always preferred, but was, as ever, a challenge due to the lack of expense he had spent on his shower. Indeed, the entire bathroom would have been better suited to the outside of the house, waiting to be collected for the junkyard. He dressed. He chose clothes that were smart but casual. It was a decision that gave him little choice. There would be no fashion show taking place from the contents of his wardrobe. He went downstairs for breakfast. Tea with milk, kindly left by Sharyn, and just enough left over to wet a bowl of cereal. He went through and sat down in the lounge.

There was some post on the small coffee table. Sharyn must have put it there. He didn't go over and examine what it was. He knew there would be nothing important. Eleven days, he thought to himself, and it's a pile about two centimetres high. That told him something. Then he noticed a sheet of paper that had been posted through the letterbox, probably overnight. It certainly hadn't been there last night. He put down his breakfast and went over to see what it was. He picked it up and, turning it over, there were written the words 'Wet Paint'.

Gavin opened the door and smiled to himself as he did so. He could smell the paint. He could see that the door had been painted and, in places, sanded too. They'd done a decent job, Big Ron, or whoever he had got to do it. And the note had been prepared in advance. It was in felt pen rather than paint and too neat to have been an afterthought. Was the man who could strangle two people in different rooms at the same time and who had also proclaimed him as dead, meat or mate, also, a thoughtful soul? People really did defy stereotyping, pigeonholing, or having some cumbersome label attached to their forehead.

Gavin closed the door and sat back down with the remains of his breakfast. He thought about his mother. Now there was a person for whom the adjectives kept changing. He couldn't abandon the negative ones, but he was unsettled by the intrusion of one or two not quite so bad ways of describing his mother. Images and thoughts of that last visit came back to him. Had she been different this time, or was it just that they had spent more time together than either of them might previously have thought healthy? It's hard when you've defined a relationship to suddenly see it sprout different wings and threaten to fly where it had never flown before. And when that relationship is with your own mother... Gavin stopped there. This was a new day and demanded new thinking and a bit of a plan. The sort of plan, he thought, that could be written up on flipchart. And by some strange coincidence, did he not have such a thing propped up against the fireplace. Cora would probably report him for stealing it. No she wouldn't, he then thought.

He read aloud the word TOMORROW, although it had been crossed out and replaced with TOMATO. Then he took that sheet down and on the one behind wrote TODAY at the top. He printed the letters clearly so there was no doubt about the word. And so, a list was written up: Ruth, Nap, Work, Sharyn. He needed to go to the hospital first to find out what was happening with Ruth. He needed to visit Nap to return his car and offer his apologies. He must contact work to find out if he'd still got a job and if he had, to start doing some real strength based social work. And he needed to spend some proper time with Sharyn, with her daughters and, if he must, if he really must, then also with the likes of the Waltons. But first Ruth.

Gavin arrived at the hospital, this time looking more like a visitor than something deposited out of the back of an ambulance. He'd gone there in his own car. It had started first time. He would have phoned either the care home or the hospital for an update first, but his mobile phone, which rather surprisingly he had discovered in the kitchen, was unsurprisingly flat.

He tried to return the way he had come the previous day, tracing his footsteps, but this was a hospital and designed so that everywhere looked the same. Doors were all over the place. Lifts weren't where he thought they were. Some doors hid lifts. Some doors hid other doors. Some doors were locked. Some doors turned out to be windows. And one door turned out to be a full-size picture of a door with a view of some faraway place where everyone probably wished they could be. Signs meant nothing. They were either pointless numbers such as Ward 31, or words that could never fit on a scrabble board. Having once found himself back where he'd started, he then found himself nearly back there again when a voice shouted to him from what he discovered was the Costa Coffee where he had been waiting the previous day.

'Can I get you a coffee?' Linda asked.

'I'll get it,' replied Gavin. 'Do you want another one?'

'I'm fine.'

Gavin returned with his coffee to sit with Linda. 'Have you been here all night?' he asked.

'Not quite. Managed to get a few hours' sleep at home but otherwise been here. Waiting.'

'That's hospitals for you. Waiting places. That's why this place probably does so well.' Gavin acknowledged their surroundings.

'You've come to see Ruth?'

'Yes. And to find out how she is.' Gavin looked at Linda. She was the obvious person to have that information.

Linda looked at Gavin. She knew she was the one to update him. 'Not good.' She stopped to assess Gavin's reaction. He waited. 'She never said anything to us, but I don't think she was that well anyway. Not unusual, of course. Or she may not have known what was wrong with her. Or she just didn't want to know. I've seen it. You get to a stage in life where you are fighting so many things that there is no point being told anything else. You're unlikely to survive major surgery so why waste time trying to get a diagnosis. You know you're not well. I think she knows and for her that is enough. Spare her the details. Carry on doing what you can do and don't worry about what you can't do.'

'And the fire?' Gavin wasn't sure what to say. He was taking it in, as best he could.

'She inhaled a lot of smoke. Something else to add to her list of ailments.'

'How bad?'

'They've got her on breathing equipment. There's damage to her throat from the smoke.'

'Will they let me see her?'

'Finish your coffee and I'll take you.'

'I'm finished.' He wasn't, but his coffee had started to taste too bitter and he needed to see Ruth to match words with presentation. He followed Linda. She seemed to go the way he thought he'd been. 'And the others?' he asked as they walked.

'Ready to return as soon as it is safe, or somewhere else can be found.'

'How easy will that be?'

'Down to who is responsible for money and insurance. Those sort of things. All above my paygrade.'

They took a left turn that Gavin was sure he had taken. 'Ruth is the worst.'

They took a right turn and through some double doors before arriving at Ward 31. It looked familiar to Gavin. Linda pressed the button, spoke to someone, and they were let it.

Ruth was asleep, or this was what Gavin assumed. She was not conscious. Linda left him on his own. She found a side room for visitors and waited. Ruth looked peaceful and comfortable except for a tube down her throat which was attached to a plastic array of leads and a montage of gadgets that looked like an old stacked stereo system. It made Gavin nervous and fearful that any movement in the wrong direction would have it all coming down, and it would be far worse than a vinyl LP being scored and repeating the same scratched mantra. He felt he ought to say something. That, and stay still. Staying still made it harder for him to speak. It all felt very stiff when really he wanted to be up close and personal. He was also self-conscious of anyone who might be listening or could walk by and catch an odd word or two, and in this situation all he could think of were odd words. Shouting odd words at a sleeping pensioner felt as awkward as a parent watching Peppa Pig and eating a bacon sandwich. He risked getting in a little nearer. He tried to be thinner and smaller. He moved forward, inch by inch, trying to calculate what was the nearest he could hope to be without being discovered underneath a pile of fallen hospital appliances. Then he crouched, neither up nor down. He couldn't have been more uncomfortable had he been trying to lay an egg. And he was well positioned to do so.

'Why don't you sit over there?' said a passing nurse. 'It would be a lot safer for everyone.' She pointed at a chair on the other side of the bed which Gavin had completely overlooked. Her voice and manner reminded him of Ruth. He had to look at her just to check. And then at Ruth. He had been so focused on the relationship between Ruth and the hospital paraphernalia to see the obvious solution. He carefully reversed back through the obstacle course and stood relieved that everything was still where it had been. Nothing had started beeping or stopped beeping or changed to an alarming different beep. He went to the chair.

'You probably missed all that,' he said to Ruth.

'You're a blithering fool,' she would have said.

'I know.'

'So, what have you been up to?'

'I've been home. My house. Back to my house. There was a welcome party. Sharyn. Cora from work. Not sure why she was there. A police officer. You'd think they have better things to do. And a neighbour. Slight over-reaction if you ask me.'

'Shows people care.'

'I know. When I think about it, I was probably quite flattered. And only one of them was being paid to be there. Cora too, maybe, I suppose. Sharyn gets paid too, but yes, you're right, she was there because she cares about me. She cares about everyone. But perhaps especially me. Well, Anna and Maria most of all, but I don't mind being third. Still on the rostrum. Bronze medal. Can't believe Cora was there. That was nice. Not sure if she was there out of choice or on behalf of work. Yes. I suppose it doesn't really matter. I was worth some time. Somebody else's time.'

'So why did you go home?'

'Yes. Why did I go home? I think it was the fire. How are you by the way. I mean you look peaceful, but it can't be good having that tube down your throat. I hope you can hear me. I hope you're okay.

'You went home?'

'Yes I did. I went home. After the fire I thought, what the hell. Face the music. You know, when you've been in the thick of it you come out less worried about being in the thick of it again. Once you get wet you don't worry about getting wet.

289

Once you get muddy you don't worry about getting muddy. Suddenly I didn't really care about getting beaten up by Big Ron. No. That's wrong. I did care, but it mattered a lot less. And eventually I had to go home, didn't I? So, I did. And there they were waiting for me. And you'll never guess what happened then.' Gavin stopped and looked at Ruth.

'Go on then.'

'Anyway. Stop interrupting me.' And Gavin laughed. 'Wish you could interrupt me. Hope you can hear. Otherwise, who am I talking to? Myself? So, before I had even got inside the house, Big Ron turned up. I know. Seems he was determined. But he hugged me and kissed me. Can you imagine. Seems one of the people I helped get out of the home was his mother. Now we're best buddies. Not sure that's exactly good news but better than getting beaten up. All got me thinking really. Life? What's it all about Ruthy? Do you see what I did there? Can't believe what's happened over these past few days. And now I've got to make it up with Nap, work and especially Sharyn. Where do I start? You can't tell me. You wouldn't anyway. You'd leave me to work that one out. So, I don't need you after all.'

Gavin looked at Ruth. Still and peaceful. 'Anyway. Get better,' he said. He got up and looked down on her and then said before he walked off, 'Thank you.'

He hadn't meant it to be a special moment or a possible final show of appreciation. The time just seemed right to thank Ruth. Gavin seemed to be in the right place, emotionally and perhaps physically, to do so. The two words were spoken without pre thought or preparation. That made them lighter to say and gave them more meaning.

'Go on then. Stop dithering. You're a blithering fool. Get a move on,' she would have said. And so he did.

Gavin found Linda in the waiting room. She looked at him. She knew it would not have been an easy visit. He appreciated the silence that she initially greeted him with.

Sometimes there is no need for words. They walked off together and kept the silence to accompany them.

'Thank you,' said Gavin as he left Linda at the hospital.

'Thank you,' replied Linda, emphasising the second word.

Nap was in. He didn't need the absence of a car to keep him at home. Gavin apologised for keeping the car for so long. Nap said it didn't matter. They were both right.

'Where have you been?' asked Nap. It was one of those questions that could be answered in simple here there and everywhere terms, with a great big 'let's move on' tagged on at the end. Or it was one of those questions that could be answered with chapter and verse and have you needing to consider instalments as the evening passed by. And for the first time, Gavin wasn't sure where to go with the answer. He could just slot nice and easy back into GavinNap world, venturing no further than who was England's best football manager, or why do some teams go up and down the leagues while others stay where they are, year on year, and should there be a law of physics to explain this? Perhaps a safe bit of politics, such as who was tallest prime minister, or how many liberal democrats does it take to change a lightbulb? Maybe even a bit of fashion, such as should you ever wear socks with sandals? GavinNap world could always be relied upon for a bit of rock music comparisons or indeed where does rock become pop or pop become rock and what would that mean for Spandau Ballet or Duran Duran? GavinNap world, where nothing really happens and nothing really matters. And we all live happily ever after.

'Nap, mate. I think it's time for us to move on.' And GavinNap world was torn into shreds, each shattered part blasting out across the universe, or at least beyond the confines of Nap's living room. What would the love child of Margaret Thatcher and Tony Blair look like? shooting off one way. What would it sound like if all The Beatles children formed a band? firing off another way. Is it worth trying to paint the socks of

Subbuteo players? ricocheting off walls. Was Cheers better than Frasier or Frasier better than Cheers? on its way to the Kuyper belt.

Nap looked shocked, as well he might. The fallen walls of Jericho looked like the final finishing touches to the newly erected Great Wall of China by comparison.

'Our friendship lasts forever but don't you think we need to grow up a bit,' said Gavin. It was halfway between a question and a statement. It was difficult territory. There was a path he needed to tread. Somewhere between the safe smooth tarmac of easy conversation and the rugged mountain treks of the ups and downs of real life.

Nap remained silent. It didn't feel right to offer his observations on the preferred size of ball when playing Subbuteo football. And that was the last piece of information in his head that had made any sense, before Nap had come back from the outer limits with all this strange talk of moving on and growing up.

'I've had the strangest days and, if I'm honest, and I want to be honest, the best days. I know now is not the time to talk about it with you. But I do want there to be a right time and I want to share with you the things that have happened.' Gavin looked at Nap. It was the sort of look that wanted to connect. Nap looked away. The moment was too intense. Gavin had said what he wanted to say. He hadn't planned this, but he knew it was the right thing. For the benefit of their future relationship, he needed to plant this seed.

'And yes, The Beatles, and football, and a whole load of nonsense are still up for hours of debate, but you're a real friend Nap and I want to move us forward, both of us.' Gavin wondered if he had gone too far. But he needed to grow up and move on. He would just have to make allowances for Nap. There was a place for triviality and superficial safe conversation, but he didn't want it to define their relationship all the time. 'Enough for now. How about a game before I go?'

'OK,' replied Nap, unsure what was happening, and feeling like Subbuteo football had been taken over by an alien governing body and they were messing with the offside rule. And surely that could never be a good thing.

They agreed to choose teams with anyone they wanted to put in.

Nap Disunited 1 Gavin's First Names Eleven 2

This felt like an end of season game with nothing to play for. The standout performance was Mick who seemed to turn up all over the place and supplied the dummy for Linda to score the opening goal for Gavin's First Names Eleven. Nap Disunited never seemed to be in the game. A second goal was inevitable and came from a nice move down the left wing. Some neat foot work from Ruth and a great cross was met by Bert at the far post. Dracula had no chance as the ball looped back over his head and into the far corner. Neither side looked interested in the second half. The only moment of note was a late goal for Nap Disunited when Frankenstein's Monster got onto a long ball from Captain Hook and poked the ball past Big Ron in the Gavin's First Names Eleven goal. The final whistle soon followed much to the relief of everyone.

Gavin ran home. He couldn't stop thinking about Nap. The changes that were taking place for Gavin were only showing up what little Nap seemed to have. He didn't want to change his relationship with Nap, but he felt some responsibility to try and give Nap the sort of kick up the backside that might have him getting a bit more out of life. He wasn't sure that it had worked out that way. He'd been kicking at thin air and Nap was further inside the closet than he'd ever been.

His run took him via the care home. He went round to where the window was. He stopped. There was an empty room. The signs were there of clearing up and preparing for whatever work was going to be needed to get them up and operating again. Would it ever be the same again? Would Ruth get to go back there? He thought about the first time he'd been up to the window. It made him think about the course of events that had led him to that first wave. He'd only known her in this part of her life, but she'd told him enough to earn great respect and make him look in on himself. He ran home.

Once home, he got out his work bag and plugged in the laptop. He could just about remember the password. Was that the thing about modern life that stood out the most? Everyone had passwords. You couldn't participate in society without passwords. And you weren't supposed to write them down. And everyone did because you were up that creek without a paddle otherwise. He typed in the password. It was correct. He sent an email to Sally Clark.

Hi Sally
Please share this message with everyone. I am well and fine. In fact I couldn't be better. But I must apologise for my absence from work, for any inconvenience this will have caused and for being a poor work colleague. This will change and I will return

with cake just to prove the point. Please forgive me and let's see what happens.
Gavin

He also sent an email to Cora.

Hi Cora
Thank you for looking out for me and thank you for caring enough to be part of what must have been a weird search party. Your five daughters are privileged to have such a wonderful mother. The world needs more Coras.
Thanks Gavin

In a final act of redemption, Gavin took Sharyn out for a meal. He asked her. He booked the restaurant. He ordered taxis there and back. He would be paying and they could talk about anything she liked, even the Waltons.

Sharyn had chosen an Indian restaurant. Gavin had realised that he was not that familiar with eating out or which were the preferred places to go to. Anything beyond a takeaway was unfamiliar territory. The waiter poured them a glass of champagne and placed the bottle in the bucket at Gavin's side. Gavin wasn't sure if this now made him responsible for the champagne or if the waiter would come back later to fill up their glasses. Could he interfere with the champagne or was he heading for a telling off if he did?

They clinked glasses. 'Thanks,' said Gavin.

'To us,' said Sharyn. They clinked glasses again.

'To us,' repeated Gavin.

They had a great meal, much enhanced by the company they gave each other. Then Gavin did the daftest thing he had ever done. He paid the taxi driver to take them to London.

Over an hour later, Gavin was stood with Sharyn looking at the Battersea Power Station silhouetted against the night sky.

'What do you think?' he said.

'I'm not sure what to think,' replied Sharyn.

'Would you rather be here with me looking at that or on your own looking at the Taj Mahal?'

She smiled at him. 'What do you think?'

That night Gavin went to bed, as late as it was, and left the curtains open. His bedroom overlooked the back garden, what there was of it, and other properties. Initially he stood and looked out. There was no Battersea Power Station or Taj Mahal. But he could see the darkened landmarks of his two escapes from the house and his one return. Then from his bed he lay and looked at the deep blue sky, a vast canvas waiting to be painted. The stars were dots that he could join, but he needed to be more adventurous than that.

Chapter 32

In the following days, Gavin started to adjust to his new normal. He returned to work. The power of cake performed wonders. It was a repeat of his chocolate cake and maybe an improvement on what even then had not been a bad effort. That he had taken the time to bake, went down as well as the cake. He visited Ruth in hospital. Sadly, she was no different, and underneath that calm exterior he suspected she was not improving. She was still attached to the stack of monitors that he managed to completely avoid this time. But she was someone he could talk to, even if she wasn't able to hear him. And maybe she was. Maybe she was admonishing him and mocking his every word. Either way, Gavin always came away feeling that his life was making the right sort of progress. He kept up his running and made himself a promise to upgrade his running gear. He might even make the right sort of progress to justify a touch of lycra. He thought about his mother. He couldn't contemplate much more than that, but even that was progress. He couldn't figure out if it was progress she deserved or not. But she wandered into his thoughts more regularly and with a lingering presence that he could not bat away so easily.

And then the news came. Linda told him over the phone and they agreed to meet at the coffee house. Linda was waiting when Gavin arrived. She hadn't ordered. Gavin ordered for both of them. He didn't fancy cake. He didn't fancy coffee, but it gave him support.

'Sorry,' said Linda. 'You were the first person I told.'

'Strange really,' replied Gavin. 'I feel sad, but I'm not surprised. I mean, I started a friendship with someone who was going to die sooner or later.'

'Still a shock.'

'And I wondered where this was going when I visited her in hospital.'

'I didn't like to say anything.'

'You didn't need to. She wasn't going to return home wearing tubes and carrying around a stack of beeping machines.' Gavin was surprised by the way in which he could be so easy about Ruth dying. 'I suppose you get used to this.'

'Not really. Somewhat anaesthetised, yes, but it is still upsetting. Part of you tries not to get attached but you do. You meet some good people. Not at their best. But the characters turn up. Just like Ruth.'

Sam brought the coffees over. Gavin had decided to try the Samiano. Considering he didn't feel much like coffee, now seemed the best time to try it. There was less to lose. A poor coffee is one of life's disappointments, but presently he could cope with that. And it pleased Sam that he had ordered it. Gavin was a bit more in to pleasing people now than he had been. It was a latte for Linda. He stayed clear of the flat white. They could be a bit hit and miss.

'She was a character,' said Gavin.

'She was,' repeated Linda.

Gavin sipped his coffee. 'I wonder what she would have made of this?' he said, in reference to his Samiano.

'Looks different. She'd have liked that.'

'True. She would.' Gavin took another sip. 'It must be strange though, only knowing people at the end of their lives.'

'I do have friends you know.' She looked at Gavin and smiled.

'I didn't mean that,' he replied. 'But you meet lots of people who can't really show you who they were or what they've achieved.'

'And you have to respect that. Whatever their situation is when we admit them, you must remember they are people and your equal and many of them may have had lives that will have surpassed anything you're going to do yourself.'

'You're right, but I think you are underestimating yourself.'

'Maybe.'

'No maybe, Linda. I've really appreciated your support and I know Ruth will have too.'

'Thank you.'

Linda shuffled on her seat and pulled an envelope out of her handbag. 'I need to give you this.' And she handed the envelope over. 'I know what's in there. I helped her to write it. But I think you should read it on your own.'

Gavin put the envelope on the table and rested his hand on it. It was thick. He sipped his Samiano again.

Linda sipped her latte and then got up. 'You need to read it on your own. Have a bit of privacy.'

'It can wait until you've finished your coffee.'

'I've finished.' She turned to leave and then stopped. 'There are other people you could visit when we get back up and running again.'

'Not like Ruth though,' replied Gavin.

'Whatever you got out of those visits, you were good for her too.'

'Thank you. That's good to know.'

'Of course you were. Anyway, think about it,' and Linda walked off, leaving Gavin to open the envelope. Its thickness was explained by two more envelopes inside, both addressed to Gavin.

He opened the first envelope. It was a card with a picture of two cats. Were they meant to be him and Ruth or was he reading too much into it? The message inside read: 'Please do a final check of the house for me. If there's anything you want, you must take it. And then give the key to my solicitors. And before you lock up check under the mattress. As I said, anything you want, please take!!!!' The four exclamation marks shouted at him.

The second envelope also had a card. This time there was an artist's impression of a bowl of cherries. The message inside read: 'Find the time to discover who you are and when you find out don't expect too much. But use this as the foundation for everything you can achieve.' She had signed it off as Saint Ruth. Who was he to argue?

Gavin had to put in a couple of day's work and then he went back to the bungalow.

He was greeted by Mick. That is to say, that as he walked up to the bungalow, Mick appeared from behind the rhododendron bush. 'You've just missed her.'

'Who? I mean hi! I mean who?'

'Horrible woman. She was asking if we had a key to the house.'

'Sounds like her niece.'

'We said no,' interrupted Daphne, also appearing from behind the same rhododendron bush. Nothing had changed.

'Hi, Daphne. You don't have a key?'

'Of course we do, but we weren't going to give it to her.' There was pride in her voice. And Mick looked at her with the same sense of achievement. 'But she'll be back.'

'But why not give her the key?'

'I don't know,' said Daphne. 'But something just made us. I think it was part her attitude and then also, Ruth gave us the key. It was a spare key anyway.'

'How did you hear?' asked Gavin.

'We didn't, but there was only going to be one thing to bring her here,' said Mick.

'Money,' added Daphne. 'We've been here ten years and we've never seen her before. Ruth said she sent her a Christmas card every year but never got one back. She wanted to see the bungalow. I guess she will get it now.'

'You need to get in there and grab anything you want,' said Mick. 'She would have wanted you to have something.'

'I'll go in and get my things,' said Gavin.

'You back again?' It was Bert.

'Can't stay away,' said Gavin.

'Just heard about Ruth. Lovely woman.' Bert looked at Mick. 'Mick told that relative of hers what he thought.'

'I didn't. I just didn't give her the key,' said Mick.

'She should have asked me,' said Bert.

'You got a key too?' said Mick.

'Of course,' replied Bert. 'I wouldn't have given it her though.' Which made Mick laugh. 'Good to see you.'

'You too,' replied Gavin. 'Just going to give the bungalow a last look over.'

'You need a key?' said Bert.

'Of course he doesn't,' said Mick.

Gavin took the key out of his pocket and waved it at them. 'Quite common around here.' He went up to the bungalow and let himself in. He was greeted by the photo of Daisy. His rucksack was in the bedroom. He put it on the bed and opened it. It became the place to deposit any items he needed to take home. He added a packet of biscuits and a couple of packets of rice. There wasn't much else. The niece could sort out anything he'd opened and left. He stood and looked out onto the garden from the large lounge window. He smiled at the fountain. He wondered what the niece would do with all this. She'd probably sell. The place needed a bit of work and some modernisation, he considered, but it would be a nice set up. The niece would make a fair packet out of it. He then remembered the card and its message.

Gavin went to Ruth's bedroom. This had been the one place he had left alone. Until now he had done no more than open the door and look without entering. This felt like a place that should retain Ruth's privacy. That would soon be discarded. But not by him. He would however check under the

301

mattress as invited to do so by Ruth. He was careful in raising the mattress and trying to keep the bedding in place. What he found were five large A4 envelopes and in them were bank notes. They were all quite thick and all containing fifty-, twenty- and ten-pound notes. He put them on the carpet and looked at them. Had she really wanted him to have these? Could he really take them? He felt both excited and anxious at the prospect. As if to get some perspective he read the message in the card again. The invitation and the message were clear. The exclamation marks hit the message home. He stuffed the envelopes into the rucksack. He smiled and mouthed a thank you to Ruth. He calculated from what he had seen that she was gifting him more than ten thousand pounds. And no one seemed to want the niece to benefit. It was a strange feeling knowing that he was walking away so much richer.

He put the rucksack outside the front door and went back in to have a final look around. This had been a place of sanctuary that had become a temporary home and now he left it as a place that gave him a final closeness to Ruth. He said goodbye to the photo of Daisy and then decided to take it. He put it in his rucksack. The niece would only bin it and that seemed wrong to Gavin. He would take it. He closed the door behind him. He stood in the garden.

'Tea?' It was Doreen. 'And cake?' She had both to offer him.

'Why not?' he said.

'You still got your key then?' Doreen said.

'Yes,' replied Gavin.

'Always got a spare one just in case,' said Doreen. He didn't doubt it. In fact, the only one without a key seemed to be Puddles, and that was not beyond possibility.

They were soon joined by Mick and Daphne and Bert. The old gang back together again.

'I hope we'll see you again,' said Doreen.

'You will,' said Gavin. He meant it.

They all sat and drank tea and ate cake in memory of Ruth.

'She'd have liked this,' said Daphne.

'She would,' said Doreen.

They knew that Ruth had died. The niece had not given them any details. She probably didn't have the details. Gavin told them about the fire and that Ruth had been in hospital. Whether it was correct or not, he reassured them that Ruth had been peaceful right up to the end. He found it a strange message to give as he had felt he was not only assuring them on Ruth's behalf, but, considering his calculated ages for Bert and Doreen, he felt he was also probably assuring them for their own future reference. Mick and Daphne looked like they had a bit longer to go.

'And were you alright?' asked Doreen.

'Why?' replied Gavin.

'The fire. Were you okay?'

'Yes. Thank you,' replied Gavin. 'Just did more than my usual share of coughing.'

'A hero then,' said Daphne.

'Come on,' said Mick. 'Next you'll be saying he has superpowers.'

'There'll be an enquiry,' said Bert. 'After something like that there's bound to be an inquiry. Someone to blame. And I bet they'll have cut corners somewhere. A missing fire blanket. An empty fire extinguisher.'

'Give over Bert,' said Mick. 'She's just died. Let's be a bit more respectful.'

'I'm just saying, that's all.'

'She'd have liked the cake,' said Daphne looking at Doreen.

'She'd have liked your cake,' said Doreen looking at Gavin.

'Gave me indigestion for a week.'

'Mick!' exclaimed Daphne, castigating her husband. They all laughed.

'What about the funeral?' asked Mick. 'Who's organising that?'

'And paying for it?' added Bert.

'The niece, who is called Della,' replied Gavin. 'She's paying. The organising? She's left that to the care home. Linda, to be exact. According to Linda, when I spoke to her earlier, Della lives in Sidmouth and that being such a distance away and the care home being on the doorstep, she thought it made sense if she took a backseat on the upcoming proceedings. The care home would apparently know much better what to do than she ever could. Linda has asked me to speak to Sharyn about taking any service.'

'Meanwhile the niece keeps an eye on things in Sidmouth,' commented Bert.

'And the money,' added Mick.

'Oh well,' said Gavin. 'At least she missed out on the cake.'

'And if she moves in next door, we won't give her any cake,' said Daphne.

'She won't be moving here,' said Mick. 'To her it's just a pile of money.'

Gavin glanced at his rucksack. It was his prompt to move. He thanked them for their companionship and set off. He also promised to return, sooner rather than later.

Chapter 33

Gavin got out of the car and wandered along the path to the chapel. It was a lot of tarmac with interspersed oases of green. Just a little bit greener as you got nearer and then the brickwork and large windows of the crematorium became conspicuous. It was a building that stood remarkably neutral in this purposeful setting. One large window had stained glass features that seemed to depict nothing of meaning but looked nice. Gavin decided that 'nice' was what it was all about.

'Nice day for it,' said Mick, appearing from behind a pillar that seemed to have no reason to be there. Unlike Mick, who looked naturally at home.

'Oh,' responded Gavin.

'We wanted to be here,' said Daphne, appearing, possibly from behind a similar pillar, although it really was not at all clear where she had come from. Thin air could never be ruled out with these two.

'We've saved you a seat at the front,' said Mick. It seemed unnecessary to Gavin.

Mick led him through a set of doors and then through a second doorway into a room that was not anywhere near as empty as Gavin had been expecting. Mick invited him to walk up the aisle to where Sharyn was stood waiting. As he paced himself, slowly and reverently, he looked at the backs of people's heads. Haircuts, ears, necks, a raised hand scratching an itch, a couple of bald patches, they were not unfamiliar to him, although not instantly identifiable. And each instant took him onto the next row and finally to Sharyn who pointed to a row of chairs to Gavin's right. There he sat. He wasn't sat long when the music started up. Gavin had suggested Beethoven, without being able to name any particular work, or opus, as Sharyn had corrected him: rather unnecessarily, he had thought. But not the one that goes 'du du du der', he had asked. He assumed the music now playing was Beethoven. It sounded like it might be. It didn't go 'du du du der'.

The coffin and the niece arrived in the doorway, and everyone looked around which once again presented Gavin with twisted backs of heads. Although this time he could put faces to one or two of them. And they included Linda and Bert and then, as she turned back briefly, sat next to Bert was Doreen. The whole gang had vacated the cul-de-sac and left Puddles in charge. The coffin was wheeled up the aisle and followed full of ceremony by the niece. She wore black for full mourning. It struck Gavin that this would have been the last thing Ruth would have wanted. He sat there in his dark blue suit, white shirt, and grey tie, with a bright purple lining on the shirt side. Gavin had deliberated over what to wear. He was going to avoid going full black. In the end only his shoes were black. This was about Ruth, not what other people would think. Although he did abandon his purple floral shirt at the last minute.

The coffin arrived at the front. The niece took a seat on the row to the left, aligned with where Gavin was sitting on the right. Gavin and Della met for the first time. There was brief contact between them. Gavin smiled at her across the empty seats between them. Della did not smile back. She offered nothing in return. Was she the sort of person that thought it was wrong to smile before and during a funeral? Could you only smile once you had given your condolences in the line out? Or was she the sort of person that just didn't smile? Gavin tried to focus back on the proceedings being led by Sharyn.

Sharyn welcomed them all. They sang a hymn. Then Linda came up to the lectern and read some poetry. Gavin watched her walk back to her seat and it was then that he spotted Nap. He missed what happened next and then missed his cue for the eulogy. That Nap was there, had thrown him completely. He hadn't realised that Nap had any smart clothes. It was stuck in his head that Nap was there. Sharyn coughed and moved forward, and then he became aware that he was out of sync with proceedings. Nap was there, he thought as he got up and went over to the lectern.

Gavin stood behind the lectern and looked out at them. Now he could see Big Ron and Jacob. How he had not spotted Big Ron earlier he did not know. He hadn't really prepared much to say. He hadn't expected much of an audience and hadn't intended making any great effort for the niece. And it was true that many of them there did not really know Ruth much, if at all. Indeed, he had only got to know her himself over the past few months. And yet he seemed to know her better than anyone. So, he abandoned the short speech that he had carried in his head. They needed to know about Ruth. They needed to know why they were here. Ruth deserved their attention. He looked at the coffin.

'Let me tell you about Ruta…' he started. He paused. Nap was here, he thought. 'Let me tell you about Ruta,' he repeated, trying to get himself back on track. And so, he told them a story about two girls, one who started her life in Germany and one, a little older, who grew up in England. A little bit about Daisy. Another little bit about Trevor. The absence of information about Della was noticeable, but he had nothing he knew to say. He told them how he first met Ruth. How they'd shared their stories. How her life had been much more interesting than his. And he ended up by saying how in one person's death we should seek to resurrect our own lives. '… We should all walk away from here today with new convictions, new dreams, new hopes. That is all that Ruth

307

would ask of you.' He paused in that poignant way that announces, through its silence, that this is a time to have a few moments to yourself. 'Thank you,' he then concluded.

Gavin left the lectern and walked up to the coffin. He kissed his hand and touched the coffin. 'Thank you,' he whispered. And returning to his seat, there was a tear in his eye. For Ruth maybe, possibly, definitely, but also for Sharyn, for Anna and Maria, for Nap, for Big Ron, for Cora, for Mick and Daphne, Bert, and Doreen, for them all. It was for all of them. They were still a small gathering, but it was the most wonderful small gathering of people he had ever seen.

Sharyn concluded with some well-chosen words which Gavin almost missed. And then he had the moment that he wanted to give to Ruth. It was not of her choosing. It was not by any prior arrangement. She probably would not have liked it. But it was Gavin set free. The stereo system started playing 'Make Some Noise' by Big Big Train. Something no one would have heard before, but it's message and rock anthemic sound were the very thing he wanted to end with. Take the morose ceremony and turn it on its head with something ringing in your ears as you leave. That was what Ruth was all about. The niece got up first to leave. It was right that she did. She also did not seem too keen to hang around. Gavin followed. She walked ahead with sufficient pace that Gavin was not likely to catch her up. Not a problem, as Gavin was enjoying the make-some-noise sentiment. That was exactly what Ruth would want. Come on everybody make some noise. Gavin moved on, but not without a little lingering, holding on to a last moment.

Outside, the niece had wandered a short distance. Gavin held the near ground. There was no line for people to walk past, to shake hands, or to offer hugs and condolences. Only two people could have formed that line and they were far from being co-ordinated. A handful of people sought out the niece to commiserate with her. Some of them meant it. Some of them were really saying enjoy your inheritance. Everyone went up to Gavin. There was one of those queues that consists of people talking to other people, all the time trying to get nearer to him and spot an opportunity to jump in before someone else or, best of all, to have reason to join a conversation he was already having with someone else. Gavin got to spend time with everyone. He thanked them individually, from himself and on behalf of Ruth, whether they had known her or not.

Nap had gone. No opportunity to thank him. There was probably no conversation to keep him. He had met Sharyn once and that was it. No reason to hang around. But the next time Gavin visited it would be different. Maybe he could even get him to go to the pub.

Sharyn came up to him. 'Nice eulogy,' she said.

'It just came out that way.'

'Sometimes the best way to do it.'

'A bit risky. I could have said anything.'

'Instead, you said everything you needed to.'

'And how come they were all here?'

'Word gets around.'

'And the girls?'

'They wanted to come.'

'I need to thank them.'

'They're in the car.'

He went over to Sharyn's car and lent in. 'Thank you for coming.'

They both smiled back at him. He wasn't going to get any more than that, but it was all more than enough to make him feel good about himself.

'I'd better let you go,' he said to Sharyn. 'Thank you,' he added.

And she smiled back at him. Without planning and mindful of the protestations of embarrassed teenagers, they kissed out of sight of the girls.

'I say vicar,' he said.

'I know,' she replied. She got into the car. Gavin watched them drive away.

He went over to his car and, as he was about to open the door, a man appeared from behind a rose bush, or so it seemed, and it wasn't Mick. Nor was he a gardener. He was well dressed, but not overdressed which, considering the occasion, made him look only a little out of place. Nor could Gavin remember him from the funeral. He came over to Gavin and offered his condolences. He gave Gavin an envelope, stiff enough to suggest there was a card inside. Then he walked off. Gavin watched him walk away.

Chapter 34

Gavin arrived at the Rose and Crown. It was two o'clock. And that was what the card had said. It was an invitation to meet if he wanted to know more about his father. Gavin had first been taken aback by both the invitation and the brief interaction with the young man. He was assuming that it would be this man that he would be meeting, but the minimal nature of the communication had left no certainty about anything. Then he had considered that it was an offer to find out more about his father. This implied he had knowledge to build on. Gavin considered that he knew nothing about his father. Of course, Gavin had deliberated about going. And, of course, he had never not intended to go.

He walked in and looked around. This was a pub he had never been to before, so he had to both familiarise himself with the setting as well as seek out who it was he was supposed to be meeting. There were people gathered at different tables and at the bar. Then at one table, he saw the back of one head and the sideways view of another head, that of the man who had given him the card. He chose not to go up to the bar to get a drink. He approached the table.

'Ah. Let me do some introductions,' said the man he had met before. 'I'm Jude.' He turned to the man sitting with him. 'And this is Tony.'

Gavin knew who Tony was. The name and especially the appearance. This was his father. A man he had not seen for over thirty years. A man, who the last time he saw him, probably looked a bit like Gavin looked now. But here he was probably well into his sixties. The well-fitted black suit attire of an ageing blues singer, trumpeter, or jazz guitarist. He had a certain coolness about his manner.

'Our Father,' added Jude. It was spoken with pride. It could have been the beginning of a prayer.

Gavin couldn't move. He was stuck to the spot. He didn't know whether to stay or leave. He wanted to cry. He wanted to laugh. He wanted to shout. All overwhelmed and coated with numbness. He had come to this place, to this table, knowing possibilities of what might be waiting for him. He had considered his father, but only amongst many other reasons for being invited to meet. He had not expected to meet a brother he did not know he had. He wasn't sure where the greatest discomfort lay. But it was both encounters. It was the whole situation. Meeting a family you had lost and one you didn't know you had.

'Sorry,' said Tony. There was a smoothness in his voice which didn't help.

'Hi,' said Jude, still standing, and holding out his hands. He invited Gavin to sit.

Gavin sat in the chair offered. All he could do was follow directions. He had lost the ability to make decisions.

Tony spoke up. It was the action of a father taking some responsibility. 'We don't have to talk. We don't have to say much. But I thought it was time we started. I have things to say. I have apologies to give. There are things I think you should know. But none of that now. You can stay a minute. You can stay an hour. I just thought we should meet. The three of us.'

'Did you know?' asked Gavin. He looked at Jude.

'That I had a brother?'

'Yes.'

'Yes. That was never a secret.'

'There were no secrets, Gavin,' said Tony. 'But I left. I chose to give your mother the space she wanted. I made the decision to remove myself. It seemed right at the time. As the years have gone by it has seemed less and less right. Now I know it was wrong. There was no one at the time but, of course, I met someone. We settled down and we had Jude.' He smiled at Jude.

'Let me get some drinks in,' offered Jude. 'The same, Dad?'

'Let me get them,' said Tony. 'Give you two a few moments alone. Gavin?'

'Yes. Pint please.'

'Anything particular?'

'Anything.' Such was his state of mind that Gavin would have accepted a pint of the pub's finest dregs. Tony hadn't asked Jude. He seemed to know. Tony walked up to the bar.

'He's a good man. Clever and funny.'

'I'm more like my mother than I thought,' replied Gavin.

'I can see that you've got Dad's sense of humour.'

'When did you first know about me?' Developing a conversation with his brother - and that itself was an unexpected label, 'his brother' - seemed less contentious than all that was swimming around in his head about his father. As brothers, and especially as sons, they carried less culpability for the current and historical situation they were in. Then again, the question was teasing that premise.

'It's easier to say that I always knew. But what you know, you understand differently at different ages. And as a child, you accept what you are told. So, yes, I knew about you. But only as an adult have I wanted to do something about it. Maybe as a teenager too, but most of what you want to do as a teenager doesn't bare thinking about.'

'But you waited, even as an adult.'

'That's the dilemma. As an adult you start to have to consider the feelings of others, so I guess I waited a while for dad to want to do something. I'm not saying he didn't want to do something, but I guess for both of us the past years of not making contact build up and then make it harder.'

Tony came back with three pints of beer on a tray. It seemed a strange thing for him to do, but Gavin noted that his father could balance three pints on a tray. Was he being ageist? Or was he just noting anything he could about his father?

He put the tray down and handed out the beer. Then sat down. 'I don't regret leaving your mother. But I do regret leaving you.'

'Why didn't you keep in touch?'

'When I left, I wanted to give you and your mother space. Then time went by and it seemed harder and harder to come back. To you that is. Not your mother. It would have made me a space invader.' No laughter from any of them. A dad joke then. 'And then so long goes by that it becomes a really big thing. And I'm not good at really big things.'

'So why now?'

'Your mother got hold of me. The timing was good. I don't know. It seemed to be the right thing to do for everyone. She might have many faults, just like me,' at which point Tony offered a guilty smile, 'but she seems to want the best for you.'

'We assumed you'd be pleased,' said Jude.

'But we know this can't be easy,' added Tony. 'Hardest of all for you, but strange for us too.'

'Meeting my brother for the first time,' said Jude. He and Gavin gave each other a look and then just as quickly they looked away.

All three of them found silence and supped their beers. There were three heads full of each other and Gavin had added his mother to that unforeseen triumvirate. Had she really contacted his father?

Here was Gavin sat with his father. He had a brother who seemed normal too. And maybe his mother did care. This was going to take time to digest. But recently his mental digestive system had been upgraded. He'd have to take these thoughts on a run with him. Probably several runs, a few walks and well, Ruth was no longer there, but he could still talk to her. And there was Sharyn. He would talk to her. He decided that it was time to leave. He didn't finish his beer.

'Ok,' said Gavin, rising from his chair. 'But I will need time.'

'We have it,' said Tony. 'I hope.'

Epilogue

Gavin pushed the tripod into the sand. He got out a red marker pen and wrote on the flipchart paper, 'Everyone should have an insect day', and then he signed off with, 'The Tomato Runner', in the bottom right-hand corner.

Oh, and the money? It made a nice deposit on a bungalow he had taken a fancy to. Sharyn had approved. And there was a fountain that he had pledged he would never repair and would be his reminder of a little German girl called Ruta.

Things had started to look a lot better.

Acknowledgements

Mark Jonathan Harris and Deborah Oppenheimer – their book, *Into The Arms Of Strangers*, contained information from the stories of the Kindertransport that enabled me to create a legitimate background for Ruth/Ruta.

Fosseway Writers – for putting up with me. Oh, and the encouragement and positive vibe that comes from sharing and learning from other writers.

Printed in Great Britain
by Amazon

27320438R00182